FIRE AND MOONLIGHT

The Lycanthrope Protection Agency

Book 6

CJ Ravenna

CONTENT WARNINGS

- Arson

- Descriptions of burn victims and people being burned

- Graphic depictions of violence and injuries

- Grief recovery

- Wolf hunting and violence against shifters in their animal form

- Dog fighting

- Torture, murder, and domestic abuse

Chapter 1

WELCOME HOME, SON

When the fire came, it spared no one.

Eddie Turner woke up choking on the ash that caked the back of his throat. His mother's arms trembled as they flew around him. "I've got you, baby. I got you." She covered his head with his wolf-patterned blanket and hoisted him into her arms. They ran.

Eddie clutched at his mother, coughing into her shoulder. He tried to ask what was happening, where was Pa, *why*, but he couldn't breathe. The blanket tumbled down to his shoulders and he gasped. Flames consumed the little house he'd grown up in, roared like an enraged beast as they devoured the homes of his friends. The fire had blazing eyes and the snarling face of a demon as fiery jaws consumed the town.

"Don't look, honey. Close your eyes and don't open them, okay?" Fear shattered his mother's voice, and he crumpled into her shoulder and sobbed. His mother tripped over something in the road and Eddie clung to her, terrified he'd fall and be left behind. She went on running. She'd tripped over a wolf lying motionless in the road as if he were sleeping, fur scorched.

"June! Eddie!" His father's voice had Eddie struggling to escape his mother's arms. He was alive!

His father leaned out the window of his truck. He was covered in blood. The door flew open, and Eddie tumbled into the back seat. His mother hurled herself into the seat beside his father and then they were driving, tires screeching over dry soil.

Eddie would never forget the ash, falling like black snow against the window. They drove past the toy shop where Eddie had bought himself his first toy with his own allowance; the roof caved in as they hurtled past.

"Pa, drive faster!" he wailed as the fire pursued them.

"Ed, put your seat belt on, and don't look!" his mother cried.

"Shit!" his father roared and Eddie flew into the front seat, his mother's arms tight around his middle as his father slammed on the brakes. The shrill yelps of wolves filled the street.

Eddie looked.

For the rest of his life, he would wish he hadn't.

The wolves were on fire, embers leaping from their scorched hair. He could *smell* them, their roasting flesh sickly sweet, and taste their burning fur at the back of his throat. His mother made Eddie look away.

"Jamison, for the goddess's sake, drive!"

His father's face had never looked so pale, the fire reflecting in his wide eyes.

The burning town disappeared behind them, but the flames followed them. The wolves howled and screamed as the forest burned. They howled for their pack, for help, screaming their anguish and fear to the smoke-blackened sky. Eddie covered his ears but he *felt* them, their pack bonds snapping like threads in his chest as they burned with the forest. He screamed and screamed and didn't remember when he stopped.

WHEN HE MANAGED TO sleep, he dreamed of the fire. In his dreams he ran as fast as he could, but he could never outrun it.

No matter where he ran, the fire always caught up to him. It burned his father, then his mother. Burned all his friends even though they were already dead—his parents wouldn't tell him, but he knew.

In his dream, he burned. He smelled his own burning skin, sweet as pork, and the charcoal taste of his burning hair at the back of his throat. The ashes rained on him like snow, and the wolves howled in the burning forest.

He woke and sobbed like a baby, inconsolable in his mother's arms. "The fire's comin'! It'll find us!" he wailed.

"Hey. Eddie. Hey, son." His father crawled into the back seat. "Here. Look at this for me, son." He pulled a ring from his finger. Eddie didn't care about some dumb ring even if it was pretty, made of ebony with a white stone in the center. Like the moon. "Know what this is, son?"

Sniffing, Eddie shook his head.

"It's a lucky charm. My pa gave it to me. He told me it was blessed by the She-Wolf herself, and that it kept him safe. Know why we survived, son? I think the goddess protected us, and she'll continue to protect us. If you wear this ring, you'll be safe."

"That's right, Ed," his mother whispered, squeezing him tight. "Go on and put it on."

Gulping, Eddie accepted the ring and put it on. It was loose on his finger. "It's too big."

Laughing softly, his father took off the gold chain he wore around his neck, removed the pendant connected to the chain, and slipped the ring on it. He put the chained ring over Eddie's neck. "Wear this, son, and you'll be safe."

Eddie didn't know if he believed him, but after he put the necklace with the ring on, the nightmares didn't bother him that night. Maybe it was special after all.

HIS PARENTS WERE TALKING at dawn, their whispers rousing Eddie from a light sleep.

"You're sure, Jamison? You're *sure*?"

"He's gone." His father sounded haunted.

A trembling exhale. "We're safe?"

"Yeah, darlin'. We're safe."

His mother's sobs were muffled as Eddie's father held her close.

Eddie didn't understand, but they were safe.

He closed his eyes and slept.

THE NIGHT AFTER THE fire, they slept in their car. It was cold, and Eddie buried himself under his wolf-patterned blanket, even though it was ruined: black in places, burnt-smelling, and smeared with ash. He hated the smell but he couldn't bear to throw it out.

Once the sun rose, they hit the road. Eddie didn't know where they were going, only that they passed a road sign that said, YOU ARE NOW LEAVING TEXAS.

He wondered if he'd ever come back.

His mother told him stories during the drive, stories she'd read to him dozens of times and knew as well as he did. Sometimes she forgot the important parts and his father would chime in. His mother would go quiet, and the salty smell of her tears made Eddie's throat ache. He missed his friends. He missed his teacher. The nice lady at the general store who always saved him a cherry lollipop. They were all gone, and he would never see them again.

Eddie's tears ran hot down his face. "Have we lost our pack forever, Pa?"

His father's lips trembled when he smiled. "No, pup. We have each other."

THEY STOPPED AT A diner for dinner, and his father went outside to have a long conversation with someone on the phone. When his pa joined them at the table, he was smiling. "I found a pack who'll take us in."

Eddie chewed a mouthful of meat loaf. "A big pack?"

"How do you know we'll be safe there?" His ma sounded unhappy.

"They know about our situation." Pa tucked into his bowl of chili. "They've been takin' in folks like us for years. Shifters who've lost everythin', who have nowhere to go."

"Are we goin' to another city?" Eddie asked hopefully.

"No, pup. It's a pack of wolves in Nevada."

"Oh." He missed living in a city. He'd been born and raised in Austin and had lived there until he was three. His parents never told him why they'd left. For a while, they'd been in Dallas. Then two years ago, his parents had packed their things and left the city without any explanation. Eddie still didn't understand why they moved around so much. It didn't seem normal. Packs were all right, but cities were more exciting, even if they were full of mean humans who only tolerated werewolves. "Is Nevada far?"

"It's a whole state away, pup. We'll drive past Las Vegas, see the lights. We'll be there before you know it."

THEY SPENT THE NIGHT in a motel and hit the road after ordering drive-thru pancakes from a roadside diner.

"What'll we do when we find our new home?" Eddie asked as they drove, a tinfoil container of hot pancakes in his lap.

"We can start over." His mother looked to the blue horizon hopefully, but all Eddie could see was endless barren desert.

"I wish we could go home." He looked out the window, his eyes stinging.

"We'll find a new home, bud," his pa said.

Eddie didn't want a new home. He wanted his old house back in his old familiar town. He wanted to see all his friends and he couldn't.

The werewolves were waiting for them just off the main highway, sitting in their cars. A hand waved out of the window at them, and then they followed the cars along a winding road. They drove past a sign that said RED ROCK CANYON NATIONAL PARK, and then another that said, NO TRESSPASSING, WEREWOLF TERRITORY. The sun was going down, and the lights of the Vegas Strip shone bright on the horizon. They drove past towers of red rocks and prickly, sparse vegetation.

"Look, honey, look!" His mother pointed ahead.

Eddie rolled down the window and stuck his head out. The lights of a tiny village winked in the night. It didn't look like much. Then one of the werewolves in the car stuck his head out of the window and howled, and the night came alive. From the village wolves ran up alongside the cars, barking and yipping and howling. All of Eddie's apprehension disappeared, and he grinned, a bit too shy to howl with them. He'd never experienced a welcome like this before.

His father was laughing when Eddie stuck his head back in. "Welcome home, son," he said.

Home. Eddie so wanted to finally come home.

They parked the cars and stepped out onto a dry dirt road that stretched through the village. Waiting to greet them at the entrance to the town was a man with olive skin. A tall woman of similar coloring stood at his side. They both smelled the same, like a mated pair. Next to them was a little girl, a big grin on her face. She threw back her head and howled, and the adults laughed.

The man stuck out his hand. "Welcome to Red Rock Springs, Turner pack. I'm Sheriff Anthony Salvatore." He spoke with an accent Eddie thought was Italian. Maybe.

"Jamison and June Turner." Eddie's pa shook his hand.

"This is my mate, Olivia, and—"

"Kassandra!" The little girl rushed up to Eddie and circled him, sniffing frantically. "Hello! Hi! Welcome! I'm eight years old and my favorite food is roasted iguana!"

"Iguana? Ew!" Eddie laughed and sniffed her in return. "I'm eight, too." She smelled like her mother's perfume. She hugged his head to her chest.

"Mama, he's cute! Can I keep him?"

Olivia laughed, shaking her head. "That's enough, darling. Vicenzo, come say hello."

Eddie hadn't seen him. He was hiding behind his mother's leg, eyes bright blue in the deepening shadows of the night. His mother stepped aside and the boy stumbled forward with a gasp. He looked scared, like a frightened animal, with his long hair and unnaturally sharp teeth. More wolf than boy.

Eddie waved. "Hello."

The wolf boy stretched out his head and sniffed, then closed his eyes and breathed in deep. His breath hitched in a hiccup, and he ran behind his mom's leg, wide eyes hidden beneath his mop of black hair.

Eddie frowned. Did he smell bad?

Olivia smiled. "He's very shy," she explained, ignoring her son's not-so-shy growl, his cheeks reddening.

With a soft sob, his ma hugged Olivia, taking her by surprise. "Thank you." The sight of his mother's tears made Eddie want to cry. "Thank you so much."

Sheriff Salvatore smiled. "Welcome home, Turners! Follow me, I'll show you to your new home."

Olivia led the way, her bright summer dress seeming to glow as it swayed around her ankles. Kassandra chatted Eddie's ear off during the walk. In the span of ten seconds, he learned her favorite color—purple—and her favorite dessert—pistachio ice cream—and the names of all her friends she couldn't wait for him to meet.

"Here you are," Anthony said. He'd stopped before a small blue house at the end of a dirt road. It was only a one-story house, but it was long.

"Our home's right over there." Anthony motioned just down the road to a much bigger two-story yellow house. "We left you some fresh clothes in the bedroom. Let me know if everything fits or if you need anything else. Once you get yourself settled in, come on over for dinner."

His parents thanked them and they stopped by within an hour.

Vicenzo looked back and caught Eddie's eye. Eddie waved and said, "See ya!"

Quickly looking away, Vicenzo ran after his parents.

Eddie didn't think Vicenzo liked him very much.

"He's just shy, hon," his mother said to him. "Give him time. Maybe someday you'll be friends."

Eddie wasn't sure but he ached for what he'd lost: friends to laugh and smile with, a place to come home to, a pack who cared for him as their own.

Maybe just maybe, he and Vico could be friends.

Chapter 2

Honey and Summer Grass

Vicenzo Salvatore didn't know why Eddie Turner smelled so freaking amazing. He smelled like the honey fresh from his grandfather's bee farm. Like summer grass in Italy. Like home and family and pack. The instant he caught Eddie's scent, he hadn't been able to speak. He never had any trouble speaking to anyone. He didn't get it.

"Vico, take a break from drawing and help set the table," his mother said from the kitchen where she drained a big pot full of pasta through a strainer.

Sighing, he set down his pencil and went into the kitchen to accept the stack of plates she handed him. "When are the strangers getting here?" The plates clinked as he arranged them on the table. "I'm starving." The sooner they arrived, the sooner they could eat.

"They're not strangers, Vicenzo. They're our new neighbors. The ones whose town burned down, remember?" His mother dressed the pasta with a white sauce while his father seared pancetta in a pan. "They seemed like nice people, and their son is eight years old, like you."

Vicenzo hummed. "I guess." They did seem nice. Especially Eddie. He almost dropped the plate as the other boy crossed his mind, an unexpected flutter in his belly.

"You were pretty quiet earlier. Do you not like Eddie?"

"I—I do. I think? But, like, what do I say?"

She shrugged. "Anything you want. Just as long as it's polite."

He sighed, still unsure. "Okay…"

His mother laughed at him. "What is the matter, Vico? He seems like a nice boy."

"He is! Probably. His eyes are super green, and his hair is so shiny and white, and—"

Kassandra snorted as she darted around the table, arranging utensils. "*Oh*, someone's got a crush on Eddie!"

This time, Vicenzo did drop the plate with a loud clatter onto the table. "I do not!"

"Don't yell, kids!" their father chided.

"Yes, you do!" Kassandra danced around him. "You want to kiss him and be his mate!"

Vicenzo's face was ready to catch on fire. He tackled his twin and she screamed and ran up the stairs with him tearing after her.

"Hey, no roughhousing!" their mother barked.

Vicenzo was still catching his breath when the doorbell rang. The Turners were here. They were wearing fresh clothes this time. Vicenzo recognized his mother's old dress and his father's coveralls. Eddie was wearing Vicenzo's clothes, ones he hadn't worn in a long time. He'd loved that old shirt with the howling wolf and those baggy jeans. He wasn't mad his parents gave them away; Eddie's old clothes had been dirty and torn, so he needed them more.

There was so much he wanted to ask. What had happened to their home, to their pack? Why did Eddie smell so good? What was his favorite color? Did he like to read or was he more into TV? Instead, he sat as far away from Eddie as possible and ate without saying a word. His heart hammered the entire time.

His parents and Eddie's talked and talked and talked.

"This pasta is delicious, Olivia!" Eddie's ma said appreciatively.

"Thank you. It's my grandmother's recipe. We butcher the chicken ourselves on the ranch."

"You have a ranch?" Eddie asked. It was the first time he'd spoken since he'd arrived.

"Yeah!" Kassie chimed in. "With cows and chickens and goats and everything! We have a garden, too. I'm gonna plant tomatoes next year!"

"Cool. I like tomatoes." Eddie smiled and something in Vicenzo's stomach flipped over.

Eddie's father asked, "Is your family from Italy?"

Dad said, "Yes, though our pack moved from Italy to America about two years ago. Italy is such an important place in werewolf history. Or it was."

"We lived in a pack town in the countryside. When the twins were born, things were peaceful, at first. But humans started invading the territory and terrorizing us," his mother explained.

A shiver ran down Vicenzo's spine as he recalled loud, sneering humans throwing Molotov cocktails at people's homes, setting cars on fire, and even shooting at werewolves, all the while the police stood by and protected the humans.

June shook her head. "That's outrageous!"

"Humans and werewolves beat each other up! I saw it!" Kassie exclaimed.

His mother shot his sister a look. "Don't talk with food in your mouth."

Dad said, "Once we moved here, we tried living in cities, but it just didn't work. Olivia and I got an offer to run the Springs Pack. It was the best choice for our pack."

Vicenzo cleared his throat. He was tired of hearing about upsetting things he'd rather forget about. "Um... Eddie?"

"Yeah?"

Vicenzo's heart tripped under those eyes. He couldn't tell if they were blue or green or a mix. Kind of like cyan, his favorite color. "I—"

"Hey, Eddie!" Kassandra chimed in. "My friend Susan says you can't lick your elbow, even if you try *really* hard!" She then tried to lick her elbow. Eddie burst out laughing while Mom and Dad scolded Kassie.

Vicenzo scowled at his plate. He couldn't think of a thing to say to Eddie, and his dumb sister kept talking to him. "Can I be excused?"

"If you want," his father said. "Just say goodnight first."

He held back a sigh. "G'night," he said to his toes.

"Hey, Vico—" Mom called.

Vico dumped his plate in the sink and trudged up to his room. He was so lame. Why couldn't he say a single word to Eddie, even though he wanted to?

He shut himself in his room after brushing his teeth. Pulling on his PJs, he crawled into bed and drew pictures of wolves howling in the desert. He wondered what Eddie's wolf looked like. His hair was so blond it was almost white, so maybe his fur matched his hair color? He drew a white wolf next to a black wolf that resembled himself. They howled at the blue moon together.

There was a knock on his door and his mother poked her head in. "Hey. You didn't look like you were having a great time tonight."

He shrugged. It had been all right. He hadn't hated it, just... "I didn't know what to say."

"Yeah?" She came and sat on his bed. "That's a cool picture."

He smiled, thinking so too. He finally felt okay about his pictures now. It had taken him a while to find it fun again after kids at school had bullied him for drawing.

"Do you like our new neighbors?"

He did. They were nice, even if Eddie made him feel a bit weird.

"Hey." She tilted his chin toward her. "It's okay, Vico. You can talk to Eddie. He's a nice boy. He won't be mean to you."

His fingers curled, wrinkling the paper. He quickly smoothed it out. "How do you know?"

"Because not everyone is like those jerks from your school. Don't be afraid to open up, okay? I think he really needs a friend." Her eyes lit up. "Hey, is your drawing finished?"

"I think so." He liked it enough as it was.

"How about you give it to Eddie? I think he'd like it."

Give it to Eddie? His insides twisted up. What if he hated it? What if he said it was bad? What if he ripped it up like the kids who'd bullied him?

"What if he hates it?"

She grinned. "What if he likes it?"

Heat bloomed in Vicenzo's cheeks. Somehow, the thought alone was enough for him to shove the picture at her. "Okay. But don't tell him it was from me!" For some reason the thought embarrassed him.

She laughed and tousled his hair. "Okay. I'll tell him it's from Kassandra."

Vicenzo's mouth dropped open. His mother hurried out, her dress swaying around her knees.

Suddenly, Vicenzo bolted from his bed and yelled, "Wait! I changed my mind! Bring it back!"

He wouldn't let his sister take credit for *his* work, he thought as his mother gave the picture back to him. Just so Eddie knew it was from him, he grabbed a pencil and wrote his name on the back, underscored for emphasis.

The night was cool and quiet, dry soil crunching under his feet as he approached the blue house at the end of the road. The lights were on inside. It had been ages since anyone had lived there. Wondering how long Eddie and his pack would stay, he reached for the doorbell and hesitated. Would Eddie like his picture? He scowled. If he didn't, he was a jerk. He rang the doorbell.

"I'll get it!" It was Eddie's voice.

"Crap!" As Vicenzo turned to run, the door opened behind him.

"Oh. Hey."

Vicenzo turned as if his feet were stuck in quicksand. Eddie's big cyan eyes were so bright, even in the dark. Geez. "Here." He shoved the picture at him.

Eddie blinked at it as if he'd never seen a drawing before in his life. "Is this for me?"

"No." Why did he say that? "I mean, yes! I mean—" His face was burning up, his words all jumbled together in a panicked ball in his brain. "Just don't rip it up! Or I guess you can if you really hate it, or—never mind!"

He took off up the road and didn't look back.

CHAPTER 3

FOREVER

Early the next morning, Vicenzo and Kassandra arrived at school. Kassandra's friends rushed up to greet her as they entered the classroom. A few of Vicenzo's friends on the soccer team waved at him. Before Vicenzo could say hello to them, the buzz of chatter in the classroom cut out when Eddie walked into the room.

The whispers stopped, but there were several short intakes of breath as the other kids scented the air, trying to get a feel for the new kid.

Vicenzo wondered what Eddie smelled like to them. Did he smell like honey and summer grass to them? Like home?

"Hey." Eddie waved and smiled, and Vicenzo's stomach did that weird flip again. "I'm Edward Turner. Everyone calls me Eddie."

Kassandra slammed her hands on her desk. "He's my brother's mate!"

Vicenzo choked as the kids burst out laughing. Eddie's face colored but he smiled good-naturedly.

"All right, everyone settle down," Ms. Elizabeth said, motioning Eddie toward a desk. "Eddie, you can go and sit next to Vicenzo."

Vicenzo wanted to sink into the floor. Why him? He shoved his nose into his notebook as Eddie's chair screeched beside him. His scent blanketed Vicenzo, reminding him of hot summer days in Italy visiting his grandparents. The sweet taste of honeycomb straight from the hive. His grandfather's tanned face and wrinkled smiles. Lying belly-up as a wolf in the grass, the sun warm on his stomach.

"*Psst.*" Eddie handed him a piece of paper. As Vicenzo took it, he noticed that Eddie's fingers were warm and slightly damp with sweat.

Hiding his hands in his lap so the teacher wouldn't see, he unfurled the paper. Written in neat handwriting was the statement, *I liked your drawing.*

Vicenzo bowed his head, smiling so hard it hurt. Pride bloomed warm in his chest. He scribbled, *Thanks.*

Ms. Elizabeth was deep in her lecture about werewolf history, so he handed back the note. Eddie scribbled something and nudged his foot, giving a start when he realized Vicenzo hadn't looked away. He handed the note back.

How'd you know what my wolf looked like? he'd written.

Vicenzo shrugged and wrote back, *Just guessed.*

Eddie smiled when he read it. Ms. Elizabeth turned to the chalkboard, the chalk scraping softly over the board. Vicenzo took the note Eddie passed him.

He'd doodled a paper-white wolf and inked in a black wolf at the bottom of the page.

It wasn't much, but Vicenzo smiled.

"Eddie, Vicenzo."

"Crap," Vicenzo said before he could stop himself. Ms. Elizabeth winked at them.

"Can either of you tell me the name of the founder of the Council of Lycanthrope Affairs?"

Vicenzo was going to get detention. He could just feel it. He'd miss recess and wouldn't get to shift and run around with the other wolves. "Uh…"

Eddie raised his hand. "Theodora Lupe."

"And the year it was founded?"

"1960."

"Very good."

Vicenzo nudged Eddie's foot when the teacher turned away. "Thanks."

Eddie's mouth quirked.

"Hey," Kassie whispered, beckoning. She scribbled something and tossed it to Vicenzo. It read, *Want to have a sleepover?*

Vicenzo passed it to Eddie. His eyes lit up and he nodded.

"Yes!" Kassie shouted.

The teacher whirled around.

"Oops." His sister had the grace to look ashamed.

She, Vicenzo, and Eddie spent recess in a hot classroom cleaning desks.

THE DOORBELL RANG. "I'LL get it!" Kassandra thundered downstairs and threw open the door. From where he sat at the table, nose in his homework, Vicenzo glanced over his shoulder.

There stood Mr. Turner with Eddie at his side, hugging his backpack to his chest.

"Welcome! Dinner will be ready in five minutes," Vicenzo's mom called.

"Smells great," Mr. Turner said, breathing in deep. They'd baked an all-meat pizza. The smells of sausage, pepperoni, and Italian spices made Vicenzo's stomach growl. His grandma loved to make personal pizzas for him and Kassandra whenever they visited Italy.

Kneeling, Mr. Turner took Eddie by the shoulders. Vicenzo's wolf hearing picked up Mr. Turner's gentle words.

"If you need anythin', just call, okay? It's your first night away from us since the fire. Are you really not nervous?"

Eddie shrugged. "I'm fine, Pa." He didn't look fine. He looked sad, his scent stifled by storm clouds.

"You don't have to stay if you're uncomfortable. Talk to Mrs. Salvatore, call us. We'll come get you. Okay?"

"'Kay." Eddie bobbed his head and his father tousled his hair and kissed his cheek.

"Behave, kiddo! Have fun." Eddie waved and watched the door until it closed.

Vicenzo pressed his pencil into his notebook until it left a small dot on the page. He'd heard the rumors before Eddie and his pack had arrived. There'd been some kind of fire. A lot of wolves died. Hunters did it, that was what Kassie's friend Derek thought. Eddie was quiet and kept to himself, but he wasn't acting like someone who'd survived a fire. Shouldn't he be more scared, or upset?

What had happened? He wanted to know why Eddie had smelled of ash.

"Hi." Eddie stopped beside the table. Vicenzo tensed, a ticklish feeling going down his spine.

"H-hey." He didn't know what to say. "Detention sucked, huh?"

"It will suck more if you don't start paying attention in class!" his mother called and Vicenzo grimaced.

"Ugh, enough about boring detention." Kassandra clapped her hands together. "How about we do something fun?"

"Like what?" Vicenzo asked.

She tapped her chin thoughtfully. "Let's have a drawing competition!"

Vicenzo grinned. "I'll beat both of you!"

Kassandra clasped Eddie's hands. Annoyance made Vicenzo clench his fists, though he didn't get why he was suddenly mad at her. "That sounds fun, right?"

Eddie shrugged. "Sure."

They followed Kassandra up to her room across the hall from Vicenzo's. It was green like a forest, with a big plush wolf on the bed as big as Kassandra herself. She'd won it during the town's supermoon festival. Once they were supplied with paper and crayons, they sprawled out on their stomachs on the woodland-themed carpet. Kassandra declared, "Let's think of a theme!"

Vicenzo sighed. "Can't we just draw whatever we want?"

"I don't mind a theme," Eddie said.

Vicenzo dropped his cheek against his arm while he waited for them to decide.

"How about nature?" Kassandra said, gazing thoughtfully at her rug. No one else could come up with a better idea, so it was decided.

Kassandra went on scribbling, tongue poking out as she concentrated. Vicenzo decided to draw some wolves and a forest at night. He wondered what Eddie would draw as the blond boy reached for some orange crayons, then some red.

"And time's up!" Kassie announced in her best TV show host voice. They laid out their drawings. "Wow, Vicenzo! Yours is really cool."

"I drew our family," Vicenzo explained. He pointed as he said, "The gray wolf is Grams. The brown wolf is Gramps. The black wolves are Mom and Dad. Those are me and you, Kassie." They all howled under a full moon.

Eddie glowered down at his drawing clutched in his hands.

"What did you draw, Eddie? Hurry. We need to decide a winner before the pizza's done."

Something changed in Eddie's face. His nostrils flared, and his eyes blinked fast. He suddenly crumpled his drawing into a ball. "Nothing." He chucked the wad of paper into the wastebasket by the door.

"Hey, kids, dinner's ready!" Mom said from the doorway, and she jumped as Eddie slipped past her and into the hall. "Come on down before it gets cold."

Kassie sighed. "I love cold pizza."

"'Cause you're weird." Vicenzo made a face at the thought.

"What was with him? Did he not like his picture?" Kassie wondered.

Vicenzo wasn't sure but the unease hanging heavy in the air made him uncomfortable. Eddie had seemed calm and quiet until that moment. Shrugging, Kassandra followed Mom downstairs. Vicenzo stood and stretched, shaking out his cramped wrist as he stopped by the wastebasket. He probably shouldn't look. He knew he shouldn't, but curiosity got the better of him.

He closed the door just in case, then reached into the wastebasket and found the paper ball. He unfurled it. In violent streaks of orange and red, Eddie had drawn a burning forest. The wolves howled with tears in their eyes to a moon choked out by smears of black smoke. The wolves had names: Vicki, Darrel, Johnathon, and Hazel.

Cold all over, Vicenzo ripped the drawing to shreds and tossed the pieces into the trash.

He wished he'd never looked.

"Vicenzo?" He jumped. His mother poked her head into the room. "Coming to dinner?"

"Yeah…" He wasn't hungry anymore.

Eddie had a secret he carried around, unable to shake.

But now, Vicenzo knew it too. And he would give anything not to know the things he now knew about Eddie Turner.

EDDIE DREAMED OF FIRE, of flames roaring and consuming the town. He lay under his blanket and smelled the smoke, choked on it as it forced itself into his lungs. But he could only lie there paralyzed as his brain screamed at him to *RUNRUNRUN*.

His mother never came for him. His blanket caught on fire, the heat searing the flesh from his bones. The wolves howled in their burning forests, screaming to the stars as their fur burned.

"Eddie?"

Sweat was icy on his skin as he woke in the dark, gasping. He lay in his sleeping bag on the floor and for a moment he thought he was back in the burning house. No, no, no! He thought they'd found a new home, a new pack. Why was he still here?

"Hey!" Warm hands gripped his shoulders and shook him. "Wake up!"

A light flickered on, casting away the darkness.

He was in a bedroom that didn't smell like his, sweating in his sleeping bag. He whimpered, suddenly aching for his ma and pa, for the home that wasn't really a home because it didn't smell like his, like pack.

Tears spilled hot down his cheeks.

"Uh... why are you crying?" Vicenzo knelt in front of him, sniffing toward him. "Did you have a bad dream? It wasn't real."

"Yeah, it was!" Eddie could barely speak, his throat was so tight. Before the fire he'd had nightmares about monsters, but those hadn't been real. These weren't nightmares. They were real, and there was no one he could turn to for a hug to tell him it was *just a dream, sweetie. It was just a dream, and no one can hurt you.*

Vicenzo sat back on his haunches, frowning at the floor. "Do you wanna talk about it? I feel better after I tell my mom about my nightmares."

Eddie shook his head and rubbed his leaking eyes, but the tears wouldn't stop flowing. It was like a dam had opened up in him. "I wanna go home."

Vicenzo nodded. "Okay. I'll wake my mom up and—"

No! He didn't understand!

"I don't want to go to that house! It's not my real home. I want to go *home.* I want to see my friends again. I want to be back at my old school with my old teachers." He hid his face in his knees as the sobs pushed out of him. Because he couldn't have any of that. It was gone, *they* were gone. All his friends were either dead or far away. All his favorite teachers. His house that smelled like pack and home and safety.

"Ma and Pa act like everythin' is gonna be like it was before b-but it won't ever be. Because of that stupid fire!"

"Who started the fire?"

Eddie hiccupped, unsure how Vicenzo knew. "I... I d-don't know. My parents just said it happens sometimes."

Vicenzo wet his lips and whispered, "People at school think it was hunters."

He sniffled, his nose so plugged up he couldn't breathe through it. "I heard people whispering behind my back. People stare. They call me weird and... and other things."

His classmates whispered, eyeing him with something like fear, smelling like mistrust. They whispered, *A hunter killed his whole pack. What if the hunter comes here?*

No one go near him. He's probably dangerous.
Stay away from him. He's bad luck.

No one had sat with him at lunch today, and his classmates had avoided him. He wanted his old friends back. But they were gone, turned to ash.

"I don't think you're weird." Vicenzo hugged his knees to his chest, looking at the floor. "You smell nice. Like sunshine and honey and summer and... stuff." His face was red.

"I smell like ash. Like something's burnt." No matter how many times he showered, he could still taste the ash sometimes and smell burning cloth.

Vicenzo's eyes brightened. "Hey! I know!" He grinned. "There's this really awesome place I like to visit. It's right in my backyard. Come on!"

Sniffling, he shook his head. "No."

Groaning, Vicenzo tugged on his hand. "It's not far. You'll really like it. I promise."

Eddie couldn't deny he was curious. "Fine. But it better not be somethin' stupid."

Shushing him, Vicenzo gripped his arm and led him out into the dark hallway. They went downstairs, and Vicenzo warned him about a squeaky step he needed to avoid. They pulled on their shoes, and then Vicenzo motioned for him to go outside.

Vicenzo led him through the trees behind his house, and they climbed a hill that overlooked the town. On the horizon was Las Vegas, a golden sea of lights glittering like jewels in the night. Breathless as he was, Eddie couldn't look away.

"Isn't it epic?" Vicenzo sat beside him and caught his breath. "It's like we have the city in our hands."

Eddie sat beside him and listened to the coyotes howl among spires of red rock. It really was beautiful, and bit by bit, he started to feel better. "It's pretty cool. Thanks."

"Y'know... maybe you could make new friends here. I really missed my house back in Italy at first. But then I met new people, and I felt better. Maybe it'll be the same for you?"

"I don't wanna meet new people." Eddie hugged his knees to his chest. "'Cause everyone else I know is gone. I don't wanna be your friend, only for you to disappear, too." He swallowed the lump in his throat, the lights blurring to golden circles from his tears.

Hands gripped his shoulders. He blinked and Vicenzo came into focus. He looked right at Eddie, his face more serious than Eddie had ever seen it and yet so fragile Eddie thought Vicenzo might shatter. His hands shook on Eddie's shoulders. "I won't leave."

"No one means to. It just happens."

"I won't!" Vicenzo's voice echoed into the desert. "It won't happen to us. Okay?"

"How do you—"

"I *know*, Eddie. I just... know." Vicenzo's voice broke, and he smelled like so much confusion and uncertainty, but his heart never faltered. "We're gonna be friends for life. I know this. I don't know how, but I've never smelled anyone like you before and I just—" He took in a deep breath, his eyes wild and desperate.

Eddie swallowed hard. "Okay," he whispered. "I believe you."

Vicenzo relaxed, his hands loosening their grip on Eddie. Seeming calmer, he turned his face to the horizon, toward Vegas. "We're forever, Ed. Just trust me." Vicenzo smiled, and Eddie was so scared but it was impossible not to believe him.

Eddie took his hand and squeezed tight. "Okay."

EDDIE DID EVENTUALLY END up going to sleep. It was a good sleep, and Vico's mom made them pancakes in the morning

When his parents came to pick him up, Eddie hugged them both.

"See you later, Ed!" Vico called as he walked away.

Eddie waved, excitement fluttering in his belly. He had a new friend.

Once he was home, Eddie ran to his room.

He unpacked his bag and smiled when he noticed Vicenzo's picture up on the wall. He'd taped it there, the drawing of two wolves howling at the moon. It was the only piece of artwork in his room, which gave him an idea.

Eddie stood and gingerly removed the drawing from the wall. He turned it over to where Vicenzo had written his name.

Eddie grabbed a pencil and added his own just beneath, then a single word underneath that.

FOREVER

CHAPTER 4

EVERYTHING CHANGED

TEN YEARS LATER

VICENZO DIDN'T KNOW HOW it had started, all he knew was that seeing Eddie Turner felt like coming home.

Whenever he saw Eddie and smelled the sweet scent of summer, he knew without a doubt where he was meant to be. If only he could find a way to tell Eddie how he felt. What held him back was that he honestly didn't know if Eddie was into him. Or anyone. Eddie had never seemed interested in dating and had never crushed on any guys or girls at school. How was he supposed to know if Eddie liked him unless he came out and asked?

Graduation came and went. Vicenzo was both relieved to be done with school for good and nervous. His future was opening up, and he wasn't sure what to expect.

His family got together with Eddie's for a big cookout that night in the backyard. They grilled chicken and some steak and ribs and had roasted corn and mashed potatoes. Even with the addition of Vicenzo's grandparents, there was more food than even a pack of werewolves could eat.

Every so often, Eddie caught his eye and smiled like a sweet ray of sunshine, causing a storm of butterflies to take flight in Vicenzo's stomach. Eddie liked him—Vicenzo was sure of it. Okay, maybe not so sure but they'd been so busy before graduation, there hadn't been much time to actually sit down and talk to Eddie.

Or, maybe, they could skip talking and Vicenzo could let all the longing of the past ten years speak for him. Then came a nagging voice in his mind. *What if I've misread things? What if he's not into me?*

There was only one way to find out.

"Just ask him out, Vico!" Kassandra said through a mouthful of bacon the next morning.

Vicenzo banged his head against the table. "Yeah? And what if he rejects me?"

"What if he doesn't? Honestly, Vico. If you don't ask him out, I'll do it for you! I'm sick of watching you pine after him like some main character in an Austen novel."

Vicenzo's face burned hot. "I do not pine for Eddie! I look at him. In the manliest, most homoerotic way possible, and he just happens to never be looking back!"

"Do you want him to be your mate?"

Vicenzo's stomach somersaulted at the thought and he wrestled to hide a dopey grin. "No."

She smirked. "I heard your heart skip a beat. You love him!"

Vicenzo punched the table. "I do—not! I do not!"

"If you kids are done yelling about Vico's relationship," their father drawled. "Vico, up and at 'em, graduate. It's time to head to the office."

Vicenzo sighed. He'd never imagined being sheriff was so boring until he realized most of it was just sitting around answering the phone and listening to the townspeople complain.

"Be grateful," his father said. "The only reason the job is boring is because humans tend to leave us alone."

Vicenzo supposed that was true. In the village he was born in back in Italy, the town had been so small, making them an easy target. The Red Rock Springs pack was larger, deterring most troublemakers. Sometimes tourists drove in by accident. Most humans stayed away from the pack territory. He liked to think the blazing desert sun wasn't worth a trip to hassle some werewolves.

"I'm happy for you, kiddo," his father admitted, affixing his badge to his shirt as they walked the dusty road to the sheriff's office. "You and Ed would make good mates."

Vicenzo's face burned, and not from the sun. "He probably doesn't even think I'm his mate."

His father slapped his shoulder. "Ask him. Go grab dinner together, watch a show at the outdoor movie theater. Have fun."

Vicenzo was still unsure about what to do when they arrived at his father's workplace. He helped himself to some icy water from the cooler in the corner of the office. Not five minutes after they'd walked through the door, the phone rang.

"Hello, this is Sheriff Salvatore. Alpha Hanson! How nice to hear from you. Yes, all's well. My youngest kid just graduated. I know—I'm amazed he did it, too."

Vicenzo snorted at his teasing.

His father chuckled and cradled the phone against his ear. He frowned. "Hold on. Where was this? Yeah, that's nearby. Do you think—hmm. I see. Well, I can send my boy over to check." His father hung up. "You wanted something to do, kiddo, you got it."

"Why, what happened?" Vicenzo sat across from his dad.

"Our neighbors at the Silver Peak Pack haven't responded to the Council's annual meeting request. Alpha Hanson called the town sheriff twice and got no answer. He can't get in touch with anybody from the town, either."

Vicenzo frowned. "Is that a bad thing?"

"It could be nothing, or it could be something. Since we're the closest, they want us to check in on them, make sure they're all right."

"What could have happened?"

His father rolled his shoulders. "Anything. Could be busy, could have a power line down that's messing with communication. Or worst case they ran into trouble with humans. We won't know 'less someone drives out there. It's about a day's drive there and back."

Though the situation could be dire, Vicenzo was excited by the prospect of getting out on the road. "I'll go."

"Will you need me to come with you? Your mother could handle things at the office in my stead."

"Nah. I'll bring Eddie. We'll make a trip of it."

His father grinned. "Smooth. You guys can hash it out, see where you stand."

"Yeah. Right." His stomach flip-flopped.

Throat dry despite the gallon of water he'd consumed, Vicenzo stepped outside and walked down the road toward Eddie's house.

"Vico!" His neighbor Derek, his freckled face red from the heat, bounded up to him.

"Hey, fellow graduate!" Vicenzo slapped him on the back.

"Right back at ya, dude." His smile vanished, lips pouting when he asked, "When is Kassie leaving, again?"

Seemed Der was still hung up on his sister. Some things never changed.

"Yeah. She'll be here another week. Then she's off to Italy." Rather than go to college, Kassandra wanted to make pilgrimage to the Monastery of the Moon in the Apennines and meditate to strengthen her connection to the goddess.

"Oh, man... that's such a bummer. You think if I tell her how I feel, she'll... stay?"

Vicenzo snorted. "Hate to tell you, but my sister's not the kinda girl to put a guy before her passions."

Derek grinned. "I knew you'd say that. That's why I'm crazy about her. Hey, what does she like to eat?"

"Uh... chicken, steak—"

Derek shook his head. "I mean, what's her favorite type of prey?"

"Oh. One time we all went hunting as a pack and caught a pronghorn."

Derek grinned. "Yes! That's it! I'll go and catch the biggest pronghorn I can find! The way to a wolf's heart is through the stomach, after all!" He gave Vicenzo a thumbs-up. "Thanks, Vico! You're the best!"

"No problem. And hey, stop calling me—"

But Derek was tearing away up the road on a quest to win his sister's heart. Vicenzo scoffed, but he admired the guy. Sure, he was loud and goofy, but he cared about Kassandra. Kassandra and Derek had been friends since they were kids. She'd never caught on to his feelings, always tottering around with her nose in a book on werewolf history while he practically drooled in her direction. And yet after all this time, he still held her in high regard and had never asked for her to return his feelings, though it looked like he was finally taking steps in that direction.

Wasn't he scared? Afraid of rejection?

And here he was, lovesick Vicenzo doing nothing to win the heart of the guy he loved. He scowled and balled his hands into fists. He could do this. He couldn't let Derek one-up him and confess his feelings first.

If it all went to shit, at least Eddie would know one thing above all else—he was loved.

Within minutes of Eddie agreeing to go, the car was packed with a change of clothes and a couple tents and sleeping bags in case they'd rather camp than stop in a motel. His mother packed some leftover lasagna for them both. Eddie hugged his parents and said, "Yes, I'll be careful," and "I'll call you!" and "I promise, Ma!"

Vicenzo chuckled and dropped his elbow on Eddie's broad shoulder. Whoa. His arms were strong. Probably from all the gardening work he did. "Someone's spoiled."

"Vico! You come and give me a hug before you leave!" his mother called from the porch.

Eddie snickered at him.

"Yes, Ma." Vicenzo hugged her quickly and let his dad hug him too.

"Proud of you, kiddo," his dad said.

"Be careful!" His mom tousled his hair.

Embarrassed, he squirmed away. "Guys, come on! I'll only be gone a couple days at the most. I'll see you soon."

He'd never been without his pack before but with Eddie at his side, he felt a lot braver about venturing away from his family. Eddie *was* his family.

His mother said, "Eddie, you look out for my boy, you hear?"

Eddie tipped his head. "Yes, ma'am."

Vicenzo elbowed him. "Suck up." Ever the polite Southern boy.

Kassandra tousled his hair. "Good luck, if you know what I mean." She made kissy noises.

Vicenzo shoved her before Eddie could see. "You're way too invested in my love life!" he hissed, seething.

"It's like a drama show!"

Rolling his eyes, Vicenzo stomped to the car and unlocked the door. The engine rumbled to life. Eddie piled in next to him and fastened his seat belt. His cyan eyes were bright, and he smiled excitedly, the sight launching fireworks in Vicenzo's stomach. "Feels great to get away from pack territory for a change."

Vicenzo hummed and grasped the steering wheel as he drove them out of the driveway and along the dirt road out of town. "If we encounter any asshole humans, I'll punch them."

Eddie rolled his eyes in humorous exasperation. The town disappeared and spires of red rock and rolling brown and barren mountains encompassed them. On the blue horizon, fat cotton-ball clouds flew like kites in the arid breeze.

"Hey, can we turn on the radio?" Eddie asked. He didn't look at Vicenzo as he spoke. In fact, he hadn't looked at him much at all today. He seemed more interested in watching the scenery than maintaining eye contact.

"Sure." Vicenzo didn't care what they listened to, so he let Eddie scan the channels until he settled on some uplifting country tune. A smile played with the corners of his mouth when Eddie's deep, low voice sang along. His syrupy Texan drawl was still as sexy as ever, making Vicenzo's heart soar. Why did Eddie have to be so adorable? Vicenzo seriously wanted to hug him... among other things.

Tapping his fingers on his thigh to the music, Eddie asked, "So, Sheriff Salvatore, did your pops tell you what to expect?"

"He's not too sure. Thinks it could be a number of things."

A frown pulled at Eddie's blond brow. Vicenzo wanted to caress it away. "I hope those wolves are all right."

"They're probably fine."

Eddie chuckled. "I know you're hopin' humans messed with 'em."

Vicenzo grinned and gripped the wheel. "They're just so damn punch-able."

With a lopsided smile, Eddie leaned over, making Vicenzo's heart lurch into his throat when Eddie slapped his leg playfully. "Keep that temper of yours in check, huh? Else I'll tell your mama I had to save your ass."

Cheeks blazing, Vicenzo swatted at him, grinning when Eddie laughed. "You know I'm her favorite."

Vicenzo barked out a laugh. "True."

Eddie sighed, a happy little sound that tugged at Vicenzo's heartstrings. "This is nice. You and me, out on our own."

"Yeah. It is." Even though he preferred to stay close to home, he liked being out on the road with Eddie.

A laugh rumbled out of Eddie as he smiled big and wide. "Shit, man. We're grown up. Well, I am."

Vicenzo reached out and pinched his shoulder. Gasping scandalously, Eddie smacked his hand. "Son of a—"

Even though they were just joking around, he fought the urge to rub Eddie's shoulder and apologize. "Turn that shitty country music up."

"Hey, don't shit talk the song of my people!"

Eddie turned up the music and they drove until the sun set on the horizon and nightfall blanketed the desert. They pulled over and set up camp away from the highway. Surrounded by cacti and Joshua trees, they got a fire going and warmed up the lasagna Vicenzo's mom had packed for them.

"I feel like a real cowboy," Vicenzo said with pride, his face upturned to the stars.

"Pretty sure cowboys aren't werewolves, and they didn't eat lasagna."

Eddie grinned when Vicenzo kicked his foot.

Companionable silence fell.

Tell him, his father's voice echoed in his mind. Vicenzo's appetite diminished.

The firelight flickered over Eddie's tanned skin, casting shadows under his high, freckled cheeks. In the fire's light, his stubble shimmered on his angular jaw like gold. His hair, untied from the knot at the back of his head, tumbled down to his broad shoulders. A tank top clung to his big chest, and showed off his thick arms and shoulders dotted with beauty marks. The sun had greedily kissed every inch of his tanned skin. The moon herself couldn't hope to hold his attention when Eddie looked so damn beautiful.

"We should shift," Eddie said suddenly.

Whatever spell had suddenly come over Vicenzo abruptly dispersed. "Huh?"

"We should shift," Eddie said with more certainty, setting aside his food. "It's been a while and it's the perfect place for it."

Vicenzo wouldn't say no. His wolf was pushing to be let out. Tossing his paper plate in a trash bag, he stood and stripped. In the quiet of the desert, every sound was so loud. He was attuned to the rustle of fabric behind him, the way Eddie grunted when he tugged off his shoes.

He's naked behind me. Eddie's naked, his brain reminded him unhelpfully. His blood simmered, breath hitching as he fought the urge to take a peek. His wolf had other ideas, shifting as soon as he'd kicked off his shoes.

He was off in a dash, scenting the cacti nearby. A coyote had been here, had pissed on the cactus. He growled and pissed right over it. His ears picked up a rustling in the grass, the distant cry of a coyote. He hated coyotes.

"Vicenzo! Pack! Friend! Play!"

His tail wagged as he whipped around. A pure white wolf, his coat so bright it glowed, loped toward him, bottom wiggling in excitement.

Vicenzo dropped into a play bow.

"Pack! Run! Chase! Hunt!"

Eddie barked in delight and pounced. They tumbled over together, nipping and licking, and then took off into the desert. Their paws kicked up a storm of dust, the wilderness a blur around them.

He lost track of how long they ran but exhaustion compelled Vicenzo to take back the reins. He collapsed, tongue lolling and sides heaving, then shifted back. Panting, Eddie sat beside him and his shift melted away.

Naked, they lay together beneath the moonlight, the earth cool beneath them. Vicenzo happened to look over at the same time as Eddie, unable to stop himself from smiling over at his friend. Eddie's smile froze on his face. When Eddie's beautiful eyes drifted further down Vicenzo's nude body, his heart kicked in his chest. Something in Eddies scent shifted. Was he... aroused? No. He couldn't be. Could he?

Clearing his throat, Eddie looked away. "That was a blast, huh?" There was an odd crack in his voice.

Vicenzo forced his eyes to the horizon and away from his friend's naked, deliciously tanned body. His throat felt like it was full of gravel and his stomach fluttered like he'd swallowed a jar of butterflies. He folded his knees to his chest and watched the faraway lights of Vegas dance across the night sky.

His skin prickled. Eddie was watching him, but when he looked over, Eddie swiftly turned his face to the stars. "I'll, uh... never forget that night you took me to see the Vegas skyline."

Vicenzo smiled. "That was fun."

Sitting up, Eddie propped his chin on his knee, sweeping wayward locks of hair from his face. "I was scared. I thought I'd lose you like I lost everyone else to the fire."

Vicenzo shifted closer to him. He hated that Eddie had believed for a second he could have lost him. From day one, Eddie had commanded his heart, found himself a place inside it, and cemented himself there. "Not possible."

Color bloomed in Eddie's freckled cheeks. He smiled. "I know. I'll never get rid of you, huh?"

"Damn straight."

"Forever. That's what you told me. I didn't believe you at first, but..." Eddie rotated to face Vicenzo, blinking fast as their eyes met. Vicenzo had to remind himself to breathe, damn it, breathe, and not to chase away his truest friend. "I always wanna be a part of your life, Vico. For a long time, I wasn't sure where my place was. But it's with you."

"Really?" With his heart in his throat, Vicenzo inched his fingers across the sand and brushed the tips of Eddie's. Eddie gave a tiny jolt, as if he'd been shocked. Vicenzo's heart thudded in his chest.

Eddie gazed at him unblinkingly, as if he was the most important person in the world. "Y-yeah, Vico. You're my home. I don't wanna be anywhere you aren't."

Vicenzo swallowed, breathless when those cyan eyes glanced at his mouth. He hadn't been imagining things. Eddie wanted him. Eddie had feelings. For him.

Breathe, damn it!

Vicenzo's heart wouldn't stop pounding. "I'm... I'm glad you think so." His face was burning up and he couldn't look into Eddie's eyes. Fuck. He was so scared. "The Springs is a nice town and all, but there was always something missing—not until you turned up." He'd actually given up on trying to make sense and was talking with his hands as much as with his mouth. Goddess, he was so stupid. "You're this light in my life, Ed. And if you take that away, I'd be blind without it. Okay?"

"Fuckin' hell, Vico." Eddie's voice was oddly breathless. "Just shut up."

Then Eddie was kissing him, big hands framing his face so gently, and Vicenzo didn't think he'd ever be able to make a coherent sentence again.

Trembling hands framed his face, their chests touching as Eddie leaned into him. Those pink lips were so soft as they moved against his. Vicenzo was only just coming out of a holy-shit-my-best-friend-kissed-me coma when Eddie lurched away. His breath wafted against Vicenzo's mouth in short, hot bursts, his lips trembling from inches away.

Eddie's eyes were so wide, the pupils blown out. He smelled like want and need. "I—I'm sorry. I didn't, I should have asked. I'm so—"

Vicenzo wouldn't let him apologize for the best moment of his life. He clasped the back of Eddie's head, curled his fingers in blond hair as soft as he'd dreamed of, and pulled him back to him. Their mouths collided and something like fireworks went off in Vicenzo's stomach. His back struck the ground as Eddie draped himself atop him, their legs tangling together.

He swiped at the salt on Eddie's lips with his tongue, his cock stiffening at the moan he received. As Eddie's stubble rasped against Vicenzo's cheek, he couldn't stop himself from moaning against his friend's lips.

A warm hand settled on his chest, wandering up to rub the short hair on Vicenzo's head. Eddie's mouth tasted like Italian spices as their tongues tangled, tickling the roof of his mouth. He found himself breathless as Eddie's mouth left his, charting a trail down his neck, sucking on that spot between his neck and shoulder.

If Vicenzo's blood burned any hotter, he thought he'd be engulfed in flames. Suddenly, something rustled near his head. He jumped out of his skin as a huge scorpion shot by and hid under a rock. "Holy shit!"

Eddie's lips left his neck. "What?" His voice was high-pitched with fright.

"That was the biggest fuckin' scorpion I've ever seen in my life." Vicenzo shoved him off. "Get up now. I really don't wanna find out what happens if a scorpion stings my ballsack."

Apparently, Eddie didn't either. The mood thoroughly cooled, they jumped up and set off for the pale smoke of their campfire. They'd run much farther than Vicenzo had expected and in the dark, with his vulnerable human toes in stinging range, he was terrified something would crawl over his feet.

Eddie took his hand. "The big bad wolf's afraid of a little scorpion?"

"That thing was a fuckin' monster!"

"Actually, it's the little critters you need to be afraid of. Their venom's supposed to be more potent."

"Not helping, Ed!"

Eddie tugged him close. "Want me to carry you back to the camp?"

"Try it and I'll bite you."

Fortunately, they arrived back to the campsite unharmed. Vicenzo didn't bother getting dressed. He wanted to go straight to bed and dream of Eddie all night. Eddie, who was still blissfully naked too and so close it hurt not to be touching him and kissing him right now.

Eddie stopped, his hand still in Vicenzo's as they approached their separate tents. Vicenzo realized he didn't want to let go either.

One more kiss goodnight couldn't hurt. Their lips met, chaste and sweet, but when they parted, Vicenzo took Eddie's hand and led him into his tent. He turned Eddie toward him as he lay down and found his lips in the dark, as easily as if they'd been doing this their whole lives. They lay side by side, Eddie curled up on Vicenzo's chest, a warm and comfortable weight.

Eddie sighed, a happy sound.

Vicenzo kissed those smiling lips, and his heart sang him to sleep.

CHAPTER 5

THE WOLVES HOWLED AS THEY BURNED

WHEN EDDIE WOKE UP, he smelled like Vico, and Vico smelled like him. It was wonderful.

He worried about what today would bring when they arrived in the Silver Peak Pack's territory. Right now, nothing mattered except that he'd woken up in Vico's arms to sleepy smiles and lazy kisses, their bodies warmed by the dim glow of the sun shining through the ceiling of canvas. A smile tugged at his mouth. Vico had been so nervous last night. How could he have doubted that Eddie returned his feelings?

Didn't Vicenzo know what he was worth? He'd reached out to Eddie when everyone at school had refused to associate with him, and he'd been there for Eddie when his demons came for him at night. With his adventurous spirit, he'd made their quiet town feel like home when Eddie had thought he'd lost everything.

He'd picked up all of Eddie's broken pieces and pieced him back into a whole, and whatever he couldn't fix, he'd cherished. And *Vico* was cherished in return. He was *home*. Eddie loved him. He always had.

"I called you Vico last night. Sorry." He knew how Vicenzo hated his pet name. Said it made him feel like a kid.

Vicenzo shrugged and squeezed his hand in a quick pulse like a heartbeat. "I liked it when you said it. It made me happy." His shy smile told no lies. He wrapped his arms and legs around Eddie. "I'm so happy, Ed. I like being your Vico."

At a loss for words, Eddie held him tight. It was hard to imagine he could ever be so happy as he was in this moment. But he'd have to trust that, with Vico by his side, there were more happy moments like this in their future.

A question occurred to him. "Have you always liked me?"

Vicenzo turned his head so he could kiss Eddie's palm, then hummed his affirmation. Eddie's heart swelled. "How long?"

With an embarrassed laugh, Vicenzo said, "Forever, feels like."

Eddie wanted to hit himself. "Were you ever gonna tell me?"

"Maybe…"

Eddie bumped their foreheads together. He'd been so lost in his mind from the day he'd arrived, grieving the life he'd once known that had been stolen by the fire, then struggling to fit in somewhere new. But Vico had been his anchor through it all. This, them… it made sense. They just fit. He pressed his mouth to Vico's and breathed in the scent of basil. His favorite scent in the world. "I think I fell for you the night you gave me that drawin'."

Vicenzo's heart raced where Eddie's ear was pressed to his chest. "Sh-shut up. You were a kid."

"Yeah, but I knew what I felt. Hey. Maybe this is silly, but…" Eddie removed the chain from his neck. "I want you to have this."

Vicenzo turned the ebony ring with the white gemstone over in his hand. "It's pretty."

"It's a good luck charm."

Vico snorted. "Bullcrap."

"Is not. Okay, maybe. But it's important to me and ever since I put it on, good things have happened for me. I met you." Eddie's cheeks warmed, but he couldn't wipe the dopey grin from his face.

"You sure you don't need it anymore?"

Eddie smiled. "What do I need with a good luck charm? I've got you."

"Sap." Vicenzo kissed him, stroking Eddie's hair back from his face. "Fine. I'll wear your silly necklace."

Grinning, Eddie put the necklace on him. It looked good on Vicenzo.

He understood now why Vico had known from the start they were forever, even when he'd been too young to explain why he knew or how. He'd just known.

And now, Eddie knew too.

Vico was his home. His mate.

Forever.

THEY STAYED IN THE tent together a while, kissing and chatting about everything and nothing. When they were ready, they packed up camp and hit the road again.

Eddie drove this time and Vico was in charge of the radio. They only had a couple more hours before they arrived. Eddie's hand left the wheel, open in invitation, and his heart sang when Vico squeezed it tight.

"Hey, you think Derek is ever gonna ask my sister out?"

Eddie snorted. "Oh, like you're one to talk."

Vico shoved his shoulder. He added, "Ed, there's nothing wrong with you wanting to travel, even if you don't want to go to college. We should make plans to go places together."

Eddie smiled. "Okay. Where's somewhere you really wanna go?"

Vico hummed thoughtfully. "Maybe New York City? My parents took me once when I was a kid."

"That sounds fun." Eddie's heart soared at the possibilities.

It was half past noon when Eddie turned off the main highway and drove for another quarter mile. He swallowed a yawn, wishing he'd had some coffee. Rolling down the window, he breathed the dry desert air in deep.

The smell of ash hit his throat and a wave of nausea rolled through his bowels. "Shit." He sped up until the blackened, skeletal remains of the town came into view. He stuck his head out the open window, slowing the car.

The small town of Silver Peak had been leveled, some buildings burned to their very foundation. He could taste charred wood and blackened metal at the back of his throat. "What the hell..." He stopped the car, threw open the door, and stepped out, his boots stirring up dust and ash.

"Ed, if you don't want to come into town, you can wait in the car." Vico walked toward him.

Eddie's hands shook but he took a deep breath. It was the hottest time of the year. Fires happened—they were inevitable—but something didn't sit right with him. "We gotta spread out, look for survivors."

Vico swallowed loudly. "Don't think there are any."

Irritation prickled Eddie's skin. "You don't know—"

"Ed, if there were survivors, they could have come to our pack for help."

"Let's just look around, okay?" Eddie set off up the street. Memories of howling wolves assaulted him, images of burning forests flashing through his mind. He curled his fingers tight. The stench of burnt fur raised the hairs on his own arms. He followed the scent and it just got stronger. "Vicenzo! Over here!"

The scent was like carrion on the breeze and he followed it to the town square where the street was flooded with debris. He froze, his heart sinking into his stomach.

The burnt remains of wolves hung by their necks from makeshift scaffolds erected in the town square. Their fur was blackened and burned, some so severely that the flesh showed beneath, a white knob of bone glistening where the flesh had been seared.

Eddie turned away and retched until his stomach cramped. Vico held his hair back, one hand firmly on his shoulder.

"Hunters." Vico's voice was thick with fury. "Sick motherfuckers."

Eddie wiped away a string of noxious spittle, spitting to rid the taste of bile from his mouth. His knees shook so badly he could hardly stand. Vico's arm went around his waist. "Come on. We can't do shit for these wolves except give them a proper burial. And we don't have time for that. We've gotta warn our pack."

"No. We can't leave them like this." Eddie's eyes stung. He hadn't been able to bury his friends. He wanted to do right by these wolves.

Vico grabbed his shoulders. "Ed, listen. Our families could be in deep shit. We can't stay. If we don't warn them, they'll be next."

The wind howled like the voices of dead wolves. The nooses creaked and flies filled Eddie's ears with their buzzing as they swarmed the dull, empty eyes of corpses. Claws cutting into his palms, Eddie turned away and marched back to the car. Whoever had done this would pay in blood. His hands shook as he got on the phone with his parents.

"Eddie?"

"Mom!" His voice came out choked with relief. "Are you and Pa okay? What about the pack?"

"Everyone's fine. Ed, what's wrong?"

"The town was burned to the ground. The wolves, they were all…"

She was deathly silent.

"Tell Vico's dad. He needs to know what we're up against. Okay? Ma?"

"Yes." Her voice shook. "Yes. I will. Drive safely. Drive fast. Don't stop anywhere. Come home, both of you."

Eddie wished he could see her, hold her tight. He was so afraid to hang up in case it was the last time he heard her voice. "Okay. Ma, I…" A lump rose in his throat, eyes stinging. Goddess, please don't let this be their last conversation. "I love you. Pa, too."

"I know," she whispered, her voice choked.

Vico squeezed his hand as he hung up.

THEY DIDN'T STOP FOR anything. The sun disappeared beyond the horizon and they drove long into the night. Eddie white-knuckled the wheel until Vicenzo took his hand and squeezed tight. "Ed, it'll be okay. My dad will call the Council. They'll help. These hunters won't get away with this."

Eddie blew out a breath, trying to relax.

"Mate, it'll be okay." Vico squeezed his hand again.

Eddie laughed, heat blooming in his cheeks. "You really see me that way?"

"For a long time. I just never knew how to tell you. Or if you felt the same, or—"

Leaning over, Eddie kissed his cheek. "I'd have to be an idiot not to, Vico."

Vico's breath hitched. Wide, shining eyes gazed at him. "You do? I'm your—"

Eddie laughed at his disbelief. "Who else other than you?"

Vico's hands trembled as they clasped his face. "Say it. Can you just say it for me?" His voice was pinched and pleading.

Eddie turned his hand to kiss his palm. "You're my mate, Vicenzo Salvatore."

Vico's lips trembled, and tears overflowed his icy blue eyes. He wrenched Eddie into a searing kiss.

Headlights briefly blinded Eddie and he yanked his mouth away from Vico's. "Shit!"

A car hurtled on a collision course toward them, driving in the wrong lane.

Eddie spun the wheel and swerved out of the way at the last second.

"What the fuck?" Vico panted, eyes wide.

Another car shot past, going just as fast.

"Somethin' don't feel right," Eddie whispered, praying he was wrong.

In the dark, lights flickered. They were close to Red Rock Springs. Almost there, and then he'd see his family, and all would be well.

And then... then he saw the smoke, clouds of it, towering over the town. Icy dread shuddered down Eddie's spine. "Fuck..." The town of Red Rock Springs was on fire.

The blood drained from Vico's face. "No. No, no, no!"

Eddie slammed his foot on the gas, tires screaming over the dirt as they soared through a wall of smoke and into the town. Eddie braked hard and grunted when his seat belt tightened around his chest. Embers and soot rained from the rows of burning buildings. Chaos flooded the streets as townsfolk ran in front of their car in mindless panic. Another car roared past, narrowly avoiding colliding with them.

Vicenzo wrestled his seat belt off. "I gotta go find my parents, help folk evacuate!"

Eddie gripped his arm so hard, Vico yelped. "Don't go. Vico, wait for me, okay? Just let me find my parents and then we can—"

Vicenzo kissed him hard on the mouth, gripping Eddie's face between his hands. "I'll find you, Ed. I'll find you, I promise."

Tears and smoke stung Eddie's eyes. "Be careful."

Vicenzo squeezed his hand.

People screamed in terror up the street. With a deafening crash, a building caved in.

"Go!" Vicenzo hauled him from the car. "Find your parents!"

Distant cracks of gunfire split the night. Wolves howled as they burned. It was a nightmare ripped straight from his childhood. Eddie ran, dodging around fleeing people. He headed down a narrow alley, taking a shortcut toward his home.

Gunfire deafened him. The pavement shattered behind him. A man thundered toward Eddie, his face concealed by a gas mask, and raised his rifle in his direction. Eddie dodged to the left, a terrified cry escaping him as a bullet hit the wall behind him. He swerved around the nearest corner just as another pop of gunfire blew apart the air.

He left Main Street behind and ran up the dirt road toward his home. The fires hadn't reached this side of town yet, and his home still stood. Relief was short-lived as heavy grunting and cursing told him the hunter was still in pursuit. "Ma, Pa!" he screamed, voice ragged and hoarse.

The door flew open. His father aimed a shotgun at Eddie and yelled, "Get down!"

He hit the dirt and the shotgun roared in his father's grip.

The hunter screamed and collapsed, writhing in the dirt.

Face twisted in a snarl, Eddie's mother stormed down from the porch. "Stay the hell away from my son, monster!" When the hunter tried to reach for his rifle, she picked it up herself. His ma pressed the muzzle point-blank into the hunter's face. Eddie couldn't look away, his stomach churning as, with a deafening crack, the gun bucked in his mother's grip. The hunter's skull shattered to pieces.

"Ed, you all right?" His father was already running toward him.

Gasping, face wet with sweat and tears, Eddie threw himself into his father's arms. His mother was there seconds later, holding him close. "Wh-what's happening?" Eddie sobbed.

His father's arms shook. "It's them. It's those fucking hunters who burned our town."

"But how?" His father had told him little of the hunters, only that he knew their leader had died years ago. "I thought—"

His father gripped his shoulders. "No, Ed. I was wrong. He's come for us, and we gotta go."

"Us?" Eddie croaked, stumbling as his father wrenched him toward the car. "But... What? Why us?"

His pa didn't answer. He hurled himself into the front seat and his ma climbed in on the other side.

"What're we doin'?" Eddie asked, feeling sick because he knew the answer.

"Get in!" his pa barked.

"We're leavin'? What about the others?"

"I said get in!" his father roared.

Eddie's heart sank to his toes. The Salvatores. Derek and his family. His former classmates. The kind men and women of this town who he'd grown up with. His father was leaving them all to die. "Wait. Just... wait a second!"

He ran back into the house, storming up the stairs to his room. There was no time to pack, but he couldn't leave without his most precious memento. He removed the frame from the picture of the white and black wolves Vicenzo had drawn all those years ago. He folded it carefully and pocketed it.

"Ed, hurry up!" his father barked when Eddie came charging out the door.

Snarling, Eddie leaped into the back seat.

His pa slammed on the gas and the car hurtled out of the driveway. "There's nothin' we can do, Ed!" His pa white-knuckled the wheel, eyes wide. "Vico's folks will call the Council, and hopefully they'll sort this mess out."

Fury brought tears to Eddie's eyes. "Can't believe you're doing this. We have friends here!"

Snarling, his father slammed a fist onto the wheel. "Ed, leavin' is the best thing we can do! He'll follow us. Maybe he'll spare the town. He always fuckin' follows us."

"*Who* are you talking about?" Eddie's brain spun. Did his father *know* these hunters? "Dad, we can't just leave! This is our pack. Our friends are here! We can't abandon them!"

Eddie couldn't breathe. His whole life was falling to pieces. Embers rained down on the car as they drove through town.

"Oh Goddess." His mother whimpered.

A person stumbled from the convenience store, wreathed in flames. Wolves tore through the streets, howling and yipping in fright. A building collapsed with a groan of wood and metal. Hunters chased wolves down an alley, guns raised.

"Pa, we've gotta stop!" Eddie screamed.

His father's nostrils flared. He accelerated, driving past the burning dead, the terrified wolves. They roared through clouds of smoke, his father leaning on the horn to warn anyone he couldn't see of his approach.

Eddie doubted he would have stopped, even if he did accidentally run over someone. Nothing mattered except saving their own fucking skins.

"Pa, stop! Please!" They were nearing the town's exit. Eddie shook the door handle, but it wouldn't open. A sob tore from him as he slapped his palm against the glass. "How can we just abandon them without helping?"

His father snapped, "We don't have a choice! Why are you fightin' me on this?"

Eddie knew he shouldn't argue, not when his father was in a mood. But he was furious, too. "Because all we do is run."

His father squeezed the wheel. "What did you say, boy?"

"We run!" The scream tore from Eddie's throat as tears coursed down his cheeks. "That's all we do! We ran when the town burned. We didn't stop to help anyone! We abandoned them!"

His father's lips trembled. Blinking fast, he shook his head. "There was no time, Ed."

In this moment, Eddie hated his father. "We didn't even try."

"Me. Is that what you mean?"

"Both of you stop. Please," his mother said through gritted teeth, her eyes baggy and tired.

Eddie held his tongue. His silence was enough.

His father released a strangled snarl. "You're right. I didn't try to save anyone. I didn't want to. You and your mother are all that matter to me and if that makes me a bad person, to hell with it."

Eddie watched the town disappear behind them and punched out a curse.

"We do what we have to in order to survive, Ed." His father's voice was hard. He stepped on the gas as they drove, hurtling up the road.

Eddie watched the town burn, as helpless as when he was a kid.

A truck tore free from the smoke and hurtled toward them.

"Pa." Eddie grabbed the back of his dad's seat. "Pa! Someone's following us!"

His parents looked back and the blood drained from his father's soot-smeared face. "No..."

The truck's window rolled down, and a man in a wide-brimmed hat leaned out the window. He had a gun.

"Down!" Eddie screamed, ducking below the window. "He's shooting at us!"

A bullet shattered the window over Eddie, chunks of glass falling onto him.

His ma screamed, gripping onto his father and urging him to duck.

"Shit!" his pa snarled.

The truck gained on them, closing the distance. With a crack of gunfire, the driver ruptured their tire. Their pace grew bumpy, slower.

"Hold on, he's gonna—" His pa's scream was cut off as the driver rammed their car with the force of a wrecking ball.

They went flying off the road. The world spun around Eddie, his mother's screams drowned out by the bellow of twisting metal as the car tumbled over and over before smashing to the ground at the bottom of a hill. Eddie was suspended upside down, flailing to free himself. He crashed down onto the roof of the car and fumbled to open the door.

"I got you, son!" His father threw open the door. He was bleeding from his forehead, a shard of glass embedded in his skin.

Eddie lunged for him and stumbled on shaking legs. He coughed as smoke burned his lungs.

"Ed, are you all right? Are you—"

Gunfire roared. His father stumbled into Eddie's arms. Eddie screamed but didn't hear it over the ringing in his ears. His father collapsed, the bullet wound smoking. The smoke burned Eddie's nose. It was silver.

Approaching them was the driver in his wide-brimmed hat, his leather boots caked with dust. The sunlight glinted off the pistol in his hands. Then his mother was there, shielding Eddie, her arms open wide. She begged, she threatened that if he took one more step—

Another blast of gunfire made Eddie's whole body flinch. His mother stumbled and fell into the dirt. Her eyes were wide and staring straight at him. Blood ran in a river from her forehead. She was— No. This couldn't be real. It wasn't real. This was a nightmare. Just another nightmare. He would wake up screaming, but his mother would be there to comfort him. She wasn't dead. She *wasn't*.

Tremors racked his body, and he was suddenly freezing cold. Blood ran between his mother's eyes as she stared and stared. His ears rang but over the ringing he heard cruel laughter, then his father's voice.

"E-Elijah..."

Vision blurred by tears, Eddie peered at his father, crumpled against the upside-down car. His wound wasn't healing. It wouldn't stop bleeding and the blood smelled like wolfsbane. Poison.

"Hello, brother," said the hunter. His voice raised the hairs on Eddie's arms. He'd never heard a sound so cold.

His mother still wouldn't get up. Why wouldn't she just get up?

The wind blew and the hat flew from the hunter's head, revealing shockingly white hair. His face was twisted by burns so severe they'd left the left side of his face disfigured, one eye sealed shut by knotted scar tissue. The hunter smiled, half of his mouth twisted in a sneer by a burn scar. "I was so hoping I'd catch you. Runnin' as always. You never change."

His mother's blood was soaking into the desert floor. "M-Mama. Please." It was all he could manage to say as his knees gave out. Sudden pain exploded throughout his skull, and he crashed to the ground, cradling his throbbing head. Blood dampened his fingers. Had he been shot? Oh, Goddess. Was he going to die?

"Don't! Don't hurt my boy! Please, Elijah. Please!"

Through Eddie's blurry vision, the hunter lowered his pistol. The grip had blood on it. He must have struck Eddie with it. "And why not? You hurt me, brother. Deeply." The hunter paced, kicking up dust. "Running off with that werewolf bitch, abandoning your own flesh and blood."

"You are not my family!" his father snarled.

Eddie couldn't understand. This hunter smelled human, but his father was a werewolf.

A hand fisted in his hair. Eddie yelped as the hunter dragged him to his feet and slammed the gun against his head. Eddie couldn't stop shaking. "P-Pa. Please, don't let him kill me. I don't wanna die. Help me!"

"Don't!" his father roared, his voice breaking in desperation. "Damn it, Elijah, I'm begging you!"

"And why should I listen to a word you say? You betrayed me! Your own brother!"

He turned the gun on Eddie's father, who howled as the bullet ruptured his knee.

No! Not his father, too. Eddie couldn't lose him. He couldn't be all alone.

Eddie struggled, screaming, "Don't hurt my pa! Don't hurt him! I'll do whatever you want!"

"Whatever I want, hmm? Now, that is a tempting offer, boy." He hurled Eddie to his knees. He crawled to his father, trying to figure out how he could make the hurting go away. The blood just kept on flowing from his father's wounds. The hunter whistled, a tuneless, eerie sound. "Are you a good hunter, boy?"

Eddie didn't know how to answer, why that mattered. His father gasped and Eddie pressed his hands over the wounds, trying to make the bleeding stop. "You'll be all right, Pa. You'll be okay. Don't leave me, please."

The hunter drawled, "I lost one of my wolves a few weeks back. Good hunter as any. Strong as hell. I asked you a question, boy. Can you hunt?"

"I can!" Eddie snapped, probably more angrily than he should have. "Why does that matter?"

The hunter grinned, revealing yellow teeth. His single bloodshot eye was as blue as the lips of a corpse. "I like you, boy. You got fire in your belly. I could use a wolf like you."

"Run, Ed, run!" his father gasped.

Eddie couldn't leave him.

"Come with me, boy, and I'll let your daddy live. He don't deserve it, but I can be merciful."

Eddie shook, nauseous with fear.

"Don't listen to him, Ed. Don't!" His father clasped Eddie's face. His hand was slick with blood. "He's a liar. He'll—" His face twisted in agony and he cried out as another bullet shattered his other kneecap.

Eddie couldn't watch his father die. His legs shook as he hurled himself to his feet, arms open and shielding him. "I'll do it! I'll go with you! Just stop hurting him." As soon as the desperate words flew from his lips, he wished he could take them back.

When the hunter's lips curled into a smile, Eddie knew his fate was sealed. "Looks like my nephew's got more sense than his pa." Gripping Eddie's elbow in a steel grasp, cutting off blood flow, he hurled Eddie ahead him.

"Ed! I'll come for you!" his father roared.

Eddie's eyes blurred as tears spilled down his cheeks.

Despite it all, his father smiled. "I love you, Eddie! Don't be scared. I'll find you! I swear it!"

The hunter said, "No. You won't."

The roar of gunfire deafened Eddie's scream. Blood dripped from his father's forehead as his chin slumped to his chest. The leather hat he always wore fell into his lap. Eddie ran, screaming for his father, and a crack of gunfire dropped him to his knees. Fire burned in his leg and he howled for his mother and father, for Vico, for someone, anyone to help him.

A high-pitched whistle split the air and wolves answered with a howl. They came from the road above, tearing down the hill in a blaze of fur and fangs. They surrounded Eddie, snapping and snarling, salivating as they sniffed at his bloody leg. Eddie couldn't tell if they'd once known humanity or if they'd ever shifted a day in their wild lives.

"Case you get any idea of running," the hunter explained, lighting a cigarette held between his brown teeth. "My wolves have a taste for it. Wolf flesh. How else am I gonna train 'em to hunt?" Grinning, he nudged Eddie as if this were humorous. Then he grabbed Eddie's shoulder. "Walk!"

Eddie put weight on his injured leg and yelped.

"I said walk!" A kick in his rear sent him flying to the ground. "Walk it off, boy. Walk it off!" the hunter roared, cackling as Eddie hurled himself to his feet.

Tears stung his eyes as blood dripped onto his father's hat. Fingers shaking, he reached down and grabbed the hat, clutching it to his chest.

"Sweet," Elijah said with a sneer. "Now walk!"

Gnashing his jaw against the pain, Eddie limped as fast as he could. Wolves pursued him, snapping at his heels, yanking on his pants. He fell and screamed his terror as they swarmed him, sure he'd be eaten. "Off, I said off!" The wolves yelped and retreated. The burn of silver hit Eddie's nose. Elijah lowered a silver whip and sneered at him. "Up. Now."

His legs shook as he stood, panting. The hunter shoved him up the hill and back to the road. An RV was parked on the other side of the road, concealed by a hill. The hunter whistled as he scooped up the metal roadblock Eddie presumed he or someone else had laid in the road in preparation for their arrival and tossed it in the bed of his truck. A hunter leaned on the truck, arms crossed as if he were bored, though a balaclava hid his face. "Good work layin' the trap for them, Royce. Take the truck. Me and the boy will go in the RV." He jerked a shoulder toward the RV. "Go on, boy. Door's open."

The RV smelled like wet fur and cigarette ash. Dirty dishes were piled in the sink and there were rows of cages for the wolves to sleep in. Old newspaper soaked in urine and spattered with shit lined the floor of the cages. The stench implied the papers were rarely changed.

"Excuse me, nephew." The hunter squeezed around him. "Sit down, and I'll fix that leg of yours." He knelt and opened the cupboard under the kitchen sink.

Eddie didn't move, squeezing the leather brim of his father's hat so hard his fingers whitened.

That corpse-blue eye glared at him. "I said. Sit. Down." The words were growled through clenched teeth.

Eddie obeyed, like a dog, sitting on the stained couch just off the tiny kitchen. Using some pliers, the hunter groped around in the wound, making Eddie gasp. Eddie held on tight to his pa's hat as the pliers pinched the bullet and yanked it free. The fire blazing in his leg subsided and Eddie gasped his relief as the wound healed.

"We got time to kill until my boys are through." Elijah kicked off his boots and propped his feet on the dashboard. His big toe stuck out of a hole in his striped sock, the nail overgrown and clogged with dirt.

"T-Through with what?" Eddie's voice was hoarse.

The hunter squinted at him. "That town of yours, of course. Never suffer a wolf to live. That's what my daddy always taught me."

Eddie made a strangled sound in his throat. Vico. Kassandra. Their parents. All the people he'd grown up with in that small town from teachers to grocers, neighbors to classmates. They would all die.

"You did it," he whispered, understanding making him sick. "You're the reason our home burned. It was you." Tears warmed his face.

"Yup. That was my finest work, I tell you. Never seen a blaze so big in my life. Killed tons of wolves, too. Exceptin' your daddy, of course. But we all know how that ended. I always get my way."

Cold fury curled Eddie's fingers but he didn't have the strength to fight. His resolve had died with his parents. He didn't care what happened to him anymore.

"Tell you what, boy, let's put on some music. It'll make the time pass by quicker." He leaned over and fiddled with the dial to the radio. "What kinda music you like?"

"I don't care," Eddie said.

"That's no way to speak to your uncle, boy. I asked you a question." A hand fisted his hair and he was forced to look into that stone-cold face. "What kinda music do you like?"

Eddie couldn't speak.

"Fine. I'll choose for you, shall I? Christ, you're as big a pain in the ass as your daddy." He switched on some country music.

Eddie closed his eyes as the music washed over him and—

He was with Vico in the car. The horizon big and blue, the hills rolling past the window. Vico said, "Turn that shitty country music up."

"Hey, don't shit talk the song of my people!"

His mate smiled and oh Goddess, was it beautiful. Eddie reached out and took his hand, warm from sunshine and the hot leather of the wheel.

Vico squeezed tight. "I'm here, Ed. I'm right here." Then he said in a low growl, "Well, would you look at that!"

Eddie's eyes snapped open. Vico was gone. Elijah leaned over the dashboard, eyes intent on the horizon. "Looks like my boys got the job done!"

A distant explosion rocked the ground. A cloud of fire and smoke burst in the night.

Vico. Kassandra. The sheriff and his deputies. They were all going to die. Just like his friends from so long ago. Like his parents.

Elijah laughed.

The wolves howled as they burned.

And Eddie put his head in his hands and screamed and screamed and screamed.

CHAPTER 6
NO ONE CAN HURT YOU

VICENZO CRUNCHED DOWN AND he choked on blood as the hunter spasmed beneath him and went limp. The smell of smoke burned his nose and silver stung his eyes. Flames roared as the hunters torched buildings, unleashing a spray of fire from their flamethrowers as wolves charged them. The smell of burning flesh and fur raised Vicenzo's hackles. Wolves howled and screamed as they burned, their thoughts a chaotic flurry of pain and rage as they died.

A howl tugged at Vicenzo's mind. It was Kassandra. He took off running, spraying dirt as his paws slammed the ground. His wolf cried out for *Kassie, pack, I'm coming, kill hunters, shred their flesh, drink their blood!*

His father howled. *"Olivia, Kassie! Hang on!"*

Whatever had happened, it was terrible.

Vicenzo shifted at the sight of his father's black wolf. He was outside a general store that had gone up in flames. Dead hunters lay in pieces around him.

"Where's Mom and Kassie?" Vico shouted.

His father's voice filled his mind as the wolf paced frantically. *"Inside! Kassie, can you hear me?"*

Vicenzo held his breath, praying his sister was all right.

"I'm here!" Kassandra's voice filled his mind. *"Mom and I are trapped. A hunter chased some kids into this building. We went in after them, but the door's blocked and—"*

His father sprang, his paws slamming against the rubble in front of the door. *"I'll get you out! Hang on!"*

A yelp came from above. His mother's wolf carried a pup in her jaws through a shattered window. She set the pup down, and he leaped safely to the ground below.

"Mom! Come down, please!"

With a whine, his mother looked back toward the shattered window and jumped inside.

Vicenzo rushed toward her. His father held him back, shifting to a man as he grasped Vicenzo's arms. His hands trembled, face pale. In all his life, he'd never seen his father so afraid.

Kassandra, shifted into a black wolf, scrambled onto the roof carrying a pup in her jaws. She leaped down from the roof and collapsed, struggling to stand.

"What happened, sis?" Vicenzo thought, kneeling beside her.

"Pups. They're still in there. They have to be saved. Mom wants to save them all!"

"Stay here, both of you!" And their father was gone, leaping as a wolf onto the crumbling roof.

"Dad!" Vicenzo screamed, and he felt like a small, helpless child.

His father looked back, eyes wild and steely with determination. *"Get our people to safety! Be the Alphas I know you can be!"* Then he was gone, disappearing through the window.

The roof creaked and shuddered, like old bones about to snap. Vico howled for them, for his parents. And then his mother collapsed over the window frame, covered in ash. Through the window, she tossed a wolf pup onto the roof. "Get him!" she cried.

The pup approached the edge and whined. Vicenzo opened his arms and caught the pup as he jumped. Kassandra yanked him back as the roof came crashing down onto the porch in a pile of flaming rubble. There was no way up now to reach the window. "Mom, come down! Hurry!" He would run to her, catch her if she jumped, anything.

His mother smiled like she had when he was a small boy and he knew that he was loved. The building came crashing in, swallowing both his parents. The scream tore from his throat and all he wanted was to throw himself on the rubble and dig, find them, and bring them back home.

Their bonds still pulsed feebly. They were alive. He could still save them. He could still—

His father's snapped first. It was like a blade had been driven into his chest. Kassandra collapsed with him, an anguished wail tearing from her throat when their mother's bond broke only seconds later.

They were gone. His mom and dad were *gone*.

A horn honked. "Vico," Kassie choked out. "We... we have to go. Now. The hunters are coming."

Vicenzo didn't care what happened to him. He couldn't imagine a world without his parents. Sudden desperation drove him to his feet, and he rushed toward the ruins of the building. Their parents were still in there. They were alive, they were only hurt. If he could get them out, if he could just— Kassandra's arms flew around him.

"Vico, stop! I can't lose you, too!" She screamed, tears coursing down her soot-stained cheeks.

His sister needed him. She was all he had. Her, and Eddie.

Kassandra helped him run to a van that had pulled up beside them. It was Derek's family car. "Get in, kids!" Der's mother Agatha called. Vicenzo collapsed into the back seat, and the van hurtled up the road. They hit a hunter and he tumbled over the top of the car and disappeared. Derek's mother, Agatha, drove, her knuckles white on the steering wheel.

"We have to go back," Vicenzo rasped. "Save them. We have to—"

Kassandra's arms went around him and she broke down. Vicenzo held her tight and cried with her until his throat ached.

"I'm so sorry, kids." Agatha's voice trembled. "I'll get you out of here. We'll call your grandparents. They'll take care of you."

There came a groan. Someone lay sprawled out in the third row of seats. They smelled of burned flesh.

"Goddess. Derek?" Kassandra's voice broke. She scrambled into the back and knelt on the car floor. Vicenzo's stomach churned. Derek was burned so badly, he was unrecognizable. One eye squinted at Kassandra. The other was burned over.

"Kassie." His voice was hoarse, dry as the desert.

"I'm here." Kassandra clasped his hand. It shook so badly it rattled her arm. "I'm here, Derek. Oh my…"

Agatha made a strangled sound that shattered Vicenzo's heart.

"E-everything hurts," Derek rasped.

Kassandra kissed his forehead. Her lips came away red.

"I'm scared. I'm so scared." He thought Derek was crying. "Please. Will you… stay with me?"

A tear slipped from Kassandra's eye. "I will."

Vicenzo couldn't look anymore. The air smelled black and burnt as it poured in through the window. Like sweet, warm grass. Like honey. Like—

"Stop!" he roared, heart in his throat. Agatha slammed on the brakes but the car hadn't stopped before Vico lurched out of the door. He tumbled over in the middle of the road and scented the air. Eddie. Eddie had been here. He was alive!

Then the stench of blood hit his nose, and his heart sank. "No. No, no, no. Don't do this, Ed. You can't do this." If anything had happened to his mate, Vicenzo didn't know what he would do. Only that he would never recover. He ran down the hill and lost his footing, sliding in the dirt. He skinned his palms as he caught himself on all fours at the bottom of the hill. A car had been overturned. He recognized the blue Chevrolet as Eddie's father's. They weren't inside. He circled around the other side and—

"No!"

Eddie's mother lay in a pool of blood, her empty eyes staring forever into the sky. Eddie's father slumped against the car, a bullet between his brows. His knees shook, bile surging to the back of his throat. He swallowed hard.

"Where's Eddie?" Kassandra whispered, arms around herself as she shivered.

Eddie wasn't here. Such tremendous relief swept over Vicenzo. Wolf tracks tattooed the ground, trailing up the hill. He smelled Eddie among them, mixed with the scent of silver and blood. He was alive. Hurt. A snarl tore at his throat. On the other side of the road behind a hill, tire tracks were embedded into the dry ground, leading off the road and then back onto it. The bastard hunters must have kept the windows open because the scent of other wolves clouded the air. He had a trail. He could follow it and find Eddie.

"He was taken," Vicenzo whispered, gut clenching. Whoever had done this had wanted him alive. His wolf howled in fury deep in his heart, and all he wanted was to follow the scent of his mate and rescue him. He looked back at Kassandra. Tears spilled down her face.

"Kassandra, I have to find him."

Her lips trembled. "You'll die, Vico. Don't do this."

Vicenzo took a step away from her, then another. "I'm sorry. Call our grandparents. They'll help. I know they will. Tell them... Tell them I'll be in touch soon."

"Vico, don't!"

"I'm finding Eddie!" Unable to look into her anguished face, Vicenzo turned and ran, following the tire tracks through the desert.

He would find his mate, and they would be reborn from the ashes.

EDDIE AND ELIJAH DROVE for days following the fire. They stopped only for gas, to sleep, or to get food. Elijah never allowed Eddie outside the RV but he brought him food: bags of chips, some water, sometimes a sandwich if the diner didn't take too long with his order.

Eddie tried to leave. He really did. One time, Elijah led the wolves out to hunt. He became distracted and chased after another wolf. Eddie's clothes ripped as he shifted and then he was running, tearing through the trees. The wolves bayed as they pursued at the command of Elijah's sharp whistle. He ran to the main road and turned back, the asphalt hot on his bare feet. He charged an approaching car, screaming, "Help! Help me!" The woman behind the wheel went pale white. She slammed her foot on the gas and hurtled away. Eddie chased her, begging her to come back, to help him.

Then the wolves were around him and Elijah panted, a sneer curling his mouth.

Eddie expected to be beaten within an inch of his life. His legs shook as he followed Elijah into the trailer. He tried to steel himself, his mind conjuring up a thousand different ways the hunter might hurt him.

Elijah opened a cage that was big enough for a wolf but far too small for a human. "Get in."

The space wasn't big enough for him to stand up in or spread his arms. Fear paralyzed him.

"I said get in!" Snarling, Elijah knocked him onto his knees. Fearing what would happen if he didn't, Eddie crawled in on his hands and knees. "You're breaking my heart, boy," Elijah crooned, but the way he smiled, so cruel and gleeful, only affirmed Eddie's belief that the man didn't have a heart. "Why would you ever wanna leave your poor old uncle? I'm your family. Don't you see? And you're stayin' in there till you remember it." He locked the cage.

And so he shifted to a wolf and found some peace within the tight, cramped space, even if it did stink. Unable to see out the windows, he lost track of where they were going, only able to keep track of time as the light outside darkened.

As the days passed, his more human thoughts became background noise. Instinct ruled him. He stopped being afraid. He stopped hurting. All he wanted was to eat, shit, and sleep in peace. Sometimes he was thirsty. He barked for water, pawing at his cage, and the hunter yelled at him to shut up.

The days blurred into each other. There was an ache inside he couldn't explain. When he slept, images flitted through his mind and he ran from roaring flames while people cried out a name or a word. *Eddie*! He didn't know who that was. He was wolf. Not Eddie. Just wolf.

Sometimes, he dreamed of another wolf, of a boy with a smile that made him want to howl until that sweet boy found him and took him home.

His name... he had a name.

What was his name?

ONE DAY, THE TRAILER finally stopped.

The cage rattled and the wolf peered up at the hunter.

"Out, boy. Come on."

The hunter reached in, and the wolf bared his fangs and snapped at his fingers. The hunter withdrew, cursing. Then he whirled around and drew his tranquilizer dart gun. Silver burned the wolf's flesh and he howled as his fur fell away and his paws turned to hands.

Eddie collapsed, yanking the dart free to ease the burning.

"Don't make me shoot you again, boy." Elijah raised the gun.

Eddie crawled out on his hands and knees.

"Still remember your name?"

"Yeah," Eddie croaked. Bits and pieces were coming back to him, re-opening the wound in his heart. He wished he'd stayed as a wolf and gone feral. At least then he'd be able to forget his mother's lifeless eyes, his father's pained screams. The last time he'd seen Vico.

"Stubborn son of a bitch, ain't you? Well, we'll fix that real soon, won't we?" Sniffing, the hunter opened the cages and the wolves tore free. "Welcome home, boys!" He motioned for Eddie to follow. His knees buckled as he stood. He couldn't remember the last time he'd stood up straight. His blond hair had grown even longer, tumbling down past his shoulders, and his face was scruffy with hair. He felt thinner, too.

He walked over to the pile of his clothes and dressed, grabbing the jacket off the floor. There was something in the pocket, a folded scrap of yellowed paper. On the back were the words, *Eddie*, *Vicenzo*, and *Forever*. Heart throbbing, he slipped the paper into his inner pocket, close to his heart. Elijah could never find this. It was all he had left of Vico, of what they'd once had, of the person he'd once been.

"Boy! Get out here!" Elijah barked.

Grimacing, Eddie followed, stepping out onto soft, damp ground. They were in a swamp. The air reeked of mud and algae. A house awaited them, a miserable thing with a lawn covered in weeds and moss growing thick on the roof. The wood looked as if it were rotting. A fence surrounded the property, crackling and humming.

"Stay on the path! I got traps everywhere," Elijah said.

The wolves were well trained, following the trail to the house in single file. Eddie didn't want to imagine how many of them had died in the bear traps that glittered among the tall grass off the path.

"Home sweet home," Elijah declared, unlocking the many locks on his door and kicking it open.

The house reeked of rotting wood. Dirty dishes were piled high in the sink, covered in bugs that were feasting on decaying food. Whatever was in the refrigerator smelled like it had rotted long ago. A stairwell led to the second floor.

"Phew! I gotta do me some housekeeping. Ah, what's the use? Another job will have us back on the road in a couple days, I'm sure." Elijah kicked off his boots and left them in the middle of the doorway. "Comin' in, boy? You're lettin' in a draft." Like that was a bad thing. This place could use airing out.

Eddie thought about running before that door closed behind him and locked him in with this unstable man. Escape wasn't worth the pain he'd endure if he were caught. And anyway, where would he go? There was no one out there looking for him. No one who cared. His family was dead. If Elijah had been as thorough as he'd been the first time he'd barged into Eddie's life, then everyone in that town was dead.

No. Vico had to be alive. Eddie couldn't accept any other alternative. Vico was alive and he was out there trying to find Eddie—he had to be. They were too far apart for Eddie to feel his bond, but that didn't mean anything. He was alive. Eddie would know it if he wasn't. Wouldn't he? Yet a part of Eddie hoped Vico would never find him because if he did, Elijah would kill him the way he'd murdered Eddie's parents. It would be best if Vicenzo stayed far away and never found him, even if Eddie's eyes stung at the thought.

Eddie stepped inside. The door closed behind him.

"Get comfy, boy. I'll have dinner ready in a few." Elijah opened the freezer and retrieved some meat. It smelled frozen but fresh.

When Eddie sat on the sofa, it creaked under his weight and something fat and furry with a long tail darted from underneath and into a hole in the wall. In the backyard, wolves snapped and snarled as they tousled. Had they ever learned to take a human form before Elijah did whatever fucked-up shit he'd done to make them go feral? His eyes darted around the room. Where were they, he wondered, hoping to find some hints as to their location. Why did that matter? Wasn't like he was ever going to escape.

A few pictures hung on the wall. One was a framed autographed sports jersey. It was black with yellow numbers on it. Eddie had never liked sports, but his father had. A New Orleans-born wolf, he'd always been a fan of the Saints.

Was his father a born wolf? He couldn't be, not if his brother was human, though calling Elijah human was a stretch and a half. Everything he thought he'd known about his family had been thrown into turmoil.

Elijah had burned the town when he was a child. His father must have known. Why had he never told Eddie? Had his mother been in on his secrets, too? He wondered how much of his own family he actually knew.

As his thoughts wandered to his family, he spotted a picture lying face down on the end table next to the sofa. Glancing to make sure Elijah wasn't looking, Eddie turned the picture face up. It was his father—there was no mistaking the blond hair and brown eyes. The sight of his smile broke Eddie's heart. Beside him could only be Elijah. His face wasn't burned and he looked eerily similar to Eddie's dad except for his eyes. There was a darkness in them and his smile didn't touch them, as if he were faking joy.

They knelt over the corpse of a wolf.

Stomach churning, Eddie dropped the picture in his shock. His breath hitched when the glass shattered.

"The hell you doin' over there, boy?" Elijah growled.

Eddie's heart slammed against his ribs. "Nothing." His voice came out a whisper. "I'm sorry." He picked up the picture and scooped up the glass, wincing as it cut his hands. "I didn't mean to. It was an accident. I—"

Elijah stood over him, his expression unreadable. Eddie couldn't breathe, terrified he'd be struck. Kneeling, Elijah picked up the picture, which was frayed at the edges. "Been meanin' to throw this out anyway. Guessin' you have questions then. 'Bout your pa. Sit down, boy. It's quite a story."

Dinner was ready. It was steak, browned and spiced just enough to give it flavor but tough and unappealing. Elijah chewed with ease, seemingly used to this particular cut of meat. Eddie had grown up on cow, sheep, pig, and chicken, butchered right on the ranch. This meat didn't taste familiar. He almost thought it was alligator meat or some other exotic meat.

"I'll tell you a story, boy." That single cold blue eye never wavered from Eddie's. He was watching. Always watching. "You should know the truth 'bout who your family really was. Bet your daddy never told you, did he? 'Bout me."

Eddie shook his head and chewed the steak.

Elijah snorted, anger flaring in his eye. "'Course not. Your daddy was a self-righteous prick, you know that? He weren't always. He and I, we were like two peas in a pod after our folks died. Our folks taught us how to hunt werewolves, like their folks before them."

Eddie's stomach churned. "My father was a hunter."

Elijah grinned. "Not just any hunter, boy. He put the fear of God in those beasts. Got himself a bounty from the Council, too. Can you imagine? I was real proud of him. But his methods... they were a bit too lax for my tastes."

Eddie's hands shook. He dropped his fork with a clatter on the table.

"He got on my ass over the years. Started pissin' me right off. Tellin' me I enjoyed the hunt too much, that Momma and Pap-pap would be disappointed in me." He snorted derisively and spat on the floor. "The hell did he know?" Suddenly, he beat the table with his fist. Eddie lurched to the end of his seat, heart hammering, and Elijah grinned as if he smelled Eddie's fear and liked it.

"We hit a pack one day. Killed a bunch of wolves and skinned 'em for their pelts. Well, I did. Your daddy never had a taste for skinnin'." He sneered. "There was one wolf. A bitch. She got into your daddy's head. He wouldn't let me kill her. He turned on me, his own flesh and blood. After everything I done for my baby brother, he chose some bitch over his own brother, his own family legacy, and he ran."

Eddie swallowed, tasting bile. He knew what came next.

"I hunted him over the years. Trained some wolves to track his scent. Next time I saw him, you know what that son of a bitch had done? He'd let the bitch turn him. Even had some brat with her. You. He did this to my face"—he motioned to the knotted scar tissue that sagged one half of his face—"and ran like a coward as I burned the town to the ground. He thought I was dead, and I let him. I'm not a patient man but my momma always told me good things come to those who wait, you know? So I waited. And waited. He got comfortable. Let his guard down. And bam!" He slapped his hands together and Eddie jumped out of his skin, flinching from him.

"You killed my friends," Eddie whispered and for the first time in so long, anger curled his fingers. "You destroyed my home."

Elijah squinted at him. "You ain't still upset about that, are you, boy? What's it matter? You got a new family now." Grinning, he stuffed his cheeks with steak and downed it with beer from a can.

Eddie wanted to hurt him. Choke him. Shatter his plate in his face. Instead, he was paralyzed as tears burned his eyes. Elijah was a human, but he was stronger than Eddie. He couldn't fight him.

"And I got plans for you, boy." Elijah pointed his fork at him. "Big plans. So eat your dinner."

"I'm not hungry." Hatred lit a fire in Eddie's stomach.

Elijah's grin fell off his face.

Fear and rage made Eddie reckless.

Elijah shrugged and chewed his steak. "That bitch of a mother of yours didn't teach you proper manners. Plenty of kids out there don't have nothin' to eat. Eat your dinner, boy." His voice was eerily calm, polite even, but his corpse-blue eye never blinked, never looked away from Eddie.

Rage gripped him, so powerful and strong Eddie felt sick. "You're not my family. You'll never be my family."

Elijah shook his head and tutted. "Weak. You're weak, boy, but I will make you strong." Elijah shot his hand out toward Eddie before he could blink, fastening his fingers into his hair and tugging hard. Pain stung his scalp.

"No," Eddie croaked. "Wait. Please, don't."

Elijah dragged him to a basement door and hurled him down the stairs. Eddie tumbled over, bruising his ribs and cracking his head on the concrete floor as he crashed to the bottom. It was dark and damp, and the basement smelled of rot.

"You're no good to me as a boy," Elijah growled. He seized Eddie's wrists and dragged him, and Eddie skinned his knees and tore his jeans on the floor. "Too weak. Too much thinkin', talkin'. It's pissin' me off." Chains clapped around his hands and feet. They were bitingly cold.

"What are you doing?" Eddie gasped. When he looked up, Elijah had his back to him. He stood before a board mounted on the wall, fitted with knives, bludgeons, chains, and lashes. Eddie's blood ran cold.

"I'm gonna hurt you," Elijah said simply, admiring a knife with a long, sharp blade. "It's a necessary lesson. Harden you up. Turn you into a killer of beasts. See, you wolves got a switch in your mind. Separates the animal from the man. Shut it off. So you don't get any wise ideas, you understand. I want you to obey."

Eddie's breath turned to gasps as Elijah came toward him, the knife gleaming in the flickering ceiling light. "I can do that. I'll obey. I'll obey. Just—"

"You don't get it!" Elijah's knee slammed into the ground as he knelt, his horrible face inches from Eddie's. "There's only one way to shut off that brain of yours. I'll hurt you, boy. Hurt you real bad. Till you're so broken, so full of pain, all you want is to make it all go away. You'll turn it all off, flash those yeller eyes of yours, and then you'll be mine. We'll be a family, boy."

Eddie begged him. He screamed. He cried. Elijah didn't care.

It might have lasted hours, days, weeks.

Eddie closed his eyes tight and formed a barrier around himself.

When he opened them, he was in a tent. The wind howled, and then he realized the howling was screaming in a voice that sounded like his.

"Shh. It's okay." Vico lay across from him. "You're safe here. No one can hurt you." His arms went around Eddie, so warm and strong. His lips caressed Eddie's forehead. "Forever, Eddie. We're forever."

Eddie closed his eyes and fell asleep in Vico's arms, safe and warm in a place that was only theirs, where nothing could ever hurt him again.

CHAPTER 7
THE HUNTER

VICENZO NEVER MANAGED TO find Eddie. For a day, he'd tracked his scent through Nevada until the trail went cold along a highway outside the ruins of town. The only thing that kept him from the brink of despair was knowing that his mate was alive. All he had to do was find him and bring him home.

Kassandra went back to Italy with their grandparents after the funeral. Vicenzo stayed with Agatha and kept her company after Derek passed away from his wounds. Vicenzo couldn't bring himself to attend the funeral of the Red Rock Springs pack. Guilt and grief consumed him, but the pain of returning to the ruins of the town he and Eddie had grown up in was too much to bear.

However, when Vicenzo heard Alpha Hanson was attending the service, he'd reached out to him for help finding his missing mate. The Alpha vowed he'd do everything he could to help find Eddie. For weeks, Vicenzo heard nothing. Anxiety consumed him day and night, and his wolf howled for their missing half. He thought about a lot of things. About his sister and how much he regretted leaving her. About his parents, their names in his contact list on his cell phone. Sometimes at night he tried to call them, to tell them where he was and not to worry about him. Then the tears would run down his face and he couldn't stop them.

He thought about Eddie and each time it was like a dagger in his heart. Was he alive? Was he hurt? He wanted to howl to him, for him, so loud until it tore at his throat and carried across the space between them. He wanted to tell him not to be frightened, to hold on because he was coming; they were forever and he was coming for him. And when they were finally together, all the shattered pieces would fall into place and he would be home again.

Finally, two agonizing months after the fire, Hanson called and asked to meet with him at a diner in Vegas. It was late in the evening when Vicenzo arrived, and the diner was mostly empty except for some friends at the bar drinking and laughing. Vicenzo sat alone by the window, watching the road for Hanson.

The waitress stopped by with his bourbon and sandwich. The bell above the door jingled. Instantly, the waitress hurried up to a man dressed smartly in a suit and tie, his salt-and-pepper hair neatly slicked to the side. She motioned to Vicenzo's table, and the man's one eye landed on him. Power rolled off this man in waves as he strode toward Vicenzo, and he fought the urge to show his throat in submission.

"Hello, Vicenzo. It's good to see you again." The Alpha slid into the seat opposite him.

Vicenzo twitched his mouth in an attempt at politeness. "Please, Alpha. Tell me you have something."

Hanson dipped his head in thanks when the waitress delivered his coffee. After taking a sip, he said, "We've determined that the hunters who attacked your town are The Beasts. For generations, they've hunted werewolves like they were prey. Last I heard, the heads of the clan had been killed and their heinous legacy was passed on to their sons. Two brothers. One of the brothers changed his name and went on the run. Death followed him wherever he went. Packs burned, innocents died." Anger thinned his mouth. "He died with his mate in Red Rock Springs. Only this time, he went by Jamison Turner."

Vicenzo's heart dropped. "What?"

"Yes, the monster finally met his end." Hanson's brow furrowed. "You knew him."

Vicenzo's hands shook. "He was my friend's father. I..."

It couldn't be true. Jamison Turner had been a good man, a second father to him, but he clearly hadn't always been the kindly man Vicenzo had once known. He couldn't believe it.

"I see... I'm sorry to be the one to break such news to you. I fear he isn't who you believed he was."

"No." Vicenzo's gums itched, his fangs longing to come out. "He spent years in that town with us. He had time to burn it all to hell if that's what he really wanted!" And yet, he'd been ready to abandon them all and spirit his son away from Vicenzo. He'd known what was coming. Vicenzo's brain ached. Nothing made sense.

Alpha Hanson touched his hand, and soothing waves of calm washed over him, easing his inner wolf's rage. "Perhaps he was a changed man, perhaps not," Hanson said gently. "But death followed his pack wherever they went and yet, they always came out the other side alive. It is suspicious, but perhaps we simply don't have the full picture. It's possible we may never know. Is it his son you're looking for?"

Vicenzo's throat tightened. He nodded.

"I can help you, but in return, I must ask you to go home to any pack you might have. You're too young to be so far away from home, and it's taking a toll on you. I can see it in your eyes."

"I don't have a home," Vicenzo said. "Eddie's my home, Alpha. I'm not leaving until I find him."

He could see the Alpha wanted to argue. He didn't. "The hunters have taken him to New Orleans. We believe they have a base somewhere in the city."

For the first time in months, a glimmer of hope shone through the darkness of Vicenzo's life. New Orleans. Eddie was there, waiting for him.

"Vicenzo, please. Step back and let the authorities handle this. Don't put yourself at risk. This is the son of a hunter. You don't know what they've turned him into."

"Thank you, Alpha Hanson." Rising from the table, Vicenzo marched from the diner.

He didn't know about Eddie's father. He'd seemed a good man, but he'd carried secrets that had brought ruin and death wherever he went. But Eddie was good. As good as they came. Whether his father had been a hunter or not didn't matter. He knew the kindness of Eddie's soul, and that was what he would put his trust in.

NEW ORLEANS WAS A big city. On every corner, some musician was crooning their soul out through a song or a saxophone. The air was hot and damp at the same time and it made him lightheaded. Damn, he hated cities. The cars stank up the air with fumes. Humans clogged the streets, all smelling of body odor, perfumes and colognes, booze or cigarettes.

Once he'd settled into a seat at a bar, he decided to call his sister. "Did you find him yet?" Kassandra asked through the phone.

"No. I'm in New Orleans. Looks like the hunters who took him might be somewhere in the city."

"Vico, I... How can you be sure he's still alive? You're risking your neck needlessly."

His jaw tightened. "He's alive. I know it. Thanks for the positivity, though. I'm glad I called."

"Just tell me you are not going to storm some hunters' den by yourself!"

"I'm not." It wasn't a lie. A plan was forming in his mind. "Listen, Kassandra. If I do go charging into a hunters' lair, I can't have them using you as leverage. I'm gonna ditch the phone, anything on me that might lead them to you. So if you don't hear from me, don't assume the worst."

"Vico." There were tears in her voice. "Don't do this. I've already lost our parents, our home. I can't lose you too. Please. Come home."

Vicenzo wished with all his heart he could. "It wouldn't be home, Kassie. Not without him." He hung up. Another word from her, and he would break in two. His mouth trembled at the sight of her name on his screen, of his parents' names. This was for them as much as it was for Eddie. He raised a glass to all he'd loved and lost and drank.

"Hey," he croaked, catching the bartender's attention. "Charge this for me?"

"Sure thing." The bartender took his phone and while he was distracted with a customer, Vicenzo walked out and left his phone and a piece of himself there, too.

He needed to find Eddie, and this city was too damn big to do it alone. He asked around at bars about hunters, asking if anyone had seen a blond boy with cyan eyes, probably hanging around some creepy motherfucker. As always, humans were useless. Time was of the essence here. He needed someone who could track, someone who could fight, so he bought himself a laptop, sat his ass in a café, and dove deep into the dark web.

Derek, rest his soul, had been the biggest nerd. He'd loved to freak them all out about his expeditions into the dark web, and the creepy, horrible forums he'd come across. As Vico searched, there was the stuff he'd expected: illegal arms trades, drugs, porn. Then there was the paranormal side of the dark web. From werewolves selling a bite for upwards of millions of dollars to humans who fantasized about being devoured by werewolves, there was something for everyone as long as they knew where to look. Vicenzo saw more shit than he cared to ever see again and truly wondered at the state of some people's minds. Really, who sat around daydreaming about werewolves taking a bite out of them?

Finally, he found what he was looking for.

Hunters. Lots of them. Plying their trade to sickos who wanted to kill their werewolf coworkers and neighbors. They weren't who he was looking for. He did want a hunter, just of a different kind. And he found them: hunters who preyed on hunters, who sought to protect werewolves by taking hunters down before they had the chance to strike. And fuck, were their services expensive.

Vicenzo didn't know how he'd afford them. He ran his fingers over Eddie's ring. His chest ached at the idea of parting with it, but he had to do whatever it took to find Eddie and make sure he was safe.

Palms sweating, he posted in the forum.

I'm looking for The Beasts. They have my friend. They're somewhere in New Orleans but I can't find them on my own and time's running out. I'll pay whatever it takes.

He posted, not sure when he'd get a message back. Less than thirty minutes later, he got a response.

I can help you, wrote the hunter. **I'm in the city. Been tracking them, too. Meet me after eight on Bourbon Street. I'll be in the Old Absinthe House on the balcony, wearing a gray hoodie. Bring payment.**

THE NEON-SOAKED STRETCH OF Bourbon Street was packed as drunks bounced from one bar to another. He passed sex shops with eye-catching displays, walked beneath beads waving from balconies above. Purple, green, and yellow lights flashed incessantly, and it was hard to find the bar he was looking for. Finally, he spotted a building that truly looked old standing at the corner of the street. A big sign announced it was the bar he was looking for.

It was packed with rowdy humans drinking Sazerac and absinthe cocktails. He bypassed the bar and climbed the stairs to the balcony, peering among the women in tight dresses and the guys laughing uproariously.

He spotted the gray hoodie at once. A man leaned against the railing, looking down over the packed streets impassively. His curly hair was long and tied back into a bun and his beard was scruffy. He turned and blue eyes splashed with gray met Vicenzo's, reminding him of the sky just before a rainstorm.

The hunter tossed back the last of his drink, glass dangling from his hand, elbows on the railing. Those stormy eyes were hard beneath a narrowed brow. "Isaac," the hunter stated, a grim bent to his lips as he shoved his hand out to shake.

Vicenzo shook and winced at the burn. The hunter had handled silver. He could smell it on him. "I'm Vicenzo. Thanks for meeting me."

"Sorry about that." The hunter wiped his hands on his pants. "The Beasts use wolves to do their dirty work. Had to prepare myself." His voice was hoarse and gravelly, as if he hadn't used it in a long time. A gold ring on his finger glinted in the light of the lamps. He didn't seem the happily married sort. Vicenzo wondered about him but quickly choked it down. "Should warn you, if they've taken your friend, there's a chance he's feral."

Vicenzo choked down a dry swallow.

"The Beasts get a kick outta controlling wolves. Breaking things. Plus side is, they rarely kill the wolves they take in. Your friend's likely their new pet. You thought about that?" Those silver-blue eyes were penetrating as they set themselves on him.

"Yeah." It was a lie. One step at a time. Even if Eddie was feral, even if they'd broken him, he would bring him back. He wasn't letting him go. "Do you know where they are?"

The hunter grunted, bobbing his head. Vicenzo supposed that meant yes. "Some wolves went missing in Monroe. Thought maybe it was my target's handiwork, but the methods were too different. Too many dead for it to have been one guy, for one thing, missing wolves for another, and lastly, the victims had been killed by silver and fangs. Fit The Beasts's style just right." He grimaced. "There's only one place a gang of hunters with a bunch of wolves might be able to hide out undisturbed. The bayou. It's a huge place but I asked some local fishermen before you got here and they tell stories of wolves howling out near Bayou Lafourche."

Vicenzo was holding his breath. He couldn't believe how close he was to finding Eddie. "Are you sure it's not pack land, or—"

Clicking his tongue, Isaac wagged a finger. "Only pack territory in the bayou is in the Black Bay Wildlife Refuge. It's The Beasts." He seemed sure of himself, and Vicenzo's heart thrummed with excitement. "My pay?"

Vicenzo removed the ring on the chain from his neck. "I don't have much money. Will this do?"

Isaac took it. Vicenzo barely stifled his growl.

The hunter held the ring to the light and grunted. "It's a good piece."

"It was my mate's." Vicenzo's voice wobbled.

As Isaac turned the ring over in his hand, something softened in his hard eyes.

"Will I get it back if you can't find him?"

"I will find him. I promise you that."

Vicenzo exhaled. "Then keep it." Parting with such a precious gift would be worth it to have his mate back.

Isaac pocketed the ring. "Thank you. Let's go. My car's parked just down the street."

Vicenzo followed.

Hang on, Ed. I'm coming.

THE HUNTER ISAAC WAS quiet as he drove, stormy gray-blue eyes intent on the dark road ahead. His car was a weather-beaten thing that desperately needed a wash. The hunter barely said a word, his expression stony, but Vicenzo wasn't afraid of him. Perhaps he should have been, considering he'd hopped into a car with a hunter.

"So... you hunt your own people, huh? That's interesting." He had to say something. His nerves were skyrocketing.

Isaac grunted.

"Are you married?" he asked, eyeing the ring on Isaac's finger.

"Once. It was a mistake."

It was like talking to a wall. He looked out the window. They were passing little towns along the Mississippi River, lights glowing faintly in the gloom of the night.

"So, why do you still wear the ring if it was a mistake? Is that a human thing or—"

Isaac rolled his eyes. "It's not my ex's ring. It belonged to my mate—"

"Your mate?" Vicenzo's jaw dropped. "Wait, hold up, you were with a werewolf? While being a hunter. Damn. That must have been complicated as hell."

"We made it work," Isaac answered, his voice rough. "I'm the idiot who ended it. Look, what's it matter? Isn't it enough I'm hunting down some assholes for you?"

Vicenzo raised his hands. "Just wanted to make conversation. It's been a long time since I spoke to anyone."

"No offense, kid, but you'd have better luck talking to drywall. I'm not in much better shape than you."

Vicenzo gave up. Outside, the houses had disappeared, and they drove along a narrow road surrounded by wetlands. Fireflies glowed above the murky waters of the swamp.

Isaac stopped the car and rolled down the windows. He listened. "Wolves. Hear 'em?"

Vicenzo shivered as their howls sounded from deep within the bayou. Their voices were tortured, full of anguish Vicenzo had never heard before. "Goddess... Eddie." His heart cracked in his chest.

"Don't you werewolves have some, I don't know, psychic connection to each other? Use it. Maybe we can locate your buddy faster."

The bonds didn't work long-distance, but they should be close enough for Vicenzo to sense Eddie. He closed his eyes, feeling for the thread that tethered him to Eddie and encountered only black emptiness. A shiver ran down his spine. "I can't feel him..." he whispered, horror turning him cold.

"What's that mean? Is he—"

"No," Vicenzo snarled, refusing to hear a word out of Isaac's mouth. Eddie wasn't dead. He would know. "Keep driving!"

They drove on through the dark, following the distant howling of wolves. Lights winked at them from the gloom. Isaac killed the headlights and the road ahead was plunged into darkness. "Think that's them." Isaac pointed with his chin into the bayou.

Wolves barked and snarled distantly, and they could see the lights of a cabin. Vicenzo thought he heard loud, drunken voices on the damp wind. They'd found the bastards. Eddie was in there somewhere, and Vicenzo would tear apart anyone who came between him and his mate. Grabbing his bag, he lurched from the car, claws out, fangs bared.

"Fuck, man, you scratched up the door!" Isaac grumbled. Vicenzo ignored his bitching. "Before you go charging in, claws and fangs blazing, we need to figure out how many of 'em there are." Isaac gripped his shoulder. "Keep our heads down, survey the property. Strike. Okay?"

Vicenzo growled.

"I'll take that as a yes. Fucking werewolves..." Isaac knelt, scooping up a handful of mud. He smeared his face with it. "Those wolves'll smell us miles away if we don't mask our scent. Especially you. You reek."

"I smell just fine, thanks." Vicenzo swung his bag over his shoulder.

Isaac suddenly grabbed Vicenzo's shoulder. "Careful." A firefly glowed just above a bear trap in the weeds. There were traps everywhere. Vicenzo smelled their silver and avoided them. They maneuvered their way around to the side of the house. The lights were on inside but Vicenzo couldn't make out anyone through the curtains.

There was a big shed to the side of the house. Barking and snarling and howls echoed from within. Vicenzo's gut clenched. Eddie might be in there, feral and afraid.

Crouching low, Isaac darted past and Vicenzo followed. They had a good view of the backyard from here. A fence encircled the property, probably electric. Hunters crowded around a bonfire, the smell of silver hanging around them like a mist. Isaac flipped the safety off his pistol. "I'll hit 'em. You go and find your friend. Check the kennels first."

Vicenzo said, "You'll be okay by yourself?"

Isaac snorted, grinning beneath his beard. "I've been on my own for five months. I'll be fine. Go. Look fast!"

Before Vicenzo could argue, Isaac took aim and fired. Despite the distance, his aim was true. A hunter stumbled, one hand to his head, and fell, twitching. The hunters flew into a panic, yelling and lunging for weapons, but since they were drunk, they stumbled around. Isaac grinned and for a moment, Vicenzo saw a wolf within him, fangs bared and hungry for blood.

"Come at me, motherfuckers!" Isaac hollered, and a blast from his pistol felled another hunter. "You wanna kill wolves? How about someone my size?"

Vicenzo ran, tearing toward the kennel as bullets struck the mud near his feet. Isaac was laughing. He sounded like a lunatic.

Vicenzo hurled open the door. A light flickered on and the wolves went ballistic in their cages. "Eddie?" he roared, struggling to be heard over the din. He ran from cage to cage, searching for a white wolf with blue, or yellow, eyes. "Eddie? It's me!" Wolves barked at him, eyes blazing yellow with feral fury, their pupils constricted to pinpricks. There had to be at least twenty of them, all beyond saving, but a white wolf wasn't among them.

His hands shook as fear left his throat painfully tight.

Eddie wasn't here. He wasn't here. He—

"I'm here, Vicenzo."

And he smelled it then for the first time since their home had burned. Warm summer grass. Honey. Home.

"Ed..." He turned—and met the butt of a gun as it crashed across his nose.

All the sound cut out as his ears rang. He fell, his head striking the floor. Blood ran thick down the back of his throat, coppery in his mouth. The light flickered as an unrecognizable man came into view, his face flashing in and out of sight. His blond hair was cut short to his scalp and a bushy beard consumed his lower jaw. His blue eyes were like shards of ice as they surveyed Vicenzo dispassionately.

He smelled like silver.

Suddenly, his face cracked, a rush of emotion dampening those hard, cold eyes. "Vico," he whispered, his voice soft and broken.

Then Vicenzo's vision went dark.

Chapter 8

A Good, Loyal Dog

Eddie fought for as long as he could. He clung to his humanity as Elijah broke him. Again and again and again. He built a fortress of happy memories around himself, somewhere he could hide away and escape to. And every time, Elijah tore those walls down. Every time he thought he'd known the extent of pain and suffering, Elijah found new ways to show him just how foolish he really was.

"Why do you do this, boy?" Elijah paced, his hands trembling. The lash in his hand dripped blood. Eddie trembled just looking at it. His tongue bled, his cheeks bitten raw and bloody from the efforts of holding in his screams. "All I want is what belongs to me. Surrender to me and all this pain will end."

And oh Goddess, it was so tempting. After weeks and weeks of never-ending pain, his mind was slipping. The wolf was surrendering even while he fought to hold on to his humanity. Sometimes, he blacked out during their sessions and woke up after Elijah had left, his claws long and fangs bared. The wolf growled deep in his chest, paced around in his mind, and whispered, *Tired, so tired. No more fighting. Give in. Give in.*

If he gave in, he didn't know if he would come back. He would forget everything that made him human. Everything he'd loved and lost would be forgotten, but the pain would end and it was such a blissful thought, not to be haunted by pain anymore, to be free...

Elijah's jowls quivered with fury. "You're a right pain in my asshole, you know that, boy?" He lunged, grabbing hold of Eddie's face and squeezing until Eddie thought his jaw would break. "I'd love to know what's keepin' you human. Whatever it is, must be right powerful indeed." He shoved Eddie's face away and paced.

Eddie caught his breath, rotating his jaw until it cracked.

"You want to give in. I can see it. Do you think I like hurtin' my nephew?" Elijah's sneer pulled at his scarred cheek, and implied he did very much enjoy their time together. "Just turn it off, boy. And the pain will be over."

Eddie spat blood onto the floor in answer. Sooner or later, Elijah would get tired. He'd kill him, set him free, and Eddie could die with his dignity intact. But Elijah had other plans.

Elijah's teeth crunched into an apple. He sat on a rickety overturned container, one leg folded over the other. "This game of ours has dragged on too long. How about another offer, hmm?"

He reached into his coat and pulled out a collar that was made of silver. Eddie stared at it, surprised. He'd been expecting more pain and suffering, not whatever scheme his lunatic uncle had cooked up. He blinked at Elijah, waiting for him to continue.

"One of my men died last week. A good hunter. We found him with his throat torn out."

The collar glinted in the flickering light.

"I need another to take his place."

Through the blood, Eddie tasted bile in his throat.

"You're a fighter, Eddie. You know how many others like you broke by now? They were weak. You are strong. I need someone like you. What do you say, nephew?"

Eddie's jaw clicked when he tried to speak. He warred with the words, choked them back as best he could.

"The pain will be over. You'll be one of us. A family, boy."

A whimper pulled from his throat. All he wanted was for the pain to end. But he couldn't give up. Vico might be alive and looking for him. He had to hold on until his mate found him.

"No." His jaw cracked from misuse and his own voice was foreign to his ears. "No. Won't hurt people. Won't be a killer. I won't do it."

Elijah shrugged, shoving the collar in his pocket. "Then I'll see you again tomorrow, Eddie. The usual time. I won't stop until I've broken you. Until you're nothing but a slobbering dog at my feet, hungry for scraps. Is that really what you want, boy? To become a feral beast? To lose your humanity and forget everything and everyone you care about? You have a choice to make, Eddie. Are you a dog, or are you a hunter?" Elijah grinned. "See you tomorrow, Eddie."

The door slammed behind him. The lights flickered and went out, and Eddie was left in the dark.

Eddie's wounds healed but he found no rest that night. He had a choice. Lose his mind and become his uncle's slobbering dog. Lose his morals and become a hunter of his own kind, no better than the men who'd stolen his childhood, his family, and his mate from him.

If he refused, he would be tortured until his mind broke and he became a feral beast. There was some peace in that, in knowing that he would forget everything he'd lost. There was terror too, knowing he would forget everyone he loved. How could he do that to his family? To Vico? Vico was the one who'd kept him holding on through day after day of unrelenting pain and suffering.

If he accepted... he would become a trained killer. He would keep his mind and the memories of those he loved, but at a terrible price.

But the pain, the never-ending pain, would finally stop.

When Elijah returned in the early hours of the morning, he had the silver collar with him. It was too small for a wolf's neck. It was for Eddie. In his other hand, he held a lash that reeked of blood.

He said, "What's your choice, boy?"

RAIN SPATTERED VICENZO'S FACE, dripping cold in his eyes. His nose had healed and the rain washed away the blood on his face.

Eddie.

The crack of gunfire echoed through the swamp. Wolves howled. With a grunt, he pushed himself onto his elbows, eyes adjusting to the dark. He smelled mud and silver. A shape moved in the dark. A figure sat on a log nearby, their eyes glowing blue in the dark. A firefly glowed and cast light upon a gaunt, bearded face.

"Ed!" Vicenzo lurched to his feet.

Eddie Turner was hardly recognizable. He'd lost weight and his clothes hung off of him. His eyes were devoid of the life and joy Vicenzo had once known. They were baggy from lack of sleep, bloodshot, and cold. A beard covered his face, bushy and unkempt. It added years to his face, emphasizing every line and the droop of his lips. They'd cut off his hair, shaved it almost to the scalp. He hardly smelled like the scent of home Vicenzo knew and loved; he smelled like silver and ash, choking out any other smells.

Tears burned Vicenzo's eyes. "Eddie. Oh, Ed. What the hell did they do to you?"

Something shifted in Eddie's eyes. Something that might have been joy. It was so hard to tell. "Thought you were dead, Vico."

"No." Vicenzo's legs shook as he took one step, then another. All he wanted was to bundle Eddie in his arms and piece him back together. "I'm so sorry. I tried to come sooner. I tried to find you, Ed. I've been looking for months. I never gave up on you. Never."

Eddie's mouth trembled. It might have been a trick of the light. His face was so guarded.

Vicenzo opened his arms. "Ed, what happened? Tell me. You don't smell like a wolf anymore. I couldn't even sense your bond. I thought—"

A wolf howled. Eddie jerked away from him, drawing silver pistols from his belt. Vicenzo froze, a trickle of fear running down his spine. His reactions, the way he moved... he was like Isaac. Like—

"You shouldn't have come here, Vico." Eddie's icy eyes scanned the shadows, glaring back in the direction of the cabin. "Should have just stayed away."

Hurt cut into Vicenzo, so strong it robbed him of breath. Why was Eddie acting this way? Why wasn't he happy to see Vicenzo? This wasn't how things were supposed to be. Nothing was turning out the way he'd thought. His hopes for a future between them cracked and threatened to shatter into glass in his chest. "What do you mean? I couldn't leave you. Eddie, you're my—"

"I'm not anythin' to you!" The words were a snarl. Eddie's eyes blazed. "Whatever connection we had—it's gone. And you need to leave before the hunters find you."

Vicenzo was paralyzed.

"Now!" Eddie lashed out, shoving him in the chest.

Denial lit a flame in his stomach. "The hell are you talking about, Eddie? I came all this way to find you. I'm not going anywhere!"

Eddie blinked hard as rain poured down his cheeks. "You came all this way for Eddie. Eddie's dead, Vicenzo."

Vicenzo lunged, latching onto his shoulders. His claws popped out, digging into the bony surface of Eddie's shoulder blades. "Listen to me. Whatever they did to you, we can fix it. I won't let them hurt you anymore, do you understand? I'll rip their fucking throats out if they ever touch you again!"

Eddie laughed. It was a terrible sound, hollow and broken, so different from the boy he'd known once, who could have brightened a room with his laughter. "Too late. It's all too late." Something in his voice cracked. "I did things, Vico." He began to shake. "Things I can't fix. Things I can't ever take back. No one can save me."

Vicenzo didn't believe that. He wouldn't. "I don't care." He captured Eddie's face between his hands. His cheekbones were so bony, there was hardly any flesh on him. "Come with me, okay? Come with me and we'll figure it out. We'll—"

The words died in his throat. Eddie's oversized sweatshirt had slipped down, revealing a silver collar around his throat. His name was carved into it. Vicenzo shook, his arms falling to his sides. Noxious disbelief roiled through his stomach.

"Oh fuck. Eddie. What did they do to you?"

Eddie's voice was a croak when he said, "They didn't. I did."

HE'D PUT IT ON himself. Like a good, loyal dog.

He'd expected it to burn, but the collar was lined on the inside to protect his skin. A small kindness. More for Elijah's benefit, he supposed. After all, Eddie couldn't hunt if he was in constant agony. But the worst pain wasn't on the outside but from within as the voice of his inner wolf faded. The collar, lined or not, cut off his connection to the most vital part of his identity. He couldn't shift even if he wanted to. He was as good as human and what a weak human he was, underfed and malnourished, nothing but skin and bones. Hardly a threat to the hunters.

Elijah slid a smirk up one half of his scarred face. "Good boy. You made the right choice, Eddie. I hope you're proud." He latched the collar tight and turned a key in a tiny lock at the back.

Eddie couldn't feel, not a thing.

Elijah extended a hand. "On your feet, boy. We need to fatten you up. Make you strong."

Ignoring the hand outstretched to him, Eddie stood on his own and nearly collapsed.

He'd thought about it for a long time. He wasn't sure of anything anymore, but if he had to choose between being a dog and a hunter's slave, he wanted to keep his mind. It was only when the collar snapped around his neck that he realized he'd sold his soul and his morality to Elijah and his hunters.

VICENZO PACED, STRUGGLING TO breathe. He wanted to kill Eddie's uncle, throttle him with his bare hands. "You did what you had to in order to survive, Eddie. Come on, we'll kill Elijah, get that fucking thing off you, and I'll get you out of here."

Eddie lurched away from his touch. "I'm not going anywhere."

Vicenzo wanted to scream. "I'm not leaving you here. Eddie, listen to me. I came all this way to find you. I had an Alpha from the Council help me. I hired this weird hunter to—"

"The Council?" Eddie's eyes darkened. "Did they tell you about my father? The man he really was?"

Was that what this was about? Vicenzo almost laughed. "Eddie, you're not him. I don't care what he did. I care about you."

Eddie gazed at his hands, his fingers twitching. "You don't know me at all, Vico. I'm exactly like my father."

Vicenzo was stunned into silence.

Eddie's mouth trembled and he spit the words like poison. "I'm a hunter now. Just like him."

"Eddie, cut the crap. No. You're not anything like him. You're good, you're—"

But all words failed him when Eddie stated, "I've killed people, Vico."

"YOU'RE A HUNTER NOW, boy. You need to look the part."

A gaunt man with hollow eyes stared back at Eddie from the bathroom mirror. Elijah stood behind him, armed with his hunting knife. He hadn't been able to find a razor.

"You're a man, not some little girl. No man's hair has a right bein' this long," Elijah grumbled.

Eddie winced as Elijah fisted a handful of blond hair. Tears pricked Eddie's eyes. His scalp stung and throbbed as Elijah pulled his hair taut and sliced away memories of Eddie's childhood. He'd been growing his hair out since he was a teenager. His mother had smiled and touched the long strands, saying, "I like this look on you, sweetheart. It suits you."

His father had liked to tousle Eddie's hair, his eyes crinkling with his warm smile. "There's a good kid," he'd rumbled.

Vico had stroked his hair when they'd kissed, assuring Eddie with each kiss that he was so deeply loved without either of them saying a word.

Eddie would never be that happy boy again. Elijah had cut it all out of him when he'd killed his parents. When he'd burned Eddie's home and his friends. When he'd torn him away from his mate.

It went on and on, chunks of hair falling like golden straw around Eddie's bare feet.

By the time Elijah was done, Eddie didn't recognize the haunted person staring back at him: his hair uneven and cut close to his scalp, in some cases far too close, eyes dead, shadows pooling in his cheeks. His scalp stung where Elijah had nicked him, the blood warm and wet against his hair. Elijah patted Eddie's shoulders, and Eddie winced, anticipating pain.

"Look like a hunter now, boy." Elijah bared his crooked, yellowed teeth in a grin. "Let's go huntin'."

Eddie dragged his feet from the bathroom to the front door and paused. His pa's hat hung on a hook by the door. Elijah hadn't gotten rid of it. Heart aching, Eddie put the hat on his head. The hat smelled like leather, and faintly, like his pa. It was stupid, but Eddie felt closer to his pa... to the boy he used to be. Adjusting the hat so it fit snugly, Eddie walked out the door after Elijah.

Outside, the air was thick with humidity. Rowdy hunters jeered from the window of their pickup truck, others making faces at him from where they sat in the truck bed.

"My nephew's one of us now, boys!" Elijah lunged, grabbing onto Eddie's shoulders. He hurled Eddie toward the trailer. "Let's hunt us some werewolves!"

The hunters roared their enthusiasm, and Eddie had never felt so ill.

The wolves barked and snarled as Elijah set them loose from the kennels in the shed, tearing across the muddy ground. They didn't have time to relish their freedom before Elijah was herding them inside, cracking a silver lash against their scarred hides.

Eddie wasn't one of them. He learned that very quickly. They drove for miles, passing over the state border into Mississippi. They stopped only at night to set up camp in the wilderness. The wolves gnawed on the bones of the game the hunters shot and butchered. Eddie's stomach groaned as he watched the hunters tuck into their venison, browned and dripping succulent juices. He couldn't remember when he'd last eaten. His stomach must have shrunk to half its prior size.

Every so often, the hunters would shoot him grins and callous looks. One of them left the fire, brushing dirt from the back of his jeans. "Here." He extended a chunk of venison to Eddie. "Help yourself, new guy."

Grateful, Eddie reached out—only to have the meat withdrawn. The hunter sneered, eyes narrowed in cruel mirth. "You want your dinner, wolf? You gotta work for it."

Eddie wanted to tell him to go to hell, but he was choking on saliva as his body betrayed him.

"Go on, boy, go on!" another hunter jeered, his beer belly jiggling as he laughed. "Sit, boy! Down, boy!"

The other hunters roared with laughter as the wolves twitched their ears and growled. Elijah's wide-brimmed hat cast his face into shadow, but the firelight glinted off his yellowed teeth.

The hunter with the venison waved it in Eddie's face. "Come on, wolfy! Do a trick for the boys, eh? Beg, boy! Beg!"

A growl rumbled in Eddie's throat. He wouldn't, his pride already so brittle. But, fuck, his stomach *ached*. No food had ever smelled so good after a month of water and plain grits in Elijah's moldy basement.

"I said beg!" the hunter roared.

Eddie's ears began to ring. He wasn't a wolf, not anymore, but the rage ate him up from the inside until all he wanted was to bite, rip, tear.

"You hear me, asshole? I said—"

Eddie lunged, his teeth closing around the hunter's throat. His nails, overgrown from a month in the basement, drove into the hunter's scalp and drew beads of blood. The hunter choked and gasped, and his fellows cried out in alarm. Eddie tasted sweat and blood as he crunched down with all his might.

A boot to his stomach doubled him over. He coughed and hacked, fumbling blindly for the meat the hunter had dropped. He drew it close, snarling at any who dared try to take it from him. Wide-eyed and pale, the hunters didn't come near him. The one he'd bitten retched and gasped, rubbing his throat. "That beast tried to kill me!"

Elijah stood, clapping. "And that, boys, is why you don't mess with a werewolf, even if it is stuck in human form. Teach you lot not to get too cocky, shouldn't it?"

Eddie crammed the venison in his mouth and chewed fast, glaring at any hunter who skirted around him. That night he slept with a full belly, and the hunters learned to keep their distance.

Come morning, they drove on until they arrived in De Soto National Forest. Eddie was happy to leave the cramped confines of the RV, a dreary environment with a filthy, sour-smelling carpet and dirty dishes every-where, and Elijah always kept the shades down so hardly any natural light spilled in. But he was fearful about what had brought them to the forest. Elijah was in an especially good mood as he cleaned his shotgun and loaded his pockets with ammo. The wolves whined and panted in their cages, itching to stretch their legs. The stench from their filthy cages made Eddie's stomach twist as he poked at the fried egg on his plate.

"There's a big pack of wolves in these parts," Elijah said, laying his shotgun on his knee and tucking into his eggs. "Locals ain't happy about them competing with the town's hunters for local game. Paid us a hefty sum to wipe 'em all out."

Eddie swallowed the acidic taste at the back of his throat. Did the stupid hunters complaining about the wolves even realize how essential wolves were for ecosystems? No, he imagined they were furious that they couldn't hunt on land that belonged to the wolf pack and all they wanted was a bloodbath. Humans couldn't stand it when wolves had something that was all their own. They had to take and take and take.

Though he itched to say these things to Elijah's face, he'd learned not to disagree with his uncle.

The chair creaked as Elijah stood, his boots clumping as he marched to the cages and unleashed the wolves. "Let's hunt."

Stomach full of lead, Eddie didn't move. His uncle didn't expect Eddie to murder innocent wolves, did he? Growing up in Texas, he'd gone to shooting ranges all the time, but he'd never killed anything living.

Elijah remained while the other hunters piled outside. "You stay put, nephew dearest. You're too green to be of any use to me yet." His grin told Eddie there was more to come. "Don't worry. I've got big plans for you. You'll be useful in other ways." He slammed the door and locked it from the outside, leaving Eddie alone in the trailer. He approached the window, which was barred and impossible to break except from the outside. He tried the door even though it was locked. He might be able to break the windshield, but with what? The furniture was bolted down.

If he was caught, Elijah would send him back down to the basement. Just the thought left Eddie shaking. The fear of the punishment he'd receive if he was caught won out over his desire to escape. Besides, Elijah was a good tracker. He'd find Eddie, and he'd go through innocent people to do it. Like he had in the Springs. His mother and father. Vico.

Feeling sick, Eddie curled into a ball on the sofa and shivered. If Vico was alive, Eddie hoped he stayed as far away as possible. He couldn't bear it if Elijah hurt Vico the way he'd hurt Eddie, or killed him like he'd killed everyone else Eddie had loved. The thought of Vicenzo was like a soothing balm, easing his tremors, slowing his heart.

Goddess, how he missed Vicenzo Salvatore. He clung onto the memory of him as he closed his eyes.

A crash woke him sometime later. Hoots and hollers echoed through the woods. A woman screamed like she was dying, and maybe she was. Eddie's blood turned to ice and he shot to his feet. From the doorway, Elijah grinned at him, covered in blood and smelling like gun smoke.

"Get on out here, boy!" he barked. He lunged for Eddie, and Eddie hated how easily he let himself be dragged out into the night. Submission was easier than fighting back. The hunters gathered in a circle, mocking and jeering.

"Move it, dumbasses!" Elijah hollered, wrestling Eddie through the crowd.

His heart sank.

The hunters had surrounded a woman, naked from her shift. Blood spattered her body, oozing from bullet wounds. Silver, Eddie guessed, since she wasn't healing the damage. She bared her blunt teeth at him, her eyes wild but wet with tears. "You monsters," she snarled, voice quaking. "You slaughtered my pack! My friends!"

Elijah barked out a laugh. "Real rich to hear you call us monsters, beast."

"I'll kill you!" She lunged for him. Eddie hoped she'd make it, that she could do what he was too scared to do and rip Elijah apart. Chains around her arms and legs yanked her back against the tree she'd been tied to.

The hunters roared with laughter.

Eddie gasped when Elijah spun him around to look into his sneering face. "Consider this your initiation, boy." He shoved a silver pistol into Eddie's hand. Eddie expected it to burn, but his wolf was so muted, the silver couldn't hurt him anymore. "Kill her."

The blood roared in Eddie's ears. Elijah wanted him to take an innocent person's life. He'd known this was the fate that awaited him the moment he'd put on the collar, but there was no way he could have prepared himself. Goddess, all he'd wanted was for the pain to stop, to keep his mind and his memories of his loved ones. The gun shook in his grip as he turned toward the woman. Sweat ran cold down the back of his neck.

"The hell you waiting for, boy?" Elijah barked. "Kill her!"

He realized now that he'd been holding out hope. Hope that someone, Vico, would come and save him before Elijah would demand such a terrible thing from him. But it was too late. The time for rescuing had come and gone.

A pistol clicked behind him. Eddie turned and found himself staring down the barrel of Elijah's gun. "I'll give you a choice, boy. You kill the bitch, or I take you both down into our special room. You'll never leave. I'll make you watch as I kill her slow. Take my time with her. When I'm done, you're next."

The threat turned Eddie's knees to liquid. He had a gun in his hand, a gun he could turn on his uncle—if he wasn't so scared he'd miss, but it wasn't his own life he feared for.

Throat too dry to swallow, he faced the woman, her teeth bared in a snarl. She would suffer terribly at Elijah's hands. Her pack was gone, her friends dead. If she had a mate, then they were dead, too. She was so much like himself, it ached. If he didn't kill her, the hunters would kill him. But first, they'd play with him, and every day until his death would be a living hell. He was not going back down into that fucking basement.

Throat thick, Eddie curled his finger around the trigger. "What's your name?"

She sniffled. "Tamara."

For as long as he lived, Eddie would never forget her name.

"Wait," she whimpered. "Tell me yours."

Tears stung his eyes. "Eddie." His voice came out a broken whisper.

"Don't do this, Eddie." She clasped her hands, eyes wide and pleading. "Please. Let me go."

Tears spilled down his face, lips trembling as he croaked, "I-I'm sorry."

His first shot missed. His second didn't. He lost all sensation in his arm. His ears rang from the gunfire, which drowned out all other sounds. Tamara fell backwards, her feet kicking, body writhing. Blood trickled from the hole in the crown of her skull.

Her twitching eyes found his before the light left them. Foam dribbled from the corner of her mouth and her limbs stopped twitching and fell limp. He wasn't ready for the finality of it. She was dead, killed by his hand. There was no turning back time. No waking up from what he'd done. The regret was instantaneous, crashing over him in waves. He fell to his knees, curled in on himself, and made himself as small as he felt.

He'd chosen his life over another living person. Nothing would ever change that, no matter how he tried to justify his reasons behind it.

What became of him now didn't matter.

The moment he'd pulled the trigger, he'd become a hunter's dog.

Eddie Turner didn't deserve to be saved.

CHAPTER 9

A SONG OF HEARTACHE AND DESPAIR

VICENZO'S FACE WAS PALE in the dark.

Eddie couldn't stand to look at him. The boy who'd loved Vicenzo had died along with his family. How could he ask Vicenzo to take him away from this place, knowing he was a shell of who he'd once been?

"Ed." Vicenzo's voice broke. Leaves crunched as he came closer, reaching out. His touch was cold against Eddie's arm. "You did what you had to in order to survive."

Eddie didn't want excuses. He'd made the choice to take an innocent woman's life, the life of a fellow werewolf. It had changed him, broken something in him. All he'd wanted was to see Vicenzo again, for Vicenzo to take him away from the pain so they could start anew. Now, he wanted Vicenzo to run as far from him as possible and leave Eddie to the fate he deserved. "What I should have done was let him kill me."

Eyes blazing, Vicenzo wrenched Eddie in close. "It doesn't matter! I'm here now, Ed, and I'm not leaving you alone with him. Not ever again! Come on, Eddie. I've lost so much." Tears filled Vicenzo's eyes, his hand shaking as he clasped Eddie's shirt. "You're all that's kept me going."

Eddie kept his jaw tight but oh, how it trembled to see Vicenzo crying for him. He wanted to cry, to break down in his arms and tell Vicenzo he'd run away with him here and now. But he couldn't. The boy who would have fallen into Vico's arms was dead and gone.

93

"Ed." Trembling hands framed his face. Vicenzo gasped, "We lost everything." Tears gleamed on his cheeks. "It's just you and me now. We can't ever get it all back. But come with me, please. You're still you. I see it."

"No." Eddie didn't recognize his own voice, gravelly and hard.

He wasn't the boy Vicenzo had fallen in love with anymore. He was a hunter, a monster. Elijah had taken his youth, his innocence, his heart, and locked it all behind a wall of silver.

"Eddie, this isn't who you are!" Vicenzo pleaded, tears on his face. "Ed, I know you!"

"No, you don't! My father was a hunter. The Council tell you that? He knew the town would burn. It's what he wanted. He sold out the pack to the hunters, hopin' Elijah would spare our family." It hurt to even say such a thing. He knew his father, and he'd changed and left the hunter's life behind. His father had thought Elijah was dead for years. The fire had been Elijah's doing, and no one else's—Eddie would believe that until the day he died. But he had to say whatever he could to make Vico leave, even if it meant hurting him.

"No." Vicenzo's voice trembled.

Eddie came toward him, aiming his gun at Vicenzo's pale, wide-eyed face. "I went with the hunters willingly. To save my own skin while everyone we knew and loved died at their hands. Like my father told me to, if he ever found us." Goddess, how it hurt to betray his father's memory like this, to hurt Vicenzo the way he was hurting him.

Gunfire echoed in the night, back toward the cabin.

Vicenzo had to leave, or else Elijah and his boys would kill him.

Worse yet, they'd make Eddie do it. And maybe Elijah hadn't turned his heart to stone yet because the thought of killing Vicenzo filled him with terror.

Eddie advanced on him, forced himself to imagine Elijah aiming his gun at Vicenzo. He wouldn't be able to save him. Vicenzo would die right in front of him.

Raising his gun to the sky, Eddie fired. "I've got a wolf over here!" he roared.

"Come with me! Hurry!" Vicenzo reached out his hand, advancing toward the shadows of the bayou. "You have a choice, Eddie. You do. Choose me." Goddess, he was pleading.

Eddie ripped his arm out of Vicenzo's grasp, tearing away a piece of his heart in the process. "No. I don't want you, *wolf*. If you don't run fast, I'll put a bullet through you!"

"Eddie..." Vicenzo sounded like he was drowning.

Eddie's pistol went off with a crack. The bullet blew apart the mud at Vicenzo's feet.

Eddie saw it. He saw the moment Vicenzo's heart shattered. The rain began to fall thick and fast around them, and Vicenzo looked frail enough to drown in the downpour. He looked as if Eddie had shot him through the heart.

Thundering footsteps came closer. The hunters were coming.

Vicenzo slumped, fabric ripping as his shift came over him. His clothes fell to pieces except for his bag, which got caught around his neck. With a wounded whine, the black wolf took off into the bayou and became one with the shadows.

He was gone. The one Eddie had come so close to calling his mate once, when they were young and foolish enough to believe their love for each other was the one certain thing in a cruel world.

The blasts from his pistol deafened his scream. He fired at the sky until the gun clicked empty. Eddie hurled the pistol into the mud. His knees shook and he collapsed into the dirt, muddy hands clawing at his face.

Over the wind and rain, he thought he heard a wolf howl across the distance in notes of such agony it cleaved right through him to hear it.

When the hunters found him, Eddie was howling a song of heartache and despair to the empty black sky.

Why?

Why would you do this?

It hurts. Goddess, it hurts so much. Make it stop hurting. Please. I don't want to feel anymore. I don't want to be anymore, I—

In his agony, Vicenzo threw back his head and howled all his heartache to the night sky. This wasn't the way things were meant to end. He and Eddie were supposed to be together. Vicenzo was meant to take him away from this place so they could heal again.

Instead, he'd lost everything. The chains binding his inner animal cracked. What he would give to let go. To forget all he'd loved and lost. A furious snarl tore from his throat. The Eddie he'd loved was dead. His family was dead. His home was gone. And Vicenzo... What was he? What did it matter what became of him?

A blackness came rushing toward him, consuming all he knew. Eddie's face disappeared from his mind. He remembered a town, burning. What was its name? It was so familiar, it was—

Home. Where was home? Was there ever a place he'd called home?

Honey.

Warm summer grass.

The wolf howled, a terrible sound of fury and bloodlust.

I can't remember. Why can't I remember?

This ache inside... where had it come from? Why was he so sad?

"Vicenzo?"

Not Vicenzo. Not anybody. Just wolf.

I am wolf.

The smell of silver made the wolf's hackles rise. He whirled around as a hunter stumbled out of the trees, stinking of the blood that spattered his clothes.

Blue-gray eyes widened. The stench of fear made the wolf's mouth salivate for blood.

"Oh shit. Your eyes... You're feral."

A snarl rumbled in the wolf's throat. He breathed in deep the smell of sweat, flesh, and blood, and his mouth flooded with saliva.

Prey. You are prey.

"It's me. It's Isaac! Hey, snap out of it!"

I will hunt you.

I will kill you.

"Shit. Get back, kid. I'll shoot you. I'm warning you!"

Snap your bones and suck out the marrow.

Drink your life's blood, tear your flesh.

Prey!

A bullet split the air between the wolf's ears. It wasn't the hunter who'd fired but another, diving behind cover within the trees. Though the wolf hungered for blood, he was without a pack. He couldn't take on two hunters at once.

He fled, spraying dirt and wet leaves behind him. He ran until his ribs ached, his tongue lolling from his mouth. Rain splashed in his eyes and soaked through his fur. Mud sucked at his paws and tried to drag him down.

The wolf ran until he found a dense clump of bushes and burrowed beneath. The branches caught the rain and kept him dry, and he closed his eyes and slept. Sunlight pried beneath his eyelids in the morning. His mouth was dry and he ached for water, and his stomach cramped from hunger. The air was hot and wet and he shook out his pelt uncomfortably as he rose, stretching his sore muscles.

Something dragged in the mud, a strap pressed into his shoulders. He hadn't noticed the bag before, so preoccupied with running. He sniffed, smelling leather but no food, and whined. Dragging the bag slung across his back, he bowed his head and drank from the murky waters of the bayou. Green things floated on the surface and got stuck on his tongue.

The heavy bag was growing uncomfortable. He shook, ducking his head until the strap fell off. Hungry, he sniffed at the bag once more. He smelled something. Not food, but that didn't matter. The scent tugged at his brain, and he felt as if he were forgetting something. Some*one.* He nosed open the flap and dug around inside, seeking more of that amazing scent.

It smelled like sun-dried tomatoes. Lavender perfume.

His teeth closed around something soft and he pulled it free. It was a cotton scarf, so soft he wanted to bundle himself in it and sleep forever. It smelled so sweet, he could have rolled in it.

It smelled familiar. It made him ache for something. For someone. For home. For—

"Vico!"

Her smile was bright as the sun. Chestnut hair billowing in the breeze. *"He's your mate. I knew it!"*

He hated it when she teased him but he was always happy to see her when she came home. His annoying sister. His sister.

That was right. He'd brought this with him.

To remember, so he could come back if he was ever lost.

To remember...

Kassandra.

And it all came rushing back. His mother's and father's smiling faces. His sister taking him by the hand, telling him that she would protect him. A sweet, lost boy with blond hair and the bluest eyes he'd ever seen, with a smile that was brighter than the sun itself.

His paws turned to tanned hands. He shivered as his fur fell away and left him naked. "Kassie." His voice was a croak. He clutched the scarf in his muddy hands. "How could I forget you?" What the hell had happened to him? Why was he here? Where was he?

The pain returned, tearing into him with fang and claw. Tears burned his eyes, and he was so scared he could scarcely breathe.

What could he do? His parents were gone. Eddie was gone.

Tears spilled down his face.

Home. He wanted so badly to go home.

As a wolf, he wandered the roads until he returned to the city of New Orleans. People stared in fear and awe, snatching their children up when he approached. Vicenzo recalled he'd come to this city in search of Eddie. He wished he'd never bothered. That damn traitor. He didn't remember much of their conversation or how he'd found Eddie, but he remembered all that mattered.

Eddie was a hunter, like his father before him, like his sick uncle. His father had sold out the town to the hunters. His brother killed him anyway—*why, though?* a doubtful voice whispered—and Eddie went with him to save his own skin.

The betrayal churned in his guts. Eddie had lied to his face for years. Why? To earn the townspeople's trust. To uncover their weaknesses until the moment came to strike. Whatever his reasons were, they'd worked—he'd wormed his way into Vicenzo's heart, then torn it from his chest.

Vicenzo wished they'd never met.

Trotting swiftly over the hot asphalt, Vicenzo ducked into a clothing store, ignoring the stares and frightened gasps. He ripped some oversized jeans from a hanger, tugged a big shirt from a rack. In the changing room, he shifted and dressed. He paid at the counter with the money in his bag and walked out. The shoes he'd picked out were too big, but at least he wasn't naked anymore.

The next thing he did was return to the bar where he'd ditched his phone before he'd gone into the bayou. The bartender recognized him from that day. "Rough week?" he asked, motioning at Vicenzo. He had no doubt he looked as shitty as he felt, despite his change of clothes.

"Guess so," he grunted. The bartender handed over his phone, and Vicenzo went into the bathroom for some privacy. Heart in his throat, he dialed Kassandra's number.

Please, don't turn me away. I'm sorry. I'm so sorry. Please, just let me come home.

Tears stung his eyes. His throat ached.

"Hello?"

Kassandra's voice nearly broke him to pieces. "Kassie," he rasped. "It's me."

She was silent a moment. Then, "What happened?" Her voice was soft and careful. She knew. What was the point in hiding it?

The tears spilled over. Gulping, he leaned on the tiled wall for support. "He... he didn't want me. T-told me to leave. He was... They'd fucking broken him, Kassie. He didn't want me. He didn't—" The sobs shuddered from him, doubling him over until he thought he'd break apart.

"Oh, Vico," she whispered, voice breaking.

He didn't think he would ever be okay again. How could he move past this? His parents, his home, his mate—everything he'd known and loved was gone.

Then Kassandra said two words that broke him and pieced him together again. "Come home."

HIS GRANDPARENTS' HOUSE WASN'T the same without his parents. Any moment now, Vicenzo expected to see them as the taxi pulled up to the countryside cottage, running down to meet him from the house. It was Kassandra that came tearing down the hill as Vicenzo stepped out of the taxi, stumbling over a root and flailing her arms madly to avoid falling. Vicenzo bolted from the car and ran to meet her, holding her tight as she threw herself into his arms.

"I'm so sorry I didn't come with you," he said, closing his eyes tight as the tears burned them. "I won't leave again. I'm staying right here."

His grandparents welcomed him home. His grandma made her famous pasta with a creamy avocado sauce and bomboloni for dessert, Vicenzo's favorite, but his appetite was nonexistent. The bomboloni reminded him of the times when his parents were alive, gathered around this very table. The table looked too big without them. He'd expected to feel relieved to be home, that some part of him would finally be whole. But his grandparents' house wasn't the same without hearing his parents' voices carrying through it. The scent of summer grass and honey from the hives wafting in through the window made him feel ill.

This house would never feel like home again. It was a cage now, full of memories from a life that had been stolen from him.

Exhausted, Vicenzo retired to his room and collapsed into bed. It wasn't even nightfall yet, but his bones ached. He closed his eyes and thought he could hear his mother singing along with Andrea Bocelli downstairs, hear the crinkle of his father's newspaper. But those were ghosts, nothing more.

A gentle knock roused him. Kassandra poked her head in.

Vicenzo lifted his brow. "Making sure I don't disappear?"

She rolled her eyes. "No. Can I have my scarf back?"

He was still wearing it, so he unwound it and handed it to her.

"Ugh. You stank it up!" she chastised, making a face.

Outside the window, the sun was setting over the countryside. Vicenzo wondered where Eddie was, what he was doing. If the hole in his head and heart would ever close. "He lied to us. All our lives."

"Vico—"

"Don't call me that." It just reminded him of Eddie, of that day in the tent when it was just the two of them and the world had seemed so beautiful and pure.

She bowed her head. "You're... different. What happened to you? When you called me, you sounded so lost."

"He took everything from us, Kassandra. His whole family. The town burned because of them, our parents died, our friends—" He bit back a snarl. The anger burned in his gut like battery acid.

"Did he tell you this?" Kassandra sat on his bed, her hand on his ankle. He couldn't feel her touch. He couldn't feel anything except rage.

"Right to my face. Told me if I ever went back, he'd kill me himself."

Tears glimmered in Kassandra's eyes. "We trusted him. He was our friend. He was your—"

"He's not!" Vicenzo snarled. He couldn't hear that word, not ever again. "He's not anything to me. Not anymore."

He wished that they'd never met, that he'd never given so much of his heart and soul to Eddie Turner.

He wished he'd torn out Eddie's throat himself, then lost his mind to feral fury.

"Vico—Vicenzo. Look at me." Kassandra grabbed his chin and gasped as their eyes met. "Your eyes... You're near feral. Goddess, how could I let this happen? I never should have left you."

Vicenzo touched her shoulder. "Not like I gave you much choice." He'd been adamant about staying behind to find Eddie. "I should have stayed with you."

"I'm your sister!" Kassandra's eyes blazed. "I should have gone with you wherever you went. If you had gone feral, it would be because I'd let you go off alone. Listen to me." She blinked furiously, her eyes never wavering from his. "We're all that's left of our pack. It's just the two of us now, Vicenzo. I'm going to take care of you."

His jaw worked, trying to find words. None came out, only a choked, broken sound. Kassandra hugged him tight, her hand at the nape of his neck like the way their mother used to hold him.

"We can rebuild. Begin again. It will take so much time, but we have each other, Vicenzo. We will be all right."

They held each other tight as the shadows deepened and the sun disappeared beyond the hills.

KASSANDRA ASSURED HIM THAT in time, his grandparents' house would feel like the home they'd lost. Five months later, Kassandra was smiling more easily and laughing again. It wasn't as big and bright, but she was getting there. She was happy with her duties at the temple and tried to encourage Vicenzo to join the monks. She claimed meditation would help him find inner peace.

Without his parents to brighten every room, the house he'd grown up in felt like a shell. He couldn't get used to it. Every day he woke up expecting to see his parents in the kitchen or hogging the bathrooms like they usually did. He waited to hear their voices calling to him from the other room. Every day, he longed to go to them for comfort so they could tell him it would all be okay.

But his parents were dead. Nothing would ever be okay again.

Hunters had shattered their pack, stolen away the life he'd once known, and turned his mate against him. Now that he'd had time for his head to cool, he wasn't sure if he believed anything Eddie had told him. He hadn't been himself. Vicenzo hadn't recognized him at all. But it changed nothing. Eddie and Vicenzo were both dead and gone, and no one could bring them back.

The void inside him widened as his grief turned to fury. The person who'd lived in this house with a loving family, the happy life he'd once had—it was all gone. He could never get it back. So why bother with this farce? Why wake every day and try to pretend that someday he would be whole and happy again? It was bullshit.

And then one day, when he was out grocery shopping for his grandparents, he heard whispers behind the shelf next to him.

"Did you hear? Hunters wiped out a whole pack of wolves in the Apennine Mountains."

Vicenzo's stomach churned as bile hit his throat.

"I heard," said another man's voice. "Beasts got what they deserved. They don't want to be hunted, they should live among a civilized society."

Hunters in the Apennine Mountains. That was far too close to Kassandra's monastery. They had to be stopped before they hurt any more wolves.

It was lunacy, but he couldn't get those whispered words out of his head as he tossed and turned that night. Couldn't stop picturing wolves like him, waking up with pieces of their hearts missing. He hadn't been able to save his pack or his home, but maybe he could save theirs.

Kicking free of his blankets, he wrenched his chair back and sat down at his desk. The pen shook in his hand and he wiped his eyes quickly to prevent his tears from splattering the paper. He wrote:

I'm sorry. I can't do this anymore. Nothing will ever be the same. There's a hole in my head and in my heart that nothing can heal. My wolf howls every night for him. For blood. I can't ignore it any longer. Kassandra, forgive me. I love you. My most precious sister.

He left the note on the breakfast table and walked out the door. He didn't look back.

The engine rumbled as he started his car. He unfolded the crumpled newspaper article from his bag and set it on the dashboard. Hunters were targeting werewolves in the Apennine Mountains. They weren't the same hunters Eddie worked with, he knew that, but hunters were hunters.

To them, wolves were prey. Vicenzo bared his teeth as his gums itched. He would show them just what it felt like to be the ones who were hunted like prey. Stepping on the gas, he drove from the garage, tossing his cell phone out the window and onto the dirt road. He didn't want to be talked back from the edge again. The fury pounding through him wasn't mindless and feral, not this time. No, there was a purpose fueling him.

The only way he knew to fill the hole in his heart was with action. He would kill every hunter he could and make sure no wolves had to know pain like this again.

The moon glowed full and fat in the sky, and the beast awoke beneath his skin, claws fastening into the wheel, fangs driving into his lower lip. In the rearview mirror, his eyes flashed, flickering from blue to yellow, yellow to blue. Yellow.

The beast thrummed beneath his human skin.

Chapter 10

A Chance for Redemption

Ten Years Later

The hunters gathered around the fire, laughing uproariously and unaware this meal would be their last. The wolf growled low in his throat, watching them. His mouth salivated for the hunters' blood.

"Vicenzo. We're ready."

His ears twitched, and he glanced dispassionately at the pack at his back. There were twenty in total and most of them had shifted, all except Roberto. He knelt in the grass, naked in preparation for the change.

"Good. Now hunker down and wait. We strike when they're asleep."

The pack settled in for a long wait. With the Mediterranean sun soaking into his dense fur, Vicenzo curled up in the shadow of an olive tree. Roberto leaned against the tree, grinning when his mate, Vanessa, stuck her snout under his arm. Vicenzo's tail wagged, the pack bonds thrumming warmly in his heart.

He was proud of this ragtag pack he'd assembled over the years. At first, he'd struck out alone, risking feral madness in his quest for vengeance against the hunters who stalked the Apennine Mountains terrorizing wolves. The wolves he'd saved had pledged their allegiance to him and vowed to follow him and help protect others.

Throughout the years, he'd earned a few names for himself, like the Beast of the Apennines, while some referred to his pack as the Wild Hunt. He didn't care what folks called them, so long as humans knew to fear him and his pack wherever they roamed.

They were good wolves, his pack. Though their scars had healed, they carried them beneath the surface of their skin. They hated hunters as much as he did and like him, they'd lost people they held dear. Without their bonds to tether him to his humanity, he knew he'd be nothing but a ravening wolf, wandering the mountains aimlessly.

Once the sun had set, Vicenzo roused the wolves and they crept from the shadows and moved in sync toward the hunters' encampment. The campfire was dying low but Vicenzo still wanted to give it a wide berth. The hunters snored and farted while they slept, tossing and turning. Vicenzo thought, *"Now, attack!"*

His pack sang a song of war and charged for the encampment.

The hunters awoke, lunging for their guns, but many were set upon by wolves before they reached them. Any remnants of humanity fled Vicenzo's mind as he hurled himself upon the hunters and lost himself in bloodlust. Bones crunched between his teeth, his fangs punctured soft flesh, and he lapped up hot, coppery blood.

The stench of silver burned his nose. Wolves yelped and cried as silver grenades detonated, blinding and weakening them. Bullets sprayed the ground at Vicenzo's feet and he ran through a haze of smoke and dust.

When the last hunter was felled by his jaws, he panted through a mouth foamy with spit and blood. The fight was over. Hunters lay dead and some of his own packmates had fallen with them, among them Roberto and his mate. He slowly returned to human form as he wrestled control away from his inner animal.

To think a few nights ago, he'd sat with these fallen wolves. They'd laughed and smiled, cried as they'd remembered those they'd lost to hunters. Now they were gone, returned home to the moon.

"We will howl for them tonight," Vicenzo promised, walking among the stricken faces of his packmates. "And we'll go on fighting in their name."

The sun was rising by the time the pack left the bloody camp. They'd buried their dead under the moonlight. If the goddess existed, if she gave a damn at all about the wolves she'd condemned to this life among humans, Vicenzo hoped she'd welcome them back to her hunting grounds.

If she existed, he hoped that was where his parents were, running forever among fields of lunar flowers.

Later that night they returned home to the ghost town in the shadows of the Apennine Mountains. It was a tiny, pitiful town that lay along a small stretch of cracked and crumbling road. It was dry and dusty, but it was theirs.

Sitting away from the pack, he tore into strips of raw meat from the game they'd hunted. Down below, the others chatted and recounted the day's hunt. Vicenzo felt a sudden jab of jealousy. They'd lost so much but they could gather and talk as if their hardships were a thing of the past. They didn't let their pain isolate them.

In the remains of the shattered window, his reflection stared back at him, bearded and unkempt. These were good people. He'd found them and they'd given him purpose, a connection. They were pack, but they'd never replace the one he'd lost the day his home burned and his parents died.

He wondered then what had become of Eddie Turner. If he was even still alive, or if he'd been killed on a hunt. He tore into the meat with a growl. He didn't care what had become of Eddie. Vicenzo hoped he'd met his end at the jaws of a pissed-off wolf.

There came a tugging in his soul.

You fucking liar, whispered his secret heart, the one buried under layers of stone.

He wondered about Kassandra. About his grandparents, and the ache became a throb in his chest. Were his grandparents still alive? What had Kassandra made of her life in the decade he'd been gone? Did she hate him? She must. He'd left her again. He deserved every ounce of her hate.

Wherever she was, he hoped her life was far better than his.

Vicenzo leaned his head back on the windowsill and slept.

THAT NIGHT, HE DREAMED of chaos.

In his dream, he ran through burning forests. Someone was calling out to him. It was Kassandra's voice. She was running so fast he could hardly keep up with her. She reeked of fear.

Her voice filled his mind like it hadn't in years, crying out, *"Vicenzo! Can you hear me? Time is running out. Can you hear me?"*

A howl split the forest, and Vicenzo had the sudden terrible feeling he was being chased. His heart pounded and in his fear he tried to run faster.

"I'm in danger, Vicenzo. I have to run fast, brother. I may never return. I just want you to know... I was so angry at you. For a long time. But the time for anger is past. I forgive you. I understand why you left, I do. I—"

Something tore free from the shadows behind him. It was a black beast, eyes blazing yellow fire. It was chasing his sister.

"I have to go, Vico. I'm sorry." Her voice broke and his chest ached as all of her pain crashed over him. *"I love you, brother. I'll see you again someday. Mother and Father, too. Farewell."*

As she vanished into the darkness, slipping beyond his reach, he screamed out for her. He was so sorry—he never should have left. He would do anything just to see her again.

Vicenzo woke, drenched in sweat and gasping for air. His head ached, thrumming with the chaotic pulse of the awakened bond between him and his sister. Her anger, her sorrow, her fear—it crashed over him in waves and left him trembling.

"Kassandra?" he called out to her in his mind but received no answer. He hadn't felt their bond in years.

That hadn't been a dream. Kassandra had been trying to send him a message. Werewolves couldn't communicate with each other across such vast distances, no matter the strength of their bond. Perhaps she'd picked up a trick like that at the monastery.

His hands shook. Kassandra was in danger. He had to go to her.

The monks at the Monastery of the Moon would know where she'd gone.

Below the building he resided in, the pack was waking to hunt. They broke off into groups and loped into the trees. Vicenzo wouldn't be accompanying them. He was grateful for the years he'd had with them. They'd kept him tethered to his humanity and he was sad to leave them.

If they noticed him walking away from town, they didn't call him back. Wolves came and went all the time from the pack. No one had any obligation to the others. Something in Vicenzo's chest ached. He wanted to be stopped, called back, asked where he was going.

Home was gone, though, and these wolves weren't his family.

Kassandra was all he had left, and he had to find her.

He descended the mountains, smelling blood and lake water from the site of their fight with the hunters yesterday. And something else. He froze in his tracks and breathed in deep. Silver. Distant voices in the woods. More hunters.

This was bad. They were too close to the pack. He had to do something, lead them away. Throwing back his head, he howled to alert the hunters to his presence and warn the pack of coming danger. Then he crouched low and moved toward the shapes wandering the edge of the lake.

This was his last gift to the pack who'd taken him in. The hunters would die before they hurt his packmates.

EDDIE DIDN'T CROSS PATHS with Vicenzo again for many years.

Not until the lone survivor of a clan of hunters called The Beasts for help. The hunter's clan had been wiped out in the Apennine Mountains by a pack of wolves. Eddie had felt a rush of savage satisfaction when he'd heard the news while his fellow hunters were enraged. Elijah had told his hunters to get on a flight to Italy, and Eddie was surprised to be going on a big hunt again.

Over the years, Elijah and The Beasts had changed their methods. They moved all over the country, changing location at least every week to cover their tracks from law enforcement. The world was cracking down harder on hunters these days. Nowadays, The Beasts were more about operating secret wolf fighting rings, which was where most of their income came from.

When he'd heard Elijah wanted to send a team to Italy, he'd been the first to jump at the chance. He must have done a good job over the years of convincing Elijah he enjoyed hunting his own kind because Elijah had agreed to let him go.

Eddie and a crew of hunters arrived in Rome late in the evening. To-morrow they would follow the trail of these feral werewolves. The attack had occurred in a nature reserve a few miles from Rome, so they would start there. Eddie and the hunters stopped at a restaurant to grab some dinner before they checked into a hotel for the night, and he was just as overwhelmed by the sights and crowds as he'd been in the airport.

"Hey, I got an idea," said Rupert, one of the hunters. "My buddy has a fur trade. I say we catch these wolves and skin them, then sell their furs. That way we earn extra on top of the client's pay!" Rupert rubbed his hands together, practically drooling.

Eddie schooled his expression so his disgust didn't show. He wanted to call Rupert out for his bloodlust, but he stayed silent. Who was he to lecture anyone on their actions? He didn't speak for the rest of the evening as they ate dinner and checked into their hotel.

In the early hours of the morning, they rented an RV and acquired hunting equipment from a smuggler outside of town. Then they hit the road and drove into the browning hills of the Italian countryside until they arrived at the enormous lake nestled within the wilderness.

Wolves had been in the area. The air smelled of urine and scat, and huge paw prints trailed around the lake. Dried blood soaked the soil where the wolves and hunters had died.

Eddie wondered what their pack bonds felt like. He didn't even remember what it felt like to be part of a pack, hadn't felt a connection to his inner wolf in years. The silver collar muted his animal instincts and senses until he was hardly better than a human. Sometimes, he remembered the golden strings of *pack* and *family* and *love,* glowing warm in his head. Those strings had snapped when his parents were murdered, when Eddie's wolf was sealed away, when Vicenzo—

His heart clenched and he closed his eyes tight. He'd promised himself never to think of him ever again. It was easier said than done, though, because the truth was he thought about his long-lost mate every single day. Where he was now. How he was doing. If he was alive, dead, feral. The unanswered questions ached so badly, it was better not to even let Vicenzo cross his mind.

They climbed a hill above the lake and a howl echoed over the woods. It was from a human throat, but there was no mistaking the call of a werewolf. Something about that howl stirred feelings in Eddie he'd long since buried.

"Shit. Get ready!" Rafael, another one of his uncle's hunters, grabbed his weapon.

"Damn wolf's howl will warn away any other wolves in the area!" another whined.

Eddie's fingers trembled on his pistol, sickness churning in his gut like it always did before a fight.

A black blur sped through the trees toward them, leaping from the shadows.

Leaping toward Eddie.

The black wolf fell upon him, and they hurtled down the hill, man and wolf tangled up together. The wind flew out of Eddie when he hit the ground. A growl rumbled above him, and he looked up into the blue eyes of a wolf. All the breath froze in Eddie's lungs because he knew those eyes. He would know them anywhere. "Oh, Vico." His old friend and the love of his life stood before him after all these years.

Vicenzo's eyes flashed, his blue eyes widening. The devastation in those eyes tore into Eddie's soul.

He had to run, had to make sure Vico followed him. So much had changed and yet one thing remained the same—Eddie would always protect Vicenzo, no matter what. He swung at the wolf, bowling Vicenzo off him. Scrambling to his feet in the grass, Eddie ran into the trees. He had to lead Vicenzo away from the hunters on the hill.

With a snarl, the wolf pursued him, his pants growing harsher, and then a voice roared, "Eddie!"

His heart froze at the sound of Vicenzo's voice. He whirled around, and Vicenzo crashed into him, arms and legs flying around him in a mockery of an embrace. As Vicenzo slammed Eddie down beneath him, his eyes flared with shock and rage.

"What the hell are you doing here?" Vicenzo panted.

"Huntin'. What else?" Eddie spat the words bitterly.

"Of course. Still a hunter's damn dog after all these years." Vicenzo laughed, the sound harsh and bitter. "Where's my sister? If you've hurt her—"

Eddie's heart sank. "Kassandra. Is she okay?"

Vicenzo's lip curled. "Like you care."

But Eddie did care. Still, after all these years, he cared about Vicenzo. "I don't know where she is. Go. Run. I'll lead the hunters away."

"Why? Don't pretend like I still mean anything to you." There was heartache within those blue depths. A part of him still cared, and Goddess, Eddie could die happy just knowing that at least a part of what they'd had once wasn't dead and gone.

"You do, dumbass. You and Kassie were my family."

Vicenzo bared his teeth. "Yeah? You sure have a funny fucking way of treating family, don't you, Ed?"

Eddie shoved, pushing Vicenzo off of him. "We ain't got time to hash it out, Vico! Get goin'. I'll hold 'em off. I'll—"

Something whistled through the trees. Vicenzo stumbled, a roar of agony tearing from his throat as he collapsed.

"No!" Eddie yelled and lunged, leaping over Vicenzo's thrashing body and shielding him as the hunters came running through the trees, guns raised. "Don't you touch him! I see another bullet fly, and I'll put a hole in you. Clear?"

The hunters gaped at him as Eddie knelt, inspecting Vicenzo's side. It was a silver dart, thank the goddess, and not one of those poisoned bullets.

Eddie turned and encountered the muzzle of a pistol inches from his face. "And why the *fuck* should I take threats from you, dog breath?" the hunter Victor sneered. "And don't be an idiot. That thing's a melanistic Italian wolf. You have any idea how rare they are?" The hunters inspected Vicenzo with interest.

"Fuck all of you," Vicenzo growled weakly.

"Let's take him to my friend's place near Milan. We'll make him shift once we're at the hideout and then we can sell his hide."

Eddie thought about reaching for his pistol and gunning them all down, but his hands were frozen at his sides. He was outnumbered by trained killers. If he died here, no one would be able to save Vicenzo. He had to bide his time and wait.

Eddie's heart sank to his toes as the hunters dragged Vicenzo away.

Who the fuck was he kidding?

How could he save Vicenzo when he couldn't even save himself?

During the drive to Milan, Eddie and the hunters sighted four more werewolves roaming the wilds and tracked them. The men's names were Gabe, Ben, and Ryan, and somehow Kassandra was with them. Eddie couldn't believe it. It was like his past was coming back to haunt him. The pack got under Eddie's skin. Ryan, especially. He talked to Eddie like he was a person. Like he wasn't a monster.

Eddie had forgotten what it was like to be spoken to with anything other than contempt and mistrust. He wasn't deserving of kindness or compassion. He was a monster. A killer. A hunter of his own kind.

Yet these fools thought he could help them.

With every passing minute, the fate of the caged wolves grew nearer. Time was running out if he wanted to save them, and he did. He did, but he just didn't know how. The hunters arrived at a cabin in the woods on the outskirts of Milan. Rupert's friends were waiting for them inside, eager to skin some wolves. There were many of them, and Eddie had no damn clue how he was supposed to free the wolves and get them all out alive.

Gabe and his friends begged him to do the right thing, to let them out. As if he hadn't heard those exact words before. As if he hadn't freed wolves only to watch them be tortured, burned, and killed.

Everything felt so damn hopeless. How in the hell was he supposed to save these wolves? What good would any of it do? He would always be a hunter's dog. A murderer. A monster.

Vicenzo exhaled shakily and said, "You know, when I saw you again after all these years, I didn't recognize you. Hated your guts, in fact. I thought the Ed I once knew was dead and gone. That he'd become an empty shell. But you're still in there. I see it. Beneath all that silver, there's still a heart in there."

Eddie let those words wash over the broken pieces of himself.

Vicenzo laughed softly. "Don't tell me you've just forgotten what we meant to each other once."

No, of course not. He would never forget. The heart he'd locked behind a wall of silver ached something fierce. "Vico, I—I'm not that person anymore. I can never go back to the way things were when we were kids."

"No," Vicenzo rasped. "No, I don't believe that. Maybe things are different, okay, but I still remember what you were like before. You... you loved gardening. Remember? Remember how we'd sit in my mom's garden for hours? Planting things, picking fresh produce."

"Stop," Eddie croaked. "Stop it. That's not me. The boy you knew died, Vico. He's dead, and he's never coming back!"

"It made you so happy!" Vicenzo's voice quaked. "You were a natural. You wanted to give life back to the earth, 'cause after everything you lost, after all the shit you went through, you still saw the beauty in the world. That's who you are, Ed. You're a fighter. You're a survivor. The boy I loved didn't fucking give up, no matter what life threw at him."

Eddie doubled over, trying to hold himself together. It ached to be reminded of all the humanity he'd lost. To be reminded of the person he'd once been and never would be again.

Goddess, he didn't deserve this, but he wanted so badly to be the person Vicenzo remembered. He wanted to be *good*.

The wall of silver shuddered, cracks forming in the surface.

Ben gripped the bars of his cage. "You're reunited with your friends. You've got the biggest shifter agency in the USA willing to take you in and keep you safe. If there was ever a fucking sign from the universe that this is your chance to be free, this is it."

The silver around his heart shattered to pieces.

He would never get another chance like this. He had a pack willing to take him in, to give him a chance at life again. He'd been reunited with his mate, even if nothing was as it had been before. If he let this opportunity go, then he was a damned fool.

A couple of hunters came in to investigate the noise. They moved to lift Kassandra's cage. They would take her into the back and torture her until she shifted. They would kill her. Vicenzo screamed for his sister, begged Eddie to help her.

His body moved before Eddie could think, and he blocked the hunters from Kassandra's cage. Eddie pointed the pistol between the hunters. "Keys. Now."

One of the hunters sneered. "You little—" His hand flew to the gun at his belt.

It was over in seconds. Eddie's hand tingled, the reverberations from the shots fired traveling up his arms. His ears rang as the hunters fell to the ground. His hand shook so badly, he dropped the pistol. "Fuck, fuck, fuck..." He'd done it. He'd stood up to the bastards.

He was going to save Vicenzo and these wolves or fucking die trying.

Eddie unlocked the cages and let Gabe and his friends out. That simple act changed his life in ways he couldn't have hoped to comprehend.

The things he'd done would always haunt him, but for the first time in so long, Eddie had a choice. And he chose to be free.

Ben, Kassandra, and the others returned to the RV. Vicenzo didn't.

"Vico... Thanks for what you said earlier." Eddie reached for him.

Vicenzo ripped his hand back, his eyes full of anger and hurt. "I said what I did to save our skins."

Pain tightened Eddie's chest. "Oh." Thing is, he wasn't sure if he entirely believed that.

"Don't you think anything's changed between us, Ed." Vicenzo's voice shook with cold fury. "We're not mates. We're not anything to each other, not anymore. You took that from us, you just remember that." He turned and walked away.

Eddie knew he was right. They could never get back what was lost between them, but they had the chance to start again.

And Eddie would be damned before he ever wasted that chance.

CHAPTER 11

FOREVER ISN'T FOR US

THREE YEARS LATER

SOME YEARS AFTER JOINING the agency, Vicenzo and the agency wolves were called out to the rugged Denali mountains in Alaska to investigate the disappearance of some wild wolves, and it turned out that hunters were responsible. At first, Eddie had been terrified it was The Beasts's doing. In the three years since they'd joined the agency, neither Eddie nor Vicenzo had heard much of The Beasts. It seemed they'd changed their methods again and had started operating more covertly.

So Vicenzo had felt he'd had to come along. Not only was he aching to put his teeth in the hunters who'd destroyed his life, but when he'd smelled Eddie's fear upon telling Ben of the disappearing wolves, protective urges he'd forgotten he had had woken right the hell up. Like hell he'd ever let The Beasts anywhere near Eddie again.

Vicenzo was always ready to kick some hunter ass, but out in the wilds, an entirely new urge awoke within him. To go far away. To forget. To stop seeing fucking Eddie every single day, a constant reminder of the foolish, lovesick boy he'd once been, a reminder of everything he'd had and lost.

He'd lived with the agency wolves for about three years now, and it was time to accept the truth: no one would ever replace the family he'd lost. No matter how much he wanted to be a part of a pack again, it was just too hard. He didn't know how to open his heart to anyone. He'd forgotten how to be vulnerable. He was sick and tired of being disappointed by others but was fed up with disappointing himself most of all.

So Vicenzo ran and didn't look back. The snow was icy under his paws, and the wind burned his eyes.

The bonds of the pack pulsed feebly in his mind, little frayed strings on the verge of breaking. With every mile he ran, the strings fell apart strand by strand. The bonds were so damn fragile. After so much time spent with the agency wolves, the bonds of pack should have been stronger, which was all the more reason why he ought to leave.

The feeble threads of the pack bonds pulsed. All except Eddies, of course.

If Eddie's silver collar weren't stifling his wolf and he could communicate, would he be asking Vicenzo to come back? With a snarl, he sprang off the ground, flying over a log, and crashed down into the snow. The threads unraveled, a strand away from breaking.

Another mile and they'll be gone, an uncertain voice whispered over the roaring of the wind in his ears. *Without a connection to my humanity, I'll be a wolf forever. I won't remember anything or anyone.*

Something churned in his gut. Guilt. He was actually feeling guilty about abandoning these people, these people who meant absolutely nothing to him. Sure, they'd had their uses—they'd put a roof over his head and some money in his pocket, he'd used their pack bonds to keep from going feral, and there'd definitely been some exciting moments. Day-to-day life wasn't exactly dull while working for the Lycanthrope Protection Agency. But they weren't pack. They'd never been.

Liar.

No! He wasn't a liar. He didn't care about any of them. Not Ben Stroud, the grumpy older wolf whose face softened as he watched over his pack; not Ryan Kelly and his mate, Zach DeShawn, always joking and supporting each other; not Max Gallagher and his mate, Gabe, both of whom smiled as if the pain of their pasts was nothing but a distant dream; not Isabella

Reyes, Gabe's sister, who always tried to include him in pack activities, even when he snapped at her.

Not Eddie. Eddie, who smelled like ash. Eddie, who reminded him of everything he'd had and lost. Eddie. Eddie. *Eddie.*

A howl tore from his throat and filled the dark, empty sky above.

They would never be his family. All of the agency wolves could go to hell. And yet...

His paws caught in a root and he flew, hurtling head over paws through the snow. His ribs ached as he panted, his tongue lolling from his mouth.

A few more steps, and the bonds would snap. In hours, days, weeks, months maybe—he didn't know when but it would happen eventually—without a pack to tether him to his humanity, he would go feral. And all right, maybe that scared him. He'd always had a pack to fall back on—his parents, then the wolves in the Apennine Mountains, now the agency pack.

But no one since his parents had felt like home. He could never have that bond again, and he was sick of trying to convince himself he could because he was wrong.

The agency wasn't his pack. They weren't his family. They could claim he belonged to them all they wanted but it wasn't true.

Yet over time, bonds had formed in his heart and mind, connecting him to each of them. Over time, he could even tell them apart. He'd ignored them for years, never reaching back across the warm, shimmering threads to connect to them. Until today, when he could no longer ignore them, when he yearned for someone, anyone, to reach out across those fraying threads and howl for him to come home.

But home was nothing but ash. It was gone, and he'd never find it again.

Going feral would be a release.

The horizon opened before him, miles of isolated wilderness. The bonds in his mind were held together by a thread, beckoning him to turn around. Vicenzo closed his eyes tight. He raised his paw and took a step forward.

They snapped all at once. He hardly felt them break. When his parents had died, he'd felt it. He'd known. The pain had been unbearable.

So there. He felt nothing for these people. Not a one.

His chest felt empty, hollow, the ache one only a lone wolf knew. It wouldn't be long now before feral madness came for him. He would forget everything and everyone, and all his worst memories would be swallowed by feral darkness. The thought scared him, but he had nothing and no one to lose, not anymore. That was true happiness. Not pack. Not love. Just the promise of an empty black abyss that would drown him like a deep, dark sea.

Vicenzo set out into the wilderness with his shadow by his side.

He walked on, and the silence of the wild became his only companion.

The sun disappeared beyond the Denali mountain ranges. Vicenzo gnawed at the abandoned carcass of an elk, his eyes darting around to make sure the wolves who'd killed it weren't returning. The scents were stale but not stale enough for him to lower his guard. Wolves always returned to an old carcass to feed.

The quiet was so deep, the wind deafened him. The shadows of the woods grew deeper, darker. He would have to find shelter for the night. A wolf howled far within the trees and another answered. They sang to each other, and Vicenzo's chest ached.

He left the carcass and walked until the land was dark. His paws ached. He found a rocky den in the woods and curled up on cold soil, laying his head on his paws. The quiet rang in his ears and the wind swept cold through his fur.

He closed his eyes and dreamed, only these dreams felt more like memories of last year.

"Vicenzo!"

He growled at Ryan's brash voice. "What?"

Ryan Kelly grinned obnoxiously as he caught Vicenzo's attention. Goddess. That goofy smile reminded him so much of Derek. Everything from Ryan's playful personality to his loud voice reminded him of that silly kid. Alarmed by the sorrow squeezing his chest, Vicenzo rearranged his face into a scowl as he turned around. Vicenzo glared down his nose at Ryan. He was short, and he wore glasses with thick frames that he probably thought made him look smart. They didn't. "Oh, come on, Vic. Have some Christmas cheer."

Vicenzo squinted at his ugly Christmas sweater. "And look stupid like you?"

Ryan puffed out his chest and turned up his nose, shoving his glasses farther up with a finger. "Rude. Guess you're not invited to Izzie and Gabe's amazing Christmas Eve party."

"Good." Vicenzo turned on his heel. What was so special about Christmas, anyway? Maybe when he'd been a kid it was fun, but now that his family was gone he didn't see the point.

"Geez, man. Remind me why we're friends with you again?"

"We're not?"

Ryan gasped, his hand to his heart. "Now that just hurt. Come on, Vic." He darted out in front of Vicenzo. "Look, man, Gabe and Izzie are throwing a party. They want everyone who's pack to come. So, if you change your mind, the door's open."

Vicenzo looked away and toward the kitchen where the pack had gathered to grab a late dinner that he'd prepared. Spaghetti and meatballs, his mother's recipe. Just the scent of Italian spices reminded him of home. He could hear his mother's voice singing along to Andrea Bocelli. He blinked away the mist that the past always seemed to leave on his eyes. It wasn't his family at the table but the agency wolves, all smiles and cheer. Eddie was with them, chatting to Luna, Max and Gabe's daughter, and Tommy, her big brother, and something inside Vicenzo ached when he noticed the gentle tilt to Eddie's lips.

What was up with that? Eddie had lost as much as he had. How could he still find it in him to smile?

"I'm not pack," Vicenzo stated. "Have fun at your party." He walked around Ryan and out into the cold.

"Party's at eight! Jerk," Ryan mumbled.

The day of the party arrived. Vicenzo hadn't changed his mind. He hadn't. He hated Christmas. He didn't want to hang out in a cramped apartment full of rowdy werewolves. He hated the city and its crowded, bustling streets. He especially hated riding the subway. He wasn't going. He wasn't, he told himself as he boarded a packed train and rode to Park Avenue.

He checked the time and cursed. He was running late. He'd stayed in the estate kitchen after hours, mixing up his grandma's Christmas cookie recipe as fast as he could. His biggest fear wasn't that the pack would give him shit for icing the gingerbread men in little coats and scarves the way his grandma used to, but that he'd miss this silly party.

He spent twenty minutes trying to find Gabe and Max's apartment. He was just bored, that was all. Besides, there'd be free food and dessert. He'd stay an hour, maybe less, and then he'd leave. He was already beginning to regret his stupid decision. At this rate, the party would be over by the time he actually got there. Not that it mattered... okay, maybe it did, just a little.

Vicenzo could still remember the last Christmas with his family. His grandma had made doughnuts for breakfast and they were even better than his mother's. Vicenzo and Kassandra ate so many, their stomachs ached. They'd spent the day opening presents and later that night his mother had cooked her signature Christmas roast, an elegant rack of lamb with potatoes and vegetables. Later, Eddie had come over and they'd exchanged presents.

This Christmas wouldn't be the same as his family's, but a part of him ached for a reminder of those simple times, for joy and for family. And so he found himself calling Ben because no, he didn't want to miss this and he was afraid he already had. Damn it. He just hoped the others didn't make him regret this.

"Hey, Vicenzo." Ben's voice was lighthearted. There was a lot of noise in the background. "Everything all right at the estate?"

"Don't know. Maybe? Uh..."

"What do you mean 'maybe'?"

"I'm not there! I'm here. Almost. Maybe. Just can't find the frigging apartment."

"Gotcha. Where are you? Look for the street signs."

Vicenzo looked up and found a street sign. "Park Avenue."

"And?"

"Sixty-ninth Street."

"Okay, you're not far at all," Ben's deep voice said. "We're on Seventy-first. Keep walking, make sure the numbers are going up. I'll meet you downstairs."

"You don't have to—" Ben hung up and Vicenzo scowled. It was already embarrassing enough that he'd gotten lost, but now he felt stupid, too. He only had to walk a minute or so before he stopped outside Gabe and Max's building. It was luxurious, with an open lobby, a doorman, and a sitting area with leather couches.

Ben grabbed the door for him as he entered. "Hey! Glad you could make it." He wore a gray sweater over a dress shirt.

Vicenzo hummed. "Thanks for... you know. I hate the city."

"I feel you," Ben rumbled, leading him to the elevator, which the doorman had called for them. "I'd lived in the country all my life before I came to the city. Talk about shell-shocked. Get off the estate more, walk around the city. You'll get used to it."

They rode the elevator up and Ben opened the door to Gabe and Max's apartment. They were all there, spread out all over the apartment and getting their scent on everything. Ryan was draped across the sofa, his head in Zach's lap. Gabe and Izzie sat at the marble countertop drinking eggnog. Max was in the kitchen with Kendra, dancing to Christmas tunes, while Gabe's parents laughed with Tommy and Luna. Max's biological mother and father had turned up, recognizable by their matching red hair and the overwhelming smell of lunar flowers. Vicenzo still couldn't believe Max's birth mom was Amaris, the deity of the moon.

In an armchair by the window, Eddie sat dunking a gingerbread cookie in a glass of milk. Vicenzo frowned. He'd made cookies, too. Now there'd be too many... His eyes met Vicenzo's and he offered a smile, and Vicenzo looked down at his feet, unsure how to react.

"Hey!" Ryan rolled off Zach's lap and hurried to the door. "Vico's here!"

Vicenzo's face warmed at the nickname. "Uh... Here. Brought these." He shoved the container of cookies at Ryan.

Ryan opened the lid and sniffed. "Man, these smell great! Did you make them?"

"Yeah. Family recipe." Vicenzo's skin wanted to crawl off. "Uh, I didn't know you guys already had cookies. Don't eat 'em if you don't want to. I don't care."

Ryan snorted. "Don't eat 'em? You crazy? Guys, come and eat these cookies before I eat all of them!" They gathered around, each fighting for a cookie.

In two seconds, Luna had eaten hers. "These are the best cookies ever!"

Max moaned. "These are delicious!"

A rush of pride ambushed Vicenzo. "They're my grandma's recipe."

Gabe crammed his cookie down his throat. "Dude, I think I love your gran."

Ben bit the head off his gingerbread man. "Damn. Putting you on chef duty was the best decision I ever made." He patted himself on the shoulder.

Shrugging, Vicenzo looked away so he didn't let the pride show on his face. They were probably just messing with him...

Ryan frowned, looking around at everyone. "Where's your sweaters, guys? Gabe said everyone had to wear an ugly sweater but I'm the only one who wore one."

Vicenzo glanced around the gathering.

Grinning, Gabe said, "I may have edited the email I sent Ry specifically."

Ryan's face reddened. "Fine. I'll rock my ugly sweater with pride!"

Squeezing past, Vicenzo went straight for the bar, wanting a drink to help soothe his rattled nerves. Gabe and Max had set up a big Christmas tree decorated with forest animal ornaments in the middle of the living room.

Pictures of their family covered the walls and filled Vicenzo with soft, fluttery feelings he tried to ignore.

There were also scented Christmas candles around the apartment, but none of them were lit. By the smell, they'd been lit fairly recently, though. Was it possible Eddie had told Gabe and Max that fire made Vicenzo uncomfortable? They seemed like the kind of people who would take the comfort of others into consideration. Vicenzo couldn't help feeling relieved the candles weren't burning. He couldn't even have them in his bedroom at the agency. Ever since the fire, being around open flames was enough to make him spiral into a panic.

Damn. Everything was so warm and festive it could have rivaled his own family's Christmas traditions. Nostalgia warred with a sudden ache of grief, and he wished he'd stayed at the estate. But before he could find an excuse to leave, Max called, "Let's open presents, everyone!"

There was a huge pile of gifts beneath the tree.

"These traditions are so interesting," a wide-eyed Amaris whispered to her mate. "I never knew the people of this land kept trees in their homes! I quite like it."

The pack crowded around the tree. Vicenzo was curious to see what everyone got, so he stayed, sitting at the counter away from the others to watch as they opened gifts. Eddie's face glowed as Ryan handed him a book on botany. Ryan explained, "I'm gonna get an herb garden going this spring so I can make everyone potions. I'd love to have you and that green thumb of yours helping me out."

"Sounds great!. Thanks, Ry." Eddie immediately opened the book. Vicenzo remembered hot afternoons spent in his mother's vegetable garden, filling a basket full of fresh produce together. A twinge of pain went through him. Those had been such simple times, when his biggest worry was that his friend since forever might not return his feelings. He'd give anything to go back to then.

Suddenly, everyone was looking at him. Max approached, a bulky wrapped object in his arms. "Here, Vico. This is for you."

Vicenzo blinked. "Me? Who's it from?"

"All of us," Ben said, raising a glass of eggnog to his lips. "We each chipped in. Was Ed's idea."

Eddie hung his head, his ears going as red as his beanie.

Max dumped the object into his lap. It was heavy. Vicenzo sure hoped these guys weren't pranking him. With some trepidation and wary looks around the room, he ripped apart the paper and—

It was a jacket, big and made of real leather, with a wool collar and lining. The leather was buttery soft. Words failed him because he couldn't remember when anyone other than his family had given him such a nice gift. His mouth opening and closing like a fish, he looked from one warm, smiling face to the other.

"You were always complaining about how cold it is in the winter here." Ben broke the silence first. "Figured you'd be a lot less grumpy if you had a real coat to wear."

"Does it fit?" Max asked. "We sort of guessed at your measurements."

"Don't know," Vicenzo said gruffly, shoving his arms through the sleeves. Warmth encased him, so soft he wanted to snuggle into it—except he wouldn't, at least not with the pack staring at him. Maybe later, when he was alone. "It's..."

Perfect, he wanted to say. Truth was, he didn't know how to put into words what this meant to him. But his heart was so warm, so full from this gesture, it ached.

Gabe whispered something to Max, who jumped. "Oh yeah! Here you go." As Max handed Vicenzo a card, he wished they'd all stop staring at him. With an awkward cough, Gabe declared, "Hey, who wants to do shots?"

The pack scrambled to the kitchen, and Vicenzo exhaled and opened the card. He snorted. It had a wolf on the front, silhouetted by the full moon. When he opened it, a pack of three paper wolves popped up from within, howling. The inscription was simple.

Merry Christmas! Here's to many more! Your Pack

That was it. So simple. Nothing more, but Goddess, Vicenzo felt so warm.

That was the night it happened, when the faint pulse of the bonds in his mind beat along with his heart, golden and warm. He hadn't felt like this since before his family was broken.

It was too much. He stood up and left without another word. No one noticed or tried to stop him. Head bowed, he walked back to the subway in the snow. The cold made his eyes water and sting and his lips tremble.

He didn't want this. He wanted to carry his family in his heart until he was long gone, and he never wanted anyone to replace them. No one ever would.

Opening the card, he brushed his thumb over the inscription.

Forever didn't exist. Forever was a promise he and Eddie had made when they were too young and dumb to comprehend what it meant. Nothing was forever, not feelings, not family, not even pain. Was it possible he could have something new? A pack. A family. A new beginning.

The ink faded beneath his thumb. When he looked up, the street was becoming a blur. He blinked but nothing could clear his vision. The streetlights went out. Darkness crept toward him.

"No," he whispered.

The street was disappearing before his eyes. A wolf prowled from the shadows with burning yellow eyes, bringing the darkness with it.

"No. Please." He clutched the card to his chest—it was gone. "No!" He closed his eyes tight and struggled to hold on to their faces, their names, but it was futile. They were fading from his mind, spilling like water between his fingers no matter how hard he tried to hold on to them. "Don't you take this from me," he snarled to the wolf as it came closer, shadows oozing from his black fur. "Let me hold on to this. Just this. Please!"

He didn't want to forget them, not even Eddie.

Why had he left? Why had he acted so recklessly?

In all his hurt and anger, he'd forgotten the good times they'd shared. He'd pushed them all away time and again, denied himself a second chance at happiness. They'd always been reaching out to him, and every time he'd acted coldly in exchange. He needed a second chance... and it was too late.

"Ben!" he roared, remembering just a little. "Eddie!" The darkness swallowed up his voice. No one answered. "Help me, please! I'm sorry! I'm so sorry! I don't want to forget!" Something ran hot and wet down his cheeks. The darkness swallowed his knees. "Please, help me! Come and find me!"

He choked on ash. The buildings around him were on fire.

"Don't," he choked. "Don't take them from me."

The wolf bared his fangs and snarled as embers drifted from his coat.

Vicenzo threw back his head and howled for someone to save him, for his pack, for his mother and father, for Eddie.

No one came. No one—

A howl split apart the night air and through the darkness, a white wolf strode toward him, its coat so blindingly bright that it cast away the darkness.

"Eddie," Vicenzo whispered. He reached out his hand and—

And he woke up, shivering as the cold gnawed into his bones. Darkness pressed in on his eyes. "No," he whimpered, more scared than he'd ever been. "I don't want this. I don't want to be alone. I don't—"

"Vico. Vico!" Hands fumbled around his shoulders and a coat flew over him.

Vicenzo smelled ash overpowering the scent of what had once been summer grass and honey. His eyes adjusted to the darkness. Eddie knelt before him, shivering in the cold. He'd given Vicenzo his coat. Vicenzo didn't understand. How could he be here? Were Ben and the others with him?

Relief swept over Vicenzo and he crumpled into Eddie's arms, clinging to him. "Sorry, Eddie. I'm so sorry. I never should have—I didn't—"

"It's okay. I'm here." Eddie's arms went around his shoulders and he helped Vicenzo stand. "Shit, it's fucking freezing! We gotta find shelter!"

He clung to Eddie, desperately seeking the warmth of his body as he followed him blindly into the thickly falling snow. Vicenzo's feet were freezing in the snow and started to become so numb he could hardly walk. Just when he thought they'd pass out, Eddie led Vicenzo to the left and into a cave where he'd set up his tent. Vicenzo faltered at the sight of the flickering campfire. Eddie gave him a knowing glance, then kicked apart the logs so the flames dispersed. Embers flared like they had when the building came down on his parents, and Vicenzo swallowed a surge of sickness at the memories.

Eddie didn't look at him. Anger rolled off him in waves, his fingers curling from it.

Vicenzo's teeth chattered when he said, "W-what's your deal?"

Eyes blazing, Eddie whirled toward him. "What the fuckin' hell is your problem?" His voice echoed through the cave.

Vicenzo's own temper flared. "You wanna fight?"

Eddie threw his hat on the ground. "Shut up, Vico. Just shut up! I've been lookin' for you for two fuckin' days. I didn't come all this way for you to act like a dick!"

Vicenzo gaped. He'd never seen Eddie so livid before. "Had no idea your face could turn so red."

"That's it?" Eddie folded his arms. "That's what you have to say for yourself? The hell did I bother freezin' my ass off tryin' to find you for?"

"Hell if I know! I sure as hell never asked you to!" Maybe his wolf had wanted Eddie to find him, but Vicenzo preferred not to think about that.

"That's right! You didn't! You just took off into the wilderness while there were werewolf hunters stormin' around, by the way!"

"How was I supposed to know you would try to find me? I didn't want to be found!" Not until fifteen minutes ago when he'd realized what he'd left behind.

"Why?" Eddie threw his hands into the air. "Why would you just assume no one would come lookin' for you? Because you're not pack, because you hate our guts? That bullshit doesn't work on me, Vico." With a strangled snarl, Eddie paced, working his hands through his curtain of long blond hair. Vicenzo grinned. It wasn't every day quiet Eddie Turner lost his temper.

"You're right," Vicenzo huffed. "I didn't think you would follow me. I haven't exactly been easy to deal with, have I? I didn't expect anyone to care that I was gone." He'd pushed the pack away since the moment he'd met them, rebuffed all their attempts to get to know him. He'd thought for sure they would give up on him, and he wouldn't have blamed them at all, even if he was the only one hurting from his own decision.

"Fuck you," Eddie spat, voice full of venom. "And fuck that. You're pack, you asshole. And you're comin' back if I have to drag your ass halfway across Alaska. Clear?"

"Fuck you, too, dog dick."

"Asshole."

"You said that already, dumbass!"

They bristled at each other, faces inches apart. Eddie wasn't a wolf with that silver collar around his neck, but he sure could growl like it. Then Eddie deflated with a long, low sigh and Vicenzo grinned, pleased he could rile him up.

"Did you really wanna go feral, Vico?" Eddie's voice was quieter and there was something raw beneath the fading anger. "Do you hate us that much that you couldn't stand to remember us anymore?"

Vicenzo gritted his teeth. "I don't hate the pack, Ed. Ben and the others are okay. Annoying, but they're not too bad. They didn't push me away when I came to them, just asking to start over. They didn't run while our home burned to the ground."

Eddie withdrew from him, eyes like ice. "Vico, I... about that..."

Vicenzo hated to even think back to those early days following the blaze that had consumed their town. At the time, he hadn't believed Alpha Hanson about Eddie's family history, not until he heard it all right from Eddie's mouth.

"The Alpha of the Council at that time told me exactly what you did. That your dad was a hunter. That death followed him wherever he went." Anger curled like a fist in his gut, shielding him from the hurt that went off like a grenade in his stomach. "Been meaning to ask for a long time, Ed. Just what did you get out of it, huh? Us."

Eddie stiffened, the breath hitching in his throat.

Vicenzo stood, not caring that he was bare from the waist down as he cornered Eddie against the cave wall. "Were you trying to get us to lower our guard so you could sell us off to the highest bidder? Black wolf skins fetch a pretty penny."

Disgust flashed in Eddie's eyes and he shoved Vicenzo in the chest. "Fuck you. I *loved* you, Vico. With everythin' I fuckin' had." His voice broke, his lips trembling in fury. Vicenzo tried to pretend he hadn't noticed.

"And you pushed me away." Vicenzo slammed his fist against the wall beside Eddie's head, and he flinched, his eyes wide and wild. "And you think coming after me now will make everything you shattered inside me okay again? Is that what this is?"

Eddie was silent.

"'Cause you can't fix this, Eddie." Vicenzo's voice broke and he blinked hard against the wetness in his eyes. "There's no fixing us. Whatever we had, it burned in the fire. Thanks to you." His throat ached. Turning his back, Vicenzo slumped against the wall, his head hanging down.

Neither of them spoke for a long time. The wind howled and filled the silence.

"And yet here we are," Eddie murmured. "You and me, Vico. Forever."

"The hell did we know about forever?" Vicenzo said, lashing out. "We were stupid kids. We didn't know shit."

"You did," Eddie said softly. "You always knew."

The pain wrapped itself around his heart and squeezed tight. "Shut up, Eddie."

Eddie didn't say any more, not about forever, anyway. "I learned about what my father was when you did. My uncle Elijah told me everythin'."

Vicenzo must have known that all along because he wasn't surprised. He just felt sick.

"My pa wasn't a good man until he met my mama. She made him good. Taught him werewolves weren't the monsters he'd been made to believe. She gave him the bite. I think after that, he decided he wanted a fresh start for his family 'cause he never told me about his past. Not even when our town burned when I was a kid. Not even the day he died. And I hated him for it, for a long, long time. But he never sold out our town. I lied, Vico, and I'm real sorry." Eddie's voice quivered and broke.

Vicenzo ached. He ached everywhere. But there was relief mixed in with all the hurt because that meant Eddie hadn't been lying to him about their relationship. "So that whole show the day I found you with the hunters... you lied to me."

"I couldn't go with you, Vico. I was broken. And even if I had, Elijah would have hunted me down just like he did my pa. Innocent people would have been hurt. You—you would have been hurt or worse. It was shitty, what I did. It was real fuckin' shitty, and I... I'm sorry."

And Vicenzo understood, more than before, but it didn't change anything because the scars were still there, deep below his skin. "I don't care, Eddie." He was so tired. "It's too late. Don't you get that? Forever isn't for us. I don't want anything to do with you." The lie tasted bitter in his mouth. Unwilling to say another word, Vicenzo lay down on his side and curled into himself, his back to Eddie.

"I'll never believe that," Eddie whispered. "Not ever."

Vicenzo closed his eyes tight and listened to the wind howl.

CHAPTER 12
LET'S START OVER

Eddie couldn't sleep that night in the cave.

Vicenzo wasn't the man he used to be. He was hard and irritable, and losing so much had left him bitter and cynical. But Eddie couldn't let him go because Vicenzo was wrong: he was pack—he'd always been. He could talk shit about how he wasn't pack, how they all meant nothing to him, but yesterday Eddie had seen right through his lies.

He'd seen the heart of Vicenzo. It was hard and scarred but it was there. And he'd watched it break as Vicenzo fought his way back from feral madness. Vicenzo had come apart in his arms, shaking with fear and cold, his face wet with tears. He'd clung to Eddie and seemed so small.

For all his tough talk, Vicenzo had been frightened by the idea of losing his connection to his humanity—to the pack. He'd regretted ever running away, and Eddie had seen it in his stricken eyes.

Across the charred remains of the campfire, Vicenzo slept, nude from the waist down with his knees curled tight to his chest. His face was pinched, his shoulders rising and falling fast. His feet twitched as if he were running. Eddie thought he knew from what. He still had nightmares about the fire, about running through the woods while Elijah's wolves pursued him.

They were both still haunted all these years later, hounded by demons they just couldn't shake. They'd found a new pack, maybe even a home among the wolves of the agency. It was time to lay their demons to rest.

Eddie knew he and Vicenzo couldn't continue this way. Something had to give, he just didn't know what.

His stomach growled. He opened his pack and retrieved a couple sticks of spicy jerky. Beyond the mouth of the cave, the storm had stopped overnight. A blanket of freshly fallen snow glittered, untouched by anything except the wind. Eddie had left markers to help find their way back to the base Manuel and Veronica Reyes, Gabe and Izzie's parents, had set up. He and Vico would be there by midday and then they could hitch a ride back to Anchorage and board a plane home.

Home. He hadn't had somewhere that felt like home for so long until the agency wolves rescued him. If only Vicenzo felt the same way toward them. Ben and the agency wolves... they were kind and warm. They would welcome them back and there wouldn't be any cruelty or pain. Things between them and Vicenzo might be strained after what he'd done, but Eddie hoped that now that Vicenzo knew what the LPA pack meant to him, things would be different. Hopefully, Vicenzo would start opening up more, accepting offers to come to pack events.

Eddie wanted that, more than anything. For Eddie, the agency had been a turning point in the blackness of his life as a hunter. A chance for a new beginning. Over the years, he'd talked to a counselor Ben had introduced him to, and she'd helped him work through his trauma from his time with the hunters and his guilt at the things he'd done.

He understood now that he'd been in survival mode all those years. Elijah had controlled him in every way possible by isolating him from others, torturing him, and breaking him down to nothing. In some sick way, he'd made Eddie dependent upon him for the resources he needed to stay alive. He'd made Eddie feel so small and hopeless. But things were different now. His uncle was out of the picture, hopefully even dead in a ditch somewhere or rotting in a cell for all the shit he'd done. It was time for both him and Vicenzo to have a second chance at happiness.

It was also time to get moving. The Alaskan wilderness could change in seconds, and Eddie didn't want the guys back at the base to wait much longer for them. Bracing himself for trouble, he went and kicked Vicenzo's bare foot. Vicenzo jerked awake so fast, Eddie wondered if he'd been sleeping at all. His eyes looked briefly yellow but with a blink they were their normal blue. A flicker of anger burned in the pit of Eddie's gut. He hated Vicenzo for a moment, hated him for letting things get so bad.

"Eat." Eddie handed him some jerky.

Vicenzo accepted the jerky wordlessly and ate it in seconds, licking his fingers free of the spices. Eddie's mouth went dry, and it was suddenly a lot harder not to notice Vicenzo was naked. Curious blue eyes flicked up at him, the tip of a finger still between supple lips.

Eddie looked away quickly and busied himself with the camping equipment, piling it back into his backpack. If there was anything that hadn't changed over the years, it was Vicenzo's good looks. He'd always been remarkably handsome, all sharp, chiseled lines and smooth olive skin. His buzz cut made his features colder, more severe.

It had been so long since they were truly alone together without the other agency wolves, much less in such a small space. They weren't lovesick boys anymore. They were broken pieces with jagged edges that no longer fit into a whole.

"Done?" Eddie asked, rolling up his sleeping bag and cramming it in his bloated pack. It barely fit.

Vicenzo grunted and stretched out his legs obscenely. It was dark but Eddie could make out the patch of black pubes between his hairy thighs, the thick base of his dick. Fucking asshole. "We need to do something about that." His face warmed. That hadn't sounded so lewd in his head.

Vicenzo's mouth dimpled when he smirked. "About what?" He scratched between his legs, his fingers rasping through dense curls.

"Gettin' you some goddamn pants? You can't move through the airport naked. You'll be arrested at the door."

"Why, would that bother you?" Vicenzo inquired. "'Cause if that would embarrass you, you know I'm gonna do it."

Eddie supposed if Vicenzo felt good enough to tease him, he was in a better headspace than yesterday. "Here." He threw some thick snow pants at Vicenzo. "Wear these. And no, you're sure as hell not wearin' my underwear."

Vicenzo wrinkled his nose at them. "Never understood humans and their obsession with clothes. They're so itchy." He tugged at Eddie's coat.

Eddie hit his head against his backpack. "Do not take that off."

"Why, would that inconvenience you somehow?" Vicenzo was grinning. Damn him.

Eddie snapped, "Do you wanna go home or not, Vico?"

"No! I don't," Vicenzo said as if Eddie didn't know him at all, which, to be fair, Eddie didn't. Not like he used to. "The HQ's your home, not mine. There's nothing for me there."

"That's bull, Vico."

Vicenzo leaned his head back against the stone wall. He still hadn't put on those pants. "Who put you up to it?"

Eddie gritted his teeth. "Up to what? Be specific."

"Who sent you to find me? Why?"

"No one did," Eddie said. "Everyone else went home. They wanted to help look, but they had priorities back home and we'd already been gone longer than anyone thought we would be. Ben and that hunter Isaac stayed after we defeated those werewolf hunters. I stayed behind to track your ass down." And he didn't regret it, even if it meant he was stuck with Vicenzo's prickly personality. "And I don't know why either, considering what a dick you've been the past three years." But the thought of returning to the estate without Vicenzo made him feel sick.

"I didn't ask you to follow me. I wanted to be left the hell alone."

Eddie snorted. "Right. That's why you were so scared when you realized what a bullshit idea it was all along."

"I wasn't—" Vicenzo scowled and hung his head. "I wanted to forget, okay? I just wanted to forget it all, everything that ever happened since the town burned down. I wish you'd have just let me."

"But you didn't want to forget us," Eddie said.

Vicenzo's nostrils flared. "Not them. Just you."

That hurt. Eddie couldn't pretend it didn't because sometimes he looked at Vicenzo and saw the boy he'd loved so strongly, the boy he could have called mate. Those memories of their time together was all that had kept him sane when Elijah had tried to tear his humanity from him—and Vicenzo wanted to forget it all.

"Me," Eddie repeated, his voice rough.

"Yeah. Just you." Vicenzo's lips thinned. "You smell like ash, Eddie. Like smoke. Like the night the town burned and we lost everything. You didn't always, but you do now." Eddie swallowed. He remembered when Vicenzo had told Eddie he smelled like home. "And I was sick of remembering everything we lost whenever I looked into your face. Sick of remembering who I could have been, who you used to be. All this shit we'll never have again." He looked out into the cold winter light. "I wish you'd just let me fucking forget."

Eddie didn't say anything. He couldn't. Vicenzo sighed long and low, his head between his knees.

Eddie couldn't take much more. "Get dressed, would you? We need to get back to base."

There came the snapping of bones.

"Oh, no you don't!" Eddie whirled around and to his dismay found Vicenzo shifting into a black wolf. "You kiddin' me, man?" he roared.

The black wolf huffed and sat on his haunches, looking smug. Eddie's hands shook. Would Ben get angry with him if he killed Vicenzo? Probably, but he was angry enough not to care.

"All right, asshole. That's how you wanna play this?" Eddie fumbled through his pack and found some feral trapping equipment: a heavy leash, thick collar, and a muzzle. Vicenzo's eyes went wide. Grinning, Eddie turned toward him. "You got a choice, Vico. Shift back and put on some pants or be my therapy dog."

Vicenzo snarled and Eddie sighed. That meant doing this the hard way. Eddie lunged as Vicenzo ran. He got his arms around the wolf's middle and hollered as the wolf dragged them both out into the snow. Eddie tossed the leash across Vicenzo's neck, trying to wrangle him into it. He grabbed both sides of the leash before he toppled off Vicenzo into the snow, and the black wolf jerked to a stop with a yelp, the leash tight around his neck.

Eddie seized the moment to hurl himself across Vicenzo's back and snap the collar around his neck. Then he forced his fingers between the collar and Vicenzo's fur, holding tight. Vicenzo's snarls were muffled with his snout on the ground, his rump high in the air, and his paws spraying snow in an attempt to free himself. Gasping, Eddie snapped on the leash. "Yes!" He spilled onto his back as Vicenzo whirled around, fangs bared and eyes blazing, and snapped his teeth.

Eddie panted, grinning. "Do I need to muzzle you now, or are you gonna behave?"

Vicenzo sneezed angrily and turned away, growling.

"Diva." Eddie stood, shouldering his pack. He fisted the leash. "Now, let's—whoa!" Vicenzo took off running and Eddie was pulled after him, spraying snow. The wilderness flew by him in a blur as they ran until they were so out of breath they couldn't possibly continue. Eddie huffed, his lungs aching from the cold. "Happy now, jerkwad?" Vicenzo panted, his tongue lolling and ribs expanding. Eddie tugged on the leash but Vicenzo wouldn't budge.

"Oh, come on!"

Dropping like a stone into the snow, Vicenzo made a sound that could only be described as a groan. Eddie slumped, his hands on his knees. "This is what you get for shifting so far from home." The wolf snapped at him. "Yeah, yeah. I get it. New York's not your home. Whatever. You need to spend some time as a human when we get back. You won't mind wearing clothes then." Eddie dragged his feet through the snow. "Don't make me carry you. I will."

The wolf eyed him warily.

"And I'll tell everyone back at the agency."

Vicenzo snarled, then stood reluctantly as if his bones weighed a thousand pounds. Eddie tugged the leash, ignoring Vicenzo's surly growl.

They made for the base a few miles away and arrived just after noon. Gabe and Izzie's parents were awaiting them along with a few helicopters that would transport them to Anchorage's airport. Manuel arched a brow at Vicenzo and the snow clotted in his fur and said, "He feral?"

"Nope, just stubborn and a pain in my ass."

Veronica chuckled. "I hope you have a plan to get through the airport with such a majestic dog."

Vicenzo snapped his fangs, not liking being referred to as a dog.

"Don't know yet. I can't pass him off as my therapy dog. Haven't got any papers or a harness. Think maybe they'll just shove you under the plane." Vicenzo whined and tugged on Eddie's jeans. "Gonna change back?" The wolf growled and sneezed. "Fine." Eddie threw the bag of clothes at him. "Then go change."

Continuing to growl, the wolf prowled away, tail down and head low. Eddie scoffed. Such a fearsome predator should never sulk so pitifully. A few minutes later, Vicenzo emerged from the tent and—

"Oh, hell no."

So many clothes. He'd thrown on every single one of the extra sweaters Eddie had packed. Vicenzo grinned, his coat wide open to show off the low-cut pink sweater he wore on top of Eddie's other sweaters. "Think Izzie's things got mixed up in here."

Groaning, Eddie said, "No. You take that all off."

"Hey. You wanted me to get dressed. I'm dressed."

Eddie wanted to kill him. How would he get through the airport with this freak show? "I'm the cause of my own sufferin'. I know it," he said, groaning into his hand.

Manuel was grinning. "Okay, fellas. Let's get you to the airport."

Eddie thought he'd jump out of the helicopter and walk all the way back to New York.

PEOPLE STARED. OH, HOW they stared. Vicenzo strutted along behind him, cocky smile on his punchable face as he returned the double takes with a sunny grin and a cock of his brow. Eddie tried to walk ahead of him, he really did, but Vicenzo had long legs and kept up easily even though he was walking stiffly and waddling. Like a freaky shadow Eddie couldn't shake.

"You're sweatin'," Eddie said. Vicenzo wouldn't last long in all those layers, and Eddie hoped he had a heat stroke. Okay, not really but he was a firm believer in karma. Vicenzo would get what was coming to him for this embarrassing display.

"It is a bit hot in here," Vicenzo remarked. "You got good taste in sweaters, Eddie. Pants, too."

Eddie stumbled to a stop. "How many of my pants are you wearing?" Now he was worried.

Vicenzo gave him a smug purse of his lips, kicking up one shoulder carelessly. "A few. No underwear either."

Eddie growled. "You son of a..." He sucked in air through clenched teeth and reminded himself he was the stupid asshole who'd demanded Vicenzo get dressed. Things would have been simpler if he'd stayed as a wolf.

They found their gate without too much trouble, aside from the walking, smirking embarrassment waddling behind Eddie. They would board in fifteen minutes. Vicenzo peeled off most of the sweaters except one and grumbled that he needed the bathroom.

Ben knew they were coming back. He'd stayed in Alaska, probably to take care of the hunter Isaac who'd been wounded in the battle against Donovan and his hunters. Eddie had called him early in the morning, and Ben had been worried about Vicenzo. Eddie had been too and still was but to a much smaller degree now that Vicenzo seemed intent on rattling his nerves. Vicenzo's humanity had slipped. This had been building for a long time. His refusal to open up to the pack had almost cost him his sanity.

Eddie's feet moved of their own accord, trailing after Vicenzo to the restroom. His inner animal feared leaving Vicenzo alone, even if Eddie would rather be anywhere else right now. Vicenzo had kicked off most of Eddie's pants—and left them on the dirty bathroom floor. He zipped up his pants in front of the urinal and turned around, his eyes narrowing at the sight of Eddie. They were still blue, for now.

"When we get back," Eddie said, "things are gonna be different."

"That so?" Vicenzo grumbled, washing his hands.

"Yes. They are," Eddie said through gritted teeth. "You were scared yesterday, Vico."

"Stop calling me that. And I wasn't."

Eddie snorted. "The hell you weren't. You were shaking."

"I was cold."

Eddie laughed. "Yeah, okay, Vico. Okay. Sure. But this can't happen again. You realize you could have been killed out there, hunted down by one of Donovan's holier-than-thou hunters?"

"I was fine."

Eddie curled his hands into fists. "You weren't. You didn't want to forget. I'm tellin' you, things need to be different. You need to start letting the pack in."

"You're not my pack." Vicenzo grabbed fistfuls of paper towels, dried his hands, and turned to walk away. The hell if Eddie would let him.

He grabbed hold of the front of Vicenzo's sweater, and Vicenzo stumbled back into the wall, eyes wide and fangs bared. "Why'd you stay all these years if you hate us so damn much?"

Vicenzo smoothed out the front of his—Eddie's—sweater. The fire that had blazed bright in him moments ago was gone and now he seemed small, lost. "It was a choice, okay? Kassie invited me to come and study with her at the temple. No way. I love my sister but I'd die of boredom. I didn't wanna impose on my grandparents. Besides, the agency had all this exciting shit going on at the time. So…"

"You chose us."

Vicenzo blinked, wetting his lower lip until it was slick. "Guess a part of me thought I could get it all back. Everything I had once." He curled his hands into fists. "I was wrong." His voice was hard.

"No," Eddie insisted. "No, you weren't." He hated this. How could Vicenzo not see it? "Look at us, Vico."

Vicenzo's jaw tightened.

"Look at us!" Eddie grabbed hold of his shoulders. "After everything around us crumbled and burned, we're still standing. You and me, Vico. Like we always said it would be."

"Stop calling me that!" Vicenzo's voice bounced off the tiles. He shook beneath Eddie's hands, then jerked out of his grip, blinking wet eyes. "No, Eddie. We're not who we used to be. I died with my parents. I died again when I came for you, asking to start over, and you fucking pushed me away." He shoved Eddie hard in the chest when he came toward him, and Eddie froze in place.

His chest ached. He didn't know what to say, what to do. Nothing he said could make right all that was so wrong between them. "I'm here now. I'm *here*. I'm not pushing you away. I'll never push you away again. Why do you think I came after you?"

Vicenzo raised his shoulders and dropped them. He'd turned away from Eddie.

"Because everythin' inside me was screamin' not to let you go, not again. Vico—Vicenzo, when you left, there was a hole in my chest. I knew if I let you leave, I'd be hurtin' for the rest of my life." Vicenzo had no reaction. Eddie wanted to scream, just so he knew Vicenzo heard him. He didn't know if he was getting through, didn't know if he was saying the right thing or even what the right thing was. "Look, I talked to Ben and he wants to do better with you. We're gonna work harder to make you feel like one of us."

Vicenzo raised his head, his shoulders dropping. "You shouldn't have to work. It shouldn't be hard. I just don't fit."

Eddie winced, hating that he saw himself that way. "No. That's not true at all. The pack's been trying for years to include you in stuff. You gotta meet people halfway—and you can't just bail on us. Ever again."

Vicenzo was silent and Eddie's gut clenched.

"Vicenzo, when we get back... you can't leave."

Sighing heavily, Vicenzo said, "I'm not promising anything."

Eddie's heart raced. "Look, let's just... let's just get home first. Then you can see how you're feelin'. Till then, let's not jump to any reckless decisions. Okay?"

Beyond the bathroom door, a voice over the intercom announced their flight was boarding. Vicenzo stepped out of the bathroom, and Eddie tried not to imagine when he might be taking off again.

THEIR PLANE GOT INTO New York late. The sun was barely beginning to rise, glowing faintly on the horizon. Vicenzo fell asleep as the taxi drove them to Fire Island. The sight of the estate filled Eddie with relief. It felt good to be back. To be home.

The pack was waiting for them beyond the gate. Ben and Isaac had returned from Alaska and stood close, shoulders touching. Eddie supposed they'd settled things between them at last. Then he noticed a bite mark peeking out from Isaac's shirt. Yup, they'd settled things, all right. On one of the swinging benches, Zach sat with Ryan's head in his lap. Zach shook him awake, fondly adjusting Ryan's glasses when the smaller man sat up. Leaning on the porch railing were Izzie and her brother, Gabe. Max appeared to be half-asleep, his head resting on Gabe's shoulder until Izzie nudged him.

Beside Eddie, Vicenzo had stopped walking. He was frozen in place, his eyes wide as he took in the pack. He'd never looked so uncertain of where he fit. His bonds with the pack must have been strained after he'd severed them of his own will.

"It's okay," Eddie said reassuringly. "They're not mad."

Vicenzo looked down, scuffing his boot in the dirt. "Things feel... different."

"Give it time."

Eddie waved and went to meet Ben and the rest of the pack. First, Ryan jumped on him, wrestling him into a hug. Then Gabe clasped his shoulder as Izzie hugged him tight. Max smiled and clapped his back, and Eddie saw Ben's mustache twitch. "Glad you found him."

"Me too."

Ben turned to Vicenzo and said, "You came back. This of your own accord?"

Vicenzo's lips thinned, and he looked down and nodded. "Yeah. Yeah. For now. If you'll have me."

Ben grabbed his shoulders. Vicenzo looked up and his head tilted back, exposing his neck, and Eddie didn't know if it had been intentional or not. Ben said, "You'll always be welcome here, kid. So don't get all shy and soft on me now."

Vicenzo smiled. It was tiny and frail.

"Now," Ben said, and it was a rallying cry.

The pack launched themselves at Vicenzo. He yelped as they surrounded him, a tornado of flailing hands and bodies. They wrestled him into a group hug, and though Vicenzo fought, eventually he stopped. He let them wrap themselves around him, touching him, hugging him, covering him in the scent of pack and home.

Vicenzo blinked rapidly, his eyes bright and wet before he hung his head, and Eddie's chest ached for him.

Please stay, he thought. *Please, don't ever leave again.*

One by one, the pack separated, Ryan with a friendly punch to Vico's shoulder, Izzie with a warm squeeze, and Zach with a hand on his shoulder.

Max put his hand on the back of Vico's neck and Gabe grinned and tousled Vico's short hair.

Ben smiled, which softened his gruff features. "Now that's all done with, I've got an announcement to make." He put an arm around Isaac's shoulders. "You and Vicenzo missed this, but it's important. This is Isaac, and he's my mate."

Vicenzo blinked. "He's human," he stated.

Isaac opened his mouth and popped out his fangs, which made Vicenzo jump. Isaac barked out a laugh. "It's a new development," he said, squeezing Ben's hand.

"Isaac is pack now, and he would be even if I hadn't turned him," Ben said. "He's one of us. You're all to show him the same respect you show me."

"But we don't show you respect," Ryan chimed in, grinning.

Ben bared his teeth in a mischievous grin. "Exactly."

Isaac rolled his eyes and shoved Ben. "Ben's bullshit aside, I'm gonna do everything I can to help this pack thrive. You're Ben's family, so you're my family. Can't say I've ever been part of a wolf pack before, but I can howl at the moon, hunt, and run as good as any one of you crazy kids." Several people looked skeptical. "Come on! I can be a wolf, too." And because this wasn't cringey enough, Isaac tipped back his head and howled. It was very... human.

Ryan sighed. "He's gonna try and be our gay dad, isn't he? Oh crap, Ben was already our dad. And now there's two of them. He and Ben are both our gay dads now!" Zach snorted and tugged Ryan close.

Ben drew Isaac to him and murmured, "That was shit, Isaac."

His mate shrugged, smiling bright as he popped a wet kiss on Ben's grizzly cheek. To the delight of the pack, Ben turned red up to his ears. "You guys got plenty of time to teach me."

"Also," Ben said, shaking free of Isaac and trying to act like he wasn't embarrassed. "Stop fucking laughing, Gabe, I swear! Isaac and me are getting married."

Izzie gasped. "Oh, Benjamin Stroud! I can't believe it!" She rushed to him, kissing his cheeks.

Gabe launched himself at Ben. "No way! Congrats, Viejo!"

"Max, control your mate," Ben said through gritted teeth.

He rushed in to pull his mate away before Ben could die of embarrassment.

"Do we really have to invite these bastards, Isaac? They're never gonna let me live it down."

"Yeah. We do," Isaac said with an arm around Ben's shoulders. "It'll be tomorrow night."

"Werewolves get married?" Vicenzo arched a brow.

"Yes," Ben said with a growl.

Isaac grinned and took his hand. "It's what works for us. We hope everyone will be there."

Ryan looked from Ben to Isaac. "So is Ben gonna be Ben Bennet, or are you taking Ben's last name, Isaac? Please tell me it's Ben Bennet. Don't let me down like this."

Ben deflated. "I hate you guys."

Eddie smiled, feeling lighter than he had in hours.

It was good to be home.

CHAPTER 13

FIERCE WOLF

THE BEAST CRAWLED UNDER Vicenzo's skin as night drew closer. The arrival of the moon pulled at every werewolf's heart, but never like this. His skin felt like paper, ready to split and let the wolf come surging to the surface. He'd only been back a day, and there hadn't been time to do any pack activities to mend his connection to Ben and the others. Once the moon was out, Vicenzo feared he'd lose control completely. It was safer for him to stay up in his room, even if he was disappointed he'd miss Ben and Isaac's wedding. It had sounded like fun.

There came a knock on his door.

"Vico? Lunch is ready."

Vicenzo growled, curled up on his bed as a wolf like he usually did when he was alone.

Leave me alone. Leave me alone...

Another knock. "You hear me?"

Why couldn't this guy get the message? Vicenzo growled louder and pawed the blankets up over his ears.

"Did you just growl at me? You're a wolf, aren't you? Ben told you no more shiftin'. You wanna go feral in your bedroom? Let me in!"

When the hell had shy Eddie Turner become such a nosy asshole?

Vicenzo buried himself under the blankets, hoping that if he just stayed quiet, Eddie would get the message and move on. To his relief, the footsteps faded and Vicenzo was left alone in silence. He closed his eyes, searching for threads that weren't there. His chest felt hollowed out. The distant voices of the pack carried to him as they laughed and chatted. He could have been down there with them. Even if he didn't talk much, they'd never held that against him. They'd been happy to include him, regardless of how little he brought to their pack. Now he'd fucked everything up.

He wished he could rewind and stop himself from running away. He was sure nothing would ever be the same between him and the pack—he would always be the one who'd run away, turned his back on them after they'd opened their den to him, shared their food, fought alongside him. A whine pulled from his throat.

There was a knock on the door. "Vico."

Vicenzo growled, but he wasn't as annoyed as he'd thought he would be. At least Eddie's opinion of him couldn't possibly get any lower.

"I brought you food."

The guy wasn't going to quit, was he? Vicenzo shook off the blankets and slunk out of bed, his toenails clicking. He tried to shift back, groping within himself for that link to his humanity. His bones creaked and strained, breaking and reforming as he thought of his home in Italy. His grandparents. The rolling Italian hills green with summertime. The smell of his grandpa's cooking.

It wasn't enough. He was shifting back before he'd even started, fingers turning back into clawed paws, hair growing and receding in a loop. He groaned, a pained sound that tore from his throat.

The doorknob rattled. "Vico? You okay in there?"

He tried to speak but the words were lost in a snarl as he became trapped in his shift.

Something slammed against the door. Once, twice, then the door burst open. The man in the doorway was pale, his eyes going wide. The wolf retreated, fangs bared, snapping his teeth to warn away the intruder in his den.

"Oh no. Vico." His voice shook. He smelled like fear and… sadness. So much sadness it threatened to kill the wolf's fury. How could he be afraid of someone who smelled so sad? "Hey. Hey, Vico. It's me. It's Eddie."

He came closer, the floorboards creaking under his smelly leather boots. He smelled like ash, like smoke, like burning. He smelled like—like—

Honey. Warm summer grass. Like… home.

The growl rumbled to silence in his throat. He needed more of that scent. It killed his fury, soothed his fears. Made him want to roll around in that sweet scent, bundle himself up in it and never leave. He took one step, then another. Those wide blue eyes never wavered from his as a shaky hand reached out. The wolf bumped his nose against the hand, and things began to come back to him like pieces of a forgotten dream.

The man—man? No, not man. Not wolf, but not man. Eddie? Eddie!—smiled and said, "Phew. Thought you were gonna bite my ass for a minute there." He stood and went to fetch something from just behind the door. "Man, I knew I shouldn't have let you sulk up here."

Sulk? the wolf thought, growling. *I do not sulk. I protect den. Protect from intruders. I am wolf. Big, scary wolf. Fierce wolf! The fiercest of all wolves, I—*

Eddie returned with a tray holding a crispy chicken sandwich slathered with spicy mayo and garnished with pickles. "Gonna shift back so you can eat?"

The wolf jumped up, his paws on Eddie's shoulders as he tried to grab the sandwich off the tray. Eddie shoved him away. "You gotta shift back, Vico!"

Vico. The name was familiar. It was… his name? No. He was wolf. He was…

I am Vicenzo!

And the understanding awoke something within him.

"I'm Eddie." He set the tray on the bed and placed a warm hand on Vicenzo's head. "You're Vicenzo. Change back. Come on now. I know you can." It was a lie. His pulse stuttered. He was afraid Vicenzo couldn't.

The hand in his fur calmed his thundering heart. He closed his eyes and whined as his bones shifted, as fur receded.

"You can do this, Vico. Come on. Whatever it is that's keeping you human, reach for it."

The bonds were too feeble. His paws turned to hands with blunt fingernails, then immediately curled back into paws. "Eddie," he croaked, just before he lost his voice in a snarl. He couldn't do it. He couldn't.

"You can," Eddie whispered. "You fight this, Vico. Fight it!"

Something burst in Vicenzo's mind. Bright and golden, but it wasn't any of his packmates. This one he knew deep in his bones.

There came a thundering on the stairs and then she was there, long hair flying back as she rushed into the room, eyes bright and full of terror. "Vico," Kassandra whispered. She ran to him, dropping onto the floor at his side. She clasped his paw. "Come on. Come back. You can do this!"

Vicenzo latched onto that warm golden thread that burned between them. His paws turned to hands, the dark fur receding. He gasped and gasped, clutching onto Kassandra's hand like a lifeline. "Kassie," he whispered, his voice hoarse but human at last.

She shook her head and pulled him into a fearsomely tight hug. "You idiot. Don't you ever do that to me again!"

Vicenzo wrapped himself in her scent. She smelled like the lunar flower incense of the monastery but beneath that she still smelled like home. Goddess, he was so glad to see her...

Eddie smiled. "Think I'll get us some more sandwiches."

"No, Eddie," Kassandra said. "Tell Ben and the others we'll be downstairs shortly."

Eddie tipped his hat. He wore it everywhere, even inside. Vicenzo thought it looked familiar. Was it Jamison's hat? If so, he understood why Eddie wore it everywhere. "Yes, ma'am."

Kassandra rolled her eyes and swatted at his hat. "Your Southern charm won't work on me. I can't believe you boys. It's been years and you're both still so stupid!" Eddie chuckled and returned downstairs. Kassandra stood, rifling through Vicenzo's dresser. "Here. Put these on." She chucked a pair of jeans and a shirt at him and threw underwear at his head. She was pissed.

Vicenzo tugged on the clothes while she paced, her wavy curls bristling and frizzy. "Are you dressed?"

Vicenzo zipped up his jeans. "Yup."

She rounded on him, eyes blazing. "You scared me to death! Ben's told me you'd run off on the pack!"

She reminded him so much of their mother, he ached.

"I didn't want to believe him. I thought you were finally settling in."

Vicenzo slumped onto his bed. He hated himself for disappointing her.

"I'll ask again, Vico. Do you want to come and stay with me in the monastery?"

"No. We've been over this."

She flung up her hands and paced. "Then should I move to America? Would you feel better if you had some family here with you?"

Vicenzo had thought about how great it would be if she lived in New York. They saw each other once every few months. He missed her, but he knew that working in the monastery gave her a sense of purpose. She loved Italy, and he couldn't ask her to leave. "You know I'd love it if you moved here, Kassie, but our grandparents need you at home now that they're older." He couldn't ask her to uproot her life, all because he couldn't get his act together.

"Then stop making me and our grandparents worry about you!" she snapped, ready to spit fire. "You can't do this, not anymore. You run away, Vico. Whenever anything gets hard, you run away."

"Not true," he said, because it bothered him that it was.

"You can't run away, Vico. Not from this, not from your pack."

"They're not my pack." Vico sat up, lacing his fingers tightly together in his lap. "Maybe they could have been, all right? But I fucked things up, Kassandra. I fucked up real bad when I tried to leave and now everything's just... They'll never see me as pack now."

Kassandra rolled her eyes and plopped down at the foot of his bed. "And you know that how?"

"I just do."

She slapped the bed. "Stop making up their minds for them! If Ben didn't want you back in the pack, he wouldn't have let you come back. So cut the crap, Vico." Sighing, she said thoughtfully, "Why did you decide to accompany them back to America? You had a pack back in the Apennine Mountains, but you chose to leave them and come live with the agency. Why? And why have you stayed?"

Vicenzo gnawed on his nails, trying to find the words. "The wolves in the Apennines... they were always temporary. Their goals aligned with my own, so we formed the ties we needed to keep our heads, and that was that." It was the truth. As for why he'd chosen to come to America... He'd lied to Eddie's face about why he'd joined the pack and why he'd stayed all these years. But he couldn't lie to his sister. "It was for him."

"Eddie," she said softly.

Vicenzo hung his head, face burning. "I went for him. I stayed for him."

"Do you know why?"

Vicenzo swallowed with difficulty. "I... No. Not really. I knew that—" Fuck. He didn't know how to say how he really felt. Once, he could have opened his heart so easily, but that was before he knew how easily hearts were broken. Kassandra waited patiently. "I knew things wouldn't be the same. But I thought—I don't know what I thought." He sighed. "That we could, I don't know? Try again. But I don't think we ever can. I think some things between us just run too deep." He unclenched his fists and made himself breathe. "If that makes sense."

"Vico," she whispered.

He said, "I'll just disappoint them. I don't know how to fix this. I'll just fuck up again." He looked down at his hands, his knuckles white as he squeezed the bedsheets.

"You have to try, Vico. You *have* to." She clasped his shoulder.

"It won't be the same." His voice went hoarse and he cleared his throat.

"No," she said in agreement, knowing what he meant. She blinked, her eyes bright and wet. "Nothing will be. But Ben and the pack, they are good people. And they care about you, Vico." She looked into his eyes, imploring him to make the right choice and fix what desperately needed mending. "Don't make assumptions. Don't push them away."

"Eddie, too?" Vicenzo sighed.

She laughed softly, more a happy sigh. "He cares too. I can tell. He reeked of fear when he thought you wouldn't come back. I know he hurt you, but he's trying to make up for it. You don't have to let him, not unless you want to."

Vicenzo didn't know if he'd ever forgive Eddie. Things were so bitter and complicated between them. It wasn't something he'd ever thought he'd feel for the man he'd once called his true love.

She took his hands. "If you can find it in you to forgive him, if you want to, then I think he'll meet you halfway."

At a loss, Vicenzo shrugged. "He sure seems intent on following me everywhere. Like he thinks I'll make for the hills first chance I get."

"Will you?"

Vicenzo gritted his teeth. "I... No. No, I won't. Not again." He didn't want to go feral. "I just don't know what's harder, staying and dealing with all the awkwardness I created or leaving it all behind."

Kassandra laughed. "You won't know unless you get down there and eat with everyone! You don't have to say anything. Just be there, let them know you're trying. Things will get easier then."

Vicenzo doubted that.

"Come on. I'm hungry. Let's go and eat."

Vicenzo's chicken sandwich was still on the tray on his bed. He'd love to just stay up here and eat alone. He wasn't ready to face the pack, and his feet wouldn't budge.

Kassandra sighed. "Come on, Vico!"

Vicenzo glared at the floorboards. The very thought of moving an inch made his feet feel like stone. But he wanted to fix this, even if he was so afraid he'd wrecked things irreparably. He knew he couldn't avoid the pack forever, even in such a vast estate. This would never get any easier until he took that first step.

"Later," he said at last. "Tell Ben I'll be there tonight for the wedding." It was cowardly, but it was a promise he would keep.

Smiling, Kassandra nodded. "Okay. I will."

She left but returned shortly and they ate their chicken sandwiches on his bed. When they were full and content, Vicenzo slumped against the plush pillows and Kassandra laid her head across his ankles. They lay the way wolves did, basking in the warmth of the bond that ran through them, connecting him to her and her to him.

"I missed you," Vicenzo said, and he lightly kicked the back of her head.

She grinned up at him. "You too."

Silence fell between them. The warm pulse of *pack* beat steadily in Vicenzo's chest, and he couldn't remember the last time he'd felt so whole. Not man, not wolf. Just Vicenzo. He loved this feeling, this contentment. He didn't want to lose it again.

And so he wouldn't.

As the moon rose, Vicenzo dressed in a tuxedo. He left a few buttons popped at the collar, never liking button-up shirts compared to cotton T-shirts or tank tops. He'd never been to a wedding before. He didn't know what to expect but given that it was a human ceremony, it was bound to be overly long and boring.

The agency sure as hell wasn't a pack like any other he'd been a part of. They welcomed everyone, it seemed, hybrids to humans. Vicenzo had lost too much to human cruelty. As far as he was concerned, wolves were better off never associating with them.

Isaac wasn't so bad for a newly turned wolf. There was something familiar about his scent, though Vicenzo didn't understand why it should be familiar since they'd never met.

Glowering at the tie in his hands, Vicenzo struggled to tie the damn thing before giving up, leaving it dangling awkwardly around his neck. Stopping at the door, he could tell the estate was full of hustle and bustle as always. He would have to face the pack tonight, try to find some way of mending everything he'd messed up. The anxiety made his claws come out, dimpling his palms and drawing pinpricks of blood. He exhaled. He had to fix this.

He swung open the door and took a step over the threshold, unsure where to look for the rest of the pack. If he hadn't stayed up in his room, he might know where the ceremony was being held. He texted Kassandra and waited awkwardly in the hallway, eyes down and staring at the floor. He scowled when she didn't text back right away.

"Hey," said a soft Southern voice.

He sighed. "Eddie." When he turned, Eddie offered him a smile. Vicenzo's mouth twitched, too nervous to commit to smiling back.

"You're comin' then?"

Vicenzo nodded, his face warming when he heard the hopeful excitement in Eddie's voice. "Looks like it, doesn't it?" He flapped his arms at his attire.

Eddie had managed to tie his own tie, which was fitted snugly beneath the collar of his shirt, the black satin trailing down his chest to his stomach. He wore a white dress shirt and a black vest that flattered his slim waistline—and astonishingly tight trousers. Vicenzo did a double take. The slim fit teased a view of his curvy thighs. Had his thighs always been so curvy? Vicenzo suddenly wanted to take a bite—not because he was attracted to Eddie. No. That had ended long ago. He just... wanted to bite him to annoy him. And not on his thigh.

"Nice job with your tie." Eddie's mouth quivered, betraying the smirk he was fighting back.

Vicenzo scowled. "Ha, ha. You go to the graduate school of pointing out the obvious? Bet you were top of your class."

Eddie rumbled a laugh, the sound smooth as whiskey. His cyan eyes twinkled. "Want me to show you?"

The thought of having Eddie's hands on him made his skin prickle. "I just won't wear it."

"I can help you if you want, Vico." Eddie's eyes widened. "Vicenzo. Sorry."

He gnashed his teeth and supposed Eddie would always slip up and call him Vico. He didn't hate it, not really. He hated the way it made him feel each time he heard the nickname Eddie had called him when they were teenagers. Like he'd been shot in the heart. Like he was back in the tent, waking up next to Eddie with their future before them.

"Fine. Show me." He was trying to get in the pack's good graces. He might as well start by not disrespecting the dress code.

This was a mistake, he realized as Eddie stepped in close. Eddie's chest shuddered with an exhale. He smelled nervous, looked it too. Fixating on Vicenzo's tie, he grasped the fabric between his fingers and swallowed, the sound loud in the quiet between them. He smelled faintly sweet, like lunar flower cologne. Vicenzo's heart stuttered. Whoa. Eddie hadn't smelled like lunar flowers in such a long time. All werewolves smelled faintly of it, blended in with their own signature scent. On nights of the full moon, that scent was more potent than ever, compelling mated pairs to fuck and bite and claim what was theirs.

Right now, that scent was scorching Vicenzo's nose. And Eddie was standing so close, closer than he ever had since they'd been reunited. The smell of him, the heat of him, the nearness of him—it was doing things to Vicenzo. As Eddie's hand brushed his chest, those cyan eyes went wide. They strayed, and Vicenzo's mouth went dry as their eyes met. Eddie dampened his lips with his tongue, his Adam's apple bobbing as he swallowed.

They'd touched before. In anger, fists bunching in each other's clothes, grabbing on hard to shoulders. And yeah, maybe those brief, heated encounters had given Vicenzo a semi. But this shouldn't have made his heart turn over. It shouldn't have. But it did.

Then he breathed in, and discovering that beneath what should have been the scent of his mate was the smell of ash shouldn't have shattered him. But it did. He didn't know if the bitterness would ever cease.

No. No way. Eddie had broken his heart in two when he'd been young and stupid enough to believe in happy ever after and soulmates, but Vicenzo would be damned before a little closeness and the stupid full moon made him so horny he forgot the havoc their relationship had wreaked on his heart.

"Okay, that's fine." Vicenzo batted Eddie's hands away and turned quickly, urging himself to breathe.

"I wasn't done." Eddie dared to sound innocent. Like that hadn't been an elaborate ploy to—what, exactly?

"Look, just—stop it, would you?" Exhausted by this, by them, Vicenzo massaged his temples.

"What?"

"Acting like nothing's changed between us." He felt like choking on the smell of ash Eddie exuded. As if they'd both burned alive long ago and hadn't realized they were walking around as ghosts.

"I know," Eddie said, impatiently but not ungently. "I'm not stupid. I know things are different, okay? Think I seriously need remindin'? That doesn't mean we can't try for a fresh start."

Vicenzo swallowed the lump in his throat. He rubbed at his neck. "Why do humans wear these? They got some asphyxiation fetish?"

Eddie stepped in front him, a determined set to his jaw. "Tell me, Vicenzo! Tell me what I can do to fix this thing between us!"

Vicenzo didn't know if there could ever be any fixing them. He didn't know if he wanted to try. "We can't, Ed. There's no fixing this. We could have. But you made sure we couldn't when you chose the hunters over me."

Eddie balled his hands into fists and his lips thinned. "I'm sorry, Vicenzo. Do you understand that?"

"I don't know," Vicenzo answered. "Don't think it even matters. The damage is done, Ed. My parents had been murdered. I was alone. I spent months looking for you. Thinking if I could just find you and take you home, I'd be whole again." Laughter—sobs?—crawled from his throat, shaking his shoulders. He leaned on the wall, staring at the ceiling. "And you... you shattered me." *And sometimes*, he wanted to say, *it's hard to hate you for that.*

Because I know you loved me, Eddie. I know you did. Whatever the hell those hunters put you through, whatever they did to you to break you... it makes me so fucking pissed, I want to hunt. Hunt and lay their broken bodies at your feet so you can kill them yourself.

Eddie bowed his head, his face so etched with sorrow Vicenzo thought Eddie would crumble before him. "I was broken. Half-crazed from all the shit he put me through in that fucking basement. I was shattered too. There was nothin' left for you to care about."

Vicenzo couldn't breathe. His chest was too tight. He'd never known the details of whatever had happened to Eddie after his uncle had taken him away. Eddie hadn't mentioned it, not to him at least. He didn't know if he had talked about it to anyone else in the pack. Somehow he doubted that, and it made him sick to imagine carrying that sort of darkness around with him. At least he had his sister to confide in, to share the pain of loss with.

Eddie had never had anyone, and as that realization set in, it hurt unlike anything else.

"I'm draggin' myself back, Vico, inch by inch." Eddie was so close, Vicenzo was cornered between him and the wall. He bowed his head, locks of blond hair hiding his eyes, his breath warm on Vicenzo's neck as he whispered, "And I'm doing it for you, 'cause you were the only thing in that hellscape that kept me human."

Vicenzo's throat ached. Everything ached.

Eddie's voice was rough, raw, but he went on. "So, no, Vico. I don't buy that there's no fixin' us. I won't ever stop tryin' to fix us. 'Cause I kept everythin' we had alive. Here." He pressed his hand against Vicenzo's chest, and his heart pounded against Eddie's palm as if Eddie held it in his hand.

Eddie looked up and his eyes were bright and damp. Blinking, Vicenzo realized his own eyes weren't dry either. Eddie's breath was hot against Vicenzo's mouth and they stood so close, their chests nearly touched with each breath.

Vicenzo's phone buzzed in his pocket. He scrambled away from Eddie and lunged for it. "Kassandra?"

"Hey! Where are you? The ceremony is starting soon. Is everything all right?"

No.

"Yeah, sure." He cleared his throat, raking blunt fingernails over his buzz cut. "Just wondering where the ceremony is."

Kassie told him the ceremony itself would take place on the beach beyond the estate, and then the guests would gather in the dining room for the reception. After telling him to hurry, she hung up. Vicenzo exhaled, already exhausted. Being around Eddie just seemed to do that to him.

"Let's get this shit over with." Vicenzo sighed, dragging his feet over the carpet. Eddie trailed behind him, ever Vicenzo's shadow. It had been that way since he'd returned. Honestly, he was surprised Eddie didn't try to follow him into the bathroom.

"Do you know where the ceremony is?" Eddie asked, his voice soft and gentle as usual but with an underlying scratchiness that betrayed their conversation was still weighing on him.

"Yeah. Follow me..."

It was unusually warm for a March night. Fireflies glowed among the palm trees as Eddie and Vicenzo walked the sandy path toward the beach beyond the estate. The salty smell of the sea washed over Vicenzo as dirt and grass turned to sand. The moon glowed bright in a cloudless night sky.

An unpleasant sensation crawled over his skin, and his wolf growled below the surface. Vicenzo hid his clawed hands in his pockets before anyone could notice. *Be cool.* He could do this. He could go one evening without ruining things for the pack. The waves lapped gently at the shore, and moonlight glimmered like gems for miles across the water.

Guests sat in white chairs with a pathway in the middle that led to a wedding arch. Eddie waved to Max, Izzie, Kassandra, and Ryan, who were sitting together. Vicenzo sniffed and smelled humans among the guests. One was Veronica, sitting beside Manuel. Another was Ronaldo, who was holding hands with his mate, Kendra, Max's mother.

He recognized Heather, who was Ben's co-parent, with her mate and Ben's sons. They sat with a human man and woman Vicenzo hadn't met before. In an empty seat beside them was an old well-loved teddy bear.

"Who're they?" he asked Eddie.

"The woman is Melissa, Issac's ex-wife. A nice lady. That's her husband, Dave."

"What's with the bear?"

Eddie smiled sadly. "Isaac told us he had a son. Beau. He died, so Isaac wanted him to be here in spirit."

Now that just made Vicenzo's heart hurt. He wished he hadn't been so dismissive of Isaac. He used to be a hunter, but it sounded like his life was more complicated than Vicenzo had realized.

Eddie sat down in the empty seat next to Ryan. Vicenzo hesitated and then sat next to him, his hands clasped tightly in his lap. He didn't know what to say and was startled when Max's low, gentle voice said, "Hey, Vicenzo."

Raising a hand, Vicenzo met Max's gaze briefly. Before he could look away, Ryan grinned and said, "Hey, look who finally left his room!"

Izzie elbowed him. "Don't be a jerk. We're happy to see you, Vicenzo, is what Ryan means."

Ryan rubbed his ribs. "Come on, we all know I am the biggest jerk. I didn't mean it that way! I know I have a hard time leaving my bedroom sometimes."

Max stepped on his foot.

"It's fine," Vicenzo said, surprising himself by smiling. "It was hard to convince myself to hang out with Ryan."

Feigning hurt, Ryan gasped, and the others laughed good-naturedly.

Kassandra caught Vicenzo's eye and smiled, looking proud.

The chattering of the crowd faded. A violinist began to play as the human minister walked down the aisle to the archway. Then Gabe and Zach took their place on either side of the altar. Heads turned and they all rose to their feet. Vicenzo stood with everyone else and faced the aisle as Ben walked down it with his father at his side. He looked unrecognizable in a black suit, his beard neat and trimmed, a smile lighting up his face as he spotted his pack waiting for him, some in the audience and some at the altar.

Ben walked past and caught the eyes of Vicenzo and the others in the audience, his eyes twinkling when he smiled. Gabe grinned and gave Ben a playful nudge when he stood beside him and Zach at the altar. When Isaac walked down the aisle, arm in arm with Ben's mother, Ben's whole face lit up. Vicenzo had never seen him look so soft.

Ben's mother kissed Isaac's cheek and he held her tight as they parted ways. The betrothed faced each other, all smiles and teary eyes, and it was as if the rest of the world fell away. It was... awkward as hell, but it made Vicenzo's chest ache.

Could Vicenzo have ever been that happy? Was this something he and Eddie could have had?

Ben and Isaac took turns saying their vows, each promising to love and provide for each other, their smiles never wavering even when their voices did. Vicenzo scoffed, though he was smiling. Eddie was crying—Vicenzo could smell the salt of his tears. Without thinking, he bumped his arm against Eddie's, and he glanced over, his eyes wide and damp. Vicenzo looked away quickly.

Beside him, Eddie sniffed. "That could have been us up there one day."

Vicenzo wished he didn't feel the ache Eddie's words caused. "Maybe—" he admitted, but he cut himself off. Maybe they could still have what Ben and Isaac did, despite everything that had come between them. But it was such a fragile hope he didn't want to utter it aloud, to give Eddie that hope in case everything fell apart again.

He hated to hear Eddie cry. Reaching out, he bumped Eddie's hand with his pinky, and Eddie latched onto it and held tight. Vicenzo should pull away. He didn't. He couldn't. His heart thundered as Eddie squeezed tight until he could feel the pulse beating in his fingers. Or Eddie's—he couldn't tell.

"Don't think forever was ever really for us, Ed."

"It could have been," Eddie murmured. "We could have..."

"Yeah." Vicenzo's throat ached. "I know."

Even Ben shed a tear, wiping it away with his thumb. He took Isaac's face in his hands and leaned in. Gabe cleared his throat. "Uh, Viejo. I gotta give you the rings first, man."

The audience chuckled, and Eddie laughed wetly beside Vicenzo.

Ben shot Gabe an impatient but lighthearted look. "Then get on with it!"

Laughing, Gabe handed them both the rings, and as Ben and Isaac slipped them on each other's fingers, the minister declared them husbands. "You may—" the minister began.

Ben lunged forward and kissed Isaac, and Isaac's arms went around him, grinning widely when they broke apart.

The crowd applauded and wolves howled. Gabe and Zach pounced on Ben and made him grimace and go bright red, and then they tousled Isaac's hair to get their scent on him. Hunter or not, whatever the mistakes of his past, he was pack now. Maybe, just maybe, Vicenzo could have that, too.

The pack and their guests migrated to the dining hall in the estate where the reception was to be held. Vicenzo had never seen the place so fancy with tables covered in white cloth and positioned away from the center of the room so people could dance. A jazz band moaned away and filled the room with a soulful sound.

Ben and Isaac sauntered up to the pack, arms around each other, and were met with a storm of congratulations and hugs. Isaac waved at Vicenzo. "Hey! I was surprised to see you again."

Suddenly, Vicenzo could swear he'd met this guy before. "I know you from somewhere."

Isaac stared like he'd grown a second head. "You hired me to track your friend down after hunters took him. Remember?"

The memories came rushing back. He'd blocked out so much of that night. "Right! Right. I remember you." Isaac had looked so different back then. "Sorry. That was a rough night."

"Did you ever rescue him?" Isaac asked, his voice nearly drowned out by the saxophone's wail. "I never saw you after that night."

Vicenzo motioned to Eddie, who was chatting over champagne with Izzie. "That's him. I... I don't remember much about that night."

Isaac clicked his tongue. "Gotcha. Well, hey, I meant to give you this." He held up a ring and Vicenzo's heart lurched. He hadn't seen it in years, but there was no way he'd ever forget it. Ebony, fitted with a white gemstone. Against his will, his eyes misted and a lump rose in his throat.

Isaac must have scented the emotions he was fighting back because he averted his gaze and scuffed his toe on the ground. "Could never bring myself to sell it. Thought about giving it back to you once the job was done, but you were gone. So, what better time than now, huh?"

He placed the ring onto Vicenzo's palm.

He closed his fist around it, lost in memories of the day Eddie had given it to him. The happiest moment of his life, on one of the worst days of his life. He'd forgotten such a good memory lay buried within the ash and smoke and devastation of that day.

"Thank you." He had to work hard to get the words out as he squeezed Isaac's shoulder.

Isaac smiled. "I'm glad you found him." His gaze wandered to Eddie. "Seen him following you around since you got back."

"He's a pain in my ass."

Isaac chuckled. "So are most of the people who love us. I should know, I married one."

Vicenzo shook his head. "He doesn't—we're not…"

Cocking his head, Isaac said, "You really think so? I've seen the way he looks at you when you're not looking back."

Was that true? Vicenzo tried to ignore the hope that flared bright and warm in his chest.

"Eddie told me about your son. I'm sorry." He worried he shouldn't have spoken when pain flickered across Isaac's face.

"Thank you," he said and took a sip of champagne. "I still miss him. I think about him every day, at least. After I lost him, I wasn't sure if I'd ever be happy again."

Vicenzo didn't have the words to say how sorry he was, but he understood exactly how Isaac felt.

"But then I met Ben, and he brought so much happiness into my life. He didn't replace Beau. He didn't heal my grief. All he did was give me a shoulder to lean on when things got tough, and it was everything I'd needed. It's possible to go through some of the worst shit imaginable and still come out the other side of it. You won't be the same as you were before, but it helps if you've got just one person in your corner. Kid, you've got a whole pack willing to pick you up when you can't stand on your own."

Vicenzo looked away, his jaw clenched tight so it wouldn't tremble.

"Lean on us. Lean on him. I know he'll let you. That's what pack is all about." Isaac's kindly blue-gray eyes and gentle smile made Vicenzo want to crumble. "For all the bad, there's a hell of a lot of joy in your life, kid. Don't forget to let it in when you're ready."

"It's hard." Vicenzo didn't recognize his voice. He sounded flayed open and raw.

"I know. But don't let him go, okay?" He squeezed Vicenzo's shoulder and went to dance with Ben. The band was playing a slow, romantic rendition of a song Vicenzo was sure he'd heard before, and Isaac leaned his head on Ben's shoulder and smiled even when Ben flushed red when he stepped on his toes.

I never let him go. He let me go.

Vicenzo balled his hands into fists, exhaled the storm raging in his chest, and let his hands relax.

Eddie had let him go, but pain in the ass that he was, he'd come for Vicenzo whenever he'd needed him. Whether it was freeing him from the hunters' cages back in Italy or tracking him through Alaska, Eddie Turner had been doing all he could to stand by Vicenzo. Eddie was trying to make it up to him.

Maybe it was time Vicenzo let him.

The crowd cheered as the band struck up a lively number. Izzie took Eddie's hand and led him onto the dance floor. Gabe and Max danced close together, Gabe smiling at Max like he'd hung the moon. Zach towered over Ryan as they danced, laughing as if they were both in on a joke. And in the center was Ben and Isaac, their faces alight with joy as their pack orbited around them. Eddie had a place among them, grinning as he twirled a laughing Izzie.

Vicenzo wanted to be a part of it, but he didn't feel like dancing, waving away Kassandra's offer. Isaac's words kept ringing in his head. He was itching to get Eddie alone and talk to him, really talk to him. Not to fight or rehash old wounds. Just talk. He squeezed the ring in his pocket, the one Eddie had said brought good luck. His life had been anything but lucky, but he did believe in fate. Fate had brought him and Eddie together again after everything that had torn them apart. It had to be for a reason.

So when Eddie's eyes landed on him from across the room, Vicenzo jerked his head toward the staircase. Eddie's eyes widened and he wet his lips. Parting from Izzie on the dance floor, he squeezed through the crowd and came toward him. Vicenzo didn't wait for Eddie to approach, too worried about what the right thing to say was. He walked away up the stairs, and Eddie followed.

Chapter 14

Eddie. Pack. Home.

Vicenzo led the way down the hall toward Eddie's room.

Eddie followed him, his boots whispering over the carpet.

"No one means to," Eddie had said once. "It just happens."

Vicenzo stopped outside Eddie's door. "Got the key?"

"I won't!" Vicenzo's voice echoed into the desert. "It won't happen to us. Okay?"

Eddie swallowed hard. "Uh, yeah. Just a moment." He fumbled in his pockets, his hands oddly shaky.

"How do you—"

"I know, Eddie. I just... know."

The door opened with a creak. Eddie walked in and Vicenzo followed.

"We're forever, Ed. Just trust me."

Eddie flicked on the light and the door shut behind them.

Silence descended, and Eddie wondered when it would break. As always, he racked his mind for the right thing to say, the perfect thing that would fix everything he'd broken between them.

When he turned around, Vicenzo had come to stand close to him. His breath caught in his chest. He noticed Vicenzo's shoulders were rising and falling quickly, but he didn't speak. Moonlight spilled onto Vicenzo's face from the gap in the curtains. His control was slipping—Eddie could see it in the thickening hair on his jawline, in the curled tips of his claws.

"Isaac gave me this," Vicenzo said through a mouthful of fangs. "I figured you'd want it back." What he held out to Eddie froze the breath in his lungs.

It was his father's ring. A lump rose in his throat, and for the first time in a long time, he had to work hard to keep the emotion off his face, a habit he'd learned among the hunters.

"I gave it to you," Eddie said. "How did it end up with him?"

Vicenzo closed his eyes tight and took a step back. "I... thought I could do this." Vicenzo sank onto the bed, panting as he curled in on himself. "Talk about this. I can't." His voice became choked with emotion. "It's so hard to forgive what you did. Even if I understand it. I still fucking hate it. I want to, but I—" His words ended in a snarl.

Eddie's eyes stung. "You don't have to." His voice wavered and betrayed him. He wanted Vicenzo's forgiveness, wanted things to go back to the way they were before. But the people they'd been were nothing but ash.

"Fuck," Vicenzo growled out. His eyes flashed from blue to yellow. "Slipping. I'm falling again." His clawed hands trembled. "I don't know how to make it stop."

Eddie's heart raced. He didn't know what to do. When he squeezed the ring in his hand, though, he got an idea. "Hold on. Just hold on!" He knelt and wrenched open the drawer under his bed.

Vicenzo's pants and snarls got louder.

"Where is it? Come on!" Eddie's hands shook as he fumbled through the drawer, searching among his hunting supplies.

"Ed? What are you doing?" Vicenzo growled, his eyes wolf bright.

"Just gimme a sec!" It had to be in here. There was no way he would have put it anywhere else. He'd put it somewhere it would be safe. Spotting a picture frame, he lunged for it. "Gotcha!" He gazed at the yellowed paper in reverence, a child's drawing of a white wolf and a black wolf howling at the moon. The edges were frayed, the paper frail enough that it might split under his hands if it weren't protected by glass.

"Eddie, there's no time." Vicenzo doubled over, driving his claws into his side. "Get out. I'll bar the door. Don't let anyone in. I'll hurt them."

No. Eddie would be damned before he left Vico alone to suffer. "Forget it. I'm not leaving you to deal with this on your own again. Here." He slammed the drawer closed and stood, holding out the framed picture.

Vicenzo stared at it. The growl in his throat died to quiet rumbles. He blinked, the yellow lights in his eyes winking on and off like stoplights in the night.

"I know things are different. I fuckin' know that, Vico, but we're still here. Through all the crap, through every hurdle life's thrown at us, it's still you and me. Just like we promised. Remember?"

Vicenzo bowed his head, his cheeks wet, his lips quivering as he wrestled with his emotions. His eyes were the bluest Eddie had ever seen as he looked at the picture. He reached for it, opened the frame, and held the frayed paper between his fingers, turning it over to read the back.

"You... kept this." Vicenzo held the drawing gently as if he couldn't stand to damage it even slightly.

Eddie swallowed thickly. "Always."

A choked, reverent sigh escaped him. "'Forever,'" Vicenzo whispered, voice cracking down the middle. His eyelashes were spiky and laced with tears.

Eddie wiped away a tear before it could fall. "I kept it with me, always. Hid it in my pocket where no one would find it. It tethered me. Reminded me of you. It kept me human."

Vicenzo's face was like granite underneath his hand until he turned his head, parting his lips against Eddie's palm and breathing hot and damp against his skin. There was still the lingering vibration of a growl buried deep in Vicenzo's chest, running through Eddie's fingertips like a rumble of thunder.

"Why?" Vicenzo whispered, and Eddie marveled at how he fit so much yearning into one single word.

Sitting up, Eddie put his arms around him, crushing Vicenzo to him, daring him to try and pull away. "You know why."

Vicenzo stilled in his arms, breathing slowly against Eddie's shoulder. His skin burned hot from fighting off his shift, like he was on fire inside. The short prickly hairs of his buzz cut tickled Eddie's hand as he clasped the back of Vicenzo's neck, squeezing tight as his own emotions caught up to him and the shaking came over him.

Vicenzo said nothing, but he breathed in deep, taking in Eddie's scent. He ran the bridge of his nose against the side of Eddie's neck, scenting him.

"I smell like ash, don't I?" Eddie mumbled, his fingernails running over Vicenzo's scalp.

He rumbled an affirmative, the sound deep and low. It went straight to Eddie's balls, and they tightened deliciously. His teeth scraped Eddie's neck, the spot where they would have claimed each other in times long past.

"Like the fire. Like silver." Vicenzo breathed in deep and let it out long and slow, his breath hot against Eddie's cheek. Eddie's blood simmered as he felt the scratch of barely there stubble against his jaw. He wanted. Oh, how he wanted. He wanted Vicenzo's mouth on his, those big, warm hands in his hair. But it wouldn't be right, not when things were still fractured between them.

"That's all?" Eddie whispered, his heart clenching in his chest.

He wanted to tell Vicenzo he still loved him, even after everything. He wanted Vicenzo to say it back with all his heart.

"Don't know," Vicenzo whispered, his hands gripping onto Eddie's shirt. Eddie wished he was still connected to his wolf so he could hear if Vicenzo's heart had stuttered. What was he to Vicenzo after so much loss? But Eddie knew, even if his wolf had been muted. Vicenzo was his mate. Nothing would change that. He must still be Vico's, he had to be.

Eddie climbed onto the bed beside him and wrapped his arms tight around his shoulders. Vicenzo hid his face in Eddie's shoulder, taking in deep breaths.

"I'm going to try," Vicenzo whispered after a few breaths. "I'm going to try and fix things with the pack."

"Sounds good."

"I know I… I don't make things easy for them. For you." Vicenzo's breath was warm against his skin. "But I'm trying, Ed. I'm going to do my best."

Eddie squeezed his shoulders. "I know you will."

Vicenzo's hesitant blue eyes found his. "I want us to give it a go. As… friends, or pack, or whatever. So—so be patient with me, yeah?"

Oh, the way Eddie's heart sang. "Yeah. Yeah, of course. I've got patience in spades."

The corner of Vicenzo's mouth lifted in a smile. He didn't speak as he leaned his head on Eddie's shoulder. They sat together for a long time in the quiet, the picture in Vicenzo's lap and his father's ring in Eddie's pocket.

It was the start of something. Maybe not what they'd once had, but something altogether new. Eddie couldn't have asked for anything better.

"You brought him back," Kassandra whispered. She leaned on the wall outside Eddie's room, her hands laced behind her back. "I felt his distress through our bond. Seems like you handled it just fine, though."

"I hope so." Vicenzo was chatting in the room with Ben right now. He'd followed Kassandra upstairs when she'd sensed Vico's distress.

Kassandra smiled. "After all this time, you still speak to his wolf."

Eddie sighed. It seemed that way, but Vicenzo's true feelings for him were so much more complex than they once were. "I can't tell if he loves me or hates me."

Kassandra laughed softly. "He lies to himself. It's how he keeps himself safe. He's afraid of failing the pack, so he convinces himself you all would be better off without him. He's afraid of you, too. Hurting you, or being hurt by you, maybe both. So he puts up a front."

Eddie's chest tightened. He didn't remember much about the night Vicenzo had come for him. His mind had been in such disarray. But he would never forget the devastation on Vicenzo's face when Eddie had ordered him away. "I hurt him. I'm trying, but he won't let me make it up to him."

"He still cares about you," Kassandra said. "You've pulled him from the darkness twice now, Eddie. Don't let him push you away. Trust me, if he truly didn't want to be here, if your presence was so unbearable, he would have left a long time ago."

She was right; Eddie knew it. He just wished he knew how to earn back all the trust there once was between them.

The door opened and Ben stepped out alone.

"Is he all right?" Kassandra asked.

"Resting. Seems like he needs it. But I told him no more locking himself in his room. He's not a teenager. I'll put him to work around the estate, keep him nice and busy. And I said if he eats dinner alone, we'll all come in and eat with him. He needs to tether himself to this pack."

"He knows." Kassandra sighed. "My brother's just a stubborn fool."

Ben rolled his shoulders and cracked his back. "Let him rest. Pretty sure they should be about ready to serve the cake by now."

Kassandra sighed dreamily. "I could so go for cake right now."

"You and me both."

Eddie stayed behind since returning to the party didn't hold much appeal. He eased open the door to check on his mate. He lay beneath the blankets, facing away from the door. Eddie slipped inside, the carpet whispering under his feet, and went and sat on the side of Vicenzo's bed.

Darkness blinded him, so he leaned backwards until his back found Vicenzo's. If Vicenzo was awake, he didn't ask Eddie to leave or acknowledge him in any way. They lay there in the darkness together and just breathed.

Eddie said, "I won't push you away, Vico. Not again. I swear it."

If Vicenzo heard him, he said nothing. Eddie closed his eyes and sat in the dark with him for a long, long time.

BEN AND ISAAC WENT away on their honeymoon for a week. As Ben's trusted friend, Zach took charge of the estate's management. Vicenzo was more active around the estate than Eddie had ever seen him. Zach put him to work on patrol duty—always with another person—but he also had Vicenzo pick up extra shifts helping out around the kitchens. Vicenzo was a competent cook and he worked efficiently if silently, the chef told Eddie during his lunch break.

Vicenzo was so busy, they hardly bumped into each other at all except maybe in the hallways on their way to bed, but even that was a rare occurrence since they worked different hours. More often than not, though, Eddie saw him at dinner, which was a pleasant surprise.

"This meat loaf is great!" Max said. "Did you help make it, Vicenzo?"

He shrugged, nudging his mashed potatoes around in the gravy. "Just chopped some onions."

Ryan dunked his meat loaf in the potatoes and wolfed it down. "Best onions I ever tasted."

The pack laughed and Vicenzo's mouth twitched in a betrayal of his happiness. Warmth bloomed in Eddie's chest. Vicenzo was emerging bit by bit from his chrysalis and spreading his wings.

Since Wednesday would be Pack Night, Ryan and Zach invited everyone to their apartment that night for a movie. They lived near Central Park, so Ryan said they should all go for a run afterward.

"Vico, you should come! It'll be awesome," Ryan said as he and Zach were departing the estate on Tuesday. Vicenzo, who was dressed for patrol duty in dark clothes and a belt with a flashlight and Taser, looked uncertain.

"Might be too busy."

Zach waved a hand. "Don't worry about it, man. I kept your schedule open Wednesday night."

Eddie smiled when Vicenzo's face lit up. "Really?"

Zach grinned. "Work is important but strengthening your connection to the pack is more important right now. See you then." He took Ryan's hand and they walked to the parking lot. A moment later, Zach's pickup drove out through the gates.

Eddie nudged Vicenzo's shoulder. "Tell me you're goin'."

Vicenzo scuffed his toe on the ground. "Maybe."

"Come on, it'll be fun. Besides, you gotta focus on mending your bonds with everyone else."

"I don't like big gatherings."

Eddie frowned. "It won't be that big. Just people we already know." "You going?"

Eddie nodded. "You bet. Never a dull moment with these guys."

As Vicenzo worried at his lower lip, he said, "I'll think about it."

Eddie left it at that.

On Wednesday, Eddie spent most of the day tending the gardens around the estate. They grew their own vegetables and fruit for use in seasonal dishes year-round, and since Ryan had discovered his druidic heritage, he'd planted various herbs for potions in a new greenhouse. Eddie had volunteered to tend to it and spent most of his time there listening to Billie Holiday croon about the blue moon, a dream in her heart, and a love of her own.

He watered the herbs and had the new seeds planted by the time Ryan arrived.

"Lookin' good." Ryan leaned over to inspect the new planters, the soil freshly turned and fertilized. He raised his hands over them and the soil churned as the herbs grew right before Eddie's eyes.

"Whoa." Eddie chuckled. "I'm still not used to that."

"It's pretty cool, huh?" Ryan said.

"Smug bastard," Eddie said, lightly tweaking Ryan's glasses. "What do you need me tending the garden for when you can do that?" Not that Eddie minded. He loved gardening, just wondered if he was truly needed.

Ryan squinted at him. "The plants thrive under your care, Eddie. I can make 'em grow, sure, but without someone to care for them, they wouldn't thrive. The plants and me are glad you're here, trust me."

Eddie sat down on a bench nearby, his gaze upturned toward the glass ceiling that flooded the room with the orange light of sunset.

"Oh, hey, you seen Vicenzo around?"

Eddie removed his dirt-stained gardening gloves. "I think he's on chef duty today."

"You know if he's coming to Pack Night tonight?" Ryan jumped as the doors to the greenhouse flew open. "Speak of the devil..." He positioned himself behind a shelf of saplings, his bespectacled eyes peeping over a row of planter boxes. Eddie rolled his eyes at his subtlety.

Vicenzo came marching toward Eddie. He was breathing hard, as if he'd been running. Eddie frowned at him. "You okay?"

"Did everyone leave yet?"

"Hello to you, too," Eddie snorted, stacking the empty planter boxes on top of each other.

Vicenzo bristled. "Would you answer the question?"

"I don't know!" Eddie grabbed a broom and swept dirt from the floor. "Check the schedule."

"Don't know where my phone is."

Eddie whipped out his phone and checked. The latest most of the pack members got off was eight, and the sun was only just going down now. "Most of us won't be off for another hour or two. Why?" He barely got the word "why" out before Vicenzo sighed with relief.

He blurted out, "I'm going. So tell them not to leave without me. I... You're coming?"

Eddie hesitated. Normally he did, but would Vicenzo not want to if he was going? He supposed he didn't have to go. He wasn't connected to his wolf, so he didn't need to worry about losing his humanity; he only went because he enjoyed being around everybody, same as everyone else. Vicenzo needed tonight more than he did.

Eddie waved a hand. "No," he said, only realizing he would have nothing to do tonight after he said it. "I'll just read a book or somethin'." He knew he'd told Ryan he'd go, but he would make it up to him some other time.

Vicenzo looked taken aback as he nodded at the floor. "Why not? You usually go."

Eddie shrugged. "Not feeling too good. I'll just sit it out."

Vicenzo smacked his hand against Eddie's forehead, and Eddie's breath hitched. His hand was warm. "That normal? Do you get sick a lot now that you can't shift?"

"N-not too often." Eddie forced his eyes to stare at the floor, his skin burning where Vicenzo was touching him. "I can get drunk, though, which is pretty sick. Kinda makes up for havin' the autoimmune system of a human. Up until I get hungover, then I regret every one of my life choices and—"

"You should talk to Luke. Make sure it's not serious." Vicenzo removed his hand from Eddie's forehead, but his fingers strayed suddenly, his knuckles rubbing over Eddie's cheek. Surprised, Eddie looked up and met Vicenzo's blue gaze. Vicenzo's eyes went wide as color bloomed in his cheeks. He tugged his hand away and scratched the back of his neck. "You got dirt on your face."

Eddie's face burned. "Oh."

Vicenzo's throat bobbed when he swallowed, tongue rasping over a plump lower lip. Eddie wasn't sure why he was suddenly so attuned to every little reaction from Vicenzo. "You don't feel warm, though. So don't worry about it. Not that I care if you get sick or anything. 'Cause I don't. Just... you know, it'd be a pain if you got sick and people started coming after the pack. Then I'd have to save your ass and... Let's just not do that."

"Good to know." Eddie thought he heard Ryan choking quietly behind the shelves.

Vicenzo stepped away, his fingers scratching over his buzz cut. "So... you're just gonna sit around and do nothing all night?"

"Probably."

Vicenzo hummed, tapping his fingers against his thigh, and Eddie wished he hadn't noticed that. It was too close to dick territory. Fuck. Why did he have to think about his dick? Now his eyes just wanted to look *there* and—

"I mean, I don't have to go," Vicenzo suddenly said. "Big groups aren't really my thing. So…"

"Okay." Eddie had no idea where they were going with this.

Thankfully, Ryan yawned and strolled casually from behind the shelf. "Oh, hey, guys! Nice nap I just had."

Vicenzo jumped away from Eddie. "Seriously? How long were you there?"

Ryan said, "I have no idea. Wow, is the sun setting already? Must have been a while! So, hey, are you both going to Pack Night?"

"Maybe," Vicenzo said.

Eddie squinted at Ryan. "Probably not."

"Oh." Ryan scratched his chin innocently. "Would you mind terribly if Eddie was there, Vicenzo?"

He stiffened. "Not really…"

"Okay, then! And Eddie, knowing he wouldn't mind if you were there, would you mind if he was there?"

Eddie wanted to strangle him. "I guess not."

"Then you can both go!" Ryan declared. "Oh, by the way, Vico, say ahh."

Vicenzo blinked at him. "Ahh?"

Ryan pulled out a small vial, yanked out the stopper, and poured the contents in his mouth. Vicenzo sputtered and choked as Ryan said, "Swallow all of it! It's great for promoting a healthy mind. It'll help those pack bonds heal that much faster!" He ran before Vicenzo could kill him.

Eddie said, "I'll see you tonight then."

Vicenzo coughed, clearing his throat with a look of disgust. "Yeah. Sure."

Eddie rode back to the city with Zach and Ryan. Vicenzo would have finished his patrol shift by the time Gabe was done, so presumably he would accompany Gabe and Max.

At least Eddie hoped Vicenzo would join them.

Once they were at the apartment, Eddie helped Zach grill some elk burgers while Ryan broke out the booze. Izzie sidled up to them, a gin and tonic in hand. "So, Ryan tells me things are getting cozy between you and Vicenzo."

Eddie flipped the burger, missing the pan in his surprise so it fell onto the stovetop with a meaty splat. That jerk. "We're not! We're the same as we always are."

"That's not what Ryan said," Izzie cooed, shimmying her shoulders. "I heard there was blushing and stammering. Touching..."

Eddie shook his head and flipped the burger back into the pan. "There's nothing going on between us."

"Ryan said you gave him secondhand embarrassment from how awkward you two were!" Izzie batted her eyelashes.

Zach snorted. "Cut it out, Izzie. It's great they're bonding."

Eddie smiled, grateful that Zach was the sane one.

"Did Ryan get any pictures?" Zach added, and Eddie's opinion of him soured. "It's just... you and Vico, touching? Blushing? I feel like I need to see that framed and laminated before I believe it."

"I hate both of you," Eddie declared without venom.

"It's about time you two started getting over yourselves and started getting... under yourselves," Izzie said, bouncing her plucked eyebrows.

Eddie rolled up a ball of elk meat and chucked it at her, laughing when she shrieked.

By the time the burgers were done, Gabe and Max had arrived. He and Max had only left a few minutes after them, so if Vicenzo had accompanied them, surely he'd be here. Disappointment panged in Eddie's stomach.

"He'll come, man," Gabe assured Eddie.

"I knew my being here will make him uncomfortable," Eddie said, taking a big gulp of a cold IP. It tasted like grapefruit and hops, fizzy on his tongue with a creamy head of foam that he wiped from his upper lip.

Gabe poured whiskey over the melting ice cubes in his glass. "Don't be so hard on yourself."

Eddie sighed, the beer bitter in his throat. "Maybe he got cold feet about bein' around all of us."

Eddie exhaled and told himself he didn't care whether Vicenzo was here or not. He would accept whatever outcome and enjoy tonight for what it was. However, his heart still jumped into his throat when the door opened.

Vicenzo lingered just beyond the threshold, one foot in the doorway to prop the door open. He'd dressed for the occasion, black jeans with a maroon button-up. Their eyes met and Eddie's stomach fluttered like he'd swallowed a butterfly. Raising a hand, he waved, his heart pounding fast when Vicenzo raised a hand too, his face determinedly blank as his cheeks flushed.

Gabe grinned and elbowed Eddie. "Sorry. He asked me not to tell you. Wanted it to be a surprise."

"Oh, your heart's racing so fast," Izzie whispered, elbowing him.

Eddie growled at her. It didn't have the power of a wolf's growl, but she got the message. He jumped up from the table and went to the door, and only when he found himself standing before Vicenzo did he realize he didn't know what to say. "Hey."

"Hi." Vicenzo dipped his head, his mouth curling into a small smile as he stared at his toes.

This was different, Eddie realized, speechless. This was so different than how they usually were. They weren't snapping at each other like they were so prone to do these days, didn't talk easily like they had as kids. They were different people, but tonight, for the first time in so long, that hardly seemed to matter.

"I'm glad you came," Eddie said, because he was. "You look... good." His stupid mouth had almost said hot. Because Vicenzo did look hot. He *was* hot. He'd always been stupidly handsome but Eddie had tried so hard not to think of him that way for the past three years, without much success.

Meeting his gaze, Vicenzo smiled. "Thanks. You look... okay."

Eddie snorted, warm to his core. Vicenzo was trying. They both were. Trying to pick up the pieces and discover how to be around each other again, without anger or bitterness. If this was their fresh start, Eddie thought it was a good one. "Hungry?"

"Starved," Vicenzo said, his eyes lighting up at the sight of all the food piled on the table. Eddie held the door for him, and Vicenzo walked in. "Uh, wait. I made these." He pulled a box from his bag and checked under the lid. His face fell. "Shit."

Eddie leaned over his shoulder. "What?"

Vicenzo huddled over the box. "Nothing! Things just got a little smooshed." He sighed.

Nudging his hand away, Eddie raised the lid and smiled. Vicenzo had made pink cupcakes. That was so fucking cute. Vicenzo's lips were in a thin line, his blue eyes looking everywhere but at his sugary confections. Eddie grinned. "They look awesome."

Ryan looked over from the table. "Vico, did you make some more of those cookies?" There was such hope in his eyes.

Vicenzo shook his hand. "Nah. Just some cupcakes but the corner of the box got smooshed, so they probably suck."

"Sucky cupcakes? Now, that just isn't possible." Eddie whisked the box out of his hands and carried it to the table. The pack devoured the cupcakes.

"These are so amazing!" Max sighed, wiping some pink frosting from the corner of his mouth.

Izzie had icing on her nose. "So worth the calories!"

Vicenzo sat beside Eddie at the table, smiling with some embarrassment as the pack helped themselves to his baked goods and Max handed him a burger. Though Vicenzo didn't talk much, that didn't matter because he smiled and laughed, his eyes twinkling as he looked around at the pack.

At some point, Gabe tried to FaceTime Ben. "If they don't answer, he and Isaac are probably fucking," he stated, just to make everyone uncomfortable.

Ben answered, his face sunburnt. "Oh no," he said as the pack crowded around Gabe's phone. "What happened?"

"Having fun in Hawaii, Viejo?" Gabe asked.

"Guys, looks like he's seen more than the bedroom ceiling," Ryan said. "Should we be concerned for your marriage?"

Ben grimaced. "Fuck off."

The pack laughed and Eddie smiled in sympathy for Ben.

"Ben, look who's here!" Ryan said, snatching Gabe's phone and turning it on Vicenzo. "We're so proud of him!"

Vicenzo rolled his eyes. "Hey. Having fun?"

Ben snorted. "I was, till you people called."

"Ignore him," Isaac chimed in, squeezing into the frame. "He's just grumpy 'cause he forgot to put sunscreen on his face."

Ben and Isaac told them all about Hawaii, their quaint beach cabin, and how beautiful the sunsets were. Isaac winced. "Ben, no shifting on the bed! Your got prints everywhere!" A silver wolf ran out of the room and Isaac smiled. "I think he wants to howl with you guys."

Zach declared they should hit the park. Eddie followed them out the door and within minutes they were roaming the dark paths of Central Park. The night was clear and the moon wasn't full but it was bright. They found an area of open woodland and one by one, the pack stripped and began to shift.

Eddie sighed as he watched them, touching the cool silver around his neck.

Zach peeled off his shirt. "I've been wanting to ask for a while now. Is there any reason you keep that collar on?"

It wasn't like it would be difficult to remove. Eddie had thought about asking someone to remove it, but he'd held back. "Guess it intimidates me. The idea of shiftin' after all these years. I haven't been connected to my wolf in a long time. I can't feel the pack bonds like the rest of you can. What if I shifted and lost control of myself?" But the question he didn't ask out loud was, *What if y'all aren't enough to bring me back?* He didn't want to hurt their feelings. He loved this pack but a part of him was terrified that their pack bonds wouldn't be enough. That he'd lost too much to find his way back to his human side if he shifted. It wasn't a risk he was willing to take. Not yet.

Zach frowned thoughtfully. "Yeah, that does sound freaky." He patted Eddie's shoulder. "Maybe someday."

Gabe frolicked off as a wolf. Eddie watched from off to the side, holding Gabe's phone. On the screen, Ben prowled the beach as a wolf, his face upturned to the same moon that shone over Central Park.

Gabe, a big black wolf, led the pack in a howl. Isaac stifled his laughter through the screen and filmed Ben, who howled along, his eyes closed and his head tilted back to the moonlight. Eddie looked beyond the phone to where Vicenzo was galloping with the pack, chasing Izzie, snapping at Ryan's heels, and tussling with Max.

Vicenzo came trotting up to him and brushed against his sides. He was panting, his tail wagging. Eddie didn't think he'd ever seen Vicenzo so happy. He sat beside Eddie, his tail thumping in the grass. "Had enough?" Eddie said.

Vicenzo huffed tiredly, his head on his paws while the pack played and howled in joyful voices. Raising a hand, Eddie dropped it on Vicenzo's big, shaggy head. Vicenzo grumbled at him but didn't shake him off.

Eddie smiled and splayed his fingers in Vicenzo's hair. "Yeah, Vico. We're home."

CHAPTER 15

TOMATOES AND SUNSHINE

EDDIE WIPED SWEAT FROM his brow, scowling when dirt crumbled off his sleeve and onto his forehead. His fingers were sore from digging, his back achy from bending over the flower beds all day. Checking the time, he realized he'd been absorbed in his work. The day had flown by and it was past time for Isaac and Ben to have returned to the estate. Taking a moment, he watched the sun set over the palm trees, and gulls crying as they headed out to sea for some fishing.

His stomach growled as he downed the whole bottle of water propped next to the empty planter boxes. He'd worked through lunch, but as he admired the freshly turned earth and the flowers neatly arranged in colorful lines, he decided the hunger was worth it.

The greenhouse door opened and Eddie's heart skipped when Vicenzo poked his head in.

"Hey." He looked around at the planter boxes. "Guess I'm too late to help you plant."

Vicenzo sounded put out, which warmed Eddie's heart, knowing that he wanted to help. "Just finished."

A frown pulled at Vicenzo's full lips. "Been a while since I worked some soil anyway. Can't imagine I'd have been too helpful. I just thought it would be like old times." He scratched the back of his neck and averted his gaze, a tell Eddie recognized. Vico was embarrassed.

He couldn't stop himself from grinning.

183

Vicenzo scowled. "What?"

Eddie chuckled at his grumpiness, but he knew he had to tread carefully. If Vico got too embarrassed, he might run off to lick his wounds. "You can still help. I got some tomatoes Ryan grew just this afternoon. Should be ripe enough to bring back to the kitchen, if you wanna help me pick 'em."

Eddie wondered if Vicenzo knew just how much fragile hope brightened his face. "Yeah. Sure."

Hoping his cheeks weren't as red as they felt, Eddie approached the tomatoes on the vine, bright red and plump.

"You weren't kidding. Those look great." Vicenzo came up beside him, appraising the fruit. He leaned in close, closing his eyes as he sniffed. Eddie took the opportunity to admire how cute Vicenzo looked when he wasn't scowling or growling. Seeing him so unguarded for a change was nice.

Eddie picked one from the vine and handed it to him. "Grab a basket. We'll fill it up."

Vicenzo returned with a wicker basket and together they picked tomatoes. The last time they'd picked tomatoes together, they'd been eighteen years old and kneeling in the dirt in Olivia's backyard. The memory stung. Glancing at Vicenzo, he found his brow furrowed.

"Been a while since we did this," Vicenzo said softly.

Eddie was surprised he'd said anything since their past was such a painful topic. He'd wanted to bring up the memory, but he'd worried about upsetting Vicenzo. "I know," he said. Silence fell and Eddie waited to see if Vicenzo would change the subject or maybe even get up and walk away. Vicenzo stared at the tomato in his hand, closed his eyes, and breathed.

Eddie took in a breath through the tightness in his chest. So much of who they were now was wrapped up in the fire that had stolen their home, their families, and who they'd been then. Eddie breathed through the ache of loss in his chest, trying to find a way not to suppress his grief but to coexist with it. The fire—*Elijah*—had stolen enough. Eddie wouldn't let him steal Vicenzo from him.

"I miss them," Eddie said. "I never got to say goodbye to them. My parents. It all happened so fast, there wasn't time. They were just... gone."

Vicenzo didn't speak. Eddie worried he'd gone too far and that Vicenzo would leave. That the hurt between them ran too deep for either of them to coexist with it—with each other. They'd promised to try and move past it, but sometimes Eddie wondered how such a thing would ever be possible after everything they'd been through.

"They were buried."

Eddie's breath caught.

Vicenzo plucked a tomato from the vine, his expression carefully guarded. "Kassandra attended the service."

Tears stung Eddie's eyes, and he tried to blink them away. He'd wondered often over the years what had become of their bodies. If they'd been given the burial they deserved or if the desert had claimed them. The wave of relief that bowled over him doubled him over, his jaw clenched to keep the storm of his grief in.

Vicenzo gripped his arm and squeezed tight. Eddie couldn't feel his wolf, but sometimes he wondered if the bond between them still persisted. Vicenzo's touch grounded him to the now, to the possibility of the future they might still have.

Clearing his throat, Vicenzo said, "I'll... I'll harvest the basil." He moved over and gave Eddie the space he needed to dry his eyes and wipe his nose on his sleeve. A weight Eddie hadn't noticed was there had lifted from his chest.

Sniffing, Eddie walked up behind him. "Thank you for tellin' me."

The corners of Vicenzo's lips flickered in an aborted smile. He scuffed his toe on the ground. "Didn't mean to upset you."

"You didn't," Eddie assured him. "I'm glad you told me."

Vicenzo's shoulders loosened and he offered a tentative smile. "Oh. Okay. Good." His fingers twitched at his side. Then he reached up and rubbed his thumb over a wet spot on Eddie's cheek. His touch tingled over

Eddie's skin, and Eddie didn't dare move in case he shattered the fragility of the moment between them.

With a gruff cough, Vicenzo turned and hoisted the basket of tomatoes into his arms. "Coming?" he asked over his shoulder.

Eddie smiled. "Yeah."

Vicenzo's eyes widened, and he was so busy looking at Eddie or maybe something behind Eddie that he walked right into the door. Eddie winced when he heard the tomatoes squelch against Vicenzo's chest. "Fuck!" Vicenzo snarled.

Hurrying over, Eddie braced himself for the full scope of the damage. Vicenzo's chest was soaked in tomato juice and seeds. Grimacing, he lifted the only undamaged tomato from the basket, then threw the basket on the floor. "Fuck's sake!"

A laugh escaped Eddie before he could stop himself and Vicenzo's head snapped in his direction. Oh no. No, no, he needed to get himself together before Vicenzo blew his top. He covered his mouth and turned away, but it was no good. Laughter bubbled from his lips until he was bent over from mirth. "S-sorry! I'm sorry, Vico—shit, Vicenzo!" Tears of laughter leaked from his eyes. "Oh Goddess. I'm dyin' here!"

A muscle in Vicenzo's jaw ticked. "Think this is funny, huh?" Then he lunged.

A tomato flew into Eddie's chest, bursting against him like a water balloon. Seeds and juice exploded over his skin. Eddie shrieked like a little kid. Vicenzo had the biggest grin on his face Eddie had ever seen.

"Bastard!" Eddie grabbed at the tomato skins on Vicenzo's chest and chucked them back into his face.

"Ugh! Stop it!" Vicenzo sputtered, his giggles the sweetest sound Eddie had ever heard. Laughing breathlessly, they wrestled until Eddie got Vicenzo's back up against the door. They were both panting and smiling now, and Eddie's mirth mellowed to affection like nothing he thought he'd feel for Vicenzo again. Vicenzo's chest rose and fell, touching Eddie's with each breath, and the heat of his body warmed Eddie's like a ray of summer sun.

His smile softened all the hard edges of his handsome face until he looked like the boy Eddie still loved so fiercely.

Vicenzo wet his lips, flicking away a seed, and Eddie suddenly wondered what the tomato juice might taste like on Vicenzo's skin.

"Shit. You're a mess." Vicenzo wiped away tomato seeds from Eddie's face.

"It was worth it." Eddie was so close to Vicenzo, he felt he could drown in those ocean blue eyes.

Vicenzo scoffed. "Really?"

"'Course. I don't mind a mess if it's from you."

Vicenzo's throat bobbed when he swallowed, and his eyes dipped for the briefest of moments to Eddie's lips. "Full of it," he muttered, his fingers curling in Eddie's shirt, urging him closer.

Eddie's heart sang, *Yes, Goddess, yes,* and *Vico, Vico, Vico.*

There was hope for them, he knew it now. Hope that they could transcend all that bad and still make something out of it. Eddie would never stop believing in that little ray of hope that shone through Vicenzo's smile, and he wouldn't let Vicenzo give up either.

Eddie's heart raced when he cupped Vicenzo's cheek, his thumb gliding over his sticky skin. Vicenzo's eyes fluttered.

Please. Please don't push me away. Please want this. Want me.

When Vicenzo closed his eyes, Eddie gasped from the sweet relief that gripped his heart, leaning in and—

Eddie's phone rang so loudly, they both jumped.

"Better be a fucking emergency," Eddie snarled, reaching back and grabbing his phone. His hands were still slick with tomato juice, and he dropped it. By the time he answered, it had stopped ringing. "Ben's back," he grumbled, not caring much. In addition to the call, Ben had left a group message about twenty minutes ago.

Ben: Got something I need to discuss with you all. Find me in my office after dinner.

Checking the rest of his messages, he noticed that Gabe had attempted to call and then had texted Eddie, saying they were meeting Ben in a few minutes.

Vicenzo checked his phone, too. "Got the same message. Doubt he wants to tell us about going snorkeling with dolphins."

Eddie sighed. "Is that really too much to hope for?"

Vicenzo snorted. "In our pack? Yeah."

Our pack.

Vicenzo scowled. "Get that dopey grin off your face. Come on, let's go see what he wants."

But Eddie couldn't quite keep the smile from his face. "See you tomorrow, little plants." He closed the door after them and walked across the courtyard, stopping along the side of the building to turn on the garden hose and rinse his hands clean of dirt.

Vicenzo borrowed the hose as well. "Gonna go change my shirt. I'll meet you upstairs."

"See ya." Drying his hands on his jeans, Eddie passed through the oak doors. The sitting room was empty, the receptionist nodding off at the desk. To the right and through the open doors, Eddie smelled the aromas of a spicy stew. His stomach roared, but he proceeded upstairs and headed to Ben's office. He knocked but didn't receive an answer.

"I'm coming in." He nudged open the office door and saw that Ben's desk was empty. Soothing music was coming from the gym just off his office. Eddie pressed an ear to the door, beyond which music played at a low volume, devoid of lyrics but relaxing. A sweet scent tickled his nose. He couldn't hear any sounds within, and even if he still possessed a superior sense of smell, the incense would have obscured any scents in the room.

"Ben?" his voice choked out as he opened the door.

Ben lay shirtless and face down on a table with Isaac standing over him, puncturing his back with needles. Ben glowered at Eddie. "Thanks for knocking."

Eddie gaped, unsure what he'd just walked in on. "Isaac, I know you're Ben's mate, but I'm not sure how I should react to you stabbin' him in the back with needles."

Isaac cracked a grin. "The airplane seat irritated his back. I convinced him some acupuncture might be helpful."

"Think he just wanted to stab me with needles for that stupid argument we had at baggage claim," Ben grumbled, wincing as Isaac tapped a needle into his ankle.

"That too," Isaac said and Ben growled.

"Someone's grumpy. Time to change your nicotine patch." He tugged the patch off Ben's arm and tossed him another one from his desk. Ben slapped it on, looking poutier than a fearsome wolf his age ought to.

"Where'd you learn acupuncture?" Eddie asked.

"I studied it when I dropped out of college," Isaac said. "Picked up a few trades before I settled on bartending, then werewolf hunting."

"What're you doing here, Ed?" Ben asked.

Eddie held up his phone. "You texted the pack. Said there was somethin' we needed to discuss?"

Ben's eyes widened. "Shit! I forgot. Isaac, get these needles outta me."

The door opened. "Hey, Viejo!" Gabe gaped, blinking at Ben with a back full of needles. Max stood behind him, sucking in his lips to keep from grinning. Then Ryan showed up and didn't hold back his laughter while Zach stood tall over everyone's shoulders and took it all in. When Izzie poked her head out from around Zach, Eddie realized they were all there except Vico.

"Well, of all the things I coulda walked in on you and Isaac doing, I'm glad it was this," Ryan said, stating what was on everyone's mind.

Ben growled and glared at Isaac, who sighed and removed the needles. Pulling his shirt on, Ben said, "Shut up and follow me."

Gabe yawned. "Better be a good reason you told us to wait around after our shift was up."

Ben dropped into his rolling office chair behind the desk.

As Isaac scrutinized Ben's chair, he said, "If you have back pain, you should probably invest in an ergonomic chair, babe. Just 'cause you transform into a big hairy beast doesn't mean you should neglect proper posture."

"Yeah, babe," Ryan said, leaning on the desk as if he owned it. "We wouldn't want anything to happen to our dear Ben's back."

Vicenzo walked in, dressed in a clean white tank top that hugged his powerful chest and showed off the rippling muscles in his bronzed arms.

Izzie nudged Eddie. "Ed, a fly's going to go down your throat."

He snapped his jaws shut and Vicenzo's mouth twitched in a smug smile.

Ben said, "There you are! I was about to put up some posters with your picture on it."

"I'm not some lost puppy," Vicenzo grumbled, reclining against the wall.

Ryan said, "Should we get him a collar and leash, too? Maybe a muzzle so he can't bite us?"

Vicenzo snapped his jaws in Ryan's direction.

Sighing loudly, Ben said, "Can we get down to business so you all can go home?" With the attention on him, he said, "A friend of mine in New Orleans needs our help."

Izzie quirked a trimmed brow. "Not just you?"

Ben nodded, his big hands folded on his desk. "All of us. His name's Phillipe. He's the leader of a small pack out in the bayou. They're being picked off by hunters."

"Assholes out there are killing wolves?" Gabe growled. "Say no more, I'm ready to feed them to the gators."

Ben said, "Not killing them, no. Not all of them, anyway. Some of them are being turned against their pack and hunting their own."

Eddie jumped when Vicenzo suddenly gripped his shoulder. He didn't say anything, didn't have to. Vicenzo knew exactly what had Eddie's heart slamming against his ribs.

"Ben?" Max murmured, but Ben didn't hear him.

Ben met Eddie's eyes knowingly. "It's The Beasts, Ed. Phillipe thinks they've returned from whatever hole they were hiding in, and—"

Eddie stopped listening as his body went cold all over. His heart was beating so fast he thought it would explode, and his lungs felt like they were in a vise.

"Eddie. Hey. Breathe, okay?" Vicenzo's gruff voice filled his ears, his hands warm and sturdy on his shoulders. His touch soothed Eddie's racing heart.

"Shit," Ben murmured. "Ed, I'm sorry. I just thought you wanted to know."

"You okay, Ed?" Izzie asked, her eyes soft and concerned. Everyone was looking at him.

He swallowed with difficulty. His fear must've smelled ripe to them. "No," he admitted, voice rough. "I..." He needed to sit. Max jumped out of the chair in front of Ben's desk and Eddie sank into it, sweat icy on his brow.

After all these years, his uncle was still up to his old tricks. He'd heard rumors sometimes, of packs being hunted by wolves. It wasn't unusual for there to be turf wars. They were one of the leading causes of death among werewolves in the wild, aside from humans. He'd started to think his uncle might have met his end, though. He'd hoped it was so, prayed Elijah had gotten his throat torn out. If he was dead, he couldn't come for Eddie. Couldn't take him away and lock him up and—

"Everyone out," Ben said, his voice low. "I need to talk to Eddie."

The pack filed out one by one but Vicenzo stayed. The weight of his hands anchored Eddie, making it easier to breathe.

"I'm good, Vico," he said roughly. "Let me talk to Ben."

Vicenzo growled his disapproval.

Ben nodded at Vicenzo. "I've got him, Vicenzo. Stay outside. I'll come and tell you all when you can come back in."

Vicenzo held Eddie's gaze and Eddie nodded, so Vicenzo removed his hands from his shoulders and walked out.

When they were alone, Ben gazed at Eddie across his desk, his silver eyes thoughtful. A moment of silence passed between them, like the quiet that comes when testing the surface of thin ice. Ben sighed. "I'm sorry, Ed. I should have been more tactful. Are you okay?"

Bile burned the back of his throat. He shuddered, suddenly freezing cold. "You w-want me to face him, don't you?" The lamp flickered, the room flashing in and out of sight. Eddie struggled to breathe. The light had flickered all the time in the basement, the cuffs cold and tight around his wrists. His wounds had ached and he would hold his breath, thinking he'd heard Elijah on the stairs. Coming for him.

Ben raised both his hands. "Eddie, hey. Listen to me."

Ben's voice came from far away, like Eddie was underwater. Drowning.

Elijah was still alive.

"I... I can't go. Don't go. You can't go." Eddie's throat thickened and he struggled to suck in even a pinch of air. "He'll kill you. All of you. He'll make me kill you. He'll—"

Elijah would find him. Elijah would take him away. Lock him up. Break him for good this time, until he lost his mind and slaughtered his pack-mates. "He'll—he'll hurt you. He'll break you. He'll make me do it for him. He'll make me. I... I can't—"

"He won't touch you." Ben was standing in front of Eddie's chair, his wolf's eyes burning bright. He didn't touch Eddie. He didn't have to. "Ed. Look me in the eyes."

Eddie did. He couldn't refuse.

Ben's eyes never wavered, burning with a promise. "You're safe. You're mine. He can't have you because you're mine, Eddie Turner. He will not touch you."

Eddie's face was wet, and he couldn't stop shaking. He leaned forward into Ben's torso, his forehead against Ben's knee. Ben did touch him then, a big hand gentle upon the back of his neck. "He'll never hurt you or anyone again. Because we're going to stop him. You don't have to come with us. I'm not gonna ask that of you."

Sucking in a gasp, he clung to the denim of Ben's jeans. No. He couldn't let his pack face Elijah alone. But if Elijah got a hold of him, Eddie was so scared he would break this time. Elijah wouldn't want him human. He'd become Elijah's dog in every sense of the word and hunt the ones he loved. If Elijah took the silver collar off, Eddie was terrified he wouldn't be able to control his shift after so many years of suppression. Elijah would own him.

"I don't know," Eddie confessed, unsure what to do. "I know him. Better than anyone. I can't let you face him alone, but…"

"Think on it." Ben's hand ran through Eddie's hair, warm and gentle. "Sleep on it. If by the morning you decide you want to, you can come with us. We can handle the likes of him. If you wanna come, we'd be happy to have you. Got it?"

Eddie nodded, unable to speak.

"Go get some rest. Let me know what you decide in the morning."

Eddie stood, suddenly exhausted.

"Come in, people," Ben barked.

The door slammed against the wall. Vicenzo dashed into the room and went to Eddie's side, looking him over.

"I'm okay," Eddie said, though he'd never felt further from it. He wanted to be alone. Raising a hand in farewell, he smiled to appease the worried faces of the pack.

Ben said, "Come morning, I need you all to be ready to leave. Pack a bag, make sure you've got what you need. If you need to take any calming medication for the flight so you don't eat the pilot, do it. Phillipe's an old friend of mine, and the attacks against his wolves can't go unpunished."

"Count me in," Gabe growled.

"My mom will take care of the kids," Max said. "I'll need to make sure Gabe doesn't get himself killed."

Izzie said, "That's a two-person job, my friend." She winked. "I'll help, Ben. Of course. These hunters will pay for messing with wolves, and for hurting Eddie."

Eddie's throat tightened when she squeezed his shoulder.

Ryan clenched his fists. "I'm always up for punching asshole hunters in the face—or shoving roots up their asses. Or burning them. Electrocuting them. You get the picture. I'm down."

Zach frowned. "I'd come, but I know you'll want someone to run the estate."

Ben said, "My father's flying in to cover for me. I need all hands on deck for this. We underestimated the hunters in Alaska and got overwhelmed. That's not happening again. We know what we're up against this time. We'll rip out their throats."

Isaac cracked his knuckles. "And here I thought The Beasts were all picked off by cops or bounty hunters. Glad they saved some for me."

Ben said, "Vicenzo, what about you? Will you be okay confronting Elijah?"

Vicenzo's jaw tightened. "I need to be okay because I have to do this. Those fuckers destroyed my home and slaughtered my family."

Nodding, Ben said, "I'm asking 'cause your bond is still healing. If you come, I need to know you can be levelheaded and that you won't lose yourself to your wolf again."

Eddie frowned. He didn't know how Vicenzo's wolf would react when he scented the monsters who'd burned his home and his family to ash. Staying here, on the other hand, wasn't a good idea, either; Vicenzo was only just beginning to take to the pack. Being separated from them would only strain the fragile bonds they'd been cultivating.

Vicenzo dipped his head. "I can do that, Ben. I promise. I'll keep my cool this time, and I won't bail."

Ryan grinned and clapped his shoulder. "That's the spirit!" Vicenzo smiled shyly.

"Good," Ben said. "Everyone get some rest. We'll leave in the morning."

Eddie dragged his feet as he headed to his room and collapsed in bed, kicking off his shoes and pants and throwing his shirt on the floor. He knew he wouldn't be able to sleep. His mind was in turmoil and he didn't want to turn off the lights. The darkness always reminded him of that damp, moldy basement, and he usually had to keep some kind of light on at night just to chase the darkness away.

When he finally did close his eyes, he dreamed. He was crawling on all fours in a dark, sprawling woods. Wolves screamed as the trees burned, embers raining from the sky. The voices of the pack howled out in terror and pain as one by one, the bonds were ripped from Eddie. Pale, dead faces materialized from the darkness. His packmates lay broken and bloody as he crawled past them. The silver around his neck burned.

No. No, no, no.

This couldn't be happening. This wasn't happening…

"I'm coming for you, boy!" Elijah's roar echoed through the burning woods.

The ground shook under heavy paws, and wolves bayed for blood as they hunted through the woods. They were coming for him. They'd drag him back to the basement. Elijah would lock him up and hurt him until his mind broke. He had to run. He had to get away, but he couldn't crawl fast enough.

Hurry. He had to hurry! He was going to die, he was going to—

Gasping, Eddie tore himself from his nightmare. The sheets were drenched with icy sweat, and he shuddered, his heart pounding as he caught his breath. The room was dark except for a nightlight by the door. Afraid to move, he scanned the shadows.

Eddie's fingers touched something soft. He jumped, astonished to find a great black wolf curled up in bed beside him. "Vico," he whispered. He didn't remember the wolf coming in, so he must have done so after Eddie was asleep. Then Eddie realized there was something to his left. A red wolf slumbered beside him, a black wolf's head draped over his back. Max and Gabe. And at his feet, another black wolf, ears twitching as she slept. Izzie.

In the armchair across the room, Isaac slumbered, a silver wolf's head in his lap. Zach and Ryan lay curled on the floor next to Ben, their paws twitching as they dreamed.

Blinking back tears, Eddie smiled and rolled over, nestling his face into Vicenzo's black fur.

He slept surrounded by his pack, and the nightmares didn't dare come for him.

C HAPTER 16

YOU KEPT IT

E ARLY THE NEXT DAY, the pack prepared to leave for New Orleans, and Ben and Isaac waited by a big white seater van. Eddie yawned and hoped he'd be able to sleep on the plane. He was so not a morning person. Ben had rented the pack a private jet for the flight, which Eddie was grateful for. Werewolves were notoriously bad flyers. Too many noises and smells crammed into a narrow space would bring the wolf out of the most composed werewolf if they didn't take some Xanax before the flight.

Eddie's stomach writhed as he set his suitcase in the van. He wasn't looking forward to confronting the man who'd burned his home twice, killed his parents in front of him, and broke him into becoming a hunter. But Elijah, if this really was his doing, had to be stopped. There wasn't proof Elijah was actually behind the killings, not yet. For all Eddie knew, his psychopathic uncle was dead and gone, and some other sick fuck had taken up the mantle. Either way, it was time to end The Beasts once and for all and put the past to rest. He only wished his stomach would stop churning.

Ryan grinned. It relaxed Eddie to see someone in a good mood. "Yo! Ready to smash in some hunters' faces?"

Eddie was pleased he wouldn't be doing this alone.

"We'll miss you, Daddy," Luna said, hugging Gabe's middle. "You too, Papa." She gave Max a hug.

Gabe opened his arms. "Come here, big guy. You're not too cool to hug your old man, are you?"

Tommy rolled his eyes but shuffled into Gabe's arms for a hug, smiling when Max piled in.

Next Max hugged his mom. "Thanks for looking out for the pups."

"Are you kidding?" Kendra squawked, planting a big kiss on Luna's cheek. "I wish you two would go away more often!" She turned and kissed them both on the cheek.

Ben growled, "Where is Izzie?"

Zach checked his phone. "Want me to call her?"

Right on cue, Izzie burst from the oak doors and hurried down the steps, carrying a bloated bag.

"Oh Christ, Izzie. You'll sink the plane!" Ben said.

"I don't know how long we'll be there. I needed a few comforts from home!" Izzie snapped, tossing her bag in the trunk of the Van.

Gabe opened the bag and held up a milk frother. "Really? When are you going to use this?"

"What a good question, Gabriel! When are you going to use *this?*" Izzie yanked open Gabe's bag and whipped out an eight-inch werewolf dildo—knot included.

Ben turned away, his hand over his eyes. "The hell do you think you and Max will have the time to use that?"

"Goddess," Zach said, eyes wide. "Which one of you is equipped to handle that thing? Seriously. Respect."

"I know who," Ryan croaked, and he looked like he'd died inside. "I wish I didn't."

Zach stroked his mate's hair. "You poor thing. Tell me everything."

Max's face was as red as his hair. "Gabe, put it away!"

Looking murderous, Gabe shoved the *thing* back in his bag. He muttered something in Spanish to his sister with a nasty curl to his lip. Izzie looked smug. "You always criticize the things I bring with me, Gabriel. It was time to have my payback."

Ben raised his hands. "If we're done with this fucked-up game of sibling rivalry, can we go? Where's Vicenzo?"

Vicenzo strode into view, his backpack slung across his shoulder. "Here. Didn't think I'd miss the opportunity to kill some hunters, did you?"

Isaac looked around and, noticing everyone was present, said, "All right, pile in."

Ryan gasped. "I forgot my toothbrush!"

Everyone groaned as Ryan tore back inside.

Ben elbowed Zach. "Aren't you supposed to be responsible for him?"

Zach shrugged, smiling fondly after him. "I did ask him if he had everything."

The pack threw their luggage in and piled into the roomy van. Eddie's stomach did flips, his mouth unbearably dry. He closed his eyes tight, not looking forward to this at all. But it was happening. Before he knew it, he would be confronting the past he'd tried so hard to leave behind.

Vicenzo sat beside him and bumped their shoulders together. Vicenzo didn't say anything or try to move away from him, which was fine. Eddie didn't want him to.

Tommy, Luna, and Kendra waved them off. The van pulled out of the driveway and the estate grew farther away.

They arrived at the airport and made straight for the private jet. His packmates were tense as they followed Ben. Already, the smells and rushing crowds must be bothering them. Eddie was grateful his sense of smell wasn't what it used to be. As they walked the tarmac toward the jet, Izzie suddenly said, "Wait! This is an Instagram-worthy moment!"

"Really?" Ben sighed.

"Yes!" she said as if he were stupid. "How often are we all together in a private jet? How often do we all get to go out of the city like this? Just because we're going to be biting hunters in their butts doesn't mean we can't make this a fun and memorable experience." She rubbed Eddie's shoulder. "Come on, gather around."

"Hell yeah," Ryan said, steering Zach toward Izzie.

"You gotta be—" Ben began, but Isaac looped an arm around his husband's neck and wrangled him behind Izzie.

Vicenzo rolled his eyes, but Eddie took his arm and said, "Come on. Get in here." Yanking his arm free, Vicenzo slouched into the frame.

Izzie held the phone at arm's length and grinned. "Hashtag Pack Life!"

"Pack life," the pack echoed, some with less enthusiasm than others, and Izzie snapped a few pictures.

Izzie sighed. "Really, Vicenzo? You couldn't look a little less murderous for once? Kassandra's going to see this!"

"No," Vicenzo said.

"It's just who he is," Ryan said, clapping Vicenzo's shoulder. "That resting murder face is part of his charm!"

Eddie stopped at the top of the stairs and looked back at the New York skyline. He exhaled, trying to steel himself for whatever awaited them in New Orleans. New York was his home and he was coming back—they all were. Eddie wouldn't let his uncle get his claws into his pack. Turning away, he strode into the jet. The pack spread out, stretching their legs as they reclined in plush leather seats.

Ryan roamed the jet excitedly, gushing over how fancy everything was while Zach read a book and Izzie and Gabe joked around. Ben leaned his head on Isaac's shoulder with their hands intertwined on his thigh. Since they hadn't taken off yet, Max FaceTimed his mother and Luna. Vicenzo had sat next to Eddie. He didn't say anything, but he'd clearly wanted to stay nearby. Eddie pretended not to notice, but he smiled all the same.

The jet took off and they flew over New York City. Everything looked so tiny, even Central Park, and the buildings were the size of anthills. The world spread out below him, from New Jersey and beyond to rolling mountains in the distance. When he roamed the streets, New York felt like the entire world, a melting pot of different cultures from all over the planet. Eddie felt so small to be reminded there was a vast world beyond the city. Yet his heart never wanted to be anywhere else. He laid a hand on the window and told himself, *He'll never hurt anyone again. He won't hurt my pack. I'll make sure of it.*

Elijah would not take his loved ones from him. Not ever again.

Vicenzo's hand settled on Eddie's knee. Closing his eyes, Eddie felt his heart rate slow, his breathing getting easier.

He would be okay.

ONCE THEY ARRIVED IN New Orleans, they checked into their hotel. It was a luxurious building, old and beautiful. Eddie thought he'd feel quite comfortable—until Ryan said it was haunted.

"What? It is. People have seen ghosts. There's this old lady that touches you at night and says, 'I'll never let you leave.'"

They would only have a day in the city. Ben had booked a boat to take them out into the bayou early tomorrow morning since the area of the bayou the pack called home was only accessible by boat. Eddie was glad they wouldn't be staying in the city too long—he'd spent years in the bayous of New Orleans.

The hunters moved around a lot, traveling from place to place on year-long hunts. The Beasts terrorized the country year-round, traveling from one end of the country to another on wolf hunts. When a hunt was over, Elijah would grin his crooked, slimy grin and take in the sight of his miserable cabin in the bayou. "No place like home, is there, boy?"

Eddie had never thought he'd find a place like home again, not until the agency wolves had opened their door to him, baggage and all. He couldn't let Elijah take his home, his pack, away from him again.

They were spread out on the same floor. Gabe, Izzie, and Max had one room with Zach and Ryan next door and Ben and Isaac's room to their left. So that meant that he and Vicenzo were sharing a room, Eddie realized with a twisting sensation in his stomach.

While Vicenzo stood in the doorway and bitched under his breath about the lemony air freshener, Eddie crossed to the window and looked out over the streets of New Orleans. They had a view of the Mississippi River as it carved through the city. He leaned his head against the glass and sighed lowly. His uncle was out there somewhere, closer than he'd been in years. The realization made his skin feel cold and clammy.

"I hate this city," Vicenzo grumbled. He'd come to stand beside Eddie, glowering down into the streets. His arms were folded tight over his chest and his nostrils flared, his breath seething from him. His blue eyes were like pieces of ice.

The last time they'd been in New Orleans... everything had ended in this city. Eddie's life as a hunter had begun here. Vicenzo had chased after him, leaving the shattered remains of his family in pursuit of a future with Eddie—only to have what remained of his heart shattered instead.

Something clenched like a fist in Eddie's gut. He'd been so wrapped up in his own foul memories of New Orleans that he hadn't stopped to think about Vicenzo's own painful memories of this city.

Yet Vicenzo had been reaching out to him, sitting next to him, touching him, albeit so subtly Eddie could pretend not to notice. He'd been uncharacteristically watchful of Eddie ever since Eddie had learned that his uncle was still out there. Ever since Eddie had brought him back from the brink of feral madness, things had been... calmer between them. Easier, maybe? Things would never be as they were. The warmth and love that had once burned bright between them would never be rekindled.

Eddie squeezed his fists. But he'd be damned if he wouldn't try.

"Beignets," he stated.

Vicenzo's bushy brows furrowed. "What?"

"We should get beignets. A big, greasy bagful with loads of Café Du Monde coffee. And we should hit up Bourbon Street and get drinks with the pack. Watch the steamboats float along the Mississippi. Ugh! And we've gotta get loads of crawfish and eat tons of Creole food!"

"This isn't a vacation, Eddie."

Eddie rolled his eyes skyward. "No, really? Here I thought chasin' down my murderous uncle and his pack of psychos was supposed to be fun! Come on, we've got a day in this city. Might as well try to enjoy ourselves, huh?"

It seemed Ben and the others had had a similar idea since the pack was waiting for them in the hotel lobby. Izzie unfurled a map and said, "We need to go to the French Quarter. So much art, food, and history!"

Ryan said, "As long as we get beignets, I don't care where we go. Oh wait! Can we go to the zoo?"

Ben scoffed. "Right, 'cause what's a better idea than letting a pack of werewolves into a zoo? You wanna give the animals a heart attack, Ry?"

Stealing the map away from Izzie, Zach said, "The World War II Museum sounds interesting."

Ben looked like he was getting a headache. "We can't do everything in one day. Besides, we've gotta keep our guard up."

Ryan threw his hands in the air. "Okay, so if I see any hunters, I'll blow powdered sugar down their throats! Come on, let's go! We're in freaking New Orleans, man!" He raced out the door.

Ben kicked Zach's foot. "Who gave him caffeine?"

Zach sighed, smiling warmly. "Guilty."

It didn't take long to get to the French Quarter from their hotel. They walked beneath the balconies of Bourbon Street, yellow, green, and purple beads waving from the banisters above. Neon lights blinked and flashed as the pack roamed past crowded bars and eye-catching sex shops. A jazz band attracted a crowd as they played in the middle of the cobblestone road.

"Oh, now we're in New Orleans!" Ryan declared, stopping to drop a tip in the jar. The jazz was toe-tapping and uplifting. Eddie had never been able to enjoy the city for the never-ending party that it was until now that he was here with friends.

Still, as he rounded the corner, a wave of memories assaulted him of drunken nights out with The Beasts hunters. Hadn't he crowded into that bar at the end of the street with them? It was vaguely familiar in a gut-clenching way. He must have visited every single one of these bars, too drunk to remember.

"Eddie!" Vicenzo's voice jolted him back to the present. The crowd clapped as the band moved on to their next song. Vicenzo had ventured away and stood on the sidewalk watching him expectantly, so Eddie sniffed to clear his head and followed him.

Jackson Square sprawled to their left as they untangled themselves from the crowds and walked the path to Saint Louis Cathedral. The cathedral overlooked the square, its pointed spires rising into the overcast sky. It was a beautiful building, Eddie thought, and one he knew well. Sometimes, while the hunters had hit up the bars, Eddie would break away and sit inside. Just sit and listen to the choir or sometimes to total silence. He didn't believe in God and hadn't believed in the She-Wolf until a few years ago when he'd learned Max was her descendant.

But it had been good to just sit and think and believe that someone heard his thoughts. Maybe a god or goddess, maybe his parents. Once, he'd asked Max if the dead existed in Amaris's realm. Max hadn't known for sure, so he'd asked his mother. Amaris had said, "There is a realm beyond mine. Beyond yours, where the wolves who have gone before us run forever. When we're finally reunited, we run forever by the sides of those we lost."

Maybe she was lying. Maybe she was saying only what she thought her son wanted to hear, but she'd looked sure and certain. If such a realm existed, Eddie liked to think his family was there, running forever, free from pain. Even if that wasn't the case, then they were at peace in death, even if his thoughts could never reach them and simply disappeared into the void. At least they couldn't see what he'd become. They would be so disappointed in him for submitting to the man who'd killed them, for not being strong enough to avenge them.

"I'll be right back," Eddie told the pack. They were getting in line to order beignets.

"We'll order you some!" Izzie called.

Vicenzo watched him, his eyebrows narrowed in a glare, though his eyes were inquisitive and searching.

Eddie slipped into the cathedral doors and his breath lodged in his throat. The cathedral looked the same. Eddie suspected the only thing that had changed was himself and his life since the last time he'd sat here. He walked down the aisle and came upon the very pew he used to sit in, halfway between the altar and the door, and took his seat, sliding into the pew. Closing his eyes, he sent out a message to his parents, wherever they were now, hoping they could hear him.

Hey, Pa. Hey, Ma.

I'm gonna make this right. He destroyed our family. He destroyed me, for the longest time. But I'm stronger now. I've found a pack. I'm gonna make him pay for what he did to our family. I wish I coulda done it sooner, before I made you so ashamed of me. I'm gonna make it better. I swear to you.

Are you ashamed of me? Are you proud of the things I've done with the agency?

Tell me. Please. Find a way to tell me. Do you even hear me?

He slumped, feeling stupid. He would never know and the uncertainty would always eat away at him.

"Hey." A brash voice blasted in his ear.

Eddie screamed.

The choir lurched to a stop. Heads turned.

Seething, Eddie stared at Vicenzo, who blinked at him with wide eyes. "What?" he snapped.

Vicenzo held up a red and white checkered basket. "We got beignets. What the hell?"

Eddie dropped his chin to his chest, his heart racing. "Great. Thanks."

Quietly, Eddie followed Vicenzo out into the muggy air. The pack had gathered around the waterfront where boats floated on the murky waters of the Mississippi River. Ben waved him over to their table, which was crowded with beignets and cups of steaming coffee. Taking a seat, Eddie dunked his beignet in coffee. He scoffed, realizing he'd been the one to suggest fun things to do and he couldn't even manage to smile.

He took a moment to watch his pack around him. Max choked on powdered sugar and Gabe thumped him on the back. Sighing, Izzie took in a deep breath, watching the boats drift over the water. The bells of Saint Louis Cathedral chimed noon and the distant sound of jazz music carried on the humid breeze. Then Ryan's laugh rang out when Ben got powdered sugar in his mustache. Vicenzo gave his beignets a cautious sniff and coughed. "What is this shit?" He poked out his tongue and licked at the powdered sugar the beignets were doused with.

"Cocaine," Ryan said. "Or close enough."

Vicenzo laughed sarcastically at him and took a big bite. His eyes widened. "Holy shit."

"Amazing, right?" Isaac said, breaking his last beignet in half and offering it to Ben. His mate shook his head, so Isaac ate it. "I bought a ton of these last time I was here."

Ben's brows bounced. "When were you in New Orleans?"

Isaac pointed a sugary finger at Vicenzo. "He hired me to track down Eddie."

Vicenzo stopped eating, his eyes going wide.

"No way!" Gabe said. "You two met before?"

"Yeah. I thought I recognized his wolf when we were in Alaska, but—"

"Guys," Ryan began, eyeing Vicenzo. For such a goofy guy, he was sensitive to others' feelings.

It was too late. Vicenzo snatched up his beignets and carried them away to the railing that overlooked the water.

Isaac glowered into his lap. "Shit. Vicenzo! Hey, I'm sorry!"

Vicenzo kept on walking.

Sighing, Isaac crumpled his napkin and dropped it onto his plate. "I shouldn't have brought that up. Sorry, Eddie. I'll have to talk to Vicenzo later."

"It's okay." Eddie nodded at his lap. "It's different, havin' y'all here. I don't think either of us thought we'd ever come back here willingly."

Isaac frowned. "Damn it. I hope we haven't been too insensitive."

Eddie shook his head. "No, no." He didn't want them feeling bad. He hated that Vicenzo was feeling bitter about being here, but at the same time, it gave him an odd sense of peace. He wasn't alone in his feelings. Eddie's chair screeched over the concrete as he stood. When he approached the railing, he left a careful distance between himself and Vicenzo as he leaned against it. Vicenzo stared out over the water, his face guarded, his eyes hard.

Eddie hadn't known. He hadn't had any idea the lengths Vicenzo had gone to in order to find him. Sure, he'd thought about it sometimes, and it had always left an ache inside that had never seemed to go away.

"You hired a hunter for me. Traded the ring I gave you for me."

Vicenzo sighed. "You kept my drawing," he said, as if that proved something.

"I did." Eddie swallowed a bite of beignet. It hit his stomach hard. "Why? Why would you trust a hunter?"

Vicenzo shrugged. "He was a hunter of hunters. Figured he wouldn't kill me."

Eddie exhaled, his stomach churning. So many hunters had posed as hunters of their own kind so that desperate werewolves like Vicenzo would hire them. Vicenzo could have been deceived and murdered, but he'd taken that risk. For him.

Vicenzo was quiet.

"How did you find it?" Eddie circled the ring on his finger. He'd never gotten an answer the night of Ben's wedding.

Jerking his shoulder at Isaac, Vicenzo said, "I traded it to him. Payment for his services. He kept it, couldn't bring himself to sell it. He gave it back to me at the wedding." He smiled and it nearly shattered Eddie. It was so full of tender sadness.

His words were like a wrecking ball through Eddie's heart. Vicenzo had traded his only reminder of Eddie in order to find him, and in return Eddie had shattered Vicenzo's heart. He closed his eyes tight against the burn. Ah, Goddess.

Vicenzo tried to move away but Eddie gripped his arm, unable to look at him but needing him near. He tried to speak around the lump in his throat. It was hard, but somehow he got the words out. "I am so sorry." He blinked and wetness rained down his face.

Vicenzo said nothing but he didn't pull away from Eddie's grip.

"I wish I'd gone with you," Eddie said, throat aching. "Every single day, I wish I'd just..." It was useless. Nothing he could ever say would make everything he'd broken that day better.

"You kept my picture," Vicenzo said again.

Eddie didn't understand. "Yeah. Yes, Vico. Of course I kept it. I kept it on me, always. Hid it from the hunters so they couldn't take it away. I think that's what kept me human." *You*, he wanted to say. *You kept me human. When all I wanted was to break, you kept me holding on and for a long time, I didn't know if I loved you or hated you for it.*

He looked at Vicenzo, who was gazing at him in something like reverence, his lips parted, his eyes wide and so unguarded Eddie almost didn't recognize him. Vicenzo wet his lips and looked away, blinking fast. Eddie's heart was racing and he wanted to reach out to him, touch the hard lines of Vicenzo's face and soften them with his fingers. He didn't, but it was close. Eddie squeezed his fingers together. Somehow, he felt like the world was tipping.

They didn't speak for several moments. From far away, a saxophone wailed. Boats tooted their horns on the water. Gulls cried. Children laughed and adults chatted. Eddie took a bite of beignet and sighed. "Fuckin' A, these are good."

After a moment, Vicenzo took a big bite of the pillowy fried dough and moaned. The sound didn't turn Eddie on at all. Not even a bit.

Vicenzo had powdered sugar on his lips and stubble. "Fuckin' A," he repeated, taking another bite.

Eddie said, "You have—stuff. On your face."

Frowning, Vicenzo dusted his face with his fingers, his stubble making a scratchy sound that Eddie barely refrained from sighing at, but Vicenzo didn't succeed in cleaning any of it off.

Eddie pointed to his own mouth. "Right there."

Vicenzo wet his lips, swirling his tongue around to coat them, leaving them silky and slick. "I get it?" He hadn't; there was a smear of powdered sugar next to his mouth.

Licking his thumb, Eddie reached out, knowing Vicenzo would likely bite him and he wouldn't be able to heal from it. He ran his thumb over the prickly stubble, wiping away the sugary residue. At his touch, Vicenzo went still, his wide blue eyes meeting Eddie's. A current of electricity ran straight down Eddie's spine.

"Gonna bite me, aren't you?" Eddie said, watching Vicenzo's eyes narrow.

Vicenzo blinked at him, his expression unreadable. "You got something on you, too."

Eddie exhaled a laugh and turned away as butterflies beat their wings in his stomach. "Really?" His hand fumbled around his face, dusting away sugar.

"No." Vicenzo sighed. "Not there. Just..." He reached out and Eddie held his breath. Vicenzo's thumb hovered inches from Eddie's mouth before brushing in a gentle stroke from the corner of his mouth to his cheek. Then his face hardened, closing off. "There. All gone." Turning abruptly, he walked away, his ears red. Eddie looked out over the water and did the one thing he hadn't thought possible since his return to New Orleans.

He smiled.

Until yesterday, he'd thought he'd never return to New Orleans. He'd thought coming back would cripple him, drag him down into all the dark memories he'd locked away. There had been some of that, sure, but as they toured the city, there'd been unexpected feelings, too.

Eating beignets with the pack until he thought his stomach would burst. Laughing as Ryan became even more hyper than usual after two cups of coffee. Zach's serious frown softening to a smile as he scoured the map. Izzie stopping to take pictures of everything. Ben and Isaac arguing over where to go next. Riding the streetcar beneath blooming magnolia trees and watching Gabe fret over Max as he stuck his red head out the window. Vicenzo's little smile as he watched the jazz band play on the cobblestone road. He thought no one had noticed, but Eddie did.

With his pack at his side, Eddie could face down his uncle.

He wasn't alone.

He would never be alone.

VICENZO HATED THIS CITY.

He might have lost his home and his family in a small town in Nevada that had been burned off the map by hunters, but he'd lost all hope for a future in New Orleans. He'd chased after the boy he loved with a broken heart, holding on to all the shattered pieces of his past. He'd offered what little he had left to the boy, offering all his broken pieces, and asked the boy to make a choice. To choose him.

And Eddie had said, "No."

Vicenzo's world had shattered and that time, there was no picking up the pieces.

That was years ago, but it had all come rushing back to him as he'd walked the city streets today. Every wound he thought he'd stapled shut bled red. Every door he'd turned his back on and thrown away the key to had come crashing open.

Come nightfall, Eddie had suggested they stay indoors. His uncle had never been brazen enough to target wolves in crowded city streets, but it didn't hurt to be cautious. Eddie had said he didn't know how many hunters Elijah employed nowadays, but Bourbon Street had been their stomping grounds after nightfall back in the day, so the pack had returned to the hotel.

"Vicenzo, you getting tired? Your face is all scowly and you're doing that thing with your eyebrows that makes it look like you want us dead," Ryan remarked.

Vicenzo blinked at him. "I don't do anything with my eyebrows."

Ryan shoved his fingers in Vicenzo's face, vigorously rubbing his brows. "Yeah, you do!" His face blanched. "You're gonna bite me, aren't you?"

Biting back a grin, he shoved Ryan in the chest. "Keep pestering me and I may take a bite."

Zach growled and tugged Ryan away as Vicenzo wheezed with laughter.

Ben yawned and stretched. "Everyone get some sleep. We'll make for the bayou early tomorrow."

One cramped elevator ride later and the pack spilled into the hallway and went their separate ways to their rooms with Eddie trailing after Vicenzo like he had when they were kids.

"You got the key?" Eddie asked. The Texan rasp of his voice made Vicenzo's blood simmer for reasons he wasn't ready to examine.

"Y-Yeah." They'd shared a room before, so Vicenzo didn't know why it was making him nervous. He swiped the key card and the lock clicked. Flicking on the lights, Vicenzo could see their room was nothing to scoff at with two queen beds and a breathtaking view of the city.

"So," Vicenzo said, trying to ignore the odd crack in his voice. "You want the one on the left or—"

"Why're you ignorin' this?"

Vicenzo's heart slammed against his ribs, and he was beyond grateful Eddie couldn't hear it hammering to escape his chest. "Don't know what you're talking about." He folded his arms as if that would stifle his stupid heartbeat and turned to confront Eddie, praying he looked calmer than he felt.

Eddie tapped his fingers against his denim-clad thigh, his cyan eyes narrowed and lips tightly pursed. "Don't do this, Vico—Vicenzo."

He clenched his jaw, willing his fucking heart to chill out. "Told you, I don't know what the fuck you're—"

Eddie crossed the room in four strides until they were chest to chest. Vicenzo's heart hammered when Eddie took his chin between his fingers and made him meet his gaze. "Don't pretend for a second you don't see what's been happenin' here." He motioned between them. Yet for all Eddie's confidence, his voice wavered, and Vicenzo could hear the way his heart raced with fear and excitement.

He made himself look anywhere but at Eddie, at his lips, into his piercing blue-green eyes.

"Don't tell me you don't feel this. Because I won't buy it, not for one second. Somethin' is different between us. I know you feel it, too." Goddess, the scent of his arousal made Vicenzo swell in the confines of his jeans.

He couldn't speak. He wanted to take all the fractured pieces of his heart and hide them away from Eddie Turner but he couldn't. It was too much, this thing between them. Too confusing. Too raw. Too big to put into words.

"You kept it," Vicenzo blurted out. "Why'd you keep it?"

Eddie's eyelashes fluttered, his eyes heavy-lidded. He hummed a question as if he was too turned on to even ask what Vicenzo meant.

"The drawing. Why'd you keep it?"

Eddie wet his lips, his throat rippling as he swallowed. "It kept me human."

Barking out a laugh, Vicenzo said, "Yeah when Elijah was torturing you. You didn't need it after you became a hunter. So, why'd you hang on to it?"

Eddie slumped over with a sigh that puffed hot against Vicenzo's damp skin. "Because."

Vicenzo waited, his patience thinning. "Because..."

For a moment Eddie tightened his lips. "Because I care about you. And our promise meant somethin' to me. Still does, I suppose."

Vicenzo suddenly couldn't breathe. His heart felt like it was cracking in two.

A few days ago, he'd almost gone feral. He had really, truly thought he would lose himself to the beast that time. Instead, Eddie had brought him back from the brink with nothing but a drawing, an old yellowed drawing and not even a very good one. Vicenzo hadn't been much of an artist when he was a kid but he'd improved as he'd gotten older. He'd thought for a time he might go to art school before it'd become apparent Kassandra wasn't interested in being the sheriff, so the duty had fallen to him.

But it was an important drawing nonetheless. And Eddie knew that.

Eddie had kept it.

He'd *kept* it.

After so much time and so much pain, after everything they'd lost and everything that had driven them apart, Eddie had kept the promise they'd made of forever. A promise that spanned years, back to when Vicenzo had been too young to even grasp what forever meant. Before he'd understood that nothing was forever.

Even after they'd stood in the rain, broken and warped by grief and change. Even after Eddie had screamed that he didn't want him, that everything they'd had was a lie. Eddie had kept it.

And somehow, for reasons he didn't know, or maybe didn't want to know, that realization had been enough to bring Vicenzo back from the brink.

"'Cause..." Eddie mumbled, his fingernail scratching at a spot on the brick wall next to Vicenzo's head. "'Cause it kept me sane when I wanted to break. Reminded me I was human? I don't know what you want me to say."

"Because you still... feel something for me."

Eddie made a strange hitching sound in his chest, his eyes widening. Nodding, he blinked fast, his eyes averted. "Yeah. Yeah, of course. That really surprises you?"

It did, Vicenzo realized as his throat ached and grew painfully tight, and that sparked a hope in him that maybe, just maybe, not everything had burned in the fire. Maybe after all this time, they could still have something. Nothing like what they'd had before, but *something*.

"I know," Eddie murmured, his voice low, the vibrations of it thrumming in Vicenzo's chest. "That doesn't mean much, or make a difference. Not now."

But it did. It meant everything. Vicenzo just didn't know how to say it.

"I've messed up so much, Vico. We can't have what we once did. I know that. I *know*. But we can have something else. Or we can try to. We can..."

"What are you saying?" Vicenzo's throat was dry, his heart hammering.

Eddie swallowed, his throat bobbing. His hand shifted, his fingers brushing up and down Vicenzo's neck. The sensation made goose bumps break out across Vicenzo's skin. He wanted more, and he didn't want Eddie to be shy. "I'm not gonna be picky, Vico. I lost the right to ask anything of you a long time ago. I'll have you however I can. In whatever way you'll have me."

Vicenzo breathed in, chasing the scent of Eddie that filled the room around him, breathing him deep into his lungs. It burned, the smell of him, like nicotine. He craved more and before he knew it, he'd leaned in close. Dragging his nose up the side of Eddie's neck, he took in a lungful of his smell, listening to the *thump, thump, thump* of the pulse point in his neck. He opened his mouth, his fangs rasping over the fluttering of Eddie's pulse.

Eddie let in a shuddery breath, and it hitched awkwardly in his throat. He splayed his fingers over the back of Vicenzo's neck, his fingertips dimpling the skin. The musky aroma of his arousal made the blood simmer in Vicenzo's veins.

A growl rumbled in his throat. Beneath his skin, the wolf thrummed, sharpening Vicenzo's fangs to points. He parted his lips around Eddie's neck, mouthing at his skin, biting down ever so slightly on his throat. Goddess, his wolf still hungered for Eddie. Wanted to bite him, fuck him, claim him. Even if he couldn't sense Eddie's bond anymore, that didn't change who Eddie was to him. Who he'd always been to Vicenzo and his wolf.

He wanted his teeth in Eddie's throat, to taste his blood. He wanted to devour Eddie's lips until they were red and sore. Eddie flat on his back, writhing as he fucked into him. Those calloused hands on his body, around his neck, his nails scraping over his scalp. He shivered when he looked Eddie in the eye. "This isn't for forever. Forever isn't for us."

"No," Eddie said, and Vicenzo tried to ignore the little break in his voice.

"So then... then what is it? This thing? Us?"

Eddie's chest shuddered against Vicenzo's. "I don't—"

Vicenzo cleared his throat and realized he didn't know what else to say either. He didn't know. Once he had but now he wasn't so sure. It wasn't what they'd once shared, a bright golden bond full of innocence. It was something else. But it wasn't nothing. It was a blank slate. A new beginning.

For a moment, neither moved. They were close, their noses brushing, sharing the same air. Teetering on the precipice over a deep sea, on the edge of being something more for the first time in so long. All Vicenzo had to do was take the plunge. At some point, Eddie's hands had fallen to Vicenzo's shoulders and were squeezing so tight, Vicenzo thought they'd leave marks. He hoped they did. Vicenzo tried to lean in, but Eddie's grip was too tight.

"Get your hands off me."

Eddie's eyes went wide, and a wounded sound escaped him. Face crumbling, he dropped his hands to his sides. "Vico—"

Before Eddie could take a single step back, Vicenzo captured his face between his hands. A choked gasp escaped Eddie, and Vicenzo captured the sound as he lunged in, falling into a kiss he never wanted to end. For a moment, Eddie was like granite in his arms.

Then Eddie came alive, his arms flying around Vicenzo's shoulders, hauling him into the warmth and strength of his firm body.

Vicenzo plunged from the precipice, and Eddie was there, drowning with him.

CHAPTER 17

PUT YOUR TEETH IN ME

EDDIE'S HAND TREMBLED AS he slid his fingers up the smooth leather of Vicenzo's jacket.

Lamplight bathed Vicenzo's olive skin in golden hues, fingers curled in the plush white comforter, his lips parted as he gazed at Eddie. The sight of him filled Eddie with a rush of giddy desire and made him want to turn and run all at once.

Of all the ways he'd imagined this happening, and oh, had he imagined it, night after night, sometimes several times a night, this was different. There'd been days when Vicenzo had gotten him so rattled, he'd wanted to slam him up against the nearest surface and fuck his brains out. There'd been nights when he woke, breathless and frightened, and craved the comfort of someone who would understand without him having to say a word. When he'd seen Vicenzo cry in the Alaskan storm, all he'd wanted was to kiss him and hold him tight and promise him everything would be okay.

They were past that, all of it. Vicenzo was no longer the boy who'd promised Eddie forever. As for himself, Eddie couldn't identify with the boy who would have said yes with tears in his eyes. Loss, heartache, and pain had stamped the tender feelings out of them both.

What they did in this room tonight was all they could ever have. Even if he burned for more, for the love they'd once had, Eddie knew he had no right to ask for it. He'd hurt Vicenzo enough. If Vicenzo only wanted this to be a one-time thing, then that's what it would have to be.

"Change your mind?" Vicenzo arched a brow.

Eddie smiled, a burst of breathy laughter escaping him. "Hell no. You?"

"Same. Just asked. Your heart's racing," Vicenzo said unhelpfully. His breath warmed Eddie's neck as he propped his chin on Eddie's shoulder.

"Really? I didn't notice." Eddie's fingers twitched, and he felt blindly until he touched Vicenzo's thigh. His leg was warm, the denim skintight.

Vicenzo's breath stuttered against his neck and then he dipped his head, tugging down the collar of Eddie's shirt to plant a kiss on his collarbone. Eddie's blood burned, currents of electricity shooting down his spine.

"Do you not wanna do this?" Vicenzo asked, his voice rumbling against Eddie's shoulder.

Eddie looked down at their feet resting on the gray carpet, then kicked off his boots, making them roll into the wall. "It's been a while," Eddie admitted. He'd caved to peer pressure from the hunters and hooked up with guys sometimes. He didn't remember any of those drunken nights, only the mornings after waking up in a cold bed, feeling used and empty.

Vicenzo's gaze prickled against his skin. "I'll get you up to speed."

Something tightened in Eddie's chest. "Not out of practice like me?"

A smirk crept over Vicenzo's face. "Jealous?"

Face hot, Eddie looked away, squeezing his hands together. It was irrational. After all, it had been years. Of course Vicenzo had been with other people, but Eddie couldn't kill the voice inside him that wished their first time had been between the two of them.

Vicenzo rolled over to the other side of the bed and opened the minifridge.

"That's expensive," Eddie said, admiring the way Vicenzo's jeans hugged his ass.

"We'll fill it up with water, put it back, and no one'll care." Vicenzo opened up one of the tiny bottles of vodka and tossed an unopened one to Eddie. "Cheers."

Eddie took a gulp of the clear liquid. The liquor burned, tingling down his arms and pooling hot in his belly. The one good thing about being more in touch with his human side? He got a great buzz from alcohol.

Vicenzo coughed, his eyes bulging. "Shit."

Eddie laughed. "Wimp."

Vicenzo cracked a grin, his teeth sharp. "Says the guy who'll be on his ass once he finishes that tiny bottle."

Taking another drink, Eddie looked away, his face burning hot, and not from the alcohol. Vicenzo hardly ever smiled, but when he did... it was like sunshine.

"You were part of a pack," Eddie said, swallowing more vodka. "Before we met again. There wasn't anyone special among those wolves?"

Vicenzo snorted as if the idea were insane. He dropped his elbows over his knees, rolling the empty bottle around in his hand. "No," he answered. "Maybe sometimes, you know? If I was lonely, if I just needed a reminder I was alive or capable of feeling more than anger and numbness. But no. Nothing that stuck."

Eddie couldn't breathe around the ache in his chest because he understood. He understood so much what it felt like to be numb, to be so angry and hopeless he didn't know what to do, how to channel it.

Inching his foot closer to Vicenzo's, he laid the sole of his foot over the top of Vicenzo's, which made him laugh softly. It was stupid, but Eddie didn't know how else to touch him, only that he needed to. He hated that Vicenzo felt that way. It wasn't a feeling he'd wish on anyone. But tonight would be different. He wouldn't let Vicenzo feel numb or lonely. And that was what gave him the courage to look Vicenzo in the eye. His heart tumbled over when he realized how close they were, sharing the same air, their noses almost touching.

Eddie wet his lips, realizing they were dry. The vodka on Vicenzo's breath burned his nose but in a good way. Vicenzo's mouth trembled as his lips parted, soft and inviting, a contradiction to his sharp nose and angular jaw.

"Goddess, I want you," Eddie whispered.

Vicenzo grabbed hold of Eddie's face and pulled him close, then gasped just before their lips collided, like a man taking a gulp of air before he went underwater. Their noses bumped, and Vicenzo kissed him hard enough to push his lips back against his teeth. Eddie didn't respond, not at first. He didn't quite believe this was actually happening, that after so much time and loss, they'd actually found their way back to each other, if only for a night.

But his disbelief didn't last long. Vicenzo's hands shook as their grip on his face softened, his fingertips brushing down Eddie's cheek to his jaw. As Vicenzo tried to pull away, his lips trembled, probably from worry at Eddie's stillness. Eddie didn't let him, though. He clasped the back of Vicenzo's head, his fingers rasping through the short hair. Parting his lips against Vicenzo's, he curled his fingers in the front of his shirt to keep him close.

Their teeth bumped together and Eddie was lightheaded as Vicenzo sucked his lower lip into his mouth. Sharp fangs dimpled Eddie's lip and when Vicenzo sucked on his tongue, he felt the scrape of his canine. It shouldn't have turned him on as much as it did, but his cock was straining against the front of his pants.

Vicenzo growled, his body vibrating with it. Their lips parted with a wet smack, leaving Vicenzo's lips puffy and slick with spit. Looking at them, Eddie nearly groaned just imagining how flushed they'd be around his dick. Eddie sucked in a gasp as Vicenzo's mouth scorched his skin, his hot tongue lapping at the shell of his ear, lips nibbling at his earlobe. Down they went, blazing a trail of hot, open-mouthed kisses against his skin. Vicenzo suckled on his neck, and the slightest press of his fangs left him breathless. Skirting around the silver collar, Vicenzo tugged down his shirt to suck on his collarbone, leaving Eddie's skin hot and wet.

"That's gonna leave a mark, you asshole," Eddie said but he grabbed hold of Vicenzo's head and pressed his mouth harder into his skin.

"Good," Vicenzo panted, sounding more wolf than man. He bit without warning, making Eddie bite down on his lip to stifle himself. "Want everyone to know that I fucked you. That you took my dick." He smoothed over the bruise with his tongue, lapping at the pinpricks of blood he'd left, then rubbed the bridge of his nose over Eddie's neck. "You're gonna smell like me. You're gonna have my marks all over your body," he said, voice raspy with desire.

Damn werewolves and their scent-marking. Damn Vicenzo for being a possessive bastard. And damn Eddie for being so turned on by it all he could scarcely breathe.

Eddie pushed his chest into Vicenzo's, urging him down onto the plush blankets. Vicenzo's legs shifted and his boots clumped onto the carpet. Crawling back to the head of the bed, Vicenzo propped himself against the leather headboard. Eddie knelt over him, his ass pressing into Vicenzo's groin as he straddled him, and he pushed his ass down into the tent in Vicenzo's jeans. Vicenzo bared his teeth, his lip curling over a sharp canine.

Claws bit into the fabric of Eddie's jeans as Vicenzo grasped his hips, then thrust up against him, groaning lowly as he ground his dick into Eddie's ass. Vicenzo's eyes were glowing in the dim lighting. The wolf was close, but Vicenzo was in control. This was good for him. Regardless of what they meant to each other, having a connection like this to his packmate was strengthening the bond between them.

Vicenzo's tanned fingers disappeared beneath the hem of Eddie's shirt, and icy dread doused Eddie's arousal. He seized Vicenzo's wrist. "Leave my shirt on."

Vicenzo's eyes widened but he gave a curt nod and didn't ask, so Eddie relaxed, releasing his grip on Vicenzo's wrist.

Eyes never leaving him, Vicenzo pulled his own shirt over his head, and Eddie was overwhelmed by him lying there beneath him. While Eddie was lean and slender, Vico was bulky with muscle, tanned skin smooth and furry with dark hair on his chest that trailed below the low rise of his jeans where a sliver of his briefs peeked over the waistline.

Eddie put his hands on him, curling his fingers in the hair on his pecs. Vicenzo's chest swelled against him. He was smug, posturing, because he knew Eddie thought he was the sexiest thing he'd ever seen. Eddie squeezed the mounds of his pectorals and pinched the dusky nipples between his fingers until they were stiff. As Eddie neared the waistline of his jeans, Vicenzo's chest rose and fell faster and Eddie's own heart rate quickened.

"Hurry." Vicenzo grunted, thrusting his hips.

Eddie reached beneath him and gave Vicenzo's ass a slap. "Shut up and let me savor this."

Vicenzo rolled his head with a low growl and didn't argue.

Kneeling back over Vicenzo's knees to give himself room to reach down, Eddie unfastened his jeans. When Vicenzo raised his ass off the bed, Eddie yanked his jeans down to his knees, and Vicenzo kicked them the rest of the way off. Eddie hooked a finger in the elastic of his briefs, tugging them down, and Vicenzo's cock sprang free, slapping heavily against his belly. Vicenzo's eyes narrowed and that was all the warning Eddie got before Vicenzo's legs snapped around his waist.

The bedroom spun as Eddie wound up on his back with Vicenzo straddling his chest, his balls heavy against him. Eddie swallowed, overwhelmed by Vicenzo as he grasped his cock and smacked it against Eddie's cheek. "Suck," he ordered.

Eddie shot him a warning look. Just because he was nearly human didn't mean he'd let a werewolf dominate him. Fuck power dynamics. Still, for now he'd let Vicenzo think he was in control. He parted his lips and Vicenzo fed him his cock, the earthy taste of him filling his mouth. He was thick and heavy on his tongue and Eddie moaned, unable to help it.

"Yeah," Vicenzo said with a groan, his eyes dark. "Yeah, you fucking love that dick, don't you?"

Whatever pride Eddie had was taking a back seat to the sheer pleasure of swallowing down Vicenzo's cock. He grabbed Vicenzo's ass in both fists and squeezed hard enough to bruise as he drowned in Vicenzo's taste and scent.

Eddie peered up from under his eyelashes as he worked Vicenzo, his nose pressing into the curls of his hair before pulling back and sucking the tip, his cheeks hollowing. Vicenzo's eyes were heavy-lidded as he held Eddie's gaze, his fingers squeezing in Eddie's hair and his claws pricking his scalp.

"Fuck. You look good sucking my dick," Vicenzo said, voice low and raspy.

A tingle of pleasure went down Eddie's spine, knowing he'd pleased Vicenzo. He tongued the vein that ran underneath Vicenzo's cock, then wrapped his fingers around what he couldn't take into his mouth and pumped his fingers in tight strokes.

Vicenzo groaned deep in his chest, exposing his throat as his head rolled back against his shoulders. Tugging on Eddie's hair, he urged him up and down, urged him faster. Eddie nearly choked on his dick a few times, slapping Vicenzo's ass to tell him to ease up, damn it. Vicenzo groaned when Eddie's palm struck his buttock. He liked it, the pain.

"Fucking hell," Vicenzo rasped, his eyes closed in bliss. "You're so good, Ed. So. Fucking. Good."

It wasn't enough. Eddie wanted to show Vicenzo the time of his life. He wanted to watch him crumble, wanted him to lose that stoic, hard-assed side and completely let go.

Vicenzo yelped in shock as Eddie suddenly flipped them both back over. He sank on top of Vicenzo, his face nestled against his abdomen. Eyes wide, Vicenzo propped himself on his elbows. He didn't struggle, his eyes fixated on Eddie. Eddie followed the musky scent of his sex, curling his fingers over Vicenzo's cock. He licked in a long stroke from the base to the tip, sucking his cockhead into his mouth. Vicenzo's hips lurched beneath him but before he could thrust into his mouth, Eddie pulled off with a wet smack and Vicenzo's cock bumped into his chin.

"Eddie," he growled, and it was a warning.

Eddie grinned at him, enjoying the lust that darkened Vicenzo's eyes, the curl of his lip that showed off his fangs. His face disappeared from Eddie's view as Eddie moved farther down, licking the soft skin of his perineum, then plunging his tongue into Vicenzo's hole.

A groan was pulled from Vicenzo's lips and he grabbed hold of Eddie's hair, urging him on. In response, Eddie parted his lips around Vicenzo's balls, swirling his tongue in a tight circle and sucking a heavy testicle into his mouth. Eddie grunted as Vicenzo's claws scratched against his scalp.

"Fuckin' hell, Eddie. Fuck. Yes!"

Relishing the praise, Eddie increased his efforts, moving lower again and swirling his tongue against Vicenzo's asshole, then pressing in.

"Fuck, Eddie. I need to fuck you. Now. Or you need to fuck me. I don't even care."

When Eddie looked up, Vicenzo was flushed and panting, biting down on his lower lip, his hands clenching the sheets. Eddie couldn't hold back, not anymore. He yanked down the zipper of his jeans, grunting his relief as his cock was freed from the restraints of his underwear. Leaving only briefly to grab lube from his suitcase, Eddie straddled Vico again and thrust the tube at Vicenzo. "Sit up. Put your fingers in me."

Vicenzo's eyes were blown wide as he scrambled to sit up, his face level with Eddie's chest. Eddie's knees trembled in anticipation, his ass hovering over Vicenzo's thighs, their dicks bumping together as their bodies shifted.

Eddie's breath hitched as the cap popped open and Vicenzo slicked his fingers, reaching behind Eddie. As a finger pressed against his hole, Eddie exhaled, then lowered his hips, his eyes rolling back as he sank down on it. Vicenzo growled, curling his finger, which sent a jolt of pleasure up Eddie's spine.

"Goddess, Ed. You're so tight."

"Hurry," Eddie said.

Nipping his collarbone in answer, Vicenzo added a second finger. Eddie bit his lower lip, dizzy from knowing Vicenzo was inside him. Vicenzo opened him up, leaving him slick and wet as he prepared him.

"Fuckin' hurry, Vico."

Vicenzo's mouth quirked against his skin as he worked his fingers in and out, curling them and leaving Eddie breathless and shuddery.

At his wit's end, Eddie shoved Vicenzo in the chest. The comforter puffed up around Vicenzo as he landed, leaning back against the headboard. Eddie felt beneath him for Vicenzo's cock, positioning his ass above his dick. He lowered himself down, gritting his teeth as Vicenzo's cock filled him inch by inch.

When Vicenzo raised his hips, Eddie pulled off and Vicenzo snarled his impatience.

"Easy big guy," Eddie panted. "Be fuckin' patient. Don't make me rush this."

"Fuck, Ed. Just ride my dick already!"

When Eddie dropped his hips without warning, Vicenzo cried out, his claws pricking Eddie's hips. Curling his fingers against Vicenzo's chest, Eddie lowered himself onto him. It burned and felt uncomfortable, but he breathed through it. He wasn't stopping. He needed this too much.

The mattress squeaked and bounced as Eddie bore down on Vicenzo until his ass was flush with Vicenzo's pelvis. Their eyes met, and Vicenzo's lidded eyes were the blue of the deepest ocean as he gazed up at Eddie in awe, his lips swollen and parted.

Lunging, Eddie crushed their mouths together, moaning as he began to ride Vico's dick in earnest. Vicenzo arched up to meet him, his hands fumbling around Eddie's neck. Their lips parted around a groan Eddie couldn't stifle, Vicenzo's deep thrusts leaving him speechless.

It wasn't gentle, this rhythm they settled into. Vicenzo's feet were flat against the bed as he fucked up into Eddie, their voices harmonizing as Eddie slammed down on him, always meeting him halfway. It wasn't lovemaking, and it wasn't forever—forever wasn't for them.

But they were together, after everything. United in the only way they could be after so much time and change, and that was all that mattered, Eddie told himself, and tried to ignore the way his chest tightened as

Vicenzo cried out his name like a prayer. "Eddie," he gasped. "Yes! Oh fuck. Yes. Fucking perfect. You're so fucking perfect."

Eddie tried to pretend he wasn't whispering Vicenzo's name between breathless kisses.

Tried to tell himself it didn't mean a thing when he grasped Vicenzo's hand and held on for dear life as he moved up and down, faster and harder.

That it didn't feel right, so fucking right when Vicenzo came inside him. That his heart didn't break at the sight of Vicenzo flushed and vulnerable and desperate beneath him.

That he didn't beg for Vicenzo to put his teeth in him. That he didn't need to be owned by him. But he did. He did. He needed to belong to Vicenzo Salvatore. He needed it so much, he *needed*—

"Bite me, baby. Please. Put your teeth in me."

Vicenzo's eyes glowed, fangs sharp as he lunged without question.

Eddie screamed when Vicenzo bit him, his fangs penetrating his shoulder. It wasn't a mating bite. Eddie's collar covered his neck, and Vicenzo had to keep away from it so he didn't get burned. Besides, it wasn't a full moon. They weren't mates, and maybe they never would be. But for right now it was everything Eddie needed.

He collapsed onto Vicenzo's chest, which was wet with sweat and slick with Eddie's cum that had been smeared between their bodies. They gasped like they were dying, a pile of slack limbs all tangled up together.

Eddie panted into the crook of Vicenzo's neck, shivering as Vicenzo dragged his tongue over the bite on his shoulder. Lazy hands smoothed down his back, grabbing his ass and squeezing.

They lay there for a long time. Eddie closed his eyes, exhausted and sated and still stuffed full of Vicenzo's cock. He realized they hadn't thought to use a condom but luckily it wasn't a big deal since Vicenzo was a werewolf and immune to STDs. In any case, Eddie was glad for it. He loved the way Vicenzo's spunk dripped out of him.

Vicenzo's throat bobbed when he swallowed, and Eddie's head moved up and down as Vicenzo's chest rose and fell with his breathing. Eddie realized he was still holding Vicenzo's hand, their fingers tangled together and their palms slick with sweat. Vicenzo looked at their hands, then back at Eddie. Swallowing again, Vicenzo wet his lips.

They weren't mates. They weren't lovers. Soon the sun would rise, and this moment would be gone. Unless… Vico wanted more? He longed to ask, but what if it was too soon? The last thing he wanted was to scare Vicenzo off by asking for a relationship. Eddie needed to be grateful and take whatever Vicenzo was willing to offer.

Eddie opened his hand and gently pulled it from Vicenzo's grasp, his fingers brushing over Vicenzo's palm. It felt monumental, and Eddie's chest was heavy as he rolled off Vicenzo onto his side. Vicenzo hadn't knotted him. They weren't tied, weren't bound to each other. Maybe once they might have been.

Eddie didn't know what to say, if he should say anything at all, if words were even meant for them.

Having regained some feeling in his legs, Eddie heaved himself out of bed, Vicenzo's gaze heavy against his back. He went to the bathroom and fetched a washcloth, wetting it under the sink. He wrung it out until it was damp and returned to the bed where Vicenzo lay. The sight of Vicenzo sprawled out among the white sheets, his cock limp between his thighs and Eddie's spunk matting his chest hair, made Eddie hunger for him again. Sitting beside him, Eddie ran the wet cloth over his chest.

"The pack's gonna give us shit," Vicenzo said.

Eddie's mouth quirked, glad they were speaking. The rag might wipe away the evidence, but Vicenzo would smell like Eddie for hours.

"Fuck 'em."

Vicenzo chuckled breathlessly.

Exhaustion compelled Eddie to lie down and rest his head, but he didn't want to leave this moment behind them.

"Do you wanna stay?" Vicenzo asked.

Eddie smiled. Yes. Yes. Yes. "Goodnight, Vico." He left Vicenzo's bed and went to his own, dumping the damp towel in the bathroom on his way there. He curled up naked beneath the sheets, his fingers fumbling for the light switch on the lamp between their beds. Closing his eyes, he exhaled, fighting down the urge to look at Vicenzo and see if he was looking back, fearing he'd break and go to him.

Eddie turned off the light and darkness covered the room.

EDDIE WOKE IN THE dark sometime later but didn't know why. His muscles were beginning to ache and the bite on his shoulder throbbed.

In the stillness of the room, someone whimpered. Eddie held his breath, thinking he'd misheard until a shuddery breath made his heart race. He fumbled for his phone in the dark and shone the light around the room. In the other bed, Vicenzo stirred restlessly under his blankets. "Vico?" Eddie whispered, uncertainty thickening his throat. "You okay?"

Vicenzo gasped, kicking beneath the sheets.

Eddie swung his legs out of bed, his feet whispering over the carpet as he stopped by Vicenzo's bedside.

He was deeply asleep, but it wasn't a kind sleep. He tossed and turned, his brows knit tight, his lips trembling. He whispered, "No, no," and "Don't, please," and "Eddie. Eddie. Eddie…"

Eddie sighed, his chest tight and painful, then eased himself onto the mattress beside Vicenzo. He reached down, holding his breath, and touched Vicenzo's arm. Vicenzo jumped in his sleep but his whimpers quieted as Eddie rubbed his shoulder, his fingers running gently over his prickly buzz cut.

"Vico," he whispered, at a loss, then leaned close to whisper in his ear. "You're not alone. You hear me? I'm here. I'm here and I'm never going anywhere again. I'm never pushing you away from me." He just wished Vicenzo could understand that. Taking Vicenzo's hand, he squeezed gently, then lay down beside him, Vicenzo's hand in his. "I promise you,"

Eddie whispered. "I will choose you this time. However you'll have me. As a friend. As more. I will always choose you."

Vicenzo's fingers twitched around his hand. His frowning mouth tugged into a smile, and it broke Eddie's heart in two.

And Eddie knew then and there he would die before he ever let anyone hurt Vicenzo Salvatore again.

CHAPTER 18

FAIS DO-DO

VICENZO WOKE UP TO the smell of peanut butter and jelly. Rubbing the crust from his eyes, he sat up. The bedroom was empty but he heard the shower running from behind the bathroom door. The sun was shining through the slit in the curtains. Far below, a jazz band played as if the city hadn't slept at all after he'd closed his eyes.

Before he could flop back down on the bed, he smelled peanut butter again. He leaned over the side of the bed and opened the minifridge. Among tiny liquor bottles and snacks that were deceptively pricey, he noticed a sandwich cut into halves. There was a sticky note on the fridge.

There's a PB and J for when you wake. Apparently, they serve those at midnight here.

– Eddie

(ps I don't know what jelly you like. I hope strawberry is ok.)

Vicenzo scoffed but there was a warmth in his chest.

His stomach growled, so he tugged the cold plate of PB and J from the fridge and set it in his lap. He took a bite of the soft white bread, and it stuck to the roof of his mouth. It was cold and delicious, the peanut butter creamy and sticky, the strawberry flavor taking him back to days spent in his mother's garden, picking ripe strawberries and eating them straight from the vine.

"Hey, Vico?" Eddie's voice was muffled from behind the door. "I think I left my clothes out there."

Vicenzo sighed. He wasn't getting up.

"You awake?"

He crammed his mouth full of the sandwich to keep from answering.

There was a sigh from behind the door. "Damn it."

And Eddie walked out in nothing but a towel.

Vicenzo choked.

"You okay?" Eddie asked, quirking a blond brow. His hair was slicked back, his beard glistening with droplets from the shower. Droplets that ran down his tanned skin, running in little rivulets over the mounds of his pecs, trickling over hard abs, glittering in the line of fine blond hair that trailed from his navel and disappeared under the towel. The towel which Vicenzo suddenly wished wasn't there at all. Goddess, he wanted Eddie all over again.

Hacking and coughing, he expelled a chunk of unchewed sandwich, his eyes tearing up.

"Oh, you found the sandwich I left for you!" Eddie said, sounding delighted, as if Vicenzo hadn't almost choked to death on it.

"Duh," Vicenzo said, voice hoarse. He reached for the bottle of water in his suitcase.

"Funny, huh?" said Eddie, still half-naked. "Near midnight, the hotel serves peanut butter and jelly. I couldn't sleep. Then Ryan texted me and told me they had sandwiches."

"You couldn't sleep? Even after what we did?" Vicenzo clicked his tongue. "Must be losing my touch."

Eddie's mouth curled into a smile. "No, definitely not."

Face burning, Vicenzo took a deep drink of room-temperature water. He'd slept but barely. He probably would have slept better with Eddie in his bed, arms around him, but he understood why Eddie had declined. After what they'd done, sharing a bed and waking up together would seem too intimate. For all he knew, Eddie hadn't wanted any of that. Last night had been incredible, apart from nightmares that had felt more like distressing memories about the last time he and Eddie had been in New Orleans. But he wondered what last night had meant to Eddie.

Had it been just a quick fuck? To Vicenzo, it had been much more than that, and he'd love to do it again. Was there any point in feeling that way, though? What if Eddie didn't want more? Their history was so complex, Vicenzo wouldn't blame him, but it would hurt like hell. The last thing he wanted was to get his heart broken again.

Just take it easy. Take things slow. Don't fuck this up.

"Bein' back here," Eddie said suddenly, breaking the quiet. "It's fuckin' with my head."

"Same," Vicenzo rumbled, tossing the water bottle back in his suitcase.

Eddie ran a hand through wet strands of golden hair.

"But it'll be over soon," Vicenzo said. "We're ending this, Ed."

Eddie's eyes were bright and focused, his lips tight as he nodded. "Yeah. We are."

He strode into the sunlight pooling across the carpet. Vicenzo's heart stuttered, and he was grateful Eddie wasn't connected to his wolf anymore so he couldn't hear it. "What's that?" The sunlight glimmered on Eddie's body, making the fine golden hairs thick on his chest shine—revealing pale scars Vicenzo had never seen before.

Eddie couldn't shift, which meant that since joining the agency, he'd never had a reason to show any skin around the pack, so Vicenzo had never seen him without his shirt on.

"Nothin'." The word was barely out of Eddie's mouth before Vicenzo's feet touched the floor.

Before he knew it, he stood within touching distance before Eddie. His wolf's acute nose picked up the smell of coconut shampoo, some fruity body wash, and the smell of ash. Always ash. Mouth drying, Vicenzo counted the scars twisting over Eddie's bare chest, twining up his arms in jagged lines, carving over his shoulders. There were too many of them, and they'd never healed. Now he understood why Eddie had wanted to keep his shirt on last night.

"Who?" Vicenzo struggled to find the words. His throat was tight, his fingers curling at his sides. "Who did this to you?" He had an idea, but he wanted specifics. If it had been one hunter or many of them. "Give me a fucking name, Ed."

Eddie's throat bobbed as he swallowed, his eyes fixated on the carpet. "Elijah," he said, his voice rusty.

Anguish tightened Vicenzo's chest. He didn't want to imagine the suffering Eddie must have endured at the hands of his uncle. Now there was no imagining needed because the proof of his torment was carved all over his body.

There was a ringing in his ears and his hand trembled as he splayed his fingers over warm, damp skin, rubbing his thumb over rough scar tissue as if he thought he could wipe it all away. But he couldn't.

It shouldn't have surprised him. He knew the cruelty of hunters and the hatred they held toward wolves. He knew, had always known, that whatever had happened after Eddie had been taken must have been truly terrible to have broken him into submission.

But he couldn't breathe. There were so many scars. Too many, covering every inch of skin below his collar. He'd give anything to have been able to protect Eddie from this.

"Vico."

"Shut up." Vicenzo's voice broke, his claws leaving dimples on Eddie's chest.

"It's okay."

"No, it isn't!" The roar tore from his throat and left his eyes burning. "No, it's not fucking okay, Ed. It isn't!"

Every breath carved like a knife through his lungs. His fangs punctured his lower lip and he wanted to bite, rip, and tear apart the hunters who'd touched Eddie.

Eddie opened his mouth, but Vicenzo turned away, panting through a mouthful of fangs. His eyes felt damp and hot. His throat ached and there was a burning in his nose. His claws cut into his palms when he curled his hands into fists. "I looked for you. I tried to find you."

"I know." Eddie's voice was eerily calm.

"I didn't... I didn't understand. I knew it was bad, whatever they did to you. I..."

"I know, Vico. I'm not angry, I—"

"Stop saying that!" It was a plea, squeezed out through a throat thick with grief and guilt. "Why did I leave you with them? Why didn't I fight harder? I should have. I—"

"Because I didn't let you. 'Cause I knew if you stayed, he'd make me watch as he broke you. He'd have made me kill you." Eddie's voice was hoarse, his eyes full of despair. "I couldn't. I just... I couldn't. Even if you hated me, even if I hurt you, it was nothin' compared to what Elijah would have done to you if you stayed." Eddie sucked in a breath.

Vicenzo ached, so badly he thought he'd shatter into pieces. "I never should have left."

Eddie's feet brushed over the carpet. He was close, his body heat wafting against Vicenzo's bare skin. He didn't come any closer, but Vicenzo wished he would.

"Will you leave again?" Eddie asked softly.

Vicenzo turned back to face him. His eyes were still damp but he didn't care if Eddie noticed. Reaching out, he cupped Eddie's cheek, shivering as golden stubble rasped beneath his thumb. Emotion brightened Eddie's eyes, chest hitching as he gasped. "No," he said. "And Elijah won't touch you. Not again. I'll kill him if he so much as looks at you."

Eddie's mouth curled as if Vicenzo were funny. His lips were still damp from the shower, plump and so soft-looking. A quiet exhale fell from Eddie's lips, which were parted in invitation, and his wide blue eyes strayed from Vicenzo's. Eddie was leaning toward him and Vicenzo was finding it hard not to lean into the warmth of his body. Then those blue eyes glanced at Vicenzo's mouth, and something like a bomb went off in his stomach.

Even after the shower, Eddie still smelled like him. Like what they'd done, but faintly. Last night was fading fast, and Vicenzo didn't want to let it go.

"I mean it," Vicenzo said, and oh, he did. There'd been a time when he'd hated Eddie, when he'd wanted nothing more than to hunt him down and hurt him the way he'd hurt Vicenzo. Now he thought that if anyone harmed Eddie, he'd kill them himself. If he saw Elijah, if the hunter raised a hand against Eddie, Vicenzo would spill his blood.

Things hadn't been simple between them in a long time but no one would ever hurt Eddie Turner again.

Sunlight glinted off Eddie's silver collar. The damn thing hadn't come off in years. Removing it would be easy enough even without the key, but he had a feeling Eddie kept it on by choice. Maybe to punish himself.

How could he breathe with the constant reminder of the monster who'd put it around his neck? He hated the damn thing with a sudden savagery. Jaw tight with anger, he touched the silver, wincing at the burn.

"Vico," Eddie began, alarmed.

Vicenzo looked him in the eyes. "After I've torn out your uncle's throat, I'll rip the key from his corpse."

Tugging his fingers away as the burn became too much to bear, he grabbed the nape of Eddie's neck and hauled him in close. Eddie grunted when their lips collided, and then his warm, damp hands clasped Vicenzo's forearms and pulled him even nearer.

Vicenzo poured everything he had into the kiss, everything he was too broken to say aloud. His heartache and fury. His desire to protect Eddie from whatever harm awaited them out in the bayou. Clutching Eddie close, he thrust his fingers into his soft blond hair. Their chests touched, Eddie's frantic heartbeat musical in his ears. Their lips tingled and Vicenzo pulled back, reeling and breathless. He wanted to linger in Eddie's soft cyan gaze, lean back in and kiss him. Instead, he forced himself to bring his hands to his sides and step away from Eddie's warmth. He just hoped Eddie understood what he was too cowardly to say.

Offering what he hoped was a confident smile, Vicenzo said, "Let me shower. Then you and I are gonna kill us some Beasts."

THOUGH THE PACK WERE clearly aware that Eddie and Vicenzo smelled like a brothel, one fiery glare from Vicenzo immediately silenced Ryan's smart-alecky remarks. Breakfast passed in pleasant, if awkward, silence.

After breakfast, Ben led the way to the docks where they boarded a boat that would take them out into the bayou. The boat's horn blared as it headed east. Vicenzo leaned on the railing and watched the city disappear behind them as they headed into the wetlands.

Ben addressed the pack briefly, saying, "Everyone, be on your best behavior. Phillipe and I have worked together before. He's a good guy, but he's very territorial and protective of his pack. Especially now."

Vicenzo said, "So no peeing on his trees. Got it."

Ben's brows, furrowed in a constant V, got somehow lower. "I'm serious, Vicenzo."

"You always are," Izzie said, touching Ben's shoulder. "We got it, Ben. We won't embarrass you. Too badly." Her ruby lips quirked in a smile.

Ben sighed, massaging his temples as Isaac rubbed his shoulders.

Beside Vicenzo, Max smiled as he leaned on the railing. The wind blew back his loose copper curls, and his freckled cheeks dimpled as he smiled. "You'll give him an aneurysm. Ben really doesn't have the biggest sense of humor."

Vicenzo grunted as he watched a fishing boat speed past.

"How're you doing?" Max's low, gentle voice asked. "You and Eddie have seemed pretty down since we arrived."

Vicenzo picked at some peeling paint on the railing. "Looking forward to this all being over."

Max hummed, blinking up at the sky. "It's been a long time coming. In the back of my mind, I guess I always thought we'd have to face Eddie's old clan sooner or later."

Vicenzo was surprised at that. "And you guys are ready to put your lives on the line to help him?"

He nodded without hesitation. "Of course. He's pack, just like you." A smile quirked his lips. "Even though I know you don't think you are. We'd do the same for you, and I think you'd do the same for us." He bumped his shoulder against Vicenzo's, and Vicenzo tried to growl at him. It was half-hearted, though Max widened his eyes and took an exaggerated step away.

"Hey," Gabe snapped. "You growling at my mate?"

Max waved him away. "No, love, just a mosquito buzzing in your ear."

Vicenzo snorted and stayed silent. He'd forgotten what it meant to belong to a pack, to be part of something greater than himself. What it was like to know he had people to watch his back, even though he didn't share their name or their genes.

"That's..." Vicenzo began. "Thanks."

Max stared out over the water, his brows furrowed thoughtfully. "For a long time, my mother and I were struggling. My father left when I was a baby. He never wanted to be a dad. Then my stepfather came into the picture, and he was..." A shiver racked Max's body, and he shook his head. "Think of every evil stepfather you've read about in a book. He was that and worse."

Vicenzo listened, surprised. He'd never spoken much to Max until today, and he hadn't known the layers beneath his shy, quiet surface.

"He kept my mom and me isolated from each other. Then he tried to have me sacrificed to some werewolf supremacy cult. That's when I met Gabe and the rest of the agency. I never thought I'd fit in anywhere. Not among humans or wolves. I never thought I'd be a part of their bonds."

"But you are," Vicenzo said. "How?"

Max smiled as if the answer were easy. "I had to trust them. It took a while but I let them reach out to me and it just… happened. They became the family my mother and I always needed. I had to go through so much pain to find them, to find Gabe, but I'd do it all again." His eyes widened and he looked away. "I'm not saying you need to feel that way. But sometimes, good can come from pain and loss. You just have to let it, which is freaking hard and so much easier said than done, but it can be worth it. You know?"

Below him, the boat cleaved through the murky waves and gulls cried over their heads. Vicenzo said, "I don't know how to do that."

Max nodded in understanding. "You'll know when you're ready, and we'll be here when you are. Unless you leave again." Max's eyes went wide. "Not that I'm blaming you or anything! Just stating the obvious, but I guess that sounded pretty blunt. Sorry."

Vicenzo managed a tiny smile. "I'm not leaving." He knew that for certain. He was tired of running, of not having somewhere to plant his feet in the earth and just *be*. He didn't know how to fix everything he'd messed up when he left. But he wanted to find a way to try.

"Good," Izzie said as she walked past. "If you leave again, I'll tell your sister." Smiling playfully, she flipped a lock of frizzy black hair behind her shoulder. The humidity was messing with her usually glossy locks. "She and I are Facebook friends, you know."

Vicenzo snorted. "You have friends?"

"I'll have you know, I have many friends," Izzie replied, unfazed. "I'm a pretty amazing friend actually, so I highly recommend you don't make me angry."

"She is a pretty cool chica," Max remarked.

Vicenzo looked down at the water to hide his smile. "She pay you to say that?"

Turning up her nose, Izzie huffed. "Well I guess I won't be giving you your pack trip souvenir."

"I'm supposed to care?"

Izzie rolled her eyes and shoved something at him. It was a small box. He rattled it and a sweet smell came from within. Unwrapping the box, he found a container of praline cookies. They smelled good, like sugar, butter, and nuts. He popped one into his mouth. It was so sugary, it made his hair stand on end. He shoved the box back at her.

"Told you he wasn't big on sweets," Eddie drawled, leaning on the railing across the way.

"Except you, of course," Max said, batting his eyes. Eddie sputtered, red-faced, and Vicenzo looked away to hide his grin.

Izzie sighed. "Fine, then. We can all share. Gabriel, catch." She threw a cookie at him, hitting him in the face.

Ben strode across the deck, his arms behind his back like a sergeant. "Don't stuff your faces. You have any idea how rich those things are? You'll be puking or bent over with a stomachache when we have to fight the hunters."

Isaac snatched a cookie from the box. Ben glowered at him. "Not gonna stand with me on this?"

Isaac chewed, sighing dreamily. "Come on, a few won't kill them."

"Fun dad is the best dad!" Ryan called, crunching on a cookie.

Leaning on the railing with an infuriating smirk, Isaac said, "You think Vicenzo here might smile more if he had some sugar in his life?"

Gabe leaned on the railing beside him with an identical smirk. "I don't know, he seems in a good mood since last night..."

They were so annoying, all of them. He was leaving. He was so leaving the minute he got off this damn boat.

JUST WHEN VICENZO THOUGHT he would fall asleep as nightfall was encroaching and darkening the swamp, distant lights flickered golden through the gloom of the evening.

Ben said, "We're here."

"And where is here?" Vicenzo asked. It looked like the middle of nowhere.

"Black Bay Wildlife Refuge," Ben said, leaning on the railing. "Home to Phillipe, leader of the Black Bay pack. Cookies away, everyone. Let's be on our best behavior."

One by one, the pack departed the boat and walked the trail through the swamp. Deep within the gathering darkness, gators hissed, strange birds called out in warbling voices, and wolves howled. The pack knew they were coming. Eyes winked at them from the darkness as they approached the village, and growls rumbled from the shadows.

A man stood in the center of the road through the village. Wolves flanked him, their eyes glowing in the darkness, and it was clear they looked to the man as a leader of sorts. He was tall and thin and radiated authority as he stood among the wolves. He had a long white beard that swayed in the wind and equally white hair tied back behind his head. He ran a freckled, wrinkled hand over the top of a wolf's head.

His face split into a gap-toothed grin and he opened his long, thin arms wide. "Benjamin! Come see, cher!"

"Come see what?" Ryan asked. "His questionable skull collection?" Zach elbowed him.

Ben grinned and went to greet Phillipe, and they slapped each other on the back.

"Everyone, this is Phillipe Delacroix. Phillipe, this is my pack."

Phillipe surveyed them, his hands on his hips. "Welcome, welcome to New Orleans!" He pronounced it as N'awlins in his thick Cajun accent. "This y'all's first time in Louisiana?"

"Oh yeah," Ben said. "We've done all the touristy stuff. How about you show us a local's perspective?"

Phillipe laughed, slapping his knee. With a bounce in his step, he led the way, motioning them along. "Allons, allons, cher!" As spritely as a pup despite the years on him, Phillipe led them to a house on stilts that overlooked the waterfront.

"Y'all get comfy now." Phillipe kicked open the door and went to the kitchen. "I got seafood gumbo on the stove."

Vicenzo sniffed, the air thick with the smell of spices. The house was cozier than the dreary swamp outside. Large windows in the living room offered views of the water. It was a big house with the living room and kitchen open to each other in a sprawling space and a dining room tucked in the rear of the house. A staircase led up to four bedrooms, which Phillipe said they were welcome to. "'Cept for the one down the hall, that there's mine," Phillipe told them with a wheezy laugh.

He was so cheerful it was hard for Vicenzo to remember why he'd called them to Black Bay in the first place.

Phillipe went outside to set the table, waving Ben away when he tried to help. They hadn't been seated in the living room for five minutes before Phillipe called them out back. On the deck outside, the pack gathered around the table, which was big enough for all of them to fit. The gumbo was hot and spicy, thick with seafood. Vicenzo loved it.

"Y'all like dancin'? It's my mate Denise's birthday and we throwin' her a fais do-do for eight o'clock."

"A what?" Ryan asked.

"A dance party! Don't tell Phillipe y'all don't go dancin' in New York!" the old Cajun said as he splashed a heaping helping of gumbo into Ryan's bowl.

Ben looked around the table, his bushy brows furrowed. "Where is Denise? And the boys?"

Phillipe's sunny smile sputtered. He sat at the head of the table and didn't speak for a moment. "The hunters got her, and my boys."

Ben's face twisted. "Shit, Phillipe. I'm so sorry."

Vicenzo looked down into his food, his gut clenching at the ache in Phillipe's voice.

"Oh, she's not dead," Phillipe added. "I'd know if somethin' happened to her, or my sons."

Isaac said, "You think they're keeping them for the fighting pits?"

"That's why I called y'all down here. My pack just ain't big enough to take on that many hunters. They come into my territory, capture my people. The law, they don't care 'bout a few missing loup-garou. Now, with you New Yorkers at my back, I think we may just have a chance."

"We are formidable," Ryan said while not looking quite so formidable as he wiped his streaming eyes and sniffled from the spice.

Ben said, "We'll do everything we can. Ed here has a history with the hunters. He knows how they operate."

Phillipe narrowed his eyes at Eddie, a smile pushing into the apples of his cheeks. "Do you now, cher?"

Eddie cleared his throat. "Firstly, may I say this is the best gumbo I ever tasted, sir? Reminds me of my mama's chili."

"Ah, a Southern boy after my own heart!" Phillipe crooned, slapping the table.

Vicenzo rolled his eyes. He was so Southern, he was about to start playing a banjo.

Eddie said, "Yeah, I do know these hunters. Their leader is my uncle. Have you seen a guy among them wearin' an old duster and a beat-up hat? Got a big burn on his face, uses wolves as pets."

"Them hunters are the meanest bunch I ever did see. But I know the one you's talkin' about. I seen him. Must hurt those wolves somethin' awful to get them rollin' over for treats."

Eddie swallowed, his eyes growing wide. The smell of his fear compelled Vicenzo to touch his knee beneath the table.

Eddie tensed, then relaxed with a quiet exhale. "Then he really is still alive. Damn. Here I was, hopin' someone put a bullet in that thick head of his. 'Course it can't be that easy. Your family is definitely alive, Phillipe."

Phillipe's eyes widened. "You think so?"

"Yeah, I do. If he wanted your pack dead, Phillipe, you'd all be dead. I know my uncle. He's usin' y'all for somethin' nasty. Probably pit fightin' like Isaac said. Wolf huntin' in recent years is a lot harder to get away with than it used to be. But fightin' pits are more discreet. He's changed his methods, but he's still a son of a bitch."

Phillipe sighed, leaning back in his chair. "I'm glad to hear it. They'll be back soon. We need to be ready for them. But the night is still young, non? You'll join us for a fais do-do, won't you? For my dear mate, and to rally our spirits for the fight to come."

Ben said, "Wouldn't be New Orleans without a party before a big battle. Why not?" Phillipe cheered and went to go fill the pitcher of water for his guests and their blistered northeastern palates.

Vicenzo was exhausted and cleared his plate, anxious for the coming confrontation with the hunters. He dumped his dishes in the sink and washed them.

"I'll save up the dishes, cher, don't you worry." Phillipe muscled him out of the kitchen. "Where ya wanna sleep?"

"Probably just take the couch," Vicenzo said. He knew the mated pairs would want to share the three bedrooms. He wasn't sure where Eddie and Izzie would sleep but they could shift and curl up somewhere, he supposed.

"Can I help with anythin'?" Eddie asked, handing Phillipe his plate.

"Well, I'd be happy if you joined us for the dance tonight."

"I may do just that." Eddie glanced Vicenzo's way and wandered from the kitchen. He looked out the living room window at the bayou. "You goin'?" he asked, glancing back at Vicenzo. "It might be fun, you know. To dance."

"Nah. I'm too tired."

Eddie hummed, and Vicenzo couldn't tell if he was disappointed or not. *Wait a moment.* Had Eddie just asked him to dance?

Izzie hurried out the door, arm in arm with Max and Gabe. "This is going to be so much fun!"

"Let's party!" Ryan said as he and Zach walked out, holding hands.

Eddie turned to Vicenzo and smiled. "Well. Sleep tight."

Vicenzo grunted, his stomach fluttering oddly at that sweet little smile. Eddie walked out the door with Ben and Isaac, and Vicenzo was left alone.

"You not going?" Phillipe frowned comically as he stopped by the door. "That boy sure looked like he wanted you there."

Vicenzo cleared his throat, picking some lint off the couch. "Big social gatherings aren't really my thing."

A musical chuckle came from Phillipe. "Ah, I know the feeling. I was like you before I met my Denise." He picked up a framed photo on the end table and rotated it to show him. In it were three boys in coveralls with blond hair, suntans, and freckles. They stood beside their mother and father. Denise and Phillipe smiled radiantly. Phillipe looked a thousand years younger, though the photo couldn't have been taken long ago; his hair was still long and white. Phillipe kissed his fingers and touched Denise's face. "My dear, sweet mate. She should be out there waitin' to ask me to dance. How she can dance..." Vicenzo shuffled at the sight of the tears misting Phillipe's eyes. His heart ached suddenly for the old man.

"Do you want to dance with that boy?"

Vicenzo's face warmed. "No..."

A chuckle. "That was a lie."

"I can't dance. I wouldn't even know how to ask him. It would be awkward."

"Take it from an ol' man, cher." Phillipe smiled, his eyes crinkled at the corners. "If the boy asks you to dance, you say oui! Life's too short."

And Vicenzo knew he was right because he ached from the truth in those words. He'd thought he would always have his parents to turn to when he needed them. The day before the fire, his parents had been talking about graduation trips and taxes and work. Kassandra had been wondering if she should ask Derek out. And his biggest problem in the world had been that he was in love with his best friend and was so scared that Eddie wouldn't feel the same way.

What had Phillipe just said? Oui? He tested out the word on his tongue, his face burning warmer with each repetition. He slumped over, his nails digging into his face. Was he really doing this? Was he really about to make a fool of himself? Eddie would say no.

Then he shouldn't have asked me to dance. 'Cause I'm gonna embarrass the hell outta him.

Heart racing, Vicenzo found his feet. He walked out the door and followed the scents of the pack and the Black Bay wolves into the bayou. He followed paw prints and footprints in the damp earth until he came across a roaring bonfire at the water's edge. Werewolves gathered around the fire, some as humans, others running as wolves within the trees. A few werewolves were readying their instrument of choice: fiddle, bass, guitar, drums, and accordion. Coolers of beer and bottles of whiskey were lined up around the fire.

Among the crowd, he spotted Gabe sitting at the fire with Max on his knee. Ben stood beside Isaac, both nursing beers, and Izzie was taking pictures for her boyfriend back in New York. By the fire, Zach and Ryan clinked their whiskey glasses together. Eddie took a gulp of beer, shoulders hunched and head down as he stuck close to the pack. The sight of him sapped Vicenzo of his courage. He should go back to the house and sleep.

At the other end of the fire, Phillipe stood, his arms open to his pack, and the wolves howled, even the human-looking ones. He said, "Y'all know Denise would love to be here for this. My boys too. Tonight is for her. For everyone we've lost to hunters. I'm sure y'all noticed our new friends. This here is Ben Stroud and his wolves of the Lycanthrope Protection Agency of New York City." Ben nodded respectfully, raising a glass as people clapped appreciatively. "And they're gonna help us get back everyone we lost," Phillipe said, his eyes burning. "The hunters ripped a hole in our heads, our hearts. Thought they could break and divide us. But we are loup-garou! And I promise you, my brothers and sisters, we will be whole again." His face hardened, his eyes cold and steely as he looked at the faces of his packmates. "There is nothin' I wouldn't sacrifice for you." He looked Ben in the eyes and smiled. It wavered. Wiping his eyes, the old man said, "Now, what are we waitin' for, my friends? Let's party!"

The band struck up a folksy, toe-tapping tune. One of the werewolves crooned in Cajun French and her packmates sang along with her. The music echoed out into the bayou, so very Cajun it was hard to imagine the gators weren't dancing along in the swamp.

Grinning, Isaac took Ben's hands and swayed him to the music. Ben resisted, red-faced, until Isaac swept him close and swayed with him. Zach and Ryan copied the werewolves around them and square-danced, and Gabe and Izzie danced while Max filmed the festivities to send to his mom. Swaying side to side, Eddie grinned as he stood alone on the outskirts.

Vicenzo took in a deep breath, squeezing his hands into fists. Head high, chest out, he strode stiffly toward Eddie. Halfway there, Eddie turned and surprise bloomed across his face. "Oh," he said. He wet his lips, his wide blue eyes drinking in Vicenzo's presence. A big grin spread across his face. "You got no idea how happy I am to see you."

Vicenzo's heart pounded fast, his face hot enough to catch fire. "Think I can guess, if your dopey grin means anything."

"I thought you didn't like country music."

Vicenzo slumped, finding it impossible to be prideful when Eddie looked so happy. "It's not that bad. It's... different. Thought it would be all country."

Eddie watched the musicians play. "It is different, isn't it? I've never heard anythin' like it." His hair glowed in the firelight, bringing out the shades of red and gold hidden within.

Vicenzo wet his lips, trying to muster the courage, trying to find the right words. Instead, he thrust out his hand. Eddie looked from his hand to Vicenzo's face.

"Want to?" Vicenzo cocked his head toward the dancers.

Eddie laughed, a breathy, nervous sound that twisted up Vicenzo's insides. "I should warn you, my dancing's a bit rusty."

"Mine too. Considering I've never done this before."

Eddie shrugged, grinning as he clasped Vicenzo's hand. "Fuck it. Let's make idiots of ourselves." He tugged Vicenzo among the dancers, and

Vicenzo had never been so aware of his arms and legs, or been so clueless as to what to do with them. Eddie wasn't much better, but he at least moved his body to the music, arms loose and feet shuffling. He jumped up and down, raised his hands to the sky, and shook his head like a wet dog. He looked ridiculous, but he didn't seem to care.

"I don't know what to do," Vicenzo said, laughing at his own stupidity.

"Who cares?" Eddie said. "Do the robot! The chicken dance. The wave. Or we could just—" He suddenly hooked his arm with Vicenzo's and Vicenzo stumbled in a circle after him. Just when he thought he'd gotten the hang of that simple maneuver, Eddie switched arms and jerked Vicenzo after him. The world spun around Vicenzo in a blur of firelight and indistinct bodies.

Vicenzo yelped, clutching onto Eddie before he fell over. Breathless, he realized he was laughing, grinning so hard it hurt as Eddie gripped his elbows to keep him upright. Their gazes met as Eddie's bangs flopped over his eyes. Vicenzo thought about brushing them away.

The music changed, the bouncy tune mellowing to something slower paced. The couples swayed together, cheek to cheek, heads on shoulders, arms holding one another close. Vicenzo didn't expect Eddie to want to dance with him that way, but before he could move away, Eddie squeezed his arm. Cyan eyes hesitantly met Vicenzo's, his throat bobbing as Eddie swallowed and his pink tongue dampened his lips. Vicenzo was too spellbound to move away, even as embarrassed as he was.

Eddie gently tugged his arms and Vicenzo moved in close, Eddie's smile widening when Vicenzo didn't pull away. To start they just swayed in place, Vicenzo's fingers curled over Eddie's elbows, the tips of their toes touching. Vicenzo almost had a heart attack when he looked in Eddie's eyes too long, and warmth ran down the back of his neck.

Gabe bumped into Vicenzo as he and Max waltzed past. Clutching Max's shoulder, Gabe motioned for him to put his hand on Eddie's shoulder. Vicenzo did, almost smacking Eddie in the face in his haste, his fingers bouncing off his ear. "S-Sorry," he stammered.

Max jerked his head toward Gabe. "*Get closer,*" he said through their bond.

Vicenzo held his breath as he leaned in, his breath catching as Eddie's hand settled at his waist. Since Vicenzo didn't know any fancy dance moves, they just swayed for a while. Looking into Eddie's eyes had gotten easier—Vicenzo didn't know when that had happened or how. Eddie nudged his foot, tugging his waist to the left, and Vicenzo jolted into action, laughing his embarrassment. They moved, swaying in a circle. Vicenzo looked down at his feet, trying to make sure he didn't step on Eddie's. He heard Gabe and Max chuckling nearby.

"You're better than you think you are," Eddie said, low and meant just for him.

Vicenzo exhaled in a laugh as he met the blue of Eddie's twinkling eyes. "You're not too bad yourself."

Eddie's other hand was resting on Vicenzo's wrist, his fingertips brushing over the skin there, then turning ticklish over the palm of his hand. After a moment, his hand settled in Vicenzo's, one arm still around his waist and guiding him in a slow circle. Beside them, Gabe twirled Max out and back in and the pair laughed.

Eddie copied them, backing up until they were at arm's length. Vicenzo tried to spin into him and went in the wrong direction. Face burning, he laughed and tried again, winding up with his back to Eddie's chest. Breathing was suddenly hard as Eddie's body pressed close to his, and Vicenzo felt the stutter of the breath in Eddie's chest, flush with his back.

Eddie lowered his hands slowly, his fingertips barely touching Vicenzo's waist as if he were worried Vicenzo would burn him. Warm breath tickled the back of his neck as Eddie's chin came to rest on his shoulder. Vicenzo reminded himself to breathe and not to lean into Eddie like he desperately wanted to. He glanced behind him and realized it was a mistake as he found his face inches from Eddie's. The flutter of Eddie's eyelashes tickled his cheek, and warm breath that smelled of Cajun spices heated Vicenzo's lips.

Eddie wet his lips before shyly meeting Vicenzo's gaze. Suddenly, they were too close. Vicenzo spun out from him and when Eddie reached out, Vicenzo clasped his hand and allowed Eddie to bring him close again, putting his other hand on the one Eddie had on Vicenzo's waist.

Smiling, Vicenzo was amazed by the ease with which they touched and swayed together. It was so easy, as if all the years of hurt and distance had melted away.

"What?" Eddie murmured.

Heat bloomed in Vicenzo's cheeks. "Thinking I like dancing with you."

Eddie laughed softly, eyes sparkling. "Me too."

As Eddie came closer, Vicenzo held his breath. For a moment as Eddie glanced at his mouth, he thought Eddie was going to kiss him, and Vicenzo thought he might even let him. Then Eddie leaned his head on Vicenzo's shoulder. Inch by inch, Vicenzo lowered his head until his cheek touched the soft golden hair on Eddie's head.

The song ended. Their feet went on moving, carrying them in a slow circle Vicenzo didn't want to stop. He didn't want to let Eddie go. Then the next song began and it was so raucous and fast-paced, Vicenzo knew he had no hope of matching it. "No way," he said.

Eddie laughed, his shoulders heaving. He stepped out of Vicenzo's arms and they hovered in the empty space where Eddie had stood a bit too long before Vicenzo dropped them. "Want a drink?" Eddie asked.

Vicenzo shrugged, too breathless to say much. Tired, Vicenzo went and sat by the fire while Eddie fetched them some beers from the cooler. He accepted the beer Eddie passed to him and took a drink of the cold, fizzy liquid. Eddie sat in the chair beside him, bottle propped on his knee as he watched the dancers go wild. Vicenzo took a gulp, unsure what to say. There was so much he wanted to say, but he couldn't decide what to go with.

"Uh... You weren't too bad. At the whole dancing thing," Vicenzo said, fixating on the roaring fire.

A smile brightened Eddie's face. His cheeks were a lovely pink, and mirth made his eyes dance. "You were pretty good," Eddie said, fanning the warmth in Vicenzo's cheeks to a blaze. In his flustered panic, Vicenzo kicked Eddie's toe, making him laugh.

The space between them thrummed, begging to be breached. There was a splotch of foam next to Eddie's mouth, and Vicenzo's fingers twitched. "Uh... You got stuff. On your..."

Eddie frowned, rubbing at the wrong side of his mouth.

Without thinking, Vicenzo reached out, running his thumb along the corner of Eddie's mouth. Eddie's eyes widened but he didn't push Vicenzo away. The touch barrier disappeared, and Vicenzo's apprehension evaporated. He ran his thumb over Eddie's cheek, making sure to wipe away the beer foam. He traced the shape of Eddie's lower lip, and Eddie's eyes dropped to Vicenzo's mouth.

"You two were incredible!" Phillipe said, materializing from the crowd. Eddie jumped, and the moment shattered.

"Looking forward to fighting beside you, Phillipe," Vicenzo said, slapping his knee as much for emphasis as with frustration. "We're gonna kick those hunters' asses." He looked over Phillipe's shoulder at Eddie, who was walking away toward the musicians.

Phillipe narrowed his eyes. "You got experience with their kind?"

"Eddie does, and Isaac's hunted them for years." Vicenzo cleared his throat. "Me too. They killed my family."

Phillipe nodded his understanding. "I'm sorry to hear that."

"So take it from me, this is personal. I understand how worried you must be, and I won't pretend your fear isn't warranted. But I'm going to do all I can to make sure those bastards never hurt your pack the way they hurt mine." He blinked away the wet sheen that had fallen over his eyes. "I'll kill those hunters. Every one of them."

Phillipe sat in the empty chair beside him. Vicenzo turned his attention to the man when he realized Eddie had gone to eat from one of the crawfish platters. "Don't underestimate them, cher. There's many of them, hearts full of hatred for our kind. If I thought me and my pack could handle them, I wouldn't have asked for your agency." He leaned on his knee, suddenly looking exhausted as he ran a hand over his eyes. "You lost everything to hunters."

Vicenzo's jaw tightened. "Yes."

"If you could go back and do it all over again, is there anything you wouldn't do to keep your home, your family?" Phillipe watched Ben and the pack dance, the firelight blazing in his eyes.

Vicenzo shook his head. "If I could have saved them, if I could have my parents here with me... No." His throat ached from the truth in his words.

"You'd even let others die if it meant their lives were spared?"

Vicenzo nodded wordlessly. "Anything."

Phillipe's hand fell heavy on his shoulder, squeezing tight. "Then we understand each other, you and me, cher."

CHAPTER 19

JUST TWO PEOPLE

THE PACK SPREAD OUT through Phillipe's house in search of a place to sleep, the couples quick to grab their own rooms. Izzie ended up rooming with Gabe and Max since there were twin beds, so there wasn't any room for Vicenzo but he'd gotten a good laugh at Gabe and Max squished into a tiny bed. Even though he'd said he would sleep on the sofa, he ended up offering it to Zach and Ryan instead since it was a foldout bed. Within his soul, his wolf howled for Eddie, and it was a call Vicenzo couldn't fight as he hesitated outside Eddie's bedroom door.

"Come on," Eddie said when he finally found the guts to knock.

Eddie, shirtless, flushed a pretty pink color. He wore low-hanging sweats that teased a view of the waistline of his boxers. "Hey."

Vicenzo tore his eyes away from Eddie's bare, scarred chest. His body still remembered Eddie's warmth, the way his firm chest had felt pressed close to Vicenzo's body. He wondered if Eddie was eager to forget that, and the thought was like a punch to his chest, making him want to bolt.

"Vico." Eddie hesitated, running his pink tongue over his lower lip, then running his hand through his hair and looking away. "You can have the bed if you want. I'll take the floor."

Right. They weren't together. Sure, they'd shared a bed, done a hell of a lot more than that—but they weren't a couple. If Eddie wanted more, surely he'd say so. Right? Vicenzo ducked his head and scratched the back of his neck. "No, that's okay. I'll take the floor. A bit too hot for all those blankets." He'd tolerate the heat in a second if it meant Eddie would let him lie close to him, though.

Eddie parted his lips. "Are you sure?"

Vicenzo just rolled his eyes because if he didn't, he'd cave and ask to share Eddie's bed. He didn't even mean in a sexual way either. Scowling, he yanked a pillow off the bed and grabbed an extra blanket from the closet. After the passion of the night before, after their dance… he craved closeness with Eddie, however Eddie would have him. But that wasn't what they'd agreed to. He didn't even know if that was what Eddie wanted. He'd asked Vicenzo to dance, but maybe it'd meant less than Vicenzo had thought. Maybe Eddie would have asked anyone to dance. The thought made him growl.

Vicenzo spread out the blanket and tossed the pillow on the carpeted floor. Eddie was still standing there by the bed, his fingers curling and uncurling at his sides, his lips still parted and brows furrowed.

"What?" Vicenzo asked, trying to make his voice more snappish than he felt so he wouldn't sound like a weak, hopeful sap.

Eddie shook his head and smiled. "Nothin'. Night, Vico."

Vicenzo shrugged and looked away before Eddie could see his disappointment. This was for the best. Things between them were complicated enough. Now that Vicenzo knew the noises Eddie made when Vicenzo was inside him, knew the way he kissed and the way his skin flushed pretty and pink… it was best not to throw in sappy feelings and sentiments. Neither of them were romance kind of guys, anyway. They'd given it a go once, back when they were young and dumb. It was best to just let the past lie.

Vicenzo buried his face in the pillow and stifled his frustrated growl. If only he actually believed any of that crap. The lights went out, and darkness blanketed the room. Vicenzo peeled off his T-shirt and jeans. The carpet was itchy against his bare skin. He sighed and wriggled atop the sheet as he listened to the ceiling fan whirring in the quiet.

"Vico?" Eddie's voice was a pleasant murmur.

Vicenzo's heart skipped a beat. "Yeah?"

"You danced real nice tonight."

His body warmed and he found himself smiling up at the ceiling.

"I'm glad you came."

Vicenzo's heart beat faster and he was grateful Eddie couldn't hear it. "It was just as embarrassing as I thought it would be." He grimaced, not liking the way his words sounded now that he'd said them out loud. It hadn't been a bad experience, not at all. He couldn't remember the last time he'd had so much fun or been so happy. So why couldn't he just say that? Why was it so hard to allow himself to be sappy and just admit he'd loved dancing with Eddie tonight? Why did he have to put up a front? He hadn't used to be so hardened. He cleared his throat and tried again.

"I... I'm glad I went, too." His face burned and he fisted the sheet, wishing he could tell Eddie that the song they'd danced to wouldn't leave his mind. Wishing he could tell him that he'd never felt so fearless around a bunch of strangers with Eddie in his arms, that the world had disappeared while they'd danced. "It was fun," he said lamely.

Eddie laughed softly. "Yeah. Yeah, it was." He trailed off and Vicenzo worried that the moment had passed. He rolled onto his side and watched the weeping willow sway outside the window, its branches gently tapping the glass. "How's the floor treatin' you?" Eddie asked, his voice light, conversational.

Vicenzo hugged his pillow. "Comfy." He wanted to be in Eddie's bed. Wanted to lie close and hold him tight until they were fast asleep.

Eddie chuckled and fell silent.

"Ed?" Something about his silence unsettled Vicenzo.

"Think Phillipe's got a bedbug problem."

Vicenzo brushed the blanket beneath him. "Shit. Really?"

"Yeah. Ew. Mind if I join you down there?"

Vicenzo's heart soared. Thank Amaris for bedbugs. "Yeah. Sure. Come on down." Eddie joined him on the floor in a rustle of sheets and the creaking of floorboards and plopped his pillow down near Vicenzo, careful to leave a little space between them. Vicenzo tried not to feel disappointed.

Eddie lay down and smiled, his hair tousled and his clothing rumpled, and Vicenzo smiled back easily, his heart somewhere between his chest and his throat.

"Thanks," Eddie said. "Can't stand creepy little critters."

Vicenzo didn't blame him. He gazed up at the shadow of the weeping willow on the ceiling. "Remember when we were kids? We had a sleepover after you moved to town."

Eddie chuckled, a deep and throaty sound. "'Course I do. I was so nervous, but you were so sweet. First real sleep I had since I'd lost my home."

Vicenzo's face warmed. "Not like now, huh?"

Eddie reached out and shoved Vicenzo's arm. His hand was warm and damp with sweat. "You're not so bad."

Vicenzo ached for those simple days. Well, they seemed simple by comparison. Reaching out to Eddie back then had been so easy. His fingers curled, and he longed to close the distance and take Eddie's hand. "I'm different."

"We both are. But I like you fine, Vico. Just as you are."

Damn. Vicenzo's chest ached. He rolled over onto his side and found Eddie, wide-eyed and soft in the moonlight. He moved his foot, draping his ankle over Eddie's. It was stupid, but it took all the courage he could muster.

Could they have something now? Not what they'd once had. But just… something, as they were now? Would Eddie like that? Vicenzo thought he'd die for a chance to see it happen.

"Like you, too, Ed," Vicenzo said. He inhaled and slowly looked Eddie in the eye. "Just as you are."

Eddie swallowed, his throat bobbing. He rolled over onto his side and their hands bumped together, lying between them and filling in what had once been empty space. Eddie's hand twitched, and his eyes strayed shyly toward Vicenzo's when he reached out and touched his face. There was no desperation in his touch, nothing rushed or rough. He touched Vicenzo like they had all the time in the world to lie like this, like they were just two people fumbling their way back to each other, as if the wounds of their past were nothing but scars.

Maybe someday they could just be two people, scarred and imperfect as they were, whose jagged edges had softened. There would always be little cracks in their surfaces, old hurts that never quite healed right. But they'd finally fit together, and nothing else would matter. Maybe then Vicenzo would find the courage to say what he was too afraid to say now.

"Vico?" Eddie's voice was soft and uneven. He cleared his throat.

"Yeah?"

"I wanna kiss you somethin' fierce. I... I know that's not what we agreed on, but—"

Vicenzo leaned in and touched his mouth to Eddie's like he'd ached to all day. Ached for years, maybe, except he'd been too angry and bitter to just be honest with himself, thinking they couldn't have this because they didn't fit together anymore. Maybe they didn't need to be perfect. Maybe even as jagged as they were, they fit just fine.

Vicenzo knew he was far from perfect. Honestly, he felt like a wreck compared to Eddie, but when he'd faltered over the right thing to say and how to say it the way he might have when he was young and whole, Eddie had met him halfway and made him wonder what the hell he'd been so worried about.

They broke apart, and Vicenzo didn't realize how long they'd kissed until he was panting and dazed, pinned beneath Eddie's warm, solid body. Eddie's eyes burned with need, but when he leaned in close, he didn't kiss Vicenzo right away. There were no rushed touches or hungry, soul-stealing kisses. Not tonight. Eddie framed Vicenzo's face in his hands and touched him like he were carved from glass. Vicenzo's heart fluttered. He couldn't remember ever being touched so gently, not in years. He'd forgotten such tenderness could ever be applied to him. That maybe he even deserved it.

Their lips brushed, setting off fireworks in Vicenzo's stomach. He ran his fingers through Eddie's hair and tugged a little, enjoying the way Eddie's eyes fluttered closed from the gentle touch. The warmth of his body blanketed Vicenzo, their chests touching as they breathed, and Eddie moaned into Vicenzo's mouth when their hips ground together.

Eddie groaned, the sound vibrating Vicenzo's lips, and Vicenzo rolled them over so he lay atop Eddie. He hated the sight of those scars on Eddie's bare skin, the reminder of the hurt he'd been through. He wanted to take it all away, in whatever way he could.

Reaching down, Vicenzo rubbed the bulge in Eddie's underwear, and he panted, his pupils blown and lips parted. Vicenzo licked his palm, his eyes never leaving Eddie's, hoping Eddie saw the promise burning him up from the inside out. No one would hurt Eddie again. Eddie gasped when Vicenzo took him in his hand and stroked in long pulls, squeezing tight beneath the head of his cock.

"Vico," he whispered, voice hoarse. He reached between them, feeling for Vicenzo, hard and aching between them, but Vicenzo shooed his hands away.

"I got you, Ed," Vicenzo murmured, tracing the crook of his neck with his mouth. "Gonna take care of you, okay?"

Eddie trembled beneath him, arching his hips into Vicenzo's hand. He whimpered and claimed Vicenzo's mouth with his, their noses bumping and their tongues gliding together.

"Tell me what you need. I'll give it all to you," Vicenzo panted. Maybe he wasn't good with words but he was a man of action anyway. If he couldn't tell Eddie how much he wanted him, needed him—he was going to show him, until there wasn't a doubt in Eddie's mind that he was as perfect as he made Vicenzo feel.

"You," Eddie said with a grunt, his lips brushing Vicenzo's and his breath scorching against Vicenzo's mouth. "Goddess, Vico. I fuckin' need you."

Eddie had him. He'd always had him, even when Vico had been too angry and hurt to level with him. Vicenzo claimed Eddie's mouth and poured everything he had into the kiss. No facades, no masking what he really felt behind gruff words and insincerity. No pretending that this meant nothing to him, to either of them.

He ran his hand down Eddie's chest, splaying his fingers over his rapidly beating heart, then clasped his hand, slick with sweat, and laid it flat against his own chest so Eddie could feel the thundering of his own vulnerable heart. So there could be no denying his feelings, not for a second.

Eddie's eyes were wide, every emotion laid bare. It was overwhelming and Vicenzo quickly brought his lips to Eddie's chest, then kissed down his chest and stomach. Once he'd wriggled Eddie's sweatpants down, he kissed his supple inner thigh. Eddie arched beneath him when Vicenzo swallowed him down, worshipping his cock from the base to the tip. His own cock throbbed and ached, but pleasuring Eddie gave him a high like nothing else. He relished it, this place that was theirs alone, a place of pleasure and tender feelings after years of grief and hurt. With Eddie's hands in his hair and his name on Eddie's lips, Vicenzo was untouchable by anyone but Eddie, and he ached for Eddie to feel the same.

He clasped Eddie's hand and Eddie squeezed so tight Vicenzo thought he would bruise. Eddie's nails bit into his back, dragged over the back of his neck, and tickled over his scalp. If there was pain, it was good pain. It was the only pain he would stand because it was from Eddie, and if it was from him, then it didn't hurt.

Eddie came with a hoarse cry that filled the corners of the room, his hand squeezing tight in Vico's. Vicenzo swallowed every drop and licked him clean from root to tip. He smiled, delighted to see Eddie so flushed and elated. Eddie's eyes were damp, his hair sweaty and plastered to his forehead. "Come here, you," Eddie panted with a dazed and beautiful smile, and Vicenzo wouldn't deny him anything.

Eddie rolled them over and tugged down Vicenzo's sweats, and Vicenzo came the moment Eddie took him in his hand and kissed him deeply. His release rocked him, leaving him weak and shuddery and utterly boneless, and Eddie held him tight, stroking and squeezing until Vicenzo was thoroughly satisfied. Afterward, Vicenzo shuddered and gasped, shattered to pieces and held together in Eddie's arms, vulnerable in every sense and yet so unafraid.

They didn't move away, not even after the sweat cooled on their bodies, not even to wipe away the remnants of their pleasure, slick and wet between them. Eddie held Vicenzo to his chest and stroked his hair, and Vicenzo listened to his heart and held his hand.

Like they were just two people, whole despite their imperfections and in love. Vicenzo closed his eyes tight and nuzzled into Eddie's neck.

Goddess. He was so in love with Eddie Turner, he could scarcely breathe.

He'd always loved him, even when they'd been bitter and spitting mad, because that had been easier than admitting the truth.

Maybe someday soon, Vicenzo would tell him.

WHEN VICENZO WOKE THE next day, Eddie was in the shower.

Downstairs, Phillipe had prepared a big pot of grits, a pan of scrambled eggs, and a plate of crispy bacon.

"Mornin', cher! Hope y'all like grits."

Vicenzo wasn't sure what grits were.

Gabe was already at the table with Max seated at his left, halfway through his food. When Gabe took a taste, his eyes widened. "Oh," he said. "It's like polenta! My mom made polenta all the time when I was a kid."

Izzie hummed her agreement as she sipped her hot coffee.

Max yawned widely and suddenly lurched forward in his seat. "Whoa."

Gabe caught his shoulder. "You didn't sleep well, mi amor?"

Blinking tiredly, Max said, "I did. Just... I'm really tired all of a sudden. Must have been last night." He winked. "That toy sure takes a lot out of me."

Everyone groaned.

"I'm kidding!" Max said, laughing at their reaction.

Wiping sleep from his eyes, Vicenzo stumbled to the table and Max passed him a bit of everything, though he looked as if the simple act of lifting a plate strained him. Vicenzo tried the grits first. They had a creamy texture and were swimming in butter, with cayenne giving them a spicy kick. There was an odd aftertaste, but he thought that maybe his palate just wasn't used to the spice.

Ben came down the stairs, yawning. "Isaac back from his walk yet?"

Phillipe wiped grits from his beard. "I don't think so. I put some grits aside for him."

"Thank you," Ben said, taking a seat.

Ryan threw himself into a chair and grabbed a pile of bacon. "You are the man, Phil!"

Zach leaned back in his chair, running a hand through his short, tight curls. "Pass the coffee?"

"Did Isaac have any coffee before he left?" asked Ben.

"Non. I can save him some." Phillipe jumped up and poured a mug of coffee from the pot on the stovetop. "How he like it?"

"Black," Ben answered, splashing some coffee into his own mug. He didn't add any milk.

"Anyone else want coffee?" Phillipe called and Vicenzo raised his hand.

"I'll have some, too." The stairs creaked as Eddie descended the steps while buckling his jeans. Vicenzo's stomach flip-flopped at the sight of him. When he met Eddie's gaze, his eyes wide and lips parted around a silent exhale, Vicenzo's breath hitched. Pink bloomed in Eddie's cheeks and he smiled, bright and beautiful, making Vicenzo's chest ache. "Mornin'," Eddie said to everyone, but he only had eyes for Vicenzo.

Vicenzo looked down into his bowl of grits to hide his smile. "Morning, you."

When Ryan wolf whistled, Vicenzo threw his napkin at him but failed to wipe the stupid grin off his face.

"The full moon's coming up in a few weeks," Zach remarked, smiling innocently. "Guessing you two will have something to share with us by then."

Ryan laughed and this time Vicenzo threw a piece of half-eaten bacon at his face.

Izzie rolled her eyes. "You boys are so stupid."

"Yeah, Ryan's a dumbass," Vicenzo said.

She shot him a look. "Oh, no. I meant you and Eddie. When are you two going to deal with it? You're stinking up Phillipe's lovely home with your pheromones."

Eddie sat across from Vicenzo, his chin propped casually on his hand as he squinted at Izzie. "Deal with what, pray tell?"

"The sexual tension. Seriously. You could cut it with a knife and spread it on my toast," Ryan said through a mouthful of said toast. "Only that sounds gross."

Max shifted uncomfortably, a hand on his stomach. "Yeah. My stomach hurts just thinking about it."

Vicenzo drank the last of his coffee and his chair suddenly felt like it was tipping to the right. He lunged to hold on to the table. "Whoa. What the hell was that?"

"Guys," Max said with a grunt. "Shit. I feel really sick."

"Max?" Gabe cried out as Max suddenly toppled to the floor, coughing.

Eddie lurched to his feet, his hands balled into fists at his sides. "What did you do?" He was glaring at Phillipe, and the older man snapped his fingers. The door burst open and two werewolves stormed in and lunged for Eddie, pinning him down.

The room began to spin, and fear and confusion set Vicenzo's heart racing. "What the hell is going on?" His voice was slurred.

A coffee cup shattered. Zach stumbled out of his chair and onto the floor. Then Ryan collapsed over the table, coughing as he reached weakly for Zach.

"Get offa me!" Eddie shouted, kicking and thrashing beneath his captors.

"Eddie," Vicenzo slurred, trying to stand. His legs were weak and he tripped over Ryan. His vision went white as he struck the floor.

"Wolfsbane. You poisoned us!" Ben snarled weakly, his face pale and sweaty. "Where's Isaac? Phillipe, damn it, if you hurt him—" Ben's furious accusations were cut off as a member of Phillipe's pack walked over Vicenzo's body and stuffed a gag in Ben's mouth.

"I'm sorry, cher," Phillipe said. There were three of him, swaying back and forth. All three of them hung their heads, their eyes pinched and remorseful. "It's the only way I can get my pack back."

"Please," Gabe wheezed. "Please. I have kids at home. Phillipe, please, don't take me away from them." Gabe's head was wrenched back and he choked as a gag was thrust into his mouth.

Phillipe's lips thinned, but he didn't say anything.

"Why are you doing this?" Zach grunted, clutching his stomach as he shivered.

And Phillipe said, "Elijah. The hunters. I offered him a trade. You for my family. You'd do the same if you were in my shoes." He looked at Vicenzo and smiled sadly. "Goodbye."

Vicenzo's body weighed a thousand pounds but he reached out, his nails digging into the wood. Eddie. He had to get to Eddie. He had to protect him when Elijah came. He wouldn't lose him. Not again. Eddie looked over his shoulder at him, his eyes heavy and skin pale.

"Vico." Eddie panted, and then his head hit the steps and he didn't move.

Vicenzo collapsed, the scent of coffee smacking him in the nose as his face splashed in a puddle of the spilled drink. "Eddie," he whispered, stretching out his fingertips. His hand thudded to the ground as a wave of numbness washed over him.

Everything went dark.

CHAPTER 20

GOODBYE

When Vicenzo opened his eyes, the world was rocking back and forth and he gritted his teeth against a cry of pain as silver cuffs burned his wrists. He was lying on the deck of a boat. Across the deck lay his packmates, motionless or just coming to. They were all awake, so the dosage must have been strong enough to incapacitate but not kill them. Isaac wasn't with them, and Vicenzo hated to think about what must have happened to him.

Vicenzo's body was unbearably heavy and he shivered, his clothes soaked in cold sweat and clinging to him. He blinked until his blurry vision finally focused. The air was thick with the smell of ash. Noxious dread formed a lump in his stomach as smoke blackened the sky and wolves howled in pain and fear.

"No," he whispered, his throat dry and gravelly, straining his neck to peer over the railing of the boat.

The village of Black Bay was on fire. Through watering eyes that were burning from the smoke, Vicenzo tried to find Eddie. He lay motionless on his side beside Max. When Vicenzo tried to unsheathe his claws, the silver burned against his efforts.

They were well and truly fucked.

Helplessness made him shake. He would have to watch as the hunters took away his pack for the second time.

Across the deck, Eddie raised his head. He was pale, his cyan eyes wide as he held Vicenzo's gaze. Vicenzo would never let his uncle harm him again.

Whatever happened here today, he had to make sure his pack got out of this alive.

Rumbles of malicious laughter echoed in the air. In a cabin toward the back of the fishing boat, shapes moved back and forth behind the windows. Hunters—Vicenzo counted at least fifteen altogether from those on deck and the ones he glimpsed in the cabin window. They were a pack of eight. They'd faced worse, but they were bound and helpless without the ability to shift, still weak from ingesting wolfsbane.

The door flew open. A man strode from the cabin, a wide-brimmed hat concealing his eyes, the flaps of his duster drifting in the hot, wet air. In his leather-gloved hands, he clutched a silver chain that connected to the neck of a wolf that was frothing at the mouth, its fur bristled and tail high in agitation. Flanking the hunter and his beast were big, brutish hunters armed with flamethrowers and protected by silver armor around their necks, arms, and legs.

Vicenzo held Eddie's gaze. Eddie was shivering on the deck, huddling into himself. Vicenzo bared his blunt teeth at the hunters as they approached, daring them to come closer. The wolf suddenly lunged at the end of his chain, his fangs snapping inches from Eddie's face, and Eddie recoiled.

"Down, boy!" The hunter cracked a silver lash across the wolf's back. The wolf yelped and lay down at the hunter's feet. "Welcome, beasts of the LPA. Must say, you're quite a pack! My wolves sniffed out two berserkers among you. Two!" Ben and Gabe could shift into gigantic bipedal wolves thanks to a gene they'd inherited. Until they got out of the silver cuffs, though, their abilities were next to useless.

"Must say, I'm impressed. In case Phillipe didn't tell you, I'm Elijah. That old fucker never did have much in the way of manners. If y'all cooperate, this'll be quick and simple. If y'all don't, I got ways of making you cooperate that I don't think you'll be so keen on."

So this was Elijah. Eddie's uncle. The man who'd burned their home and tortured Eddie until he was broken. Vicenzo shook with fury at the sight of him.

The hunter grinned a smile full of yellowed teeth beneath a long beard, his single eye fixed on Eddie. "Well, hello there, dear nephew. What an unexpected surprise."

Eddie shook violently, but his eyes were full of fury. "Did you know I was coming?"

"Can't say I did." Clicking his tongue, Elijah shook his head. "You know, it hurt me somethin' awful when you never came home from your little trip to Rome. I feared the worst. Turns out, you been alive all this time and runnin' around with wolves. After I opened my home to you, taught you everythin' you know. Made you strong." Anger thickened Elijah's voice, his knuckles whitening as he clenched the wolf's silver chain. "You betrayed me, Eddie. And you know how I feel about betrayal."

Vicenzo's heart slammed against his ribs.

Eddie's teeth chattered when he said, "Y-you didn't teach me a fuckin' thing. You k-killed my family. Tortured me."

Elijah lunged for his pocket and drew out a lighter. With a click, it ignited, the flame burning inches from Eddie's eye. "You," Elijah snarled, "don't know the first goddamn thing about torture, boy. But you will. Oh, you will!" He grinned.

"Leave him alone!" Vicenzo demanded.

Eddie's eyes went wide and he shook his head at him.

Elijah whipped his head in Vicenzo's direction.

"Touch him, and I'll rip your fucking arm off."

Jaw tight, Elijah stood, his fingers curled around the lighter. He clicked it on, and the sight of the flickering flame made Vicenzo's heart sink. "Made some friends, Eddie? This one's quite protective of you, ain't he?" He knelt, his knee slamming into the deck, and he scrutinized Vicenzo. Half of his face was marred with severe burns that left him disfigured.

Vicenzo's heart slammed against his rib cage as he tried to anticipate an attack. Elijah's mouth curled into a smile when he noticed Vicenzo eyeing the flame. "Don't like fire, boy?" He held the lighter close to Vicenzo's face, and the heat made cold sweat break out all over him. The flame licked at his skin, tearing a gasp from Vicenzo, but just before it could become painful, Elijah withdrew the lighter. Panicked gasps clawed at his chest when Elijah brought the flame back, closer and closer to his eye. The pack shouted their fury and alarm.

"Elijah, leave him alone!" Eddie snapped, straining against his chains. "You're pissed at me, so take it out on me!"

The hunter glanced Eddie's way. "Huh. Seems this one's special to you. How sweet." He cocked his head to the side, his wide eye squinting as he looked Vicenzo over. "Now, ain't you a fine specimen. Young. Powerful. Got a fire in your belly. Show me your teeth again, boy."

Vicenzo didn't listen.

Elijah pulled a break stick from his belt. "Show me your teeth, boy," the hunter said, a grin curling his mouth, "before you ain't got none at all."

Vicenzo opened his jaws wordlessly, hoping his eyes conveyed every ounce of his contempt for him. The hunter grabbed his jaw in a steel grip and Vicenzo grunted his discomfort.

"Good. Very good. I dare say you'll be a formidable beast once I've broken you in." Grinning, he patted Vicenzo's cheek before he shoved him into the railing with a cackle of laughter.

The river spray cooled his face and his breath hitched as Isaac waved at him. He was drifting along in a boat below view of the hunters. Some blood matted the side of his head, but he was still standing. He raised a hand to his mouth and motioned for Vicenzo to stay quiet.

"And what's this? We got a lady wolf, boys!" Elijah jeered to the cackles of his men. Izzie's eyes blazed and she didn't cry out as he fisted her hair and inspected her, snapping her neck from side to side.

A furious snarl came from Gabe, who was tied up on the other side of the deck.

"This one your mate, beast?" Elijah sneered. "Don't see a bite on her. I never did have much appreciation for female beasts but you, my dear, are a firebrand. I'm sure my wolves would love to get to know you."

Izzie spat in his face. "Fuck you!"

The hunters guffawed.

Elijah wiped away the spittle. "Well, that wasn't very nice, was it? I'm a busy man, my dear. I ain't got time to waste breaking beasts. You might just be too much for me to handle."

The silver around Vicenzo's wrist tingled and for a moment he felt the call of his wolf. Across the deck, Ryan's forehead was furrowed in concentration, though the hunters might mistake it for a glare. While the silver was weakening the connection to his wolf, Ryan was also a druid, and druids existed to serve their pack with their magic.

The boat lurched suddenly and the hunters yelped. The waves were growing restless as Ryan commanded the elements to his will. There was warmth in Vicenzo's head as Ryan's magic reached across the pack bonds and pulled magic from them to strengthen his abilities. The pull in his head got stronger but it wasn't painful. It felt warm and right, so Vicenzo didn't fight it.

"I don't have use for so many of you," Elijah declared. "Torch 'em. Keep that one alive." He pointed at Vicenzo. "Maybe the girl. The females are usually quite resilient in the fighting rings. Kill the berserkers. They'll be too much damn trouble." He motioned to Ben and Gabe. "And that one looks too soft." He pointed at Max. "Keep Glasses there. Him too." He sneered at Zach.

The hunter aimed the flamethrower at Max. He was breathing hard, but he stared down the hunters in contempt.

Vicenzo nearly choked on the bile rising in his throat. He would have to watch all over again as his pack burned before his eyes.

Gabe's eyes went wide and he panted hard around the gag in his mouth.

Ben shouted through his gag, thrashing against his restraints.

"No!" Izzie shouted, her eyes glassy with terror. "Please, don't!"

Elijah barked a laugh. "Such dramatics."

Lips moving silently, Ryan bowed his head.

One of the hunters howled as the flamethrower exploded in his hands. The flames crawled over his body, consuming his clothing as kindling, then melting the flesh from his bones. Elijah gaped and his wolf strained against the chain and took off running.

Though Elijah stamped at the fire on the deck, the flames wouldn't be quenched. They spread across the deck and the hunters retreated. The flames licked at the wood but didn't touch the pack as they zeroed in on Elijah and the other hunter. Then the cabin door crashed open and more hunters pounded across the deck, armed with fire extinguishers to combat the blaze.

"What in the holy hell is this?" Elijah roared.

The chains around Vicenzo's wrists vibrated. They shattered, and one by one the pack leaped to their feet. The flames roared up into a wall of fire as Ryan raised both his hands, the fire reflected in his eyes. Zach stood beside him, a hand upon his shoulder to offer him the strength he needed to sustain his magic.

From down below, there came a howl. It was a human sound and Izzie cried out in delight. "It's Isaac! He's got a boat!"

"Go!" Ryan shouted. "Hurry! I can't hold this much longer!"

Ben's eyes blazed as he grabbed Ryan's shoulder. "I got you, Ry. Everyone get to Isaac!"

Izzie and Gabe, Max's hand in his, leaped over the railing and crashed onto the lower deck. Vicenzo grabbed Eddie's arm.

"Boy!" Elijah roared. "You think you know pain? You ain't seen nothin' yet!" Eddie froze, looking past the wall of flame. "You won't get away alive, not this time!" Elijah's eye blazed, his face etched with fury.

"Go!" Vicenzo snapped, shoving Eddie toward the railing. He jumped over after Eddie had landed below. Isaac motioned wildly at them to hurry as one by one, the pack joined him in the fishing boat. It was a squeeze, especially when Zach leaped down into the boat, Ryan in his arms.

Ryan grinned, his face covered with a sheen of sweat, and made an explosion gesture with his hands. "Boom." There were multiple explosions and screams coming from the lower deck as Ryan ignited whatever flammable material the hunters possessed, and the windows became obscured with black smoke.

"Hell yeah, I did that," Ryan croaked, pale and exhausted.

Zach kissed his forehead. "You're amazing."

Isaac sped his boat past a few motorboats surging in a formation in front of Elijah's flaming boat. Vicenzo counted five of the boats hurtling over the algae-covered water toward them. "Shit."

Ben roared, "Get down!"

Something slammed into the back of their fishing boat. It was a harpoon.

"What the hell?" Vicenzo growled.

"Get us outta here, Isaac!" Ben said, his hand upon his mate's shoulder as Isaac increased the boat's speed. They flew over the water, zigzagging between trees to avoid the harpoons and crossbow bolts flying after them.

A boat pulled up beside them. There were two hunters inside, and one of them aimed down the sights of a crossbow. Gabe charged, shifting to his enormous berserker form. Black fur rippled over his skin as he leaped into the boat and tore apart the hunter with his fangs and claws.

"Gabe!" Max called out a warning and Gabe leaped back into their boat just as the hunter's boat smashed into a tree and exploded on impact.

"Behind us!" Izzie cried just before they all jerked forward as a boat rammed them.

Digging into a box full of hunting equipment on the ship's deck, Isaac threw Izzie a silver grenade, and she pulled the pin and chucked it at the boat. He put on a burst of speed and they escaped the explosion, but so did the three hunters, who'd leaped onto the back of the pack's boat seconds after Izzie had tossed the explosive. A wolf leaped, its jaws open wide, and a bolt from Isaac's crossbow pierced the beast's skull. It's teeth missed Vicenzo's scalp by inches as the wolf fell out of the air and crashed below the surface of the water.

Shifting to his berserker form, Ben roared, the sound bowling over Vicenzo, then seized a hunter by the throat and hurled him overboard. Izzie's claws flew across a hunter's eyes, blinding him with blood. She kicked him in the stomach and sent him flying into the murky water. On the other side of the boat, Zach covered Ryan with his body as the third hunter loomed over him, a silver blade in his fist. Vicenzo slammed into the hunter and sent him flying into the water.

A motorboat roared up behind them, closing ground fast, and Vicenzo realized Elijah was in it. The boat had been fitted with a harpoon gun that was aimed right at Eddie. "Got you now, boy!" Elijah let the harpoon fly.

There were no thoughts. No time to hesitate. Vicenzo had promised that these bastards would never hurt Eddie again, and it was a promise he would keep. Even if it meant dying for him. Vicenzo threw himself at Eddie, who crashed to the deck, and pain punched through his shoulder. The harpoon arrow was made of silver and burned like a hot iron in Vicenzo's body.

"V-Vico," Eddie croaked, eyes wide and mouth slack in horror. "No. No, why would you—"

There was so much Vicenzo wanted to say but he never got the chance.

Elijah swerved his boat sharply to the right, and the harpoon yanked viciously in Vicenzo's shoulder. The deck disappeared beneath him. Eddie screamed for him, reaching out to grab him even though there was no stopping what was about to happen. Vicenzo flew over the side of the boat and toward the murky waters of the bayou. All he could do was grit his teeth against the howl of pain so he didn't choke when the water crashed over him.

Water roared in his ears. The barbed arrow in his shoulder fastened into his flesh and *pulled,* dragging him against his will. The pain darkened his vision until he thought he'd pass out. Finally, the tugging sensation eased, and he drifted to a stop in the water. Flailing with one arm, he broke the surface, gasping for air. Hands seized his shoulder, and he yelped as he was lifted from the water and hurled down onto the hard deck of a boat.

Blinking away the water in his eyes, he squinted up at Elijah. The hunter towered over him, teeth bared in a sneer. "You," Elijah snarled. Vicenzo saw white as pain cracked across his jaw from the dirty toe of Elijah's boot. "Wasn't you I fucking wanted! You'll have to do. Least I got one damn wolf outta that fuckin' mess." He gripped the barbed hook lodged in Vicenzo's flesh, and Vicenzo howled his anguish as Elijah yanked him by the harpoon across the deck.

Two other hunters in Elijah's boat jeered and laughed at him. The chained wolf snapped and snarled, its mouth frothing, barely held at bay by the hunters as it lunged for Vicenzo's shoulder. "Take the wheel and get us to solid ground," Elijah said conversationally as he lugged Vicenzo along behind him. "I gotta have a word with our guest."

The pain was so immense, Vicenzo's vision went dark. Agonizing pain had him waking, howling when Elijah tore the arrow from his shoulder and chucked it onto the floor. Vicenzo was inside the fishing boat's cabin. Tight cuffs attached to a railing overhead dug into his wrists, keeping his arms suspended at a painful angle. A hunter steered the boat while Elijah stood over him with an unfriendly leer. At least the cuffs weren't silver. On second thought, that concerned him. Surely the hunters would want his wolf contained. So why hadn't they used silver?

"Vicenzo? Are you okay?" Ben's voice carried across their bond, but it was faint. With each passing second, Elijah was taking him farther away from the pack.

Heart racing, Vicenzo glanced out the window but didn't see anyone following him.

"For now," he answered.

"Lookin' for your pack, wolf?" Elijah sneered. "They ain't comin', I'm afraid. By now, my boys have probably killed each and every one of 'em. If they have any sense, they'll bring my nephew to me."

Vicenzo growled low in his throat. "Won't touch him. I won't let you."

Elijah barked out a laugh. "How're you gonna do that when I've turned you into a drooling dog? I got big plans for you, beast."

"I'll fucking kill you, you son of a—"

Elijah flicked his lighter on and torched Vicenzo's healing wound.

A roar pulled from Vicenzo's throat, one of terror and agony as the fire blazed into his skin. It burned a small hole through his wet shirt, and his flesh began to smoke. Vicenzo screamed as he never had before, his fangs sharpening to points. Just when he thought he'd pass out, Elijah withdrew the lighter. Vicenzo's whole body slackened, and he sucked in gasps of air.

Fuck. This was going to be hard to endure, but he had to. He had to hold on. His pack would come for him. He needed to be strong until then. Closing his eyes tight, he felt for the bonds of his pack, still fragile in his heart.

"Ben. Everyone. I'm okay. Tell Eddie I'm okay. Tell him to stay the fuck away from this madman."

"We're gonna have fun together, you and me." Elijah flicked open a silver switchblade with jagged edges. Vicenzo's stomach turned over, and when Elijah held the flame beneath the blade and heated the metal, he tasted bile in his throat. "You'll shut off that pesky human mind of yours, till you're nothin' but a slobbering beast."

Vicenzo's growl became a whimper when Elijah brought the tip of the blade inches from his eye, the heat making his eye water.

"Vico, hang in there, kid," Ben said.

"We're coming for you. Don't be afraid," Max said.

"We're here, my friend," Izzie said. *"We're here. It will be okay."*

Vicenzo couldn't stay connected to them. They would feel his agony, his terror, his despair. He couldn't do that to them.

"Don't let him hurt Eddie," he pleaded with them. *"Promise me."* And then he muted the bonds, silencing the voices of his pack, cutting himself off from them. This way, they wouldn't feel his pain and fear, but without them, despair wrapped around his heart.

He was alone with the monster who'd burned his home and slaughtered his family.

Elijah ran the tip of the blade over Vicenzo's forehead. He gasped as his skin split like it was paper, then gritted his teeth against the burn. The searing blade cut into his cheek. Flicked over the bridge of his nose. Licked across his jaw. Blood dribbled into his eye, obscuring his vision.

The wounds stung and burned, but it was nothing, not yet. The terror left his heart pounding as he tried to anticipate Elijah's next move. He ground his teeth together when the cuts got deeper, the blade scorching his flesh until he had to bite his cheek to keep from screaming. Blood soaked his shirt, and he tasted it on his tongue from his lacerated cheek. Tears stung his eyes.

"What's this?" Elijah crooned. "Your wolf eyes are showing."

The wolf paced below his skin. The trauma Elijah's presence stirred within him and the pain from his wounds was making his wolf volatile. If Elijah carried on like this, he would have one pissed-off wolf on his hands, and Vicenzo would lose control. Possibly for good. The terror only pushed him closer toward feral madness. Fuck. This wasn't what he wanted. He couldn't lose himself, not again. The bonds of his pack were still healing, they weren't strong enough to keep him from going feral. If he'd just had a little more time to fix everything he'd broken, if he'd just let them in sooner—

"Well now. This should be easier than I thought. I knew you was a wild one, wolf, but I didn't know how hard your wolf was ridin' you." Elijah opened a drawer. He held up some pliers.

Vicenzo's teeth chattered, his fangs sharp in his mouth.

"This should speed things along nicely." He hooked the nail of one of Vicenzo's trembling fingers with the pliers and pulled.

Vicenzo told himself to be strong, that he could take this, that he'd been through worse. He still screamed when Elijah ripped his fingernail out. Fur rippled over his arms, his face elongating into a snout.

"One down," Elijah said, inspecting the bloody nail with interest. "Nine to go. But that's not countin' the ones on your toes."

It went on and on until Vicenzo was incoherent from the pain, only managing to howl and snap and snarl as his wolf wrestled for control. The wolf wanted to come out and fight, but at what cost?

There were things Vicenzo didn't want to forget. Dear things, precious things.

His father's smile as he picked Vicenzo up and twirled him through the air.

His mother's soft, gentle voice as she read him to sleep.

The way Kassandra laughed when he told her his tooth was loose. "It'll come out. Soon! I can feel it!" She'd offered to yank it out for him, and he'd run and hid from her for the rest of the day.

His grandpa's hands, big and warm as he picked Vicenzo up and sat him on his lap. The way he cheered or groaned while they watched soccer together.

Grandma's cooking, pizza with homemade tomato sauce using tomatoes fresh from the garden. With her warm smile, she would give him tomatoes straight from the vine and they'd eat them whole, juices and seeds and everything.

The day a shy, lost boy came to town, smelling of honey, summer grass, and home.

A picture of a white wolf and a black wolf, howling at the moon. The word *forever* written on the back beneath their names.

The night he'd kissed Eddie Turner for the first time and understood what forever meant and what he truly wanted. Eddie. Always Eddie. He would do anything for Eddie. It was a promise he thought had died long ago, burned to nothing but ash along with the boys they'd once been. He loved Eddie. Goddess, Vicenzo loved him so much. He should have told him.

Beneath his skin, the beast strained against Vicenzo's control. That control had gotten stronger than it once was thanks to his pack, but in the midst of so much pain and trauma, it was coming apart fast. It would be easy to let go, to surrender all of himself to the wolf.

He closed his eyes tight and breathed in and out. Everything hurt. This was supposed to be their beginning, his and Eddie's. This wasn't how they were supposed to end, divided by hunters yet again. They were supposed to find their way back to each other, no matter how long it took, no matter how stupid and stubborn they were about it.

Closing his eyes, he found the warm bonds of the pack and unmuted them. They were frightened. They were looking for him.

"Don't come for me," he whispered across the fraying threads. *"Stay away, Ed. Please, Goddess, stay away."* Eddie couldn't come after him. He deserved nothing but peace with their pack. Their beautiful, crazy family who'd chosen them time and again, and given them a home when once they'd had nothing.

"I love you, Eddie."

Eddie couldn't hear him, but Vicenzo had finally spoken his truth.

"Vico!" Ben said. *"Hang on. Hear me? We're coming!"*

"Goodbye," he told them. *"Thank you for everything."*

"Vico?" It was Max. *"What are you doing?"*

"Don't," Ben croaked. *"Don't do this."*

Vicenzo felt for each of the threads that bound him to his pack. They cried out to him, they begged him, told him they were coming, to hold on, please hold on, they were coming, they were—

He severed the bonds connecting himself to his pack and felt as if an axe had been driven through his skull, through his heart. He roared from the pain. It happened quickly. His fangs pierced his lip. Knuckles cracked as his bloody fingers spasmed and his torn nails regrew into claws. Fabric ripped and tore as his body shifted, fur bursting from his skin. His head snapped to the left, then to the right as the wolf's jaws burst from his face.

"It's happenin'. Let him outta those cuffs. Get a collar. Hurry!"

Everything faded as he closed his eyes and—

He stood in the middle of a burning forest. Wolves howled as they burned, the smell of their burning fur and flesh making Vicenzo's stomach roil. Yellow eyes blazed from within the trees, their light as big and bright as the moon. The wolf came for him, shaking the earth with each slam of its paws over the cracked desert floor. It was huge, towering over the trees and blocking out the moon's light.

The wolf opened his jaws wide and darkness engulfed him.

EDDIE'S VISION BLURRED WITH tears. Gabe had a hand on his shoulder, squeezing tight. Their boat had crashed during the fight with the hunters, and they'd been wandering the muddy shore, trying to catch up to Elijah's boat. Ahead, Ben sagged against a tree, his shoulders shaking.

"What happened?" Eddie said, his voice raspy and dry.

Max touched his chest. "Vicenzo broke the bonds between us. He…" Max swallowed hard, eyes damp. "He had a message for you, Ed. He said he—that he loves you."

Vicenzo loved him.

Oh, goddess, his Vico loved him.

Tears stung Eddie's eyes and he had no hope of fighting them back as they spilled down his face. It wasn't fair. Eddie should have been the one to hear those words. Vico should have told him face to face and Eddie should have been there to kiss him and tell him that he loved him, too.

It sounded too much like a goodbye. Elijah wouldn't kill him. No, but he would make Vicenzo wish he had. He would torture Vicenzo. Probably was already torturing him right now. Elijah wouldn't stop, not until he'd broken Vicenzo's mind and forced him to go feral. Eddie knew, because he'd experienced that pain himself.

A scream tore from Eddie's throat and he lashed out, striking the nearest tree with his bare fists. He wished he had claws so he could tear the trunk to shreds. He swung again and again until the bark tore his knuckles and blood dripped down between his fingers. Gasping, he slumped against the tree, choking back sobs.

Izzie touched his back. "Eddie, this isn't the end. We can still save him. We'll get him back."

He sucked in shuddery gulps of air. She was right. This wasn't over. "What if he goes feral?"

"Ed. Look at me." Ben's voice was scraped as raw as Eddie's knuckles, and Eddie nearly broke into pieces when he saw the tears in Ben's eyes. "We will find him and get him back. I promise."

Sniffling, Eddie wiped his streaming eyes. "I've seen what happens to the wolves my uncle breaks. They don't come back."

Ryan shook his head. "I can help bring him back. That's what druid magic is for, to help werewolves. Let's not be all Debbie Downer here."

Ben said, "That's right, Ed. We've brought ferals back before, and this time is no different."

Ben was right. They could do this. He and Vicenzo had come together and been pulled apart. They'd wasted years being angry and scared, hiding behind the wounds of their past. This wasn't how it ended. This wasn't their goodbye.

"It'll be a challenge," Eddie said, "but I don't care. Gabe, did you and Max give up on each other when you were separated in Italy?"

Gabe took Max's hand. "Hell no."

"And Ryan and Zach, you didn't give up on each other when Ryan moved away. You fought like hell."

Zach propped his elbow on Ryan's head. "We sure did."

Eddie looked to Ben and Isaac. "You two were separated for twenty years. Did you let that stop you?"

"Almost," Ben grumbled.

Isaac kissed his sour-looking mate's cheek. "No. We made it work."

Eddie looked to Izzie. "And you..."

With her hands on her hips, Izzie glared at him. "My work with the LPA is way more important to me than any guy. Except Enrique. He's a keeper. But you have a point. We don't give up on our own. It doesn't matter if

Vico's feral. We'll fight like hell to bring him back to us. That's what we do."

Eddie smiled.

Ben clapped Eddie's shoulder. "Then let's find out where that bastard uncle of yours took him."

CHAPTER 21

A PACKMATE TO SAVE

By the time they finally found a way back to New Orleans, Eddie was exhausted. As the pack piled into a booth at a 24-hour diner, Eddie hung his head between his knees and prayed to Amaris that Vicenzo could still be saved.

"Hey." Ryan kicked Eddie's boot under the table. "No matter what shape Vico's in, he's got a hell of a good reason to come back." He batted his eyelashes.

"You look stupid," Eddie said, his face warming.

Ryan rolled his eyes. "You're mates! I'm so proud of my sons for finally pulling their heads outta their asses!" He tousled Eddie's hair, and Eddie snorted and batted his hand away.

Zach smiled exasperatedly. "What he means is Vicenzo's got more reason than ever to come back. Look, man, we've been through way worse than this. Remember when Atticus nearly drove us all feral? When MacCready and his wolves attacked New York? And look at us. We're stronger than ever. We'll get your boy back, and we'll stop your uncle."

Zach held up a hand and Eddie leaned over the table and slapped their palms together. "Fuck it. Let's do this."

The pack ordered a big breakfast: plates of eggs of different styles, hash browns, sausages and bacon, bowls of grits, and a plate stacked high with biscuits. Ben hardly ate since he was on the phone with the local police, and Isaac had to hand him chunks of biscuit to remind him to eat. The call lasted over an hour. Finally, Ben hung up with a sigh and eagerly accepted the mouthful of hash browns Isaac gave him. There were chuckles but Ben glared and quickly silenced them.

"Good news?" Eddie asked. His grits were a lump in his stomach.

Ben said, "There's only one suspected underground fighting pit the cops know of within driving distance from New Orleans. It's in Mississippi. They suspect it's being held in some barn in Kentwood. The owner of said barn's got a history of wolf fighting. The cops are going over today to shut the fight down." He grinned, his eyes alight. "They wouldn't mind if we helped."

"Hell yeah!" Ryan said, spitting eggs across the table and making Izzie roll her eyes. "Let's shut those fuckers down!"

Eddie balled his hands into fists in his lap.

Hang on, Vico. I'm coming for you.

THE SUNSET STAINED THE sky blood red by the time they arrived in Kentwood, Mississippi. They sped through sleepy rural streets as Ben followed the coordinates relayed to him by the officers until they stopped near a cornfield. Ben led the way toward the silhouette of a barn and silos that reached toward the skies, casting long, deep shadows.

Wolves and dogs howled from within the barn, their voices full of misery and fury.

"What's the plan?" Zach asked, marching beside Ben.

"The cops are undercover and they should already be inside," said Ben. "We wait for their signal."

Eddie closed his eyes. If anything happened to Vico—

Gabe gripped his shoulder. "Easy there, Ed. We got this."

Ben opened the barn doors and a rush of sound washed over Eddie as he followed him inside. Men and women formed a ring around a barrier in the center of the barn. The ground within the ringed-off pit was stained with old blood that had seeped into the wood. Eddie couldn't imagine how many wolves and dogs had lost their lives beneath the indifferent eyes of humans while they drank beer and made bets. The thought made his fingers curl into fists.

Max sniffed the air and growled low. "This place makes me sick."

Gabe put his arm around his shoulders, jaw tight.

Ryan was bristling, and Zach tugged on the hood of his sweatshirt to keep him close. The druid was short but his temper ran hot, and Eddie felt intimidated just seeing the fury behind his glasses.

Ben said, "Keep your heads on, people. Wait for the signal."

Izzie nudged Eddie. "Do you see Vico?" She stood on her toes, trying to see over the crowd.

He could see some cages within the pens further back but couldn't identify who was inside them. "No," he whispered, his heart thudding hard in his throat. He scanned the crowd, going from one bloodthirsty face to another. He couldn't see Elijah, but he was sure his uncle was here somewhere.

This was it. His uncle's reign of terror ended today.

"This is the police!" boomed a voice from a loudspeaker somewhere in the barn. The excited buzz of the crowd cut out abruptly as eyes went wide and heads turned in all directions. "Put your hands in the air and line up against the wall!"

Ben shouldered through the crowd, his badge in hand as he went to stand with the group of undercover officers near the door. Side by side with the police, Eddie readied himself for resistance.

What happened next happened fast.

A hunter peered around a bale of hay up in the hayloft and fired. The bolt cut through the air and penetrated an officer's shoulder. She went down as her fellow officers opened fire on the hayloft. Taking the opportunity to scatter, the crowd ran for the back doors or any side entrances. Ben roared, his fangs and claws out. The wolves in the back of the barn went crazy, hurling themselves against their cages and rattling them side to side.

Eddie charged, leaping onto a haybale and climbing up into the loft. He seized the hunter by her throat and threw her to the ground.

A bolt flew past Eddie's head as he dove for cover behind a bale of hay. There were more hunters in the back near the cages. One popped up from behind the pen where he was taking cover. Eddie's bullet split his skull and he slumped over the gate to the pen.

Once the hunters blocking the way were dead, Eddie ran for the cages. Panting, Eddie knelt next to the wooden gate of the pen. A wolf snapped and snarled in his ear, its paws slamming against the gate. He leaned around and took a shot as a hunter ran past for the back door. The bullet caught the hunter in the ankle and he fell with a yowl, clutching at his leg.

While their comrades opened fire, keeping the cops at bay with bullets and silver grenades, the hunters escaped. Ben roared and his song bowled over Eddie.

"Find the ones who hurt you." Ben's berserker voice filled his mind and even though he wasn't connected to his wolf anymore, Eddie still wanted to submit and obey. *"Find them and hurt them like they hurt you, but leave them alive."*

The feral wolves answered Ben's command, howling their bloodlust and fury. Eddie reached around and flipped the latch on the pen door, and a wolf hurled itself against the gate and ran free. Then the hunters firing at the cops suddenly shrieked and screamed as the ground shook beneath their feet. Ryan advanced on them, hand raised. Roots exploded from beneath the ground, wrapping around the hunters and binding them to the floor.

"Set them all free!" Izzie called, and she unlocked a wolf's pen. The pack scattered, freeing wolves from their enclosures, and the wolves charged, pursuing the hunters. Eddie ran toward a pen near the back door and his heart stuttered. A black wolf snarled at him, yellow eyes burning bright.

"Vico," Eddie whispered. The wolf's lips pulled back from his fangs, his snout wrinkled in fury. There was no recognition in those wild eyes, and it made Eddie's stomach churn. "Easy. I'm gonna let you out, and we're gonna make those sons of bitches pay." His hand trembled as he fumbled with the latch. The door sprang open and the black wolf charged, turning into a smoky blur as he pelted past Eddie in pursuit of his captors.

A white wolf with streaks of black on his back and snout tore past—Ryan. A big brown timber wolf followed—Zach. Izzie and Gabe raced past as wolves, and Max's red fur was like a fireball as he hurtled after the hunters. Feet slamming the dirt as he ran into the night, Eddie fired shots after the hunters as they fled like prey.

Two of the hunters tried the handle of a car and when it wouldn't budge, they climbed atop the vehicle and huddled there as Ryan and Zach threw themselves against the metal. Vicenzo tackled a hunter to the ground, shaking her leg between his jaws as she screamed. Gabe and Max chased a hunter up a tree and another barricaded himself inside a silo as Izzie hurled herself against the door, barking. Isaac pointed his pistol in a hunter's face and the hunter went deathly still, hands up. Ben hoisted a hunter off the ground in one enormous claw and threw him into a tree.

A wide-brimmed hat flew through the air and landed in the dirt at Eddie's feet. Elijah. Looking in the direction of the wind, Eddie spotted the old hunter as he knelt beside a trailer. Elijah looked around with a wild expression as he unhooked the trailer from his truck. His single eye met Eddie's and the blood drained from his face. Snarling in primal fury, Eddie raised his gun and fired, blasting Elijah's pistol out of his hand. Elijah ran, hurling himself into his truck.

Eddie took aim at Elijah's tires. His gun clicked empty, and there wasn't time to reload. Lunging, Eddie latched onto the back of Elijah's pickup truck. Eddie's feet dragged in the mud as Elijah hurtled toward the cornfield, crashing through the wooden fence and barreling through the rows of corn. Stalks of corn slapped Eddie in the face and beat at his shoulders and head. He ducked into the truck bed and took a moment to catch his breath.

When he sat up, Elijah slammed on the brakes. Eddie tumbled over the hood of the truck but latched onto the windshield wipers. He ducked his head as Elijah fired through the window, shattering the glass. Eddie struggled, trying to crawl his way on top of the vehicle. When he looked up, he was staring down the muzzle of Elijah's pistol. Elijah grinned and Eddie saw white as gunfire erupted.

All the oxygen in Eddie's body was knocked out of him as what felt like a fist slammed into his neck. He went soaring through the air, tumbling over until the world blurred around him. He spasmed, feeling like he was dying as his windpipe throbbed. As he fumbled for his throat, he was certain he'd encounter slick, hot blood from where the bullet had entered his neck and—

The silver collar cracked in two, the halves falling into the mud beside him. A cold nose pressed against his ear and a growl rumbled in his eardrums. Looking up, he saw three black wolves above him. He blinked and the three became one as his dizziness faded. Vicenzo blinked yellow eyes at him.

There was no recognition in the wolf's eyes. He scented the air and licked his chops, no doubt smelling the blood from Eddie's scrapes and cuts. The wolf flattened his ears and growled at him. Heart racing, Eddie said, "Hey. Easy there, Vico. It's me. It's Eddie."

The wolf's yellow eyes flared brightly.

"Hey, come on. Snap out of it! You know me." Eddie's voice wobbled and broke. Vicenzo had been fighting off feral madness for weeks now. He couldn't give up—Eddie wouldn't let him.

"Ed," Zach began, approaching slowly.

Ben gripped Zach's shoulder. "Hold on."

Eddie shivered under those furious yellow eyes. "We grew up together. Remember? We promised we'd be together forever. You promised me, and I ain't lettin' you break it. Not now, not ever."

The wolf stopped growling and tilted his head at Eddie. Then he sat down, his posture more relaxed even though his eyes were still feral yellow.

Relieved tears stung Eddie's eyes. Vico had recognized him. "You're still in there, Vico, aren't you?" He caressed the wolf's cheek. "I knew it. Thank the goddess. I knew you weren't so far gone."

"You okay, Ed?" Ben stopped beside him.

Eddie nodded, closing his eyes as exhaustion weighed him down. Ben extended a hand and Eddie reached out and froze as his sleeve rolled back. The scars were fading, healing before his eyes. Scars his uncle had given him. Scars he'd received from wolves he'd hunted. His past was disappearing before his very eyes. It would always live there under his skin, but Eddie was surprised how good it felt to have the physical reminders finally wiped away.

"Your collar," Ben said, brow raised.

Eddie nodded, watching the scar tissue fade into smooth skin. "Yeah. My healing is kicking in." He closed his eyes, searching, but encountered a black space in his head and heart where he'd hoped to feel the pack threads. "I can't feel any of you." Eddie's voice shook. Fuck. It was just as he'd feared. He could go feral if this wasn't addressed, and soon.

"Easy." Ben squeezed his shoulder. "You won't shift until tonight when the moon is out. We'll get this fixed, Ed, but we have to get home first."

Vicenzo cocked his head, his eyes flashing yellow.

Eddie said, "Are you controlling him?"

Ben frowned. "Bit of a negative word choice. But yeah, I guess so. Him and the others, keeping 'em from losing their shit and attacking us. It's temporary until Ry can help restore them. We need to get all of them back to the agency for treatment."

Disappointment walloped Eddie in the chest. Vicenzo hadn't recognized him at all. His calm was Ben's doing. Was there any hope for him?

Eddie reached out, his fingers settling on Vicenzo's snout. His chest ached as the wolf remained unresponsive to his touch. "Can we help him?" He needed Vicenzo to be okay, and it wasn't only for Vico's sake now. Eddie's wolf would need their bond to anchor him to his humanity. However they got Vico back, it would have to be before the moon rose.

"Ben, if we can't help him, I'm done for, too. He's always been my anchor. Always." Eddie's eyes stung. "If I don't have him, then I'm as good as lost to my wolf." If Vico couldn't come back, then Eddie didn't want to either. A world without Vicenzo Salvatore wasn't a world he wanted any part of.

"We've done it before. We can do it again." He patted Eddie's shoulder. "Now, help the others get the wolves caged up. I'll talk to the cops and tell them your uncle's on the loose."

Dismay tightened like a fist in Eddie's gut. "I tried, Ben. I really did."

"I know," Ben answered. "He won't get far. Now, let's go. We got a packmate to save." He walked away and Vicenzo loped after him. Eddie watched the black wolf go, hoping and praying they would find a way.

He wasn't giving up on Vicenzo Salvatore. He wasn't losing Vico, not again.

EDDIE AND THE PACK were flown back to Fire Island in a helicopter. It would be a few days before the other wolves arrived at the agency for treatment but Vicenzo had been able to travel with them. During the flight he slept curled up at Ben's side while his eyes darted nervously around the once familiar faces of his pack. Eddie wished his own connection to the pack had been fixed, wished there was a thread connecting him to Vico so he could reassure him that everything would be okay.

The fear twisted up his insides and made him feel sick. Vicenzo couldn't leave him. He had to come back so Eddie could tell him how much he loved him and hear him say it back. So they could make up for all the years they'd wasted, being so stupid and angry and bitter.

The helicopter landed with a bump at the heliport located near HQ.

"Home." Ryan sighed, digging a finger in his ear as they departed the heliport and climbed into cars waiting to pick them up.

New York didn't feel like home, Eddie realized bitterly. For so long, home had been temporary. Back when his father was on the run from the Council and The Beasts, they'd moved from place to place. Red Rock Springs had been the first place that felt like home, and Elijah had stolen that from him, too. Now his uncle was once more on the loose, and at any moment he could come and take Eddie's home from him again. It was a fear he'd lived with constantly even after joining the agency, made flesh and blood after his encounter with Elijah. Nowhere would ever feel like home again unless Vicenzo was with him and his uncle was gone.

The agency's gates opened as they drove up. Vicenzo growled as the staff approached with a collar. Ben flashed his eyes and Vicenzo stilled but continued to growl as the staff snapped the collar around his neck and led him away. Eddie blinked against the burn in his eyes.

As Vicenzo disappeared around the corner, Eddie swallowed around the lump in his throat. A glance up at the setting sun made Eddie's heart sink. His time was running out, and so was Vico's. He prayed they could bring him back, for both their sakes.

CHAPTER 22

FIRE AND MOONLIGHT

THE EXAM ROOM ON the second floor of the estate was quiet when Eddie arrived. Zach and Ryan sat on the floor with Vicenzo who growled around the muzzle as Ryan reached toward him.

Ryan said, "Easy, bud. I'm not going to hurt you." Slowly, he reached for Vicenzo's snout and touched the spot between Vicenzo's yellow eyes. His fingers began to glow. Quiet fell as Ryan bowed his head and closed eyes glowing golden with magical energy.

Zach put his hand on Ryan's back. Zach didn't have magic, but Ryan claimed his magic was stronger when Zach was around.

Ryan yanked his hand back as if he'd been burned, and Vicenzo took a few steps back, growling around the muzzle.

"Okay?" Zach asked, massaging Ryan's shoulders.

Ryan gnashed his teeth, raking a hand through his hair. "Damn it! I can't get through to him!"

"What do you mean?" Zach asked, the calm to Ryan's storm.

Ryan sighed, rubbing his glasses on his sleeve. "I'm trying to use my magic to make a bridge between him and us. To restore the bonds he shattered. Without magic, we'd do a Humanity Restorative Treatment using objects he might have an emotional attachment to in order to jump-start that connection to his humanity." He motioned to some of Vicenzo's things he'd laid on the ground in front of the wolf, like his favorite shirt and the drawing he made for Eddie. "Even with the objects and the magic,

288

he's fighting me. I need to try something else. He's too feral for what I'm trying to do."

Eddie squeezed his fingers together. "But you can bring him back."

Ryan nodded. "I will."

Kneeling behind him, Zach touched his forehead to Ryan's hair. "You got this."

Ryan exhaled, eyes bright with determination.

"Maybe he doesn't want to come back." Eddie hated himself for saying that but maybe staying as a wolf was simpler due to their past.

Ryan waved a hand. "Let's not go there, Ed. Okay, let's do this..." He began to chant in what Eddie thought was Gaelic. Vicenzo's fur rippled and his eyes glowed, flashing a bright, human blue.

Eddie's heart stuttered. Ryan had done it. He'd brought Vicenzo back, he—

A wave of yellow filled Vicenzo's eyes, choking out the blue. He lunged, straining the chain tethering him to the wall.

Zach yanked Ryan back. "Ry?"

Ryan was doubled over, clutching his head. "Son of a bitch," he said with a grunt.

Eddie smelled blood. "Are you bleeding?"

Rubbing his nose, Ryan said, "Shit. That ain't good." There was a smear of blood on his fist from his nose. He dropped back onto his butt with a defeated sigh and chewed on his lip, his brows furrowed and glasses askew.

Zach said, "I think that's enough." His knuckles whitened as he gripped Ryan's shoulder. "Even I felt that. Like a throbbing in my head. That's not normal."

Eddie slumped, anxiety churning his insides. "What happened? I saw his eyes turn blue! You got him back, so what happened?" He sounded more accusatory than he felt. He needed this to work, so badly.

His face paler than usual, Ryan said, "He's not as feral as I thought. It's his own choice. I heard his voice—he told me to go away."

Crossing his arms, Eddie glared at his stubborn mate. "Piss off, Vico. We're not giving up on you." He had no idea if the wolf understood him.

Zach ran a hand over his short stubble, his brown eyes glazing over as he thought. "Maybe it's not you he wants to talk to, Ry."

Ryan cracked a grin. "But I'm so fantastic."

Zach bit back a smile, sucking in his lips. "Ed's the one he's got the connection to. Maybe he'd like to talk to Eddie?"

Ryan slapped his forehead. "Duh! Why the fuck didn't I think of that?" He flapped a hand at Eddie.

Eddie wasn't sure how he could be of any help, but he knelt beside Ryan. "What do I have to do?" Whatever it took, he would do it without question. He wouldn't stop until he brought his mate home.

Ryan said, "So, there's this theory. Well, it's not really a theory. Gabe told me that when he became a berserker, he had to go inside his own freaking mind to confront his inner wolf. A lot of spiritual Zen bullshit I didn't buy at the time, but now that I've been using my magic to help wolves, I've been there. It's like... Hmm. How do I say it?" He snapped his fingers. "It's like there's a place inside all werewolves where our wolf dwells. When we've got a strong connection to our humanity, our human selves are in harmony with our inner wolf and we... coexist. When we lose ourselves, when the wolf takes over, there is imbalance and chaos."

Eddie didn't understand. "Where are you goin' with this, Ry?"

Ryan said, "I'm going to send you into his mind. Into his inner world. And you're gonna help him restore the balance."

Eddie gaped. "Like... teleport me?"

Ryan shook his head. "Well, sorta. You'll be here physically, but your minds will be linked."

Eddie wasn't sure he liked the sound of this. "That sounds dangerous for him, maybe even for you."

Ryan chuckled softly. "It might be. I read some ancient texts of an account. This druid tried to restore a wolf's humanity by linking them and fried both their minds. Like, their heads actually exploded and—"

Zach shook his head. "No. Absolutely not, Ry. If it's that risky, we need to do something else."

Eddie's heart sank. "But this might be the only way we can reach him, Zach!"

Ryan grinned. "I've done this before. I can do this. Besides, that druid probably didn't have a very, very handsome mate."

Though he coughed with embarrassment, the corner of Zach's mouth hooked up. "What he means is his magic is strong because we are strong. He can do it, Ed."

Eddie breathed in and out. "Let's do this."

Ryan said, "Kneel in front of him."

Eddie did, looking the black wolf in the eyes. Vicenzo's ears flicked but Ben's berserker powers still had a hold on him, and he was calm.

"Put your hands on him."

Eddie did, one hand on Vicenzo's head, the other on his shoulder.

"Deep breaths in and out. Try and clear your mind. And..." Ryan began to murmur in Gaelic.

Eddie focused on his breath, curling his fingers in Vicenzo's fur.

Something burst in his mind, a thread connecting him to Vicenzo that burned bright.

His eyes flew open and he gulped, racked by vertigo as his vision spun. The air was hot. He smelled burning leaves and wood, the charred stench of burnt flesh and fur and—

Eddie knew where he was even before the howling began. The wolves screamed as they burned along with their homes.

He pushed himself up onto his hands and knees. Soot covered his fingertips. He raised his head to the smoke-blackened skies as ash fell like snow over the desert. "Vico?" he called, his voice drowning among the roar of the flames and the howling of the wolves. Something tugged in his mind, black and burning. Vicenzo was in here somewhere.

As wolves tore toward him, their bodies wreathed in flame, Eddie pushed himself up and ran, choking on ash. Smoke curled near his foot and he jumped and looked down. His pant leg was burning. *He* was burning. He'd been burning for years, suffocating on the memories of everything and everyone he'd lost. Somewhere, Vicenzo was burning, too.

And Eddie was tired of burning in the past.

"Vico!" he roared, running past the shadows of hunters armed with flamethrowers, past wolves who flailed and howled as they burned alive.

Shapes loomed ahead of him. Eddie thought he recognized one of those silhouettes. It wasn't Vicenzo, but he recognized the camo jacket, the choppy hair. Was that... himself?

Eddie reached out, touching his own shoulder and—

And he knew this moment because it had haunted him, haunted them, for thirteen years.

He stood where his silhouette had stood, but it wasn't Vicenzo who stood before him. A huge wolf stared back at him through blazing yellow eyes. Smoke curled from his body, embers and ash raining from his fur.

"Leave," the wolf snarled. The voice was feral, fearsome, but the creature trembled. "Go away, Eddie. I told the druid to stay away."

Eddie dropped the silver pistol in his hand, struggling to breathe around the silver choking his throat. "Vico," he whispered, his voice hoarse from smoke. "Why? Why are you doing this?"

"Leave me here." The wolf growled and backed away, his huge paws igniting the grass underneath him. "Can't you see? Don't you get it, Ed? There's no salvaging this. Us. Go away and never come back. Find a way to be happy without me."

Eddie dropped to his knees, shaking too badly to stand. "I won't do that."

"Just leave me!" The wolf howled. "Live your life without me. Just let me burn."

"I'm tired," Eddie croaked, his voice cracking down the middle. "I'm tired of burning, Vico. I know you are, too. We've been trapped in this moment all these years. Struggling to move past this. The moment you came to me wanting to start over, and I..."

He swallowed thickly. The fire had reached his knees, but it didn't hurt, even though everything below the knee had turned to ash.

"I pushed you away. Because I was broken. Because I was lost. Not because I didn't love you." His eyes burned, and smoke stung his nose and ached in his throat. "I love you, Vico. I never stopped. I always have, and I..."

Words failed him. He reached out, opening his hands. The wolf raised his hackles, backing away. The tips of his fur were burning, embers glowing within his dense coat like fireflies.

"We're not who we once were. I used to think if you'd just let me in, we could be who we used to be. It would erase the hurt I caused you, the damage that had been done to me. It won't. Vico, nothing will ever erase any of the things we went through. Who I was, who you were—they died with our families." Something ran wet and hot down his face.

The wolf whined deep and low, his ears flattening as flames licked at his paws.

Once, Eddie hadn't known what to say to make Vicenzo forgive him for pushing him away. How he could erase years of bitter pain, anger, and grief with just the right word. And he knew now he couldn't, and he knew now he didn't care to.

"I want us to start again, as who we are now. Broken. Haunted. Damaged. But with the pack who chose us again and again despite it all. Nothing else matters but that. So..."

He couldn't breathe. Everything hurt, and he didn't know if it would ever stop hurting but with his pack, with Vico, he knew they would be okay.

"So I'm choosing you, Vico. I'm asking you to come back with me. Back to them. To our family, to our home. 'Cause home ain't home unless you're right there with me. And... and if you can't, if it just hurts too damn much, then I will stay here and burn with you."

The wolf's eyes flickered. Yellow... yellow...

Eddie crumpled, his chest tight and throbbing.

Trembling hands clasped his face, brushing away tears and ash.

Breath hitching, Eddie looked up.

Vicenzo knelt before him. His eyes were big and bright, glistening with unshed tears. Lips trembling, Vicenzo leaned in, bumping their foreheads together. He exhaled and smoke rose in a cloud from his mouth.

"I'm not..." Vicenzo's voice was rough and scratchy from smoke. "I'm not the same person, Eddie. I'm cynical, and dark, and I say shit I don't mean—" He exhaled harshly. "There's parts of me that are all smashed up. I don't know how to put it together again."

Eddie clasped his face. "I know. Okay? I know, 'cause that's me, too. You think I'm perfect?"

Vicenzo snorted. "You sure seem like it." And he meant it. He looked at Eddie like he'd hung the sun, moon, and stars. Blinking hard, Vicenzo set his lips in a tight, trembling line. "I told myself you'd come for me. I wanted to believe you would, even though I also wanted you to stay away from that monster."

Eddie exhaled shakily. "Did you believe I'd come for you?"

Vicenzo shrugged, but a tear tumbled down his cheek. "I wanted you to, Ed."

Eddie kissed Vicenzo's forehead and tasted ash. "I'm here now. I found you, and I'm never pushin' you away again. I'm never lettin' you go. Do you believe me?"

Vicenzo's eyes were so wide and damp, catching the orange glow of the fire raging around them. "I do," he whispered, and Eddie couldn't fathom how two little words could hold so many tender emotions.

"So come back, Vico. Will you come back with me?" Eddie held his breath.

Vicenzo leaned in, enveloping Eddie in his arms. He said, "Okay, Eddie. Okay."

Eddie closed his eyes tight and flung his arms around Vicenzo's shoulders.

They held each other tight as the forest burned, as their clothes caught fire and their flesh smoked.

They burned together, until they were nothing but ash.

VICENZO OPENED HIS EYES to a white ceiling with cold tile against his back. There was a warm weight atop him, and for a moment he couldn't breathe. He wondered if he'd died and been reborn like a phoenix, trapped beneath the ashes of the life he'd left behind and the person he used to be.

He wanted to be better this time. He didn't want to be angry anymore, or bitter. He wanted to start over. With Eddie. With the pack, the family he'd found. If they'd let him.

"Hell yeah! I did it!"

"Ry, shush," said a deep voice, though not without a touch of humor. "Ed, Vico? You guys okay?"

The weight atop him shifted. "Oh shit! Can you breathe, Vico? I'm sorry!"

Vicenzo gulped in oxygen as Eddie's shoulder came away from his nose. He blinked up into a pair of bright blue eyes, locks of golden blond hair falling over them.

"Eddie..." Vicenzo whispered. His arms weighed a thousand pounds but he managed to lift one. He brushed his fingers over Eddie's cheek. It was damp, and the salty smell of his tears clung to his skin.

"You're back," Eddie whispered, voice trembling. He smiled, and it was blinding. "You're really..."

Vicenzo smiled, though he couldn't remember going anywhere. His memories were fuzzy after Elijah had taken him. All the missing spaces must have been from when he'd given himself to his wolf. It scared him to realize how much more he might have missed, because he didn't want to miss this. He never wanted to be anywhere else but here, with Eddie, with his pack.

"Yeah, Ed." He dropped his arms around Eddie's shoulders and held on tight. "I'm back. I'm home."

Eddie kissed him, and he poured his all into it. Vicenzo was overwhelmed by him, the passion with which he kissed him, his tongue brushing his lips and their teeth bumping, his joyful tears as they rained onto Vicenzo's cheeks.

"Your collar... it's gone." Vicenzo touched his bare neck.

Eddie nodded, his heart skipping. "I'll shift tonight for the first time in years."

Vicenzo grinned. "That's awesome."

Eddie hummed, too worried to say much.

"Hey. It'll be okay. Ed, listen to me. I can feel you," Vicenzo whispered. "Faint but... I can finally feel you." Their bond was fragile and tenuous, but for the first time in years, Vico could feel him. It wasn't like when they were kids. It was blackened and burned but warm in his heart.

Eddie rubbed his own chest. "Me too. A little." He was frowning. "It's not as strong as it once was."

Vicenzo squeezed his arm. "It's okay. This is our new start. Our new beginning. We'll nurture our bond day by day. It will be enough to bring you back when you shift tonight."

"You think so?"

Vicenzo cupped his cheek. "Yes. I know so."

Eddie hiccupped when their mouths parted, his trembling lips working into a fractured smile as tears glittered on his lashes. "Welcome home."

CHAPTER 23

FAMILY

THERE WAS NO TIME for celebrations. It was a fact that lay heavy on Vicenzo's heart, but there it was. Eddie knew it too. He could see it in his mate's eyes, and in the heavy smile he presented to Ben.

Eddie said, "My uncle's hunters are gone. His wolves are gone. He doesn't have any allies he can turn to. He never trusted anyone outside his own clan. So..."

Vicenzo took his hand. "We're gonna go after him. Eddie and me. We can take him on our own. And we're gonna make sure he's stopped for good."

It was a plan they'd discussed together, sitting on the cold tile after Vicenzo had regained his humanity. Neither of them had wanted to leave after everything the pack had been through, the bonds that Vicenzo had shattered only just beginning to heal. But they had to be the ones to end this.

Eddie's hand tensed in Vicenzo's, his eyes wide as he scanned Ben's face for his reaction.

"So, that's it," Ben said, his hands folded on his desk. Vicenzo couldn't smell anger or disapproval that they'd made this decision without the pack's input.

Eddie added, "We'll be careful, Ben. I swear it. And I know where he is, too! I think so, anyway."

Vicenzo bumped their shoulders together. "He knows so."

Eddie nodded, his face red. "Elijah had this place out in Nevada, somewhere he'd go if he needed to shake the cops. An abandoned military bunker built back in World War II, I think. It's the only place I can think where he might have gone, especially since traffic cams caught him headin' in the direction of Nevada. So I'd like to ask for your permission to hunt him down, just Vico and me."

Ben nodded, running a hand through his bushy beard. "To think I'd see the day you two would make decisions together behind my back and assume I'd say yes." He grinned. "Have to say, I'm damn proud of you boys."

Eddie blinked and Vicenzo's chest warmed with satisfaction.

"You'll let us go after him?" Eddie asked.

Ben said, "I hate to see you go, but you're mine, both of you. And we're yours. You'll come back to us."

Vicenzo said, "We will."

Eddie leaned forward in his seat. "Of course. And look, this isn't because we don't love you guys or because we think you'd slow us down, or—" He took in a breath. He was afraid; Vicenzo could smell it. He was afraid of losing his family again, of making the wrong choice like he'd done before and pushing people away. Vicenzo squeezed his hand.

Eddie blinked fast. "He took everything from us, Ben. Our home. Our families. He drove Vico and me apart. We need to settle this together. And we'll be careful. I'll look after Vico. We'll nurture the connection between us so no matter how long we're gone, we have something to remind us of home."

Ben nodded, gazing down at his desk. "I've already given you my permission, Eddie. And I promise you both, no matter how far you go, no matter how long, you will always have a place here." He looked up and smiled. "Just watch yourselves out there. Elijah's a cornered animal, and we all know how those get."

Eddie slumped, blinking down into his lap. "Thank you, Ben."

"There's just one thing." Ben gazed at Eddie, his brows furrowed. "Once the moon rises, you'll shift tonight."

"You sure it won't be until the next full moon?" Vicenzo asked. That was when the urge to shift and mate was the strongest for werewolves. After all the shit he and Ed had been through, he wished they could catch a damn break. His poor mate had enough to worry about.

Ben dipped his head. "Positive. This isn't Eddie's first shift, and his wolf has been caged for so long even a glimmer of moonlight could make him shift at this point."

"He's right, Vico," Eddie admitted. "I can feel it. The moon isn't even at its brightest but I've felt it tuggin' at me."

Ben's beard made a scratching sound as he ran his hand through it thoughtfully. "You can't leave, not until you've had your first transformation. Your wolf needs to come out and strengthen his connection with the pack. You'll need a powerful shifter like me there to help you through it, and someone"—he looked pointedly at Vico—"to remind you to come back."

Eddie nodded, worrying at his lower lip until it was pale. "This is gonna suck, isn't it?"

"It'll be painful," Ben said, eyes intent on Eddie. "Your wolf will take control, but we'll be there to bring you back."

Vicenzo squeezed Eddie's shoulder, hating to see him worry. "Till then, how about you throw us a mean going-away party, Alpha?"

Ben slapped his shoulder. "Fuck off with that alpha shit, and now you're talkin'."

It was a Wednesday, which meant the pack would gather before the full moon like they always did. Usually they went to Gabe and Max's house in Duchess County but there was no time to make the drive, so they'd celebrate after hours at the agency.

Kendra and her husband, Ronaldo, drove over to see everyone, bringing Tommy and Luna with them. Gabe's parents, Veronica and Manuel, greeted their son, daughter, and grandkids. The doorbell rang and Izzie's eyes lit up. "I'll get it!" She answered the door, and a young, handsome man with glasses grinned as Izzie rushed over and took his arm.

"Everyone," Izzie said. "This is Enrique. My boyfriend."

Enrique waved. "Hey, everyone." He smiled brightly at Veronica and Manuel. "Hello, Mr. and Mrs. Reyes."

Veronica's face lit up. "I think I like this one, Izzie."

Manuel clasped Enrique's hand and shook it. Tightly. "Hey, Enrique. My daughter's told me so much about you." His nostrils flared as he sniffed Enrique.

Eddie sniffed too. "Whoa. My sense of smell is so strong now. I can actually smell that he's human." Vicenzo smiled, pleased by how happy Eddie sounded.

"Wolves are my favorite animal," Enrique squeaked. "I'm totally cool with the whole werewolf thing. Like, really cool. I think werewolves are awesome, and your daughter's awesome, and—yeah."

Veronica flashed her teeth in a grin. "We think so, too."

Manuel barked out a laugh. "Then I think you'll like us very much."

And that was that. Enrique joined the pack at their table in the courtyard for a feast. Gabe and Max grilled up a stack of elk burgers with a variety of buns and toppings. Ryan brought so many cases of beer, Max joked he'd robbed the local grocery store blind. Veronica had made her beloved tres leches cake.

While they ate, Max and Gabe told the story of how they'd first met since Vicenzo realized he'd never asked. Max said, "I was lost and scared and hurt, but then I smelled him and a part of me knew that I was going to be all right."

Luna snorted through a mouthful of cake. "That's not what happened, Pa! You almost ripped out Daddy's throat."

Gabe and Tommy laughed.

Ryan's upper lip was covered in beer foam when he earnestly said, "You guys are a pain in the ass, but there's nowhere else I'd rather be. I seriously hate it that Gabe and Zach had to suck face so I could find out about the

LPA, but hey, looks like it was worth it. What? What are you guys laughing at?"

Zach took a sip of wine. "Seriously, though. This agency, this pack, you guys changed my life. I mean it. I'd be in land development if it weren't for you guys. A werewolf, bulldozing forests. Have you seen how ugly my father's buildings are? Cheers, guys." He raised his glass.

Isaac wiped his mouth with a napkin. "This cake is amazing, V. Babe, open wide." He held up a forkful to Ben, who growled. Isaac rolled his eyes. "Cut the crap and eat the cake. You know you want to."

Ben let out a long-suffering sigh. "I've gotten so soft since we got married." He ate the cake and glared at anyone who laughed, his fingers curling over Isaac's hand. Turning to Izzie he said, "How'd you two meet?"

Holding Enrique's hand, Izzie said, "We met at the diner in town. I had to do paperwork and I was starving, so I stopped by for a bite."

"I'm a cook there," Enrique added.

"Makes the best omelet I ever had!"

Affection brightened Enrique's eyes as he kissed Izzie's fingers. "It was quiet that night, so I was also waiting tables. The moment I saw her, I knew she was somebody special. There was this intense urge to talk to her that I'd never felt before. Makes sense now that I know I'm her fated mate." When the pack cheered, Enrique and Izzie smiled at each other and exchanged a sweet kiss. Gabe and their parents rushed to hug and congratulate Izzie on finally finding her fated match.

Eddie took Vicenzo's hand beneath the table and Vicenzo squeezed tight. Eddie raised his voice to be heard over the laughter and chatter. "We're leavin', Vico and me."

A lull fell over the crowd, all eyes landing on them. There was surprise in each of their eyes, except for Ben—and Enrique, who mostly looked confused.

Eddie wet his lips and continued. "Elijah took everything from us, and he's still out there. Vico and me, we talked and we decided that the only way we can move on is if we're sure he can't ever take our family away again." Eddie's voice faltered as the pack looked on with wide eyes.

Izzie said, "And we're not coming with you, are we?"

Vicenzo cleared his throat. It was tight. "No," he stated, and it was harder to say than he'd thought it would be. "This is something we have to do. But we're coming back to you, both of us. Ed called you family, 'cause that's what you are to us. Maybe we don't share genes or surnames, but you chose us." Vicenzo swallowed as his throat ached. Warmth burned in his chest, in his eyes. "We'd lost everything, we'd lost who we were, but you gave us a home. Put all our broken pieces back together into something resembling a whole. And we chose you. So..." It ached deep in his chest to say goodbye.

Because he loved them, all of them. So much. This family he'd found, perfectly imperfect, each bent and broken in their own way and with the scars to show for it or hidden under their skin.

Eddie's hand was warm and heavy on his shoulder. Vicenzo had lost his voice, overwhelmed by his feelings, so he bowed his head so no one would see. Eddie said, "We love you guys. All of you. Enrique, you're new here, but you're gonna be pack. I can feel it. 'Cause that's what this pack does. No matter who you are, where you come from, whether you're a human, hybrid, or wolf or a hunter, how many scars you carry—they take it all in stride and give you a home. So thank you. All of you. This isn't goodbye." Eddie raised his glass. "We'll see you all soon."

The pack raised their glasses and drank. Izzie was the first to stand and run to Eddie's side. She threw her arms around him and Vicenzo, almost tipping their chairs over. Chuckling, Vicenzo blinked fast and put his arm around her too. Ryan came next, wrestling Eddie's head to his chest, and Zach came up behind them, putting his hands on both their heads and lightly bonking them together. Isaac squeezed Vicenzo's shoulders as Ben clapped Eddie on the back, and then Gabe hugged Vicenzo while Max hugged Eddie.

The void that had yawned inside Vicenzo since the death of his family didn't close. The hurt would never truly fade away, but where there'd once been pain, there was love, blooming bright and warm like summer roses, and everything that was once lost was found again.

EDDIE STAYED INSIDE, AWAY from the moon's light, while the others prepared to shift. The pack would go for a run underneath as was tradition, but Ben wanted to know Eddie was in control first. Nerves churned like snakes in his belly. Eddie couldn't remember the last time he'd transformed—it had been that long ago.

The call of the wolf thrummed in his veins. The moon tugged at him, calling out to the beast within, telling him to throw his head back and howl, run and hunt. His claws came out, scratching the countertop. Eddie tried to urge them back in, taking deep breaths, but the animal within wouldn't be soothed. His wolf had been caged too long, and he was about to let it free for the first time in years.

What if when he shifted, he lost himself completely and could never come back? What if he destroyed the bonds he'd formed among the pack? What if he hurt someone?

The fridge door slammed. Ryan stood in his Timberwolves sweatshirt, his head tilted back as he wolfed down a slice of V's cake. Eddie smiled, biting back a laugh. Ryan shamelessly sucked some icing off his thumb. "Nervous?" he asked.

Eddie ran a claw over the marble countertop. "Yeah," he admitted.

"Don't be. You got this." Ryan gave him a sticky thumbs-up, his fingers glossy with sugary sweet icing.

Eddie snorted. "How do you know that?"

Ryan shrugged, and Eddie craved his confidence. "Gotta have faith, man. I believe in you."

Eddie's mouth tugged into a smile. Ryan had always believed in him, seen something in him, even when he was a lowly hunter of his own kind. "I know," Eddie said. "Thanks, by the way."

Ryan raised a brow, wiping his fingers on his sweatshirt. "No problem. What for?"

Eddie shrugged because he couldn't figure out what to be thankful for and it wasn't for lack of options but because there was an abundance of things in his life to be thankful for. He started from the beginning. "For seeing something in me. For believing I was capable of more than being a hunter's dog."

Ryan blinked. "Oh. Yeah, man. No problem."

Eddie wasn't done. "I mean it, Ry. You treated me with kindness. Probably 'cause you were scared of dying, sure. But you made me want to be better. To be a hero instead of the villain of my own story. Without you, I wouldn't be a part of this pack. So, thanks."

Ryan flushed, running a hand through his wavy hair. "You weren't a villain, not to me. You just seemed lost, like your life wasn't yours, hadn't been yours for a long time. I guess I thought if I was in your shoes, I'd want someone to be kind to me, to help me find my way back. You know?" He shrugged as if it were nothing, but to Eddie, that simple act of empathy had saved his life. "Besides, I think you'd have found your way back eventually."

Eddie chuckled. "Well, you definitely helped. So thanks, Ry."

Ryan scuffed his toe on the kitchen tile. "Hey, uh… good luck tonight. Your first shift in a long time, right? I don't even know what your wolf looks like. I can't wait to see it."

Eddie wished so, too, but Ben thought it would be overwhelming if he was surrounded by the pack. He was probably worried Eddie would hurt someone. "We'll be able to shift and run together once Ben's sure I'm calm."

Ryan chuckled. "Yeah, that's true."

A howl echoed from within the woods, and the wolves in the yard howled back. Eddie stood, clasping the counter as his knees trembled. "That's Ben."

Ryan raised a hand. "See you later, Ed."

Eddie smiled, surprised by how easy it was. Ryan had that way about him. At times he could be all bombast and sarcasm, but he was loyal and supportive when it counted. Eddie waved. "I will. See ya, Ry."

Vicenzo was waiting for him outside at the stone firepit. He stood as Eddie closed the back door. "Ready?"

Eddie exhaled, his body wired tight with tension. He didn't have to say anything. Vicenzo took his cold hands in his and leaned in, pressing his mouth to Eddie's. Clasping Vicenzo's face between his hands, Eddie ran his fingers over his angular jaw, his thumb brushing Vicenzo's cheekbone. He closed his eyes tight and couldn't believe that finally, they could have this. It was too good to be true, and Eddie put his arms around Vicenzo and held him close, afraid that once he shifted, he'd destroy the tenuous bond flourishing between them and undo so much progress.

"You'll be okay, Ed." Vicenzo took Eddie's hand as they walked across the estate grounds, their hands clasped tight between them as Vicenzo led the way into the woods.

Even with the moon concealed by clouds, Eddie's gums itched and he tried to pull his hand away as his claws lengthened, worried he'd cut Vicenzo without meaning to. Vicenzo held tight and said, "It's gonna be okay, Ed. I'll be here, and I'll make sure you come back."

Throat dry, Eddie nodded and squeezed his hand tight.

Ben waited for them in a clearing a mile from the house. He leaned against a tree, his arms folded, one foot propped against the trunk. "Ready?"

Eddie couldn't speak, so he nodded instead.

"I'll talk you through it," Ben said. "And if needed, I'll keep you calm if you lose control. Vico, offer as much support as you can. Reach out to him through your bond and remind him of his humanity."

Vicenzo nodded, face grave.

Ben turned his face to the skies. The cloudbank was beginning to break, the moon's light glowing around the soft edges of the cloud. Ben said, "It's almost time. Hurry, take off your clothes."

And because Eddie was nervous, he said, "You take that tone with Isaac?"

Ben rolled his eyes, and Eddie stripped, kicking off his jeans and tossing his shirt aside. When he was nude, Ben told him to sit, so Eddie sat down on the cool forest floor, the grass tickling his bare skin. Ben said, "Breathe in and out. Focus on keeping your heart rate steady. Good. Find a memory, a strong, happy one. Use it to anchor you."

Eddie thought back to when he and Vico were children, the lights of Las Vegas aglow on the horizon. Vicenzo looked him in the eyes and said, "We're forever, Eddie. You and me." And Eddie felt like he had come home.

Then the moonlight touched his skin and an electric current swept down his spine. His back arched, forcing Eddie to look into the light of the moon. His canines lengthened to points and his claws burst from the tips of his fingers, but it wasn't painful yet. His heart slammed against his chest, racing so hard and fast Eddie thought it would burst in his chest.

His leg jerked out from beneath him and the bone snapped, and a scream was pulled from his throat. White fur burst from his arms and receded. His fingers shattered, remaking themselves into paws or *trying* to, and Eddie crumpled into the dirt, howling as his hand turned into a clawed paw. The pain left him in spasms as his bones shattered and reformed. Eddie gnashed his teeth, digging his fingers and claws into the dirt, trying to make it stop.

"Don't fight it," Ben said. "I know it hurts, but if you fight it, that'll just make the transformation last longer. Breathe. Okay? Breathe and let it wash over you."

"I got you, Ed." A hand closed over his paw and squeezed. "I got you. You can do this. I know you can."

"Vico," Eddie whimpered, his eyes watering as his muscles spasmed. "It hurts. It hurts, I can't—" His head snapped to the side and he howled as his face elongated into a snout. His tailbone burst from his lower back but before the blood could flow, flesh grew along the tail, his skin itching unbearably as fur sprouted. His skin burned hot as if he were on fire inside, and Eddie thought he must be dying.

The moon said, *"Sing to me. Sing to me, wolf of mine. You've been away for so long and I've missed you so, Edward Turner, but you're home. You're home now. Sing to me!"* The She-Wolf's voice was so sweet and Eddie had to answer. Because he was hers. He was a wolf. He was—

The howl pulled from his throat as the transformation completed and he sang to the moon above. Smells... there were so many smells! Somewhere within the trees, he smelled meat and blood and deer flesh. He smelled the green of the trees and sweet pine sap, pollen tickling his nose and making him sneeze. The earth beneath his paws was soft and cool, the grass ticklish between his toes. He wanted to roll around in the dirt and get the sweet-smelling leaves in his fur and—

Squirrel. There was a squirrel! Up there, in the tree. He bolted, his paws slamming against the bark. He woofed, clawing into the trunk of the tree. He would kill the squirrel. Eat it and crunch its bones, then roll around in it.

"Uh, Ben, I think he's good. He's definitely not aggressive."

"Not unless you're a squirrel."

His ears flicked and he turned and saw two men standing behind him. One was big and strong with a furry face. He smelled like power and something woodsy. The wolf wanted to roll over on his back and show his stomach because he was a good wolf. A nice wolf. He didn't want to hurt anybody.

"Oh hell, kid. I don't need to see your junk." The older man looked away, his hand over his eyes.

He whimpered, flat on his back as he showed his belly in deference. He was sorry for trespassing in this place. The trees smelled like another pack of wolves, but he couldn't remember how he got here.

Beside the older man was another, tall with suntanned skin and short fur on his head. He smelled... good. Really good. It made his tail wag, made him want to roll around on top of the wolf and sleep on him. Protect him from everything and everyone. Because he was the most precious of all, because he smelled like home, like pack—

Pack. There was an emptiness inside him. And the wolf realized he was alone. He had no pack. He had nothing. He had no one. No. He'd had people once. He could remember their faces, a man and a woman. Mother and Father wolf. They'd loved him so.

Then they were gone. A bad man came toward him, smelling like silver and death. He locked the wolf up. Hurt him. Tortured him. Made him do terrible things. No. That wasn't true. No one had made the wolf do terrible things. He'd done it himself. Put the silver collar on. Took the gun the bad man thrust into his hand and killed other wolves like himself to save his own skin.

A whine shuddered from him. He pawed at his face. He didn't want to remember these horrible things. He wanted to forget it all. He would feel so much better if he could just run away and forget.

As the man that smelled like home, like the pack he'd once had—did have? could have?—came closer, a tremble racked him. The wolf was scared, but he didn't growl. He would never hurt this man, and he didn't think this man would hurt him. Before his eyes, the man abandoned his human form, changing to a black wolf with blue eyes. The wolf bumped his nose to Eddie's forehead and whispered words only for him.

"It's okay. You're okay. Nothing you did was your fault. You're not alone, Eddie. You'll never be alone or hurt again. You're mine. My love. My mate. Find us. We're your pack. We're your home. Find us."

Something glowed warm and bright in his head and heart. Their bond was ashen and frayed but he latched onto it. The thread connected him to the black wolf, and through him to others, faint threads of light that glowed brighter. Voices called out to him, rippling like waves along the threads wrapping tight around his heart. They howled to him and everything inside him wanted to howl back, so he did.

Because he was theirs, he realized, and he wasn't alone at all. He howled and his pack answered until the night was alight with the song of pack and family and love. He howled, and his pack came to him from within the trees, their eyes glowing bright. A red wolf loped beside a male black wolf. Two pups leaped and frolicked, watched closely by a female black wolf. A brown wolf snapped playfully at a white wolf with streaks of black on its snout, ears, and back. A gray wolf with streaks of black and gray-blue eyes bounded up to Ben.

They howled as one, calling out to him, guiding him home to them.

And Eddie broke from his shift with a gasp. His elbows shook and he crumpled into the dirt. His body ached, his eyelids heavy. He'd done it. He'd done it... Eddie closed his eyes, ready to sleep. A cold nose tickled his ear and Eddie laughed, trying to swat Vico away. The wolf nipped his fingertips and lay down, his body flush against Eddie's back.

Before Eddie knew it, the wolves had gathered around him in one big puppy pile, keeping him safe and warm. Ben shifted and plopped down next to Isaac and the pair cuddled. Eddie put his arm across Vicenzo's back and buried his face in his black fur.

There in the woods underneath a full moon, Eddie settled down to sleep surrounded by his family. He closed his eyes and whispered across the bonds that tied them all together, stronger tonight than they'd ever been before.

"I will come back. I will come home to you, all of you. I promise."

Chapter 24

WHERE WE BEGIN

THE SUN WAS RISING as Eddie and Vicenzo drove into the Holland Tunnel, and Vicenzo looked back just as the city disappeared behind them. Chuckling, he said, "I used to hate cities. Now, I can't imagine living in the country again."

Eddie was pleased he'd had a change of heart, but his mind was foggy as he gripped the wheel to anchor himself in the now. Doubt was creeping in. Elijah wasn't stupid—he had to know they were coming for him. Would he even be in the bunker when they arrived? What if this was all for nothing?

A hand gripped his arm, and Vicenzo arched a brow, showing a hint of teeth as he smiled. It was like the sun peeking out between dark clouds. Vicenzo squeezed, his thumb running over the fabric of Eddie's sleeve. Vico didn't say anything because he didn't need to—the touch of his anchor calmed Eddie's swirling thoughts. He exhaled, focusing on the warmth burning between them, like the sun. They hadn't mated, not yet. Eddie wanted to, but not with so much hanging over them.

Once Elijah was dealt with, once they were home, then Eddie would ask. If he could even find the words. A part of him feared Vico would reject him because he wasn't good enough, because of their past, because of anything, really. Now when Vico touched him, though, Eddie wondered why he'd worried at all. He loved Vico, he always had, even when they'd been at each other's throats, and Vico loved him. It had taken them years to find a way back to each other, to even begin to dream of a new future after all they'd lost and as the men they'd become. But that future was within Eddie's grasp. All he had to do was reach out and take it.

Las Vegas was thirty-seven hours away and from what Eddie remembered, the abandoned bunker was in the Mojave near Lake Mead, hidden in the hills. Vicenzo turned on the radio, scanning through the channels until he came upon some old-timey tunes from the sixties. The Monkees sang "I'm a Believer" and Vicenzo hid a smile by looking out the window. His hand fumbled, covering the top of Eddie's hand over the gear stick.

"Mom and Dad loved this song," Vicenzo said. There was an ache in his voice.

Eddie's chest hurt. He'd been trying not to think about the last time they'd been in Nevada together, but Vico's words made it real. They would be within driving distance of the ruins of the town where their childhoods had ended. With a painful ache in his chest, he wondered if something else had been built in its place, over the bones and ashes of all those who died in the massacre.

"We should visit their graves," Eddie said, his throat full of gravel.

Vicenzo didn't have to ask who or look at him when he shook his head.

"Then I'll go," Eddie said, understanding his reluctance. "I never got to say goodbye to my parents. It's only right."

Vicenzo squeezed his hand. It hurt. "Like hell I'll let you go alone."

Eddie blinked fast, the road clearing before his eyes. His eyelashes were damp. "We don't have to stay long. I just... I need to do it. Finally say goodbye to them. Let it all go."

"Yeah. I know." Vico loosened his grip on Eddie's hand, his thumb smoothing over Eddie's knuckles. Tapping his fingers on the wheel to the rhythm of the music, Eddie sang along under his breath. He thought he heard Vicenzo whispering each word.

They stopped for gas near Pittsburgh around midday, the sun high and hot in the sky. Vicenzo took the driver's seat and on they went. He'd grabbed them some snacks and they munched on them as they passed over the state line into Ohio, the state of Ben's birth and where the first LPA had been founded.

They drove on, skimming the border of Indiana as the skies darkened and the sun began its descent. Exhausted, Eddie declared they'd stop for the night at the nearest hotel in Chicago. Sighing, Vicenzo said, "Let me keep driving. I don't wanna stop."

"You're runnin' on gas station coffee," Eddie said, reclining his seat as far back as it would go.

"Yeah, but we'll make more progress."

Eddie groaned. "For fuck's sake, I'm tired, Vico. You are too. Let's just stop in Chicago and get up bright and early."

The muscles in Vicenzo's jaw ticked, and his eyes pierced the darkness of the road ahead, the lights of Chicago getting brighter and brighter. "And if Elijah gets away? What'll we do then?"

Eddie gritted his teeth. "Fuck if I know! He could be gone already."

"Then what the hell are we doing?" Vicenzo squeezed the wheel. "He might not even be there. He'll slip away again and who knows when we'll find him next? We have to keep going."

Eddie exhaled, trying to keep a level head. "Think about it. We got back to New York a hell of a lot faster than Elijah. He's a wanted man, and all he can do is drive. We got a head start on him, and he can't be that far ahead of us."

Vicenzo stepped on the gas. "So, if we go faster and cover more distance, we'll catch him."

"And what good is that if we're dead on our feet by the time we find him?"

Vico sighed, raking his fingers over his prickly buzz cut. "Fine. Where's that cheap hotel?"

Eddie checked the GPS. "Frontage Road and West 172nd Street."

They stopped on the way there for Chinese food. Once they were in their hotel room, they ate their fill of chicken lo mein and sweet and sour pork. Eddie had just enough room in his stomach for a few dumplings.

Then they shared the sink to brush their teeth, kicked off their clothes, and crawled into bed. Vico turned off the lamp and the room darkened. A warm body nestled close as Vicenzo nuzzled the back of Eddie's neck, wrapping his arms around Eddie's waist. Eddie laid a hand on Vicenzo's wrist and kept it there until he was asleep.

AFTER ANOTHER NIGHT IN a hotel, they drove until the lights of the Las Vegas Strip lit up the night sky, glowing like a setting sun on the horizon. Eddie's stomach was in knots as they drove through the city. Finally, they parked the car within the Mojave National Reserve.

Hoping he remembered the way, Eddie led them deeper into the desert. Vicenzo clutched his hand as they roamed the dry, dusty terrain in search of the bunker. Eddie's heart raced, and Vicenzo was squeezing his hand tightly enough that Eddie felt the pounding of Vicenzo's own heart through his fingertips.

"Smell anything?" Vico asked, nose to the air.

All Eddie smelled was dry, cracked soil and a few desert hares. Then he realized he'd stepped in a footprint in the dirt. He knelt and sniffed, catching Elijah's scent. "He's been here." For the next few minutes, he and Vicenzo followed the tracks.

"Whoa. Hard to miss." Vicenzo gazed at a heavy round door, tinged copper with rust, that was built into the side of the hill and was barring the way. Grimacing, he said, "Getting in there's gonna be a pain in the—"

Eddie pushed against the door and it opened.

Vicenzo shrugged, smiling wryly. "Okay. Guess not." Darkness filled the entrance, so Vicenzo turned his phone's flashlight on. "If you get scared," he began.

Eddie knocked their shoulders together. "You're the one who'll scream if a spider falls down your neck."

Vicenzo's eyes popped. "There are spiders?"

"Probably." Eddie shone his light on the ceiling, covered in brown stalactites that dripped, making puddles on the ground. Straining his ears, Eddie listened. His senses were more acute than ever, picking up Vicenzo's rapid heartbeat. It was loud, telling him that Vicenzo was nervous. Straining his ears further, he detected another heartbeat from deeper within the tunnels. He smelled leather and silver burned his nose. "Elijah," he growled.

With a snarl, Vicenzo turned to bolt.

"Wait!" Eddie grabbed his arm. He shone the flashlight over a trip wire covering the width of the hallway. A bundle of silver grenades swayed overhead. Vico gulped.

"Yeah. Should have expected that."

"Move slowly, keep your eyes open. He's cornered down here." Like prey.

They passed over the trip wire and proceeded deeper into the bunker. A door loomed ahead. Vicenzo got on one side, Eddie on the other, and he pressed his ear to the door and listened. His uncle's heart beat slowly, his snores rumbling like thunder. He was asleep. Eddie whispered, "Be ready." Vico nodded, his eyes bright and wide.

The door opened. From previous visits with his uncle, Eddie knew it creaked sometimes, so he opened it as slowly as he could. His eyes quickly adjusted to the darkness beyond the door. Elijah snorted in his sleep and didn't wake. The smell of silver bullets burned Eddie's nose like bleach—as always, his uncle slept with his gun within reach.

Eddie thought through their bond, *"Take his gun away."*

Vicenzo crept up to his uncle's bed, clasping the pistol and sliding it off the nightstand and into his grasp. Eddie's shoes whispered over the ground as he approached, looming over the man who'd torn apart his family and broken Eddie into becoming a hunter. The rage washed over him, rage for everything this man had taken from him, for all the lives he'd destroyed. Lunging, he threw his shoulder into Elijah's chest, pinning him, then slapped his hand over Elijah's nose and mouth, pressing down with every ounce of strength he had.

Elijah's panicked snarl was muffled by Eddie's hand. He struggled, tossing and turning, but Vicenzo turned the gun on him. Elijah's breath hit Eddie's hand in hot, frantic puffs as he tried to suck in air. The cords on his neck stood out. Eddie growled, his fangs lengthening. "Hello, Uncle." Drawing back his fist, he slammed it into Elijah's face.

Bones cracked as Elijah's nose broke. Blood pooled hot and wet under Eddie's hand. Elijah gurgled on it, his good eye bulging. Eddie bared his fangs and there was fear in his uncle's eyes, fear that left him shaking against Eddie, his face pale. Finally, the hunter knew the terror he'd inspired in Eddie.

Eddie had hit him so hard his finger broke but the bone had already snapped back into place before Elijah tumbled out of bed, spitting blood across the ground as he choked and gasped for air. A bloody sneer twisted his mouth as he looked up at Eddie, teeth crimson as he snarled, "Boy!"

Eddie slammed the toe of his boot into his uncle's face, toppling him back to the floor, and his skull struck the concrete with a crack. Dropping down beside him, Eddie yanked on Elijah's shirt, forcing his uncle to look him in the face. Eddie roared, fangs bared and eyes burning as, for a heart-stopping moment, he felt the fury of the wolf within. Elijah's eyes went wide.

"Your collar," he whispered in understanding.

"I'm not a boy anymore," Eddie snarled and then he grinned. "I'm a wolf, Uncle. And right now, you look an awful lot like prey."

"Beast," Elijah spat, specks of blood hitting Eddie's face.

"I am," Eddie said. "You created this the day you burned our home and ripped me from my family."

"I gave you a new family!" Elijah blurted out, and the sour smell of his fear was pungent. He was close to pleading. "I took you in. I saw somethin' in you! Fed you from my table. Taught you everythin' I know, didn't I, boy?"

"You tortured him!" Vicenzo roared, eyes blazing.

"I made him strong!" Elijah coughed, choking on blood.

"You taught me hate," Eddie spat. "For myself, for the world, for who I am. But my pack taught me love. I will never allow you to hurt the ones I love again!"

Elijah huffed a cold laugh. "So kill me, then. It don't matter to me. I will haunt you, boy. After I'm gone, I will haunt both you dogs. And that'll make me rest easy."

He was right. The scars on Eddie's skin had healed, but they would always be there beneath his skin. The nightmares would come for him, nightmares of unending pain and helplessness. But he would have Vicenzo sleeping beside him to hold him close, and he'd found a family he could turn to in good times and bad. Elijah might have taken his home, his parents, but he couldn't take Vicenzo away. Eddie wasn't the hunter this man had broken. He was whole.

Eddie's voice shook as he said, "No one will mourn you. No one will remember your name. No one will ever be hurt by you, or live in fear of you. I will never live in fear of you. Not again."

And he took his uncle's pistol from Vicenzo and aimed at Elijah's head. This man would never hurt his family again. "Goodbye, Elijah."

There was a crack as the gun kicked in Eddie's grip. Elijah's head snapped back as the bullet entered his skull right between his eyes, and Elijah Turner was no more.

AFTER LINGERING TO RIDDLE Elijah's body with bullets, Vicenzo ran after Eddie from the dark bunker and out into the Mojave. "Ed?" He looked around and spotted him hunched over, body spasming as he retched. Vicenzo came up behind him and laid his hands on his shoulders until the storm had passed, though Eddie still shook beneath his touch.

"He's gone," Eddie whispered, and his voice was so small. "He's gone. He's—" A broken sound escaped him and he collapsed to his knees and crumpled, his forehead to the dirt. Vicenzo fell with him, draping himself across Eddie's back. He held his mate tight and kissed his hair, his hands stroking up and down his back.

"Yeah, Ed. He's gone. He's gone forever and he'll never hurt you again. He'll never hurt anyone again, I swear it. I've got you. I've got you, Ed."

Vicenzo lost track of how long they lay like that beneath the star-strewn sky. Finally, Eddie stirred beneath him and Vicenzo opened his eyes. They were damp. Eddie shivered feverishly, but the sharp hitch in his chest had evened out to slow, shaky breaths.

"It's over," Eddie whispered, and a fresh wave of grief surged inside Vicenzo. He wished this had happened sooner, that they hadn't had to lose their families, their homes, and their love for each other to get to this point. He wished nothing had ever been taken from them.

"What is it?" Eddie asked, touching Vicenzo's face.

He swallowed, his throat aching. "We had to lose everything to find each other again, to find Ben and the others. If Elijah had never come, our lives would be so different. Our families would be whole. You and I wouldn't have been separated..."

"I know," Eddie whispered. "It's hard. If our families were still alive, we wouldn't know about Ben and his pack. We wouldn't have had the experiences we did, the adventures we've been on. But sometimes I think I would trade just one day to see my parents again. To smell the smoke from Pa's pipe and hear my mama singin' along to Elvis Presley songs. To sit down and eat dinner with them as a pack..."

Vicenzo put his arm around Eddie's shoulders. "One day wouldn't be enough."

Eddie sniffed, rubbing a fist across his eyes. He laughed quietly in acceptance. "No. No amount of time would ever be enough."

Vicenzo squeezed his shoulders. "We can see them, you know."

Eddie smiled, his eyelashes wet. "I'd like that."

Vicenzo didn't want to. He was afraid, terrified that, at the sight of his parents' headstone, he would break and no one would be able to salvage what was left of him. But Eddie wanted to go, and he wouldn't let his mate do this alone.

They would never be alone, not ever again.

THEY RETURNED TO THE car and drove past the glowing lights of the Strip. Eddie's hands were tight on the wheel as he drove toward Red Rock Springs. Vicenzo couldn't drive, not there. He thought he'd lose his courage once he caught sight of that familiar dirt road that led into the town.

Beside him, Eddie's breath hitched, and Vicenzo looked ahead. There was an old sign at the fork in the road welcoming them to the Red Rock Springs Pack Memorial, and Eddie eased off the gas and they idled there. Eddie smelled of grief, and his heart raced fast in Vicenzo's ears. Reaching out, Vicenzo took his arm.

"Come on, Ed," he said with more confidence than he felt. "Let's go home."

Eddie took a breath. In and out. In and out. Then he stepped on the gas, and they were driving along the winding road past towering red rock spires and rolling brown hills. Arid desert wind blew in through the window and for a moment Vicenzo thought he could still smell the smoke. He took another breath and realized he was mistaken. The land had healed from the fire all those years ago, plants and cacti and shrubs growing from what had once been charred earth. Life went on.

"I remember," Eddie said, stopping to clear his throat. "I remember driving up this road in the back of Pa's truck. He said, 'Welcome home, son.' I didn't want to be here. I wanted my old home in my old town with my friends, but they were gone. Then all these wolves came to greet us, howling and running up beside our car."

Vicenzo smiled. "I wanted to run with them, but my dad told me we had to wait and greet the new family."

Eddie chuckled. "I was overwhelmed. There were all these new smells, all these people I didn't know. And then I saw your parents standing on the dirt road. I saw you, this weird little kid hiding behind his mama's legs. I was sure you hated me."

Vicenzo's face warmed and he shook his head. "Nah. I smelled you and you smelled like honey and warm summer grass. I don't know. I felt like everything was gonna be all right. It blew my eight-year-old mind."

"What do I smell like now?" Eddie asked.

Vicenzo leaned over to get a whiff of him. He pressed his nose into the cotton of Eddie's shirt and breathed in deep. Eddie squirmed, chuckling. "Like mine," Vicenzo said. "Like home."

Eddie turned his head to kiss his cheek, and then his eyes swept back toward the road. Vicenzo loved how they sparkled. "You do too."

Vicenzo followed his gaze toward the road and all the fluttery feelings disappeared. The skeletal remains of a town rose up from the hills. Eddie stopped the car abruptly, his knuckles white as he squeezed the steering wheel so hard, Vicenzo heard the wheel creak dangerously.

"It's still here," Eddie whispered.

Vicenzo couldn't speak. Memories choked him. He closed his eyes and saw his mother leaning out the window of the burning building. She'd smiled, and he knew he was loved. Then she was gone in the rubble.

A car door opened and shut. Footsteps crunched on the dry ground. The door on Vicenzo's side opened and Eddie stepped back, waiting. Vicenzo was frozen. He didn't know if he could do this. He didn't know if he *wanted* to do this.

"Do you wanna wait here?" Eddie asked, his eyes gentle and concerned.

Vicenzo tightened his jaw. He stepped out of the car and slammed the door behind him. He wasn't leaving Eddie alone again.

Though the streets were clear, Vicenzo felt as if he were stepping over the ashes and bones of the burned and dead. They walked past the gutted remains of the general store where Vicenzo had bought candies with his allowance money. The remains of the schoolhouse, blackened and crumbling, brought back memories of how stuffy the classrooms were in the summer, his hands damp as he passed notes to Eddie. Derek's house was nothing but rubble, and Vicenzo remembered the way Kassandra had held him as he died slowly in her arms. They walked farther, but they didn't take a right at the next fork in the road. Vicenzo knew where that road led, and he couldn't stand to see his family home. He couldn't.

Instead, they went left and encountered the sign that pointed the way to the cemetery. Heart sinking, Vicenzo squeezed Eddie's hand and followed him up the hill. Tombstones rose from the dry, cracked earth. Others had come before them recently, leaving fresh flowers or lighting candles for their lost loved ones that still smoked.

They walked among the graves until Eddie stopped before two graves, side by side. His mate's throat worked as he swallowed, eyes blinking fast. Sniffing, Eddie let go of Vicenzo's hand and knelt before the graves of his parents. Fingers shaking, he reached out and ran his fingers over the engravings of each of his parents' names.

"Hey." His voice broke and he tried again. "Ma, Pa. I came home, finally. I'm sorry. I'm so sorry I couldn't come sooner. I'm sorry I didn't fight harder, that I couldn't do anything to save you." Vicenzo knelt beside him and touched his shoulder. Eddie's mouth trembled, his eyes bright, but he was holding himself together. "I hated myself for being so helpless. Sometimes, I thought I hated you both for never telling me the truth 'cause I thought if you just told me, I could have been prepared. I could have stopped Elijah."

Eddie exhaled, holding on to a headstone to keep himself from falling. "Now I understand. I do. You both wanted a better life for me than the lives you led before. After I lost you, I didn't think that was possible." He smiled, broken and beautiful. "Then I found Vico. Again, after so much time. We were different people, broken and scarred, but we found a pack who made us whole again. And when I see you again, I'll tell you all about them, and we'll run under the moon and nothing will hurt us again." Eddie blinked fast and a tear slipped down his cheek. "I love you, both of you."

Eddie touched both of their headstones, placing his hands on a paw print engraving. Then he stood, reaching for Vicenzo's hand. "C'mon. Let's go say hello to your folks."

A while ago, he texted Kassie and asked where his parents were buried. She'd sent him a picture of the grave, so he knew where to look. When he caught sight of the tallest headstone in the cemetery, Vicenzo knew they'd found them. A stone wolf howled atop the grave, jaws parted forever in a never-ending song. Two names adorned the smooth surface of the grave: Olivia and Anthony Salvatore, beloved wolves, parents, and friends. They'd been buried together, as inseparable in death as they were in life.

Vicenzo had thought he could be strong for them. His heart was fuller than it had been in so long but the sight of their grave tore it clean in two, like it had never healed at all. He tried to speak, to tell them hello, that he missed them so much. *I love you, I love you, I love you.*

All that escaped was a broken sound as the ache in his heart crawled up into his throat, burning his eyes and nose. His shoulders shook, his breath hiccupping in his chest. He put his arms around the stone wolf and cried like he'd lost them all over again.

The grief shattered him, and he didn't know how he could ever be whole again when they'd lost everything. Nothing would ever take that way, and he didn't know how to move past this.

Vicenzo's knees buckled and he fell into the void. He thought he'd closed it off, thought he'd shut the door and thrown away the key. Now it was wide open and he didn't know how to close it, if there would ever be a time when he would be whole and happy again instead of shattered into so many shards of glass.

Arms went around him. Eddie gathered him up and held him tight and close, holding him together as the world around him fell apart.

"You're not alone," Eddie whispered, and his voice shook. "We're not alone. This isn't how we end, Vico. Don't you see? This, this right here is where we begin again."

Without hesitation, Vicenzo clung on tight and believed every word Eddie said.

Some time later, when Vicenzo could breathe again, they lay in the grass at the foot of his parents' grave and watched the stars. Vicenzo closed his eyes and listened to Eddie's heartbeat beneath his ear, sighing as gentle fingers ran over his hair.

"Beautiful," Eddie whispered, gazing up at the stars. "You just can't see them like this back in New York."

And because Vicenzo was feeling a tad pessimistic, he said, "I heard once that the stars we're seeing might already be dead and we wouldn't know it. That depressed me."

Eddie's chest rose and fell as he sighed. Vicenzo thought he'd bummed him out. Before he could apologize, Eddie said, "But we can still see their light. They might have been gone a thousand years, but they still shine for us. They don't leave us. Like the ones we loved."

Vicenzo hadn't thought of it that way. "I like your way of looking at things."

Eddie hummed sweetly.

There was still an ache in Vicenzo's heart. Maybe it would always be there. Some days it would hurt worse than others, a reminder that he'd loved and been loved. Maybe he would always be haunted by what he'd lost, the way Eddie would be haunted by Elijah and the things that had been done to him.

But for all they'd lost, they'd found so much.

"Eddie."

"Yeah?"

"I wanna go home."

And Eddie smiled. "Yeah. Me too."

When they were ready, they stood, turning their backs on the graves. They walked in the dark back to their car and climbed in. The headlights illuminated the ghosts of burned-down homes but they didn't look back when Eddie reversed and pulled onto the road. They drove from the town like they'd done so long ago when they were teenagers and so excited to be together and away from their parents for a few days. Back when Vicenzo's biggest problem was that he had a crush on his childhood friend.

Beside him, Eddie switched on the radio and country music played. Vicenzo smiled at him because for all they'd lost, Eddie Turner was here right next to him. For all the lies and hurt, all the bitterness and sorrow that had come between them, their promise of forever had never changed.

"Hey," he said.

Eddie looked at him, his eyes aglow.

Vicenzo grinned. "Turn that shitty country music up."

Eddie smiled, turning the dial as he leaned over the gear stick. Their lips met and it was like they were eighteen again, their futures as wide open as the road that reached for the endless horizon.

They were here, together, and Vicenzo would do everything he could to make sure it stayed this way. That it was always him and Eddie, forever.

THE PACK KNEW THEY were coming. The bonds burst bright and warm inside Vicenzo's heart, as strong as they'd ever been. As the estate came into view and they drove beneath a canopy of palm trees like a green tunnel, Eddie rolled down the window and howled.

The pack answered his song, howling them home.

The gates opened at their approach and they were there, all of them. Ryan waved from Zach's back. Gabe and Max ran up to meet them as they pulled into the driveway. Izzie threw her arms around Eddie as he jumped out, and Ryan steered Zach over and collided into both of them. He wound up on the floor while Zach rubbed his back. Ben stood on the steps, a light in his eyes and a secret smile hiding beneath his mustache. Isaac was by his side, his arm around Ben's waist.

Isaac tugged Eddie to his chest and tousled his hair. Gabe and Max bombarded Vicenzo with questions, demanding to know all about what had happened. Vicenzo batted them away, unable to shake his smile as he and Eddie stopped before Ben, standing tall on the step above them.

"It's done?" he asked.

Eddie bowed his head. "It is. We're home."

Ben bared his teeth in a smile. He opened his arms and crushed them both to his chest.

"Puppy pile!" Ryan shouted, crashing into Vicenzo's back. The pack gathered around them, pressing close, enveloping Vicenzo and Eddie with their scents.

"Welcome home, sons," Ben Stroud rumbled.

Vicenzo closed his eyes tight and the void inside him filled with warmth and joy.

Home.

He was home.

EPILOGUE

"Eddie. Stay with me."

Eddie jumped, tuning out the distant sounds of the estate: Gabe and Max chatting with their kids. Ben on the phone in his office with Isaac. Zach and Ryan debating who would win in a fight, Batman or Spiderman, because they were kids. Izzie and Enrique, being sappy—he would really rather not hear them.

"Sorry." He took in a breath and blocked it all out. Even four weeks later, he was still adjusting to his connection to his wolf. The full moon was just beginning to peak and soon they would run as a pack beneath the moonlight.

"Are you with me?" Vicenzo arched a brow. He lay beneath Eddie on silky white sheets. There was so much suntanned skin, Eddie could scarcely breathe.

"Yes," Eddie rasped. "Yes, Vico."

Vicenzo reached between them and Eddie gasped as Vicenzo took hold of him. "Claim me," he whispered. His breath burned against Eddie's ear, his lips hot and wet as he sipped at the shell of his ear, then down his neck. "Do it now. Hurry."

Eddie didn't appreciate being rushed, not about this. "Be patient."

Vicenzo showed his teeth, his canines sharp. He nibbled at the spot between Eddie's neck and shoulder. The skin there burned, and Eddie growled deep in his chest. There was a pounding in his head that hadn't been there before, a primal urge that lengthened his claws and made him want to bite.

He would satiate those baser urges, but he'd be damned if he'd rush this. He reached for the lube in the drawer. They'd already gone through half the bottle this week alone, their bodies wired with need and anticipation as the full moon approached. As he coated his fingers, a growl rumbled from Vicenzo's chest as he opened his thighs, baring himself to Eddie.

Eddie pressed inside. Vicenzo was tight around his fingers, hot and perfect. A hand curled around the back of his neck, and Vicenzo squinted up at him, his eyes heavy-lidded and his pupils the blue of the deepest ocean.

"Are you sure the fire is okay with you?" Eddie glanced over his shoulder at the flickering flame in the hearth. Lighting it had been Vicenzo's idea.

"Yeah," Vicenzo rasped. "I'm good, Ed. I promise." He grinned, his eyes alight with mirth. "Besides, now when I see fire, I'll just think of your fingers in my ass."

Eddie snorted. "So romantic."

Vicenzo kissed him, hard and desperate, his tongue licking into Eddie's mouth. Eddie poured his all into it, his joy, such joy that he could have Vico as his mate. That they were here after all this time, after everything that had come between them, because they were meant to be together.

"Eddie," Vico whispered, his breath hot against Eddie's mouth. "You've gotta. I need you to—"

Moonlight pooled over the bed, tingling over Eddie's skin as he pulled his fingers from Vicenzo. White fur thickened on his arms. His fangs lengthened. The spicy scent of arousal had him driving his claws into the mattress, ripping at the sheets. It was time.

Panting as he drew his knees to his chest, Vicenzo offered himself to Eddie. His eyes burned yellow as the wolf flared to the surface, contained but wanting, needing, to be claimed. Eddie grasped himself, his breath hitching from that slight touch, and worked himself until he was slick and ready. He rocked his hips and watched as he filled his mate, his hands gripping Vico's hips, his claws dimpling his skin. Taking his time, he worked Vicenzo open bit by bit. He rocked his hips forward and back, forward and back, mesmerized as he glided in and out of his hole.

Vicenzo arched off the bed, hungry for him, squeezing the sheets between clawed fingers. "Yes," he whispered, his eyes closing. "Fucking yes, Eddie!"

Eddie wanted to make him howl. He dropped onto his elbows, his claws fisting the sheets on either side of Vico's broad shoulders. Vicenzo threw back his head and snarled as Eddie filled him with his cock, his pelvis ramming Vicenzo's hips. Eddie thought he'd hurt him and tried to apologize, but Vicenzo grabbed his hair and yanked him down. Their mouths crashed together, their fangs scraping and cutting into tender, swollen lips, their tongues so tangled Eddie lost track of which was his.

Folded in half beneath Eddie as their bodies collided again and again, Vicenzo raised his hips, his cock slapping against Eddie's stomach. Vicenzo panted, his arm between them as he worked his cock in hard, fast pulls. He tightened around Eddie, his fangs long and sharp. The salty smell of Vicenzo's sweat and the earthy tang of his sex tangled with the sweet scent of basil that emanated from his neck. Eddie wanted to put his teeth in him, leave his mark so everyone would know Vicenzo belonged to him.

Their bodies burned hot, slick with sweat. Fur sprouted dark on Vicenzo's arms. It was happening. It was really happening. Eddie's mind spun with the realization that they were here, together, so close to being one. Grabbing Vicenzo's hands and pinning them to the bed, he fucked his mate harder.

"Put your teeth in me," Eddie said, but it was a plea because he needed this. He needed Vico. He needed to finally fulfill their promise of forever. "Vico, do it. Please, baby. Make me yours."

"Eddie," he whispered. Vicenzo's eyes burned yellow, and the whisper of his name became a shout as Vicenzo's hips arched off the bed. He came, hot and wet all across Eddie's stomach, then Vicenzo's teeth found Eddie's neck, lighting Eddie up from the inside out. The bond between them, nourished with blood, sweat, and tears, blazed like the sun, wrapping itself around Eddie's heart. This was it. They were one. They were forever.

Pounding into his mate's tight perfect body with abandon, Eddie drove his fangs into Vicenzo's neck as he came. Vicenzo cried out as Eddie's cock swelled at the base, knotting them and tying them together. Vicenzo caught him as Eddie fell into his arms, gasping and shaking. Weak as he was, Eddie pulled back because he needed to see proof of his claim. There, at the juncture between Vico's neck and shoulder, was a perfect wolf's bite, already healing to a scar since mating bites never faded.

"I have one?" Eddie whispered, because he wasn't sure. All his other scars had faded but he needed to keep this one.

Vico snorted, smiling sweetly. He reached out, tracing the tender spot between Eddie's neck and shoulder. "Yeah, sweetheart. You're mine, Eddie Turner." He said it with such savage pride, it made Eddie want him all over again.

Eddie touched where Vicenzo's fingers were and felt the raised, rough bump of scar tissue shaped like Vicenzo's fangs. Tears misted his eyes and his heart swelled in his chest to twice its size like the Grinch on Christmas morning. He crumpled into Vicenzo's arms, kissing him over and over as he cried the happiest tears he'd ever shed.

Vicenzo laughed at him, kissing his hair as his arms held him tight.

"This is it," Eddie whispered, sniffing stubbornly as he met Vicenzo's gaze. "Our forever."

"I can't wait," Vico whispered, and his smile trembled on his face.

Eddie kissed him, holding Vicenzo's face in his hands. He slumped against Vico's chest, laughing and crying happy tears as Vicenzo stroked his hair. Outside their window, the pack howled beneath a full moon. Eddie and Vicenzo would join them when they were ready, and they would run and sing a song of love and family, a song of pack. But for now, there was nowhere else Eddie would rather be than here with Vicenzo.

Across the bedroom, the firelight illuminated a drawing, frayed and yellowed with time, of two wolves, one white and the other black. Written on the back was a promise, hidden and known only to them, and the wolves howled their secret song to the paper moon above.

A song of forever.

The End

THANK YOU!

Thank you for reading! I sincerely hope you enjoyed Ed and Vico's story and this series. These characters have a special place in my heart and got me through some rough times.

If you enjoyed, please consider leaving a review on your preferred platform of choice. Indie authors like me depend on word of mouth reviews like yours. Additionally, please consider recommending this series if you enjoyed it! Thank you again!

WANT A FREE EBOOK?

Sign up to my newsletter to receive a free prequel to The Lycanthrope Protection Agency series, Before Moonrise. This novella features forbidden love, friends to lovers, possessive werewolves who adore their mates, and sexy times on a beach, in a barn, and a broom closet just to name a few locations. Additionally, you'll receive bonus content, cover reveals, and news about new releases. What are you waiting for?

Sign up now by clicking the link if you're on an e-reader, or on my website at CJRavenna.com.

ALSO BY CJ RAVENNA

The Lycanthrope Protection Agency Series

Before Moonrise (Jin & Marcus. Newsletter exclusive)

To Hunt A Moonborn Beast (Gabe & Max)

Child Of The Moon (Gabe & Max)

The Moon Aways Rises (Gabe & Max)

The Moon Over The Oak (Zach & Ryan)

Redemption Under The Moon (Ben & Isaac)

Fire and Moonlight (Eddie & Vicenzo)

ABOUT CJ

CJ Ravenna loves to tell stories where the ordinary meets the extraordinary. Her books often feature an explosion or two, possessive and protective werewolves who adore their mates, steamy and swoony romance, and of course a happy ending. Connect with me on:

My website: cjravenna.com

My Facebook group: Ravenna's Ravens

Instagram: @cjravenna

TikTok: @cjravenna

Goodreads: goodreads.com/cjravenna

Bookbub: bookbub.com/authors/cj-ravenna